UNLEASHED
THE UNSPOKEN TRILOGY
BOOK THREE

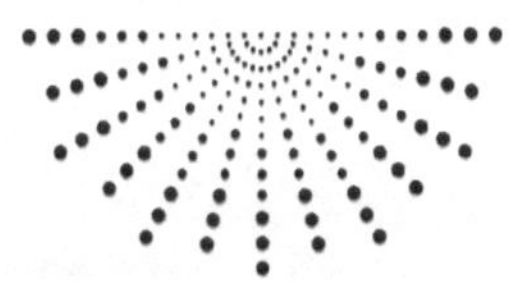

CELIA MCMAHON

Parliament House Press, LLC

ISBN 978-1-956136-73-9

Edited by Loni Crittenden and Erica Farner

Cover by Shayne Leighton

CHAPTER ONE

I could almost taste his blood on my tongue.

I rose to my knees and peered over the roof of the Old Hen tavern. He was walking away—or rather, stumbling away, most likely wasted from ale and exhaustion. The sight of him elicited a growl from deep in my throat.

I've been waiting for you.

The sky was blue-black: a full moon with a light shower that plastered my short hair to my forehead. I wiped the water drops from my eyelashes and stood. I found level footing and leapt onto the roof of the next building, landing feather soft. When the man turned to look my way, I crouched and pinned my hood closed across my face, hoping for the cover of night. I heard him cough, and spit something thick onto the street. I dared a look to be sure.

Archibald Grayson Apatimi looked more pathetic now than he had been a few months ago, his pock-marked face even more cavernous with eyes so unfocused, it was on my luck alone that he now walked in the right direction. He had been Ashe's captain of his personal guard and a traitor to Mirosa. He was thinner and sickly. And yet, despite the man's fragile state, I felt no pity. Branch, the older wolf from the Den who taught me to fight, was a voice in the back of my head. *Don't be fooled. Even injured or sick wolves can bite.*

The sight of the traitor dragged me into memories I'd rather have forgotten. If I could, I'd have chalked them up to nothing but a long and horrible dream. But being here in Stormwall made that impossible. Not only was I forced to remember, but also see with my own eyes what I'd done to my kingdom.

I could feel the pain coming off the city, like a sentient thing gathering under my skin. A sudden, ferocious pain made me struggle for breath. The loss of life during Dal Paratheon's invasion swirled around like a blackened cloud. How many more had died since? It was difficult to discern, with every one of Stormwall's people moving through the destruction of their home.

Every one of *my* people.

Their fear was a palpable thing, invading every inch of space in this city. If not for the storm of Peek Island soldiers and Gwylis, but for the shockingly large amount of missing children; posters begging for their return nailed to buildings and walls all around the city. This terror permeated the air, the earth, in the very breath of the lungs of the people I should have protected.

This regret panged in every rise and fall of my chest. My people deserved a better ruler.

I drew in a long breath and leapt to the next roof, following Archibald's solitary path through the city. He turned down an alley and stopped to piss. I cringed against the scent of urine. I could kill him now, though this close to the main square, it would be entirely too reckless. All my killings were lured from the city and, sometimes, to the privacy of a bedroom.

But before I could stop myself, I crouched and sprang from the rooftop.

I didn't land as softly as I intended. Archibald finished pissing and looked over his shoulder, seemingly unconcerned of the woman standing behind him, watching him soil the brick of the wall. The rest of his body followed until he faced me, a grin spreading across his gruesome face. "The whore returns, after all."

In my former life, I'd be distracted by the insult. Often, it would send my temper flaring and soaring with reckless abandon, doing anything and everything to defend myself. But now, I had demon magic inside of me. It flared there now, in the hollow of my stomach like an inextinguishable fire.

I met the former guard's eyes and matched his grin. "You know who I am."

He held my gaze. "Don't think for one moment, the shadows of my past do not come calling at one point or another."

I ground my teeth together. "I am no shadow."

"Could have fooled me."

I drew in a sharp breath. *No time for arguing.* "Where is Prince Ashe?"

Archibald threw his head back and laughed. "No wonder you're covering the city in red." He casually anchored a hand on his hip. "I don't know anything about the prince. As far I know, he's dead."

My eyes widened. For weeks, I'd lured and tortured soldiers and guards alike for information from behind the palace walls. I'd taken a knife to my face, healing, and then repeating it every evening. For weeks, I'd sunk into a blood-red fury only the threat of daylight could stop. If Dal Paratheon's own traitorous fiend didn't know where Ashe was, what hope was there in finding him?

Ashe should have sent word. A crow. Anything. But I waited for days before donning the hood and stalking the city under the cover of night. I hunted men as they came out of taverns, loose and drunk. I tempted them into inns, I took them beyond the city boundaries, and for what? I didn't know how many I'd killed, or which ones still churned around in my belly. I did not regret the killing, because the demons did not allow me to feel shame or guilt. I only regretted the time wasted.

But I refused to believe him, gritting out the words, "You're lying."

"Are you sure?" Archibald asked. "I've been in the palace, and there's been no one-armed prince strutting the halls. As far as everyone knows, he died during the Battle for Stormwall."

I scoffed at the ridiculous name. It sounded like my father and his forces even had a chance at keeping the throne. They didn't. "So, you wish to die for your lies."

"I'm going to die either way, Princess. Best by your claws than the king's noose."

He was right. If he went back and reported me, Dal would certainly kill him for not taking me back there with him. Dead or alive.

He was better off dead, and better for my conscience.

Wargave would tell me how I was wasting my time and effort. No news would come from the palace, especially not anything useful and convenient for myself. He'd said those exact words just days ago when I'd come crashing into his little shop bucking like a wild horse, angry that I could not find what I needed. *The world doesn't bend for you, Isabelle Rowan. Stop thinking it will.*

Suspicious shopkeepers with fake eyes shouldn't speak like wizened old men. There was nothing more unnerving.

"You ruined everything for me, bringing your traitor king to my kingdom," I said. He blinked at the last word, clearly misinterpreting my absence. As much as I thought I'd left the New Kingdom behind, it was always there waiting for me, very much mine by blood and rights. "It didn't have to happen the way it did."

Before I finished speaking, I moved. Changing into a wolf here would only attract attention, as it did in a bedroom for example, but my strength as a human matched the bite of my teeth. I grabbed Archibald's arm and slammed him against the opposite wall. He went for his weapon—a dagger, perhaps—but I knocked it away too quickly. He tried to drive a fist into my belly, but I sidestepped, knocking him off-balance. I drove a fist into his neck and a knee into his midsection, sending the older man crashing onto his knees.

This cat and mouse game was fun, and only for the truly sadistic. I was playing with my food.

Archibald heaved. "Your mother wasn't quite so feisty. Where did you get such fire?"

I drew my dagger. "You slept with her, didn't you?" Images of their shameful flirting across the table flashed before me. I'd first spoken to Ashe that night. Lulu had been gushing the entire night.

"Like mother, like daughter, slumming with the palace scum," Archibald spat. "Some likeness after all."

My pulse kicked up a violent rhythm as the darkness pressed on me, my fire lashing out from beneath my skin, sizzling the very air between me and the guard.

"What was the boy's name? Fray Castor?"

I thought hearing his name would freeze me to the spot and flood with my mind with all the things I'd done to him—the things he never deserved. The full weight of it should have subdued me, but the demons reacted with a hiss and a whisper: *Forget about him. You never needed him.*

"Shut up," I snapped, addressing both the Uncanny and Archibald. "You don't know him, and you don't know me."

This only made the man smile wider. "Oh, I know women like you. The sick kind of females who lust after monsters because it reflects what they are deep down inside."

My hand trembled. *Don't think about him. Don't.* "I said, shut up!"

"They talk about you, you know. They call you a monster."

I lunged for him, but blinding anger made me careless. He grabbed hold of the necklace holding the jewels and ripping it from my neck.

I barely heard them fall to the ground, back against the alleyway, before my vision flashed with shadows.

My throat went bone-dry, my tongue leaden in my mouth. The feeling of being filled up like a wave and then like a deluge. I swear the ground tipped beneath my feet. My hands curled into a fist around my dagger hilt. My control over my magic slowly shattered.

I am not a monster.

A burning sensation swamped me. Flames licked my fingertips. Embers sprouted from every hair on my body. But I did not burn. This magic was from demons, born of choice and desperation.

Yes, you are.

An inky black figure came into view to my left. I knew what it was, I did not have to ask. And I was too weak to fight against it. Fire, wrath, and hatred.

Shadows drank up the enormity of the scene, and in one swift motion, I drew a straight line across Archibald's neck. The scent of blood soaked the air; a familiar scent, and a good one at that.

Archibald's head rolled to the side, his eyes still wide, as if death came as a surprise. I picked up my necklace and tucked it into my pants pocket. The demons shrank away, but not entirely. They danced in my peripheral, awaiting the next call.

Another smell hit me right away. Not Voiceless, but not the typical Gwylis scent either. Something earthy, like a kindling fire and cheap bracelets. The sound of jewelry clacked and bounced off the light of the moon as she approached and dipped her head to the guard's body. "I see you couldn't stay away long. What mess have you dredged up now?"

I swiped my blade across my pants and sheathed it. "That's none of your concern, soothsayer."

Abiyaya laughed. She stepped further into the street to gain sight of me, but I kept putting space between us until there wasn't any more. "Visit me," she said and turned her back. "The stars are bright tonight."

Finished talking, the old soothsayer disappeared down the cobblestone street and out of sight. I held up my hands in defeat and looked back in the direction of the Barge and then in the direction of impoverished homes where Abiyaya lived—where I ultimately made my destination.

~

I KEPT A SLOW PACE BESIDE THE SOOTHSAYER, WINDING DOWN THE city streets until we approached the poor section of Stormwall.

A voice cracked the air moments later. "TOBIAS!"

I craned my neck over a small grouping of people. There, I found a Peek Island guard restraining the screaming woman while the rest watched helplessly.

Panic assailed me, fueled by the silver fish upon the guard's breastplate. From what I could tell, Dal Paratheon cared very little for the people of Mirosa. This could end in tragedy.

The woman screamed, her eyes bloodshot, her body going limp as she sobbed for a name. *Tobias.* Who was Tobias?

I leaned into Abiyaya, keeping my face hidden in my hood. "What is happening over there?"

Abiyaya took a moment to listen. "She cries for her son, Tobias. He was seven years old. Taken, probably."

I turned back to the woman, who was now out of the guard's arms and on the ground in a heap. I watched as a man, a commoner, low-born in a threadbare cloak came and lifted her, looking vulnerable and apologetic to the onlooking guard.

"I'll take her inside," he said, his tone rushed. "She will cause no more noise, I promise you. Don't kill her. She is only grieving."

Grief took hold of my body. Familiar grief. "The missing kids," I whispered. At first, I'd thought they were being smuggled out of the city, but the missing posters and now this; I could no longer deny something far more sinister was happening. People were getting hurt. More than I could save.

Abiyaya met my fraught expression. "Twenty-two children."

I loosed a breath. Twenty-two children, vanished. This had to do with Dal Paratheon, I knew it. But what would he want with children? Was he punishing people? Surely not this woman. She was not a palace worker. She hardly looked like a business owner, and by the state of her clothing, she did not have much money. What would Dal want with her son?

There was something there, but I filed it away for when I had more information.

We neared the soothsayer's home and I let all of questions drift away.

"Come. Sit." Abiyaya motioned to one of two chairs at the table where I'd once dropped my blood into a dish; it had turned black as tar. It was only at this moment, I finally understood why.

I wanted to say, "I'm not your dog," but instead, I stayed silent and took the seat.

When enough time had passed, Abiyaya came out with it. "So, you went ahead and became the thing your family hated." She smirked, and her deep wrinkles wrinkled further. "That's quite the achievement."

Yes, quite. I folded my hands on the table. The dish sitting on the table in front of me dredged up memories of the first time I'd come to the soothsayer's house. "You called me beautiful and cruel."

"And you called me a witch."

I curled my lip, smirking. "Well, you made predictions that came true. That makes you a witch."

"You speak of things you know nothing about."

I looked up at the soothsayer, to her scarred hand. "Are you a Gwylis?"

Abiyaya kept her mouth in a thin line and slowly raised her powder-white eyebrows. "Do I smell like a Gwylis to you?"

I'd be able to smell her some distance away, but I sniffed the air anyway for good measure. It stunk of damp earth and something I could not identify as either pleasant or offensive. "No. But you smell like you crawled from the center of the world."

She laughed at this. "Maybe so. Maybe so." She gestured to the dish. "Another go?"

I snorted. "Why, so you can tell me my heart is a shriveled carcass roasting in the summer heat?"

"That's why you came, isn't it?"

"I came because I thought you'd have information for me."

Abiyaya cocked her head. "Information is what you need?"

I smirked and gestured to the room. "That's why I'm *here*."

Abiyaya sat back in her seat. "Why are you really here?" she asked. "It is to kill Dal Paratheon's soldiers, is it not?"

"Because my home was threatened, and good people died." I blocked my mind from conjuring Ghetee. I couldn't show weakness. Not now.

"*This* home was threatened. What did you do to stop it?" She waited for an answer, but I kept silent. "You ran is what you did. You ran to a place you thought was better." She leaned forward, her eyes locked onto mine. "Was it better?"

"It was led by a someone unfit to rule who deserved to die." I nodded. "I suppose not."

An infinitesimal smile crawled across her lips. She knew of Rixon's death. Of course, she did. "And who should rule?"

"I will rule. This is my kingdom."

"You wish to be queen?" Her words ignited my skin, sending a jolt into my head and I let the feeling ride.

I am Isabelle Victoria Rowan, and I would be Queen of Mirosa.

Gone were the days of running from my problems. I would no longer let usurper kings invade my land. I would defend it with my life.

"I am the only answer," I said simply. "I am the right answer."

Abiyaya weighed my words, but remained neutral. She pulled her lips together and said, "The dead are reflected in your eyes. This grief will kill you."

I stood up. "If you're done, I have places to be."

Traitors to kill.

Abiyaya stopped me with one quick hand to my forearm. "I will tell you of the prince if you amuse me just this last time." She motioned to the dish once again.

My gaze jerked back to the soothsayer, my breathing erratic, my mind swirling with images of the one-armed Ashe Paratheon. Once a prince. Always a traitor. "You know of Ashe?" I hated the desperation in my voice.

"You two had a plan, did you not? Did it ever occur to you maybe that plan did not go the way you wanted it to? Maybe the prince betrayed you. Again."

Again.

Yes, the thought crossed my mind, more times than I liked. It kept me up at night and rattled me in the day. I could still hear his words. *"I can get him to trust me again and then I'll kill him,"* he'd said. He knew as well as I did the only way to destroy Dal Paratheon was from within. We did not have the forces yet, and Dal seemed to conjure them from thin air.

Are you listening?

How could I deny the determination in such words? Ashe looked as though he could destroy the world from its core if he had the chance.

The one-armed human prince with the heart of a beast.

I now lived in a world where enemies lurked in every corner. I'd left my allies in another world, far past the Archway. My throat tightened. I was alone, but I'd done it to myself. This loneliness, like two fists squeezing my neck, evaded only by hunting down soldiers and guards throughout the city and letting death become my own companion.

Well, other than the demons living inside of me. Not many people could say that.

I shook the thought away, forcing myself to focus. I had nothing left now but to trust the prince, and to see him back safely.

"Fine." I thrust out my hand. She ignored it, and suddenly, she was moving so fast, she might as well have been a blur. She unsheathed my dagger and pressed the tip of the blade into my skin.

The demons recoiled, spouting poisonous words with voices mingling like a chorus.

Gwylis Queen, why do you let the bitch hurt us?

I gritted my teeth until Abiyaya withdrew the steel from my finger.

"Aquarius won't speak with you yet, will he?" Abiyaya asked as she squeezed my blood into her dish. I watched a drop, two, three, and then she released my hand. I caught my breath as the demons still cursed into my ears.

"That's none of your concern." Aquarius did refuse to speak; not because of who I was, but merely because he needed time to think, I assumed. Wargrave undoubtedly informed him of the happening back at the Den. But each day passed, and I waited, sitting on rooftops, and with each day I grew more anxious. Nothing got done. And I made excuses for the Gwylis king when he might be a filthy coward like my father.

Questions wracked my brain. How long until the Den pack came for me? How long until I'd get into the castle and shred apart Dal Paratheon for all he'd done? What of Pyrus? Crim? I shook my head. *This is too much.*

I shouldn't have come alone.

I didn't think I'd be alone. I thought Aquarius would stir from his depression—from his cramped and hidden life in Wargrave's cellar. I'd expected too much too soon.

The world does not bend for you, Princess.

"This dagger will subdue the demons," Abiyaya said.

I knew this, of course; I'd used it to kill Rixon and her very own evil inhabitants. But I never thought of stabbing myself to shut them up.

"The necklace too," she added.

My fingers curled into the emerald and ruby necklace resting in the hollow of my neck, heavy and warm against my skin. I had to find the last gem to call upon the heavens to fight the Uncanny and break the Gwylis curse. It sounded simple enough until I said it aloud to the skanky shop owner, Wargrave. He laughed and laughed, but offered no insight. It was all right anyhow. I didn't need him. I needed Aquarius.

Both Henry's dagger and the gems did nothing but delay the inevitable. I could not control the demons, and sometimes, I did not want to. Not when brute force took precedence over polite conversation.

"What of the boy?" Abiyaya asked, pouring the strange liquid from a bottle she produced. She mixed it with my blood and stirred it with her finger. "Was this all worth it?"

I bared my teeth, but said nothing. There wasn't anything *to* say. I'd done what I'd done and there was no taking it back.

Don't think about him.

"You can say his name, you know," Abiyaya said. "Your heart may be bleeding, but it's not emptied yet."

Do you think you could love me the way I love you?

I could hear the question, spoken by someone who used his words only when needed. Only when his heart told him to speak. I'd nodded to his question as the ball continued without me outside those hedges.

He'd come back for me, risking his own life. The cure had worked, and he used his first words on me. *Let me save you, Izzy.* His words had purpose.

No, I didn't think it possible now; the saving and the loving part. Not after killing his own mother. Not after putting everything else before him. I saw him through a looking glass, turned the opposite direction. So, so far away.

He was better off nameless, or else I would break.

"Our paths have split," I said, keeping my voice steady.

"Love has no place in war. It's for the best."

I flicked my eyes away, suppressing the sting of tears those last words threatened to set free. *Stop thinking about him!* "You see war." I kept my voice as steady as possible.

Abiyaya stirred the dish with a noncommittal sound. "I see the same things I saw before, but..."

As she trailed off, she stood. With the dish in her hands, she turned her back to me. "You love too strongly, too fiercely, and it will be your downfall."

"Will I still bring nothing but death?"

Abiyaya turned, her eyes foggy with...tears? "Yes, but most of it will be your enemy."

I drew breath into my lungs, the relief crashing into me like a wave. "And Ashe?"

Abiyaya set down the dish and took a breath. "The only thing I've heard about the prince is that he is here in Stormwall and he is alive."

A small tear made its way down my cheek, but I only allowed one. I wiped it away and sat up straighter. Steeled myself. "But you don't know what will become of him?"

The soothsayer shook her head. "Do you trust him?"

I said nothing.

Abiyaya scoffed. "He is human. Incapable of trust."

I shook my head, but no words came.

She nodded. "But you *want* to trust him?"

I did. Every part of me wanted to know that he would not side with his father again. But would the promise of power deem too much for him? Would he succumb to the weight of a crown? Men were weak when presented with the choice of power. But Ashe was alive, and that was something.

I stood to leave. "I have to send another crow."

Abiyaya clucked her tongue. "How many would that be? No crow will reach him. He is beyond your reach."

I tilted my chin to my chest and sagged into my chair. Humans, incapable of trust, had let me down before. If the gods were listening, they would have heard my prayers. I would have known Ashe was still with me, that he was still on my side. But as the days wore on, those prayers faded, and along with them, my hope.

"I do secret coding in my messages," I said, finding my voice. "I take precautions, so even if they were intercepted...they'd be...all right." My breathless words didn't make sense. They sounded far away and weak. When did words become so worthless?

"I have often been wrong," Abiyaya said, rousing me from my thoughts. "Even I'm not perfect."

My posture slumped. I killed Archibald tonight, but I may have lost Ashe. Why must it be that when my best intentions were fulfilled, the world deemed to punish me? Death surrounded me like a storm cloud, thundering its way into my life, cascading floods into everything I held dear.

Hope was an ember in the back of my mind. All could be well if I held on a bit longer. But how long?

I did know why they came to me now, but I recalled the words Abiyaya said back in the alley while Archibald bled out atop his own urine.

The stars are bright tonight.

The phrase sounded familiar. I'd heard it three days after I'd arrived in Stormwall. The fact that they were spoken in the daytime should have alerted me to something amiss, but at the time, I was stalking a soldier and had no time to dwell on something insignificant. Now, those words did not seem so pointless.

"What did you mean by saying the stars were bright tonight?" I asked. "Is it code for something?"

Abiyaya smiled and her eyes brightened. "That, my girl, is why you will never be alone." She bowed her head. "But also, why you need to get through to Aquarius. There can be no revolution without a leader. There are those who defy the king, those who can be stirred with the right motivation. You know as well as I do Gwylis hide within this city and beyond, but they will not last long if you waste time waiting on the prince. You must take matters into your own hands."

"I need to get to Hassara."

Abiyaya paused.

I narrowed my eyes. "Do you know anything about that city?"

"City?" The question hung there, but she did not elaborate. Time crushed me, and I did not have time to poke and prod this old sooth-sayer. I had things to do.

After a while, she finally said, "But you cannot make the journey alone."

I bowed my head. How right she was. I'd taken missteps all too often and gotten myself into more trouble than necessary. I did not listen to reason, and my arrogance sometimes clouded my vision. But I'd come this far with nothing but my own two hands, albeit a body full of demon magic, but still, alone.

I still had the Gwylis cure, concocted by my good friend Pyrus, the best healer in all Mirosa. I missed him so much, it hurt even to think about him. Without his wisdom and encouragement, I felt as lost as I probably looked at times. But I had this cure—enough to save a dozen or more I expected, more if I could get more of it made. I wasn't sure how to go about doing that. I couldn't access the castle. I didn't know if he even lived.

Or Crim. My former Voiceless guard whom I left behind, who told me not to come back the last time we'd seen each other. Would he be angry for my return or would he ask to see my new dance routine? I smiled to myself.

I'd practiced, after all.

But instead of friends, I had an old shopkeeper with a fake eyeball and a wolf king who would not speak to me. Useless, the lot of them.

All my life, I wanted nothing more than to break free of my parents.

To belong somewhere. But I'd learned that you belong in the places you left the pieces of your heart. In Stormwall, I left them with Crim and with Pyrus and in the grave where my cousin Lulu rests. I scattered them in the Old Kingdom with Olio, Branch, and Sonia, and then I bled the pieces over the young wolf, Ghetee and over my brother's resting place in the Lonely Fields.

With new allies, I risked losing again. I risked loving again. I put my entire heart in peril.

But I'd already sold it, didn't it?

"I expect a crow will arrive at the Barge soon," Abiyaya said.

"All right." My heart raced in my chest. In these last few stagnant weeks, I finally felt something was about to happen.

Abiyaya cleared her throat. "The Uncanny will use what you feel and throw it back at you tenfold. Do trust others, but do not trust yourself."

CHAPTER TWO

If I'd been paying attention, I would have seen how much of a monster my father was. Instead, I sat at supper at a table that did not belong to him, in a castle he had stolen, surrounded by people I did not care for who thought of me as their heir apparent.

I am going to die in this place.

I painted on my best smile and focused on a man who seemed content as I nodded along to his words. These people, they spoke to hear their own voices. It was nothing of value. Nothing of heart.

I missed being around people who only spoke when there was something worth saying.

"My son," my father said, dabbing at his mouth. My father looked nothing like me with his hollow eyes and gaunt face. When he smiled, I flinched. He looked like a corpse, dressed in someone else's skin. "What do you say about the offer?"

The food turned to dust in my mouth. I swallowed and took a swig of wine. It burned all the way down my throat. "What offer, Your Majesty?"

A bubble of laughter erupted from the table. Drunk, I assumed, the lot of them.

My father eyed me with disdain, but kept his smile pasted on his face. His line of sight traveled to my missing arm. I instinctively tucked it away beneath my cloak. "The offer of marriage from the Lord of Kine's daughter. She's of a pretty age. Just shy of fifteen."

I felt the blood rush from my face. Since the day I'd arrived in Stormwall, I'd been treated like a prize to be won. Servants doted on me, trailing me day and night. And the meals. So many meals with so many people I did not recognize. Were they sympathizers? Were they Gwylis? It wasn't like they spontaneously shifted to ease my worries. Not one person was ever introduced to me, and they came and went so quickly, I never had time even to ask.

But I was the heir to Mirosa. Since nobody had ever seen me leave Stormwall after my father attacked, it had been easy. But my father assumed I'd been taken, and I didn't say a word to refute that. Not one person knew what happened to me beyond the Archway.

At least none here with me in this room.

I tapped the tip of my nose and fit on my best smirk. "Fifteen, has she not had her first blood yet?"

Raucous laughter filled the room.

My supper churned in my stomach.

"Indeed, she has," the man beside me replied, downing a cup of foul-smelling ale. Ah yes, now I remembered; this was none other than the Lord of Kine himself. "I can attest to that."

I swallowed the taste of sour bile.

"I cannot see how you can frown at such a wonderful gift," my father said, his lips thinning.

The Lord of Kine waved off my father. "Leave him be. Let him grow from your shadow."

I exchanged a look with the lord, brief, barely there. Was he defending me?

"To be bestowed such a gift is a great honor," Lord Kine intoned. "You are half a man. You should be grateful for anything you are gifted."

I cleared my throat. "I am not frowning at the gift, but only that I have to wait weeks for the gift to arrive."

The table was pleased. They went back to eating and drinking and fell into individual conversations. My gaze moved from my cup, across the table to my father who stared back at me with the cold displeasure

I'd come to know. Nothing would ever be good enough; the evidence lay in a scar across my lower abdomen, given to a boy not yet man enough to my father's taste. Although he marched me around like a hero, he found my existence disappointing.

A man who let himself get captured was not a man at all.

But I was his only son, and he needed to keep posturing if only to show his people he was a king whose blood would continue to rule long after this death. My father was a bully, tried and true. He knew Mirosa would not bend to a usurper king, at least not right away, but far be it for him to accept it. He'd keep on posturing until the day he died, denying that he did not have Mirosa's love and never would.

A young man came from the kitchens—a servant, from the look of his bland grey uniform—signed to another servant on the other side of the table. Had I known how to communicate with the Voiceless, I would know what they were discussing, but from their actions, I assumed it was only to refill the cups on the supper table and to clear away empty plates.

I had never given the Voiceless a second thought, even before Isabelle had told me what her father had done to them. I never truly looked at them. Not until the day the former princess and I found Fray Castor bloodied and dying in the forest during our hunt and disastrous almost-kiss. It would've been terrible for me to think that it had been the first time I truly looked at them as people.

Sometimes I could be a terrible person, but at least I was a sorry one.

The young male Voiceless picked up my plate. He blanched at the sight of me and looked a little too long. A little too searching. His eyes were a clear blue, like the waters around the Peek Islands. I knew he was Voiceless, but I couldn't find it in me to speak a word. The sound of my father clearing his throat had him averting his eyes quickly and rushing off with haste.

"If you had a thing for the Gwylis, I could arrange something for you," my father said, quirking an eyebrow. He said this loud enough for all to hear, as he always did when belittling his own son. "Ah, here she is now."

I looked up from my scowl to see the tallest woman I'd ever seen. She had at least five inches over my father, who stood at six-foot-ten. She was around my age, with blonde hair, cut short like a man, and light eyebrows to match. Her eyes were two different colors: one blue and the other a dark brown. Although she wore a neutral expression, something about her suggested coiled power.

There was a man behind her, his pace slowed, dark brown skin slick with sweat. He appeared to be panting. The tall woman barked orders for him to hurry or he'd, "spend another night tied up to the bedpost." If this man hadn't looked the way he did, I'd have thought this woman's words to be raunchy bed humor, but this was a whole different beast.

Something happened to this man.

She sat down at the table and leaned back in her chair. The sweating man stood behind her, failing to keep upright. He used the tips of subtle fingers on the back of her chair to keep himself from falling over.

"Ashe," my father said. "Meet Katka. The leader of the Greatwolf Pack."

"Pleased to make your acquaintance." I struggled with the words, my voice breaking like a pubescent boy. I'd yet to see any Gwylis in the weeks I'd been in Stormwall. At least not ones with voices. The sight of Katka brought something locked away to the surface; *I'm not safe within these walls, no matter what side I choose.*

Still, the Gwylis took on a role far beyond what I knew, and my father made sure I was kept in the dark. The man who had captured me the morning on the cliff was never seen again. His name I knew, and I'd asked for him once, only for my father to shake his head as if he'd never known the man at all. That soldier had seen me speaking to Isabelle and the way she had to tear herself away to let me go. If it ever got out that Dal Paratheon's son had ties with the Gwylis, well, I'd probably end up by way of Henry Rowan. Dead by my own father's sword.

Not the way I wanted to die.

Rumors circulated about what I'd seen in the Old Kingdom. Some of my own friends from the Peek Islands had sat down to discuss it in length. They wanted to know what it was like and how badly the Gwylis suffered without their king. I'd arrived in Stormwall with a bushy beard and cloaked in animal fur. It took long looks to determine I wasn't Gwylis myself.

So, I made up lies. I told them I spied on their city. I told them I watched as they killed and ate and mated without regard. I painted them the savage beasts these soldiers wanted them to be. But to my surprise, they never questioned why my father had brought in the very people they hated to fight at their side. Did they tolerate them? Or did my father have a different plan for the Greatwolf Pack?

The crows proved a useless tool, as messages in and out of the castle were strictly forbidden. If Isabelle had lived up to her part of the deal, she and the others should be somewhere in Stormwall right now, hiding, and waiting for me. The thought kept me up at night and plagued me like an illness. The old healer who kept crows down in the dungeons had not been seen and all, but the king was allowed down there. Sometimes, I'd hear screams, and I wondered if they were torturing the man called Pyrus. But they'd go on and on, deep and filled with rage and hunger. They were not human sounds. *That* I could attest.

I was not allowed past the castle grounds. Most days, I'd sit in the cemetery, at Henry's false grave and imagine; if Isabelle could be anywhere, it would probably be here. I'd noticed, some two weeks after my arrival, that there'd been a loose stone in the cemetery wall. But I'd not been vigilant, and a guard had seen me loitering about and had the hole duly repaired. Now, if one tried to move the rock, it would not budge an inch.

The supper conversation died down and the guests bade their good-byes as they headed to bed. The man standing behind Katka's chair groaned audibly, as if something pained him. I would have asked if he needed help, if not for the fact that my father never let his smile slide when looking upon the poor man. Katka ate and drank without even a glance at the man.

I nodded to my father by way of goodnight. He said nothing as I moved across the hall, but Katka's calculating stare bore through my back. I looked once over my shoulder to meet her dark gaze, only for her to turn away a moment later.

But it wasn't the Gwylis's icy stare. It was the look Isabelle gave when the soldeir dragged me away at knifepoint; the vulnerability she'd let slip, and although she had an intense bond with Fray Castor, I knew part of her cared for me. And that was the only thing getting me through my days. The hope, the sadness, and everything in-between.

The same feeling shadowed me as I moved through the castle, to my room on the second floor. The carpet in the halls had all been ripped up, after having been burned to a crisp by Isabelle I assumed, and the paintings and tapestries along the walls stripped and thrown away. Now there was nothing but the sound of my boots on the stone and the cold loneliness nipping at my heels.

My father must be poisoning people. It was the only thing I could think of to make that man behave the way he did. My father loved to watch others' suffering. Letting a person slowly die in front of him would be his own form of entertainment.

I let the thought form and found that I could not rebuke it. My father was the one giving the orders, but the tall woman—Katka—enacted it. What was she? Were there more terrifying things in this world besides giant wolves?

Yes, there were...and some of them wore human faces.

In the hallway leading to my room, I ran into Lord Kine loitering in front of his guest chambers. His large frame took up the space in the corridor. Sweat gleamed from his face. He wasn't the kind of man I wanted to exchange pleasantries with, even after his offer of his daughter.

But I remembered his words at dinner, and it gave me pause.

"Your Highness," he said, bowing at the neck. The light of the torches on the walls made his face shine. "I thought you could join me for a drink."

I shoved my hand in the pocket of my pants. "I don't drink."

"Good man."

I waited.

"I do not wish to give you my daughter," Lord Kine said, squaring his shoulders. "In fact, the thought gives my cramps. Not because of your"—he gestured to my missing arm—"unfortunate shortcoming, but because I am taking her far from here. Your father is evil."

I shifted on my foot. An invisible line drew itself between Lord Kine and myself. This could be a test of sorts; another one of my father's cruel games. "That is treason."

"You should know treason very well, I expect."

I flexed my hand, hyperaware of the one I'd lost to Fray Castor. The memory slammed into me anew: Castor ripping my flesh, my words, begging for someone, anyone, to cut off my tainted arm so I would not become a monster.

And Isabelle.

Innocent, ferocious Izzy.

She was so determined. She'd thought she'd save me the pain. Now, the Gwylis didn't feel as much of a threat. The man with whom I shared blood frightened me more.

Inside me swelled a fury of what I'd let myself become. Hatred for what my father had done. But Izzy broke free. I could do the very same.

If I took a chance.

"I thought—" I cleared my throat and lowered my voice. Something in this man's eyes told me he knew I'd been lying, that I was not hear for love of my father or my land. "I thought perhaps I misinterpreted something this evening at dinner. Something—"

The lord dipped his chin to his chest and smirked. "You did not misinterpret."

I leaned in closer. He smelled stale, like a day-old ashtray. "Could you get a crow to someone in the city for me?"

The Lord of Kine held my stare, and my heart went from its place in my chest to down into my belly. Had I made a mistake?

Finally, he tilted his head, surveying me as if I were a child showing him a simple trick. "When I find you worthy, I will help you. But if only you are worthy."

With that, he turned and left me alone in the room, staring at the space where he'd been.

I'd messed it up. I'd messed everything up. I'd taken the first chance I'd had in weeks and still, I'd failed. The Lord of Kine wanted a worthy man? Surely, he wouldn't find it here in this hallway.

I went to my room and closed the door behind me. Servants came in and out all day long, cleaning up dishes or dirty clothing or patting down the wrinkles on my sheets for the hundredth time. Everything was perfect always. I sighed and cast a look over my chambers from the four-poster bed on one side to the sitting area with a table and four chairs on the other.

Nothing could have been out of place, except the person sitting there.

Teal robe, an excess amount of jewelry, and all-knowing eyes all belonged to the soothsayer called Abiyaya. She leaned forward, crossing an ankle over her knee, her robe falling between. "The Lord of

Kine's loyalties are not so cheap. But he does not deal in riches, but in esteem."

I stood there, open-mouthed, saying nothing.

"You're surprised to see me."

"I—um..." My stammer did nothing to allow my thoughts to catch up to what I was seeing. Stormwall was locked down so tightly, not even a crow could enter, so how did an old woman who walked no faster than a wounded deer get through all that security?

"At a loss of words." She raised a brow and sat back in the chair. "You weren't so silent the first time we met. If I remember correctly, you said I was ill-mannered."

"You are in a prince's room without permission, so I think I'll stick with that assumption."

Abiyaya gave a gap-toothed grin. "I know you, Prince; don't forget that." She eyed the place where my left hand had been, and grunted. "Such a pity. You had very strong hands."

Heat flushed my cheeks as I moved my arm out of sight beneath my cloak once again. "How did you get in here?"

"On the wings of a crow."

"Impossible."

Abiyaya stood, sucking the air from the room. "A lot of things that seemed impossible for you have happened, and what do you say, Prince of Stormwall? Do you still deny the magic that runs under everything in this land? The gods, the demons, the humans who wanted to become gods? Do you deny my predictions?" She glanced at my left arm again. "With one hand, you can still bring down your father, even though you sink down into despair night after night. You vowed not to hurt anyone ever again, but you must."

I recalled the words. I'd spoken them to Isabelle on the mountainside while on our way to see the Gwylis queen, Rixon. At that time, I'd felt a certain freedom there in the Old Kingdom, and whether or not the queen wished for me to stay, I knew even alone I would feel better than I would beside my father.

That day on the cliff, when I'd first seen Isabelle with Fray Castor, I lost myself. My head swam with confusion and furious jealousy of seeing her with him; along with the pressure of my captain of the guard, Archibald, I'd sided with my father. I'd made a choice, and that choice rippled across the entire kingdom. Even as I laid bleeding from my wounded arm, I did not feel sorry for the Gwylis servant. I had wanted him dead.

And in doing so, I'd broken the trust of the one person I loved the most.

Now I stood before the soothsayer, as broken as I should be, given the things I had done. She exhaled dramatically, closing the distance between us. Her jewelry clinked as she moved, and she stopped at arm's length. "Weak things are easily broken, Prince, and the king wants to break you. You cannot be weak, not now. You must be strong for her."

"But I cannot contact her outside this damned castle," I bemoaned.

"You must do what needs to be done on your own. Sit. We have much to discuss."

I shook my head. Isabelle and I had a plan. Killing my father would do no good if I did not know what plans he had for Mirosa. Something sinister lay in those dungeons, and the lack of Gwylis told me my father had secrets, and I was not trustworthy enough for him to confide them in me.

Are you listening?

Isabelle had nodded to those words, agreeing to everything I proposed. If I could not follow through, would my actions drown the kingdom?

Abiyaya cleared her throat, drawing my attention back to her. "You wish to accompany Isabelle Rowan to Hassara, do you not?"

Hassara—a place she'd been instructed to go by her dead brother, Henry. I'd never heard of the place, and although I found it on a map one night, I couldn't help but listen to the tiny, uncertain voice in the back of my mind.

All of it sounded absurd. If I knew anything, I'd say she were running herself right into a dead end.

"Are you listening, Prince?"

The world felt unbalanced, shaking beneath my feet. I thought of the Gwylis of the Den and how they'd brought me back to life after traveling through the wintery mountains.

They'd saved my life.

I owed them mine.

Paper rustled. There were stacks of blank parchments and a feather with an accompanying bottle of ink at the table in front of me. The soothsayer slid a piece between her fingers. "Prince?"

My throat tightened, but I sat down nonetheless.

Abiyaya pushed the ink toward me and handed me the feather. "We have much work to do. Will you listen closely?"

I took the feather and dipped it in the ink. "Yes, I'm listening."

CHAPTER THREE

I hurtled down the back alleys of Stormwall and slinked my way down into the damp and dirty section of the city. The Barge offered nothing good to good people. This was a place of dark dealings and hidden Gwylis kings.

Thanks to my training with Branch, my breath remained steady despite my head wanting to shake out of pure adrenaline and panic. Besides, after facing armies not once, but twice, I sort of had a knack for how much I could take. But still, facing Aquarius and begging him to speak to me shouldn't have been all that nerve-wracking.

Except it was.

The Gwylis king, who'd been holing up in the cellar of Wargrave's for who knows how long, became the key in bringing the Greatwolf Pack to our side. Or at least I thought. Lulu always said my thoughts sometimes had wings, able to soar so high they almost felt unbelievable. Maybe I was wrong about all of this. Maybe I didn't care.

I had to try.

I veered down the dingy streets and stopped at the bottom of the stairs to Wargrave's shop. I took a deep breath, mastering the fear and disappointment had now become my life, and slipped inside.

The shop looked as it always had with its clutter and dust. The counter in front was empty save for some old-looking vases, but the clothes rack to my left looked fairly full from the last time I was here. Which was...yesterday.

I spotted a missing child poster tacked on the front counter right over the last one and closed my eyes, the hysterical mother's cries echoing in my mind.

How horrible of a person did I have to be to force myself to ignore this? Not ignore, but more...shove it aside while I took care of bigger things. A part of me wanted to know more, wanted to invest a bit more time into these children's disappearances, but time was not a thing I had to spare. But perhaps someone would know. Wargrave, perhaps, or if he would speak, Aquarius.

I moved further into the shop. Wargrave must be in his room in the back, sound asleep, as I should be.

I pushed the heels of my hands into my eyes, exhaustion finally catching up to me. If I truly were to expect a crow from this rebellion, I should probably get some rest.

But my room was in the cellar in the very same place I went through the change. That one window room with the dingy mattress became my home. It was a wonder Wargrave let me stay with him to begin with. I bet it was the story of me killing the queen that did the trick. He was a sympathizer, after all, and did not care for Dal Paratheon as he didn't for my father. But he didn't look at me like everyone else did when I first arrived at the Den. He didn't see me for a name that caused so much bloodshed. He looked at me as a person.

Which was disturbing; Wargrave had been the last person I'd expected to become an ally since he did rob me of my money for the sabrecat tooth for the Voiceless cure. But if he saw any sort of hope in me, I saw the same in him. He housed a lot of it there in this cellar.

Hope came in the form of an old grey wolf who refused to speak a word to me.

Words were so important. I needed them now, even if this was the hundredth time I tried.

I squared my shoulders and descended the stairs to the cellar. At the bottom, I had two choices. If I went left, I could fall into bed and dream this all away for a few hours, or I could turn right and face a Gwylis, who may do nothing but annoy me further.

I did some truly stupid things in my life, so today was no different.

With a great exhale, I turned right.

I'd told Aquarius everything that had happened over the past few months. When I got to the part where I made a deal with the Uncanny, I clammed up. I did not know why speaking of it made me feel such shame. I supposed it was because I saw Aquarius as my father, and I did not want his judgements. I didn't know what I wanted from him to be honest, but it wasn't silence.

I opened the door to his room, refusing to let the enormity of the first Gwylis hit me—at least for now. The torches were lit, and he opened his eyes. "It's a full moon, but you wouldn't know, because you stay in this room like you're caged," I said.

Aquarius did nothing but let out a sigh. The wind from his nostrils blew wisps of hair against my forehead. I would have giggled at the action, but all I felt was sadness.

I leaned against the wall opposite the giant wolf and frowned. "I killed Archibald Grayson tonight. He was Ashe's former guard. He had no information for me, though, but I avenged Lulu and that's enough for me." I blinked away some unshed tears. "Gods, I miss her. Sometimes, it doesn't even feel real."

Aquarius didn't lift his head. He had his white and grey muzzle right on top of his two front paws. He might as well have been a statue, for all anyone knew.

I remembered the first time I'd seen him. I was overcome, thinking Wargrave had been keeping him prisoner, but I soon found out the shamed king had sequestered himself, abandoning his people, and every-thing he sacrificed and fought for. He left them to be poisoned and to die. People like Crim and like...

Ghetee. I added his name to memory, so when I went to speak of those I loved that left me too soon, I now had three to whisper to the wind.

Henry. Lulu. Ghetee.

If one more life must be lost, let it be my own.

I interrupted my own thoughts and told him about what Abiyaya had told me and how I was going to join a rebellion, because I could not wait for Ashe any longer. And I could not sit here on my ass doing nothing but eating lemon buns and hopping on rooftops. I still didn't tell him about the Uncanny and what they planned to do with the Gwylis. It only dredged up feelings of sadness for Henry, since he had been the one who told me. It was a miracle I felt anything at all.

I cleared my throat. "So, there you have it. I'm joining a group of people I hope are allies, and I'm taking my kingdom back. But then I'm leaving it to find a jewel to break the curse. Sounds silly, right? Like something out of a bad fantasy book."

Aquarius should have laughed. Lulu would have. I bet Olio would. That man would cut off his own finger just to watch his twirl in the air, for a laugh.

The dead are reflected in your eyes. This grief will kill you.

Speaking to the old wolf was purposeless. If I had any kindness left in me, I should have put him down weeks ago.

I threw a hand to my chest to suppress the sorrow of thinking such a thing. Those were not my thoughts.

I looked back at Aquarius. There was so little left of the wolf I once thought was powerful. He had not been much when I first saw him, but he was a mere shell now. What had happened to make him this way?

"I don't expect anything else from you," I said on a breath. I was so tired. I wish I could fit myself into the old wolf's body and sleep. But instead of doing just that, I turned to leave. "I'll undo what you did. You cannot stay a wolf forever." I gestured to the doorway. "You have to be human to fit through this. Remember that."

I didn't wait for a response. There wouldn't have been one, anyway.

HUNGER DRAGGED ME FROM BED THE NEXT MORNING. FROM THE position of the sun. I'd only slept a few hours. Still exhausted, I followed the stairs up to Wargrave's shop in hunt of breakfast. The shopkeeper had a tiny kitchen in the back of the shop was a stove, a wash basin, and a small table with a crooked leg. There was a pot of something mushy on the stove. It smelled all right, sort of like cinnamon. It was cold and maybe a day old, but I couldn't be choosy. I grabbed a bowl from the shelf above and helped myself.

With my bowl in hand and my spoon in my mouth, I peeked into Wargrave's room, but his snores told me he was still asleep. The man slept like a baby. Must be nice.

The oatmeal went down smoothly, even though it could have used some sugar. I set my bowl in the sink and moved to the front of the shop. There, I backed open the front window, just enough to let in a breeze. It stunk in here. I wondered how much of it belonged to me.

As I went to smell my armpits, something swooped down from the sky and landed on the sill in front of me. A crow. Tied to its leg was a rolled piece of parchment. I carefully undid the bindings and gave the crow's head a pet with my first two fingers. "Good girl."

The crow nodded and took flight.

Wasting no time, I unrolled the letter and read it aloud. "We dance tonight when the stars are bright in the thing that belongs to you, but people use more than you do."

A riddle. My heart picked up, pacing along with my thoughts. I'd never been good at riddles. Lulu used to tell me I lacked the brain capacity to think outside what is logical. If it wasn't clear and upfront, I did not see it at all.

I wasn't seeing it now, and the panic set in.

"Shut the window; it's cold as death."

I started at Wargrave's harsh and dry voice. He'd gotten worse since I arrived. His cough was almost constant, and his skin had taken on strange and unhealthy pallor. What never changed was his constant judgments of me.

I don't need this right now, I thought. I needed silence.

I turned my back to Wargrave and recited the riddle. My neck ached, and my mind went fuzzy. Why couldn't I solve a simple riddle? Why did they have to make it so difficult?

I felt impotent. Powerless.

"If I solve it, will you move out of my cellar and leave me be?" he rasped. He moved to the back of the shop where he continued his grumbling. I heard the clang of a kettle and then some cursing about eating all the oatmeal.

"There's enough in there, you old fool," I muttered, reading the note over. What was something that belonged to me that people used more than I did? I crumpled the parchment in my fist helplessly and peered out the window as dismay roiled through me.

Oh, Ashe, where are you?

"Murder should not be a tool for children."

I stared at Wargrave, and he went on despite my unwillingness to listen.

"What you're doing is not right," he said. "Hunting soldiers, killing on a whim like a wild animal. You kill when your life is threatened, yes, all right. But not this. This is depraved." He gestured to me. "A young person, no matter the wolf inside, should not be out there killing for sport."

"You..." I paused, letting his words sink in. I suddenly felt like a small child caught sneaking food from the kitchens. I knew he was right. I did hunt those men, and I killed them, justifying it with evening the score. Pike Ivo had killed Ghetee. Gwylis had killed Lulu. My father killed Henry. I deserved my jug of blood.

But I slumped at Wargrave's words. I may have demons wiggling around in there, but I didn't have to let them influence me, if they were influencing me at all.

How much control did I have?

What I was doing was not in self-defense. It was more than revenge. It was unadulterated evil, and no matter the demons that crawled around between my bones, I had to be better than that. "I'll try harder."

He huffed. "Give it to me, then."

I handed the note to Wargrave's bony hand. One eye watched me while the other looked at the riddle. He little hair he had left on his head floated above his scalp, as though threatening to flee at any moment.

"Your name," he said.

"Isabelle."

Wargrave sneered. "That's the answer, you idiot. Your name."

Oh. Something that belonged to me, that people used more than I did. "All right," I said, pondering. "Makes sense, but how can that be a place? Where—"

Wargrave raised his eyebrows and nodded along with me. "The Queen Isabelle."

The Queen Isabelle was a ship, not named for me specifically but for my great-great-great grandmother. It was a trade ship, and moved across the waters along the south of Mirosa, docking in cities along the coast. It didn't seem like a wise location for a secret meeting. Not with how busy the docks can be, at all hours of the day. Not with so many soldiers milling about.

He knew all of this already. He was, after all, a Gwylis sympathizer.

"You didn't tell me." I took no liberties in controlling the growl in my voice. But Wargrave wasn't fazed. His good eye looked straight at me.

"The way I see it, you want to start wars, you do the leg work," he said.

"You're a terrible human being."

"Never said I wasn't."

I sighed. "I am not getting through to Aquarius, and I don't think Ashe can complete his mission. I am moving on to Plan C."

Wargrave crooked an eyebrow. "Which is?"

"Wash the taste of day-old porridge from my mouth, find some proper tea, and plan my attack on the Traitor King of Mirosa."

I'D SLEPT PISS-POOR LAST NIGHT, BUT I FELT MORE AWAKE THAN ever. My mind swirled with thoughts of Ashe and what he could be up to behind the castle walls. To block out the fears, I recalled his words to me the last time I saw him, being dragged into the woods with a knife to his throat.

Trust me.

Trust was such a hard thing to come by, which was why I needed to tread softly around this...rebellion situation. I pulled my hood deeper over my head as I approached the docks. I climbed up to get there and immediately saw the sails of the Queen Isabelle. They stood straight, like perked wolf ears.

The ship made a beautiful silhouette against the night sky.

Henry took me out to the docks once. I remembered every detail, even now, from the smell of the saltwater and the sound of the water sloshing against the great ships. We watched traders and fisherman for the entire afternoon, and a kind man even let me up on the deck. But only for a moment. There was the risk of him drowning a princess that kept his hands on my waist, counting three seconds until he lifted me off. The same man told my brother and I how they used the stars to navigate, and how they sometimes saw sea creatures longer than their own vessel.

My mother discovered what Henry had done, and scolded him until the late hours, and after, he came into my room and told me stories of brave sailors and vicious monsters they conquered. He told me about the stars and the moon and how they felt alive when sailing in the middle of the great ocean. I swear, on this night, he fell asleep before me.

There were too many stories to remember now. But sometimes, when the night was quiet enough and I could see the stars in the sky, I recalled snippets of Henry's stories, and suddenly his voice was there, lulling me to sleep.

But recalling these memories now only threatened tears. There was no room for crying. Not when so many people depended on me.

I observed the scene. There were few people out on the docks now. Torches lit the docks as far as my eyes could see. Along the boardwalk, there were several shops and taverns, but only the taverns boasted customers. As usual. Three men carried crates onto a ship to my left. I couldn't see the name of it. It didn't matter. The only ship I cared about was right in front of me.

I clutched my necklace under my cloak and pushed off from the wall. Keeping my head down, I slowly followed the street onto the wooden platform leading to the dock and stopped when another pair of boots appeared. "Sir," I grumbled and brushed past. No use making any sort of conversation. The less my face was out there, the better.

I'd just approached the ramp leading up the ship's deck when a voice called from behind me. "Aye, boy, where do you think you're going?"

Boy? My hair was short, but come on.

Sighing, I tilted my head to the sky. "The stars are bright tonight."

The pair of boots I'd passed were attached to a man who came toward me. "Yes, miss, they are," he said. He looked at me through one eye. The other, gone long ago by the looks of the healing. The socket, nothing more than a pinched hole of skin. There were crumbs in his long beard. The scars on his face crisscrossed like rivers on a map. How did he manage scars like that? I shuddered to think.

"Tell me why you came here," he said. The sound of the water against the hulls of the ships mesmerized me; I began to dream that none of this was happening. That I stood on a beach of white sand and crystal-clear water. I was reminded of Ashe's stories of the Peek Islands and shot back to reality.

I crossed my arms in front of the stranger. He was taller and wider, and a belt of polished steel hung at his hip, but I wasn't about to go down in a place like this. I was primed to die in a flurry of battle against the sounds of teeth and steel. Something along those lines. "What is your name?"

The man laughed mirthlessly. "You come to my dock and demand my name?"

I sucked on my teeth. "You can ask questions and waste my time. It's no wonder you've done nothing so far."

"I heard what you did. News travels faster than the wind. You killed your own people." That stiff face of his held firm. "You kill anyone who stands against you. You have no allies and you are all alone." He paused long enough for me to hear the drunken chorus of men stumbling down the pier. "Please, forgive me for not bowing. Bad back and all."

A knot of profound anger swamped me. I gritted my teeth, fury thick and potent in my veins. I'd already had a verbal smack from Wargrave over my murder spree. No need for one here.

"I thought I was protecting my family," I said.

"What have you done to protect the one you have here?" He waited for an answer that I refused to give. No man would goad me. I was here now. Wasn't that what mattered? "What use are you to us?"

I went back and forth on shoving the man into the ocean and decided it was best not to commit murder tonight. I was a changed woman, after all. Instead, I offered him something else. "You sent the crow, didn't you? There is something you want."

The vial containing the Voiceless cure hung heavy in my pants pocket. The man's eyes dragged down my body and settled just about where it sat. I shoved my hand down and closed my fist around it. If this was a trap, I'd done a stupid thing by bringing it here. But deep in my bones, I knew there was always a way out of any situation. Especially now.

The man took a step toward me and watched as my hand flew to my dagger. Heat coursed through my body, and a sizzle of fire ignited at my fingertips.

He smiled and retreated. "The princess has indeed returned."

~

THROUGH ALL ITS SPLENDOR, BELOW THE DECKS OF THE QUEEN Isabelle was a mockery of her name. The lulling quiet as we walked by torchlight did nothing to distract me from the cramped corridors and dirty floor littered with sludge and fish parts. I smelled more than fish. There were men here. Lots of them. Sweat and bodily fluids assaulted my senses. I almost missed the familiar smell of a Gwylis.

My pulse kicked up. What pack were they from?

The one-eyed man was called Derwin, and he led me as far down as we could go. When I thought we were about to jump into the ocean, he stopped at a door and rapped twice. "Where's your other half," he asked as we waited for the door to open.

"I'm not a half."

He grinned. "Fair enough."

The door swung open to a room filled with pipe smoke and moon ale. I would have puked right then and there had I not been busy memorizing the details of every person in the room before I even crossed the threshold.

There were two men in the room, and they sat around a large, round table. A lantern on the ceiling swung back and forth as the ship held itself against the tide. Its flickering lit up every man's face in turn.

One of the men wore a black cap and had a wiry grey beard. He squinted at me accusingly. But little did he know, I had learned to hold my own against judgmental old men. In fact, it was probably my specialty. I held his stare until he broke away.

The second man was my age, with light eyes and a frown. His chestnut hair was long and pulled back with a tie. He only gifted me a quick glance before averting his eyes. I couldn't tell if he was rude or not.

Irrelevant, I thought. The smell I picked up from him was of Gwylis, but before I could celebrate for finding my wolf kin, I realized something important.

The young man was Voiceless. He didn't have to lift a finger to sign for me to know.

"Hello," I said, as I removed my hood. I dragged a hand through my hair and shook it out. "Isabelle Victoria Rowan. Wolf-Princess. Little Wolf. Whatever you want to call me doesn't matter. I'm here."

The old man stood and took off his cap. He held it to his heart. Was he going to bow to me? Heat flushed my body. *Please, don't.*

Instead, he clutched his cap tightly in his fist and threw it onto the table, where it landed in a bowl of cold slosh from an earlier meal. "Where have you been?"

It took effort not to flinch. "Here. I've been here for a month!"

Derwin ushered me in and closed the door. He took one of the empty seats, but didn't offer me one, so I stood by the door. "Isabelle is here to help us, Flea; don't disrespect the girl."

I couldn't fault these men. I'd seen the distrustful looks before, when I first arrived at the Den.

Suddenly, it was in the air—something my senses were too overloaded to notice. "You're both Gwylis." I looked at the young man. "But you're the only Voiceless."

He nodded and averted his eyes. Shy, I determined. What was he doing with the rebels?

"We'd waited for help for months," Flea said, taking his seat back. He left his soiled hat in the bowl before him. "For months, I've dreamed of murdering that king and his prince in their sleep."

"Seems you're in need of some sun."

Nobody laughed, which was fine. I didn't need an audience. I studied the three men in the room, feeling strangely like I was back in the Den, being assessed like a horse at auction. But something about what Flea said nagged at me.

"Months?" I asked. "Ashe has only been here for over three weeks."

They all looked at me.

"He followed me though the Archway and made his own way in the wilderness before—" I swallowed. Why was my throat so dry? "Before he gave himself up. The plan was to take Stormwall from within. To inform me of his father's plans. But none of that has happened. No crows. No word. Nothing."

The silence in the room was suffocating.

"What?"

"You made our work really hard," Derwin said. "Out there killing soldiers, leaving messes for us to clean up. The king's men been sniffing up and down these parts. We have to anchor outside the continent most times."

I snorted. "Don't pretend that was my doing." Dal had had this city on lockdown ever since he took the throne. How dare they blame that on me. "What sort of rebellion are you, anyhow?"

"The kind you need."

I clicked my tongue. "I don't typically *need* anything," I crowed. "Unless it's cake. You...don't have cake, right?"

Nobody spoke.

Tough crowd.

I cracked my neck and refocused.

"So, what do you offer us?" Flea asked, as he eyed his discarded hat with dismay. "We ain't looking for new members."

"But you don't have a plan, right?" I looked from man to man. Even the Voiceless man met my gaze, interested. "I have one. A new one, and it involves your king. Your real king."

The Voiceless man's head swiveled to Flea, and he signed something I didn't catch quick enough.

"Tyron is right," Flea said. "Aquarius is dead."

A sudden feeling of excitement rushed through me. "What if I tell you he's not?"

Derwin laughed. "You're talking out of your ass," he said. He poured ale from one of the pitchers and downed in. "Prove it."

"I don't have to. He's the one who changed me."

Tyron, the Voiceless man, signed: *She's telling the truth.*

Derwin shoved his chair aside and approached me. I was reminded of my first meeting with Olio and the way he practically licked me up and down to find out who I was. Derwin didn't do that, but he did inhale when he got close enough and let my scent truly sink in. He nodded, and all at once, the tension in the room was gone.

"Dal promised them everything Aquarius did," Derwin said. "But Dal followed through. Aquarius ran and hid. What makes you think the Greatwolf Pack will follow Aquarius? They have many reasons not to."

"Because he's the strongest." The words came out weak. What was I doing? I didn't come here to pass off Aquarius as a leader, but I was using him as one. But maybe, maybe if the rebellion took interest...if they began to see Aquarius for who he truly was, the Greatwolf Pack wouldn't be far behind. I could do what Ashe couldn't. I could unite the Gwylis so when the time came to break the curse, they would not act on behalf of Dal Paratheon. They would be one.

At present, we were outnumbered, and that was including the wolves beyond the Archway.

"I can't leave here without taking Stormwall," I said to the room. "I have a mission beyond these walls, and I cannot waste any more time." I slipped the tiny vial containing the Voiceless cure out of my pocket and onto the table in front of Tyron. "A drop is all you need. You should be able to cure at least twenty to thirty from this."

"What is that?" Flea asked, as he leaned forward.

"The cure for the Voiceless," I answered, and drew my brows together. "I'm sorry I took it with me and I'm sorry there isn't any more. My friend who made it... The one who created the poison to being with, he's dead now, maybe, but if you know someone who is good with potions, maybe—"

"Isabelle."

Tears had come to rest on the tops of my cheeks. I pawed at them and looked away. I knew I'd been selfish in what I'd done. I'd left the Voiceless behind—the ones who needed me, who I'd always cared for. My arrogance knew no bounds.

"I have magic," I said, my voice breaking. "I have strong magic."

Flea scoffed. "Magic is a word for things you don't understand," he said. "You know nothing of sacrifice. Of love. When you do, come back and talk to me."

"How dare you speak to me that way." The words came without thinking, and with them, a cloudiness to my vision. My senses attuned to everything in the room. The sweat from Derwin's body, a stale piece of bread inside Tyron's pocket. The underlying fear in the room stunk worse.

Deep breaths. Count to three. A soreness in my gums. A deep, flaring hatred rose from the pit of my stomach. I turned my back to orient myself. I felt as though I had no control over my body.

Demons could do many things if we gave them permission. They could tear the world apart if given the right conditions.

I'd sold my soul to them. I shouldn't have been so surprised.

I fought against it, as one would when internally fighting demons. I pressed the ruby and the emerald into my chest, thought of destroying the Uncanny, and found myself calmed. I turned back to the men, swallowed a lump in my throat, and prepared to apologize until I saw the look on Tyron's face. It wasn't fear. No, I smelled no fear from him. It was understanding.

We were both demons wrapped in human bodies.

Derwin sighed. "I'm afraid some men do not trust words. Actions are another story."

Tyron waved a hand to get my attention, and signed. *What did you think happened to the prince once he returned here? They passed it off as if he never left, lousily as he did.*

"I thought he'd play his father's game," I said. "I thought he'd somehow take down his father." Speaking them aloud made the words sound so ridiculous. Was that what we really planned? It was absurd, and these men thought so. "I made a mistake."

Trusting him?

I shook my head. "No, the entire thing in general. I shouldn't have agreed to it. It gave me nothing but false hope."

Tyron's face remained impassive as he signed: *The prince betrayed you.*

"It doesn't matter anymore." I've waited long enough for my crown.

Tyron raised his brow.

Derwin leaned against the wall and propped up one foot. "Tyron works in the castle. In the kitchens."

Something large and heavy fell into the pit of my stomach. The kitchens. Unbidden, a memory forced its way into my mind, that of a certain scowling servant with brilliant blue eyes. He drew his name in the dirt and told me I had a horrible sense of fashion.

The one I left behind.

I shook the memory away, the name. It was too much. "Tell me what you heard."

Tyron answered without hesitation. *The prince came in, not bound, but walking as if he'd never left. He told his father about the Den. He told him you were there and that you'd return here. Dal made it sound like the prince had gone with the army in pursuit of you, not that he betrayed his father.*

I felt like the ground dropped from beneath me.

"You think Tyron is wrong?" Derwin asked me. "You put your trust in someone you loved, and they let you down. Sounds like life, to me. You should not be surprised."

"Don't tell me how I should be," I snapped. "You don't know anything about me."

"If the prince told his father about the Den," Flea said, "the pack is going to be slaughtered, mark my words. He knew what he was doing when he told the king everything. Don't think for a moment he didn't."

I overheard him, Tyron signed. He cast his eyes downward. *He described the buildings, the number of wolves he'd seen. Everything.*

The room spun around me. My palms grew sweaty, and my lungs nearly ceased to exist. Ashe would not stand in the way of my birthright. His weakness would not be tolerated, and in turn, I could not be weak. I'd forgiven someone before, and they nearly cut my head off. I could not take the risk I took with my father. Never.

I sucked in a staggered breath; the demon's life-sucking anger flickered beneath my skin. "I'll kill him."

Derwin sighed, his jaw working. "Agreed."

Tyron nodded. *Thank you for this,* he signed, and took hold of the vial I'd given him. *If you wished to recruit, you're going about it the right way.*

I tried to smile, but it felt impossible. I was in a room with three other people, yet I'd never felt so alone.

"So, what is your plan?" I asked, marshaling in my emotions. "You're a rebellion. What have you done to rebel?"

Derwin didn't overlook the bitterness in my tone, but he did choose to ignore it. "The king is holding a ceremony to announce the prince's betrothal in two weeks' time. It will be quite the party."

Tyron clicked his tongue. *The archers are already standing by.*

Archers?

Flea answered before I could open my mouth. "Stationed on the rooftops, far enough away from the others Dal will most likely have guarding his precious cargo. Only the best. Long range."

"Gwylis?" I asked.

Derwin nodded. "Voiceless."

But now, I can bring more to the rebellion, Tyron signed. *The cure alone is enough for them to pledge allegiance to you.*

My heart stuttered. *No, not to me! I wasn't their leader.* "Part of my goal was to unite the Gwylis," I said. "Aquarius is alive, and he is king."

Tyron shook his head. *We have no king. Just you.*

CHAPTER FOUR

Tyron came the next night, and nothing about his arrival was what I expected.

I'd spent the day in a daze, wondering how much of a disappointment I was and if I really wanted to face the Voiceless at all. Would they look at me the way Flea had looked at me? *Where have you been? Where have you been?* The words bounced around the walls of my mind, and still I did not have an answer.

I was here now. Would that be enough?

Wargrave tolerated my presence in the shop as one would a fly. I stayed out of sight as customers came and went, and spent most of my time in front of Aquarius's room, wanting nothing more than to beat the words out of him. Stupid wolf. I needed council. I needed his words more than ever. Never had I felt so unsure.

I managed to wrangle my emotions into one solid thought: *Take back the throne.*

I laughed inwardly. As if it were so easy. I tried not to think of this plan including killing Ashe, because when I did, my resolve shattered.

Wargrave had just finished with the last customer out when there was a cursory knock on the door. Tyron stepped in, and four men fled in behind him. They all wore simple commoner's clothes of loose-fitting tunics tucked into pants and worn boots. They were all young—

my age, maybe a few years older. They all wore daggers in plain view at their hips, dangerous if pushed too far. If they were trained anything like Fray had been, I had no worries about how skilled they might be.

Tyron greeted me with a slight bow and signed, *Sorry for the lateness. These things take time.*

Time pressed upon me with an iron fist.

There were four other men, one of which I noticed was a woman when she drew closer. She wore her hair short, cropped close to her scalp, but her eyes were such a light green, they reminded me too much of Ashe. She took me in with a frown and examined me from head to toe. I was thinner than I used to be, with much of the muscle I gained training with Branch all but whittled away. My hair grew back fast, but choppy and greasy from lack of proper care. I wore no makeup, but she didn't either. Her face was fresh, freckled along her nose and under her eyes. She was shorter than me and dainty in her build, but the hardness in her eyes and the way she stood told me there was nothing dainty about this girl.

After her thorough examination, she signed with two hands flat, palms facing the ground and swiftly moving them apart. *Floor.* At my questioning look, she bent down and brushed a hand across the floor at her feet. *My name, but with only one* o.

Flor. I nodded. "It's good to meet you, Flor," I said. I offered my hand, but she didn't take it. It was for the best. My sweaty palms pulsed with every beat of my heart.

The remaining Voiceless were called Rowell, Stark, and Brill. After a brief introduction, I turned and led them to the cellar while Wargrave watched from the front counter, silent. As we took the first stair, I heard another knock on the shop door. I shot a questioning look to Tyron, who smiled. *We have more,* he signed.

In awe, I stepped back upstairs to find at least a dozen more people entering the shop. Before I knew it, it was full, wall to wall. Wargrave watched with indignation as the guests touched his wares and fiddled about, waiting for direction from Tyron.

"How many more?" I asked, doing a count in my head. I got up to thirty-seven before another knock sounded.

"One more," Tyron said, so suddenly that it knocked the breath from my own lungs. I nearly jumped into the boy's arms, but instead, I opted for an awkward body shake.

"It worked!" I exclaimed. "How many did you get from that vial?"

Tyron grinned as his eyes roved over the full shop, to all the men and women watching and waiting. "All of them."

I stumbled back a step. "You found a healer to make more from the vial?"

Just then, the door to Wargrave's Wares opened for the last time tonight, and in walked a man whom I assumed to be dead. A man, who was one of my greatest friends.

"Pyrus."

A bottled up sob escaped my throat as I weaved through the tight crowd and lunged into him. He caught me and nearly stumped back out the door. "You're alive."

Pyrus squeezed me tightly. "It appears I am, and I often wondered why until this moment."

He released me, and I had a chance to get a good look at him. He'd lost weight, mostly in his face, though his belly remained. He wore the same thin-framed glasses, but his cheeks had lost their apple red color. His skin was paler than I remembered. It was almost as if he hadn't seen the sun in months.

"I may not look it," he said with a laugh. I blinked, and he still he was there. Pyrus was alive!

"Come." I took him by the sleeve and led him to the back where Wargrave kept his kitchen. We slid into his tiny bedroom and shut the door.

I lit a candle as I found my words. When I finally managed to speak a coherent thought, I spilled out everything that had happened since the moment Pyrus saw me leap from his infirmary window to escape my parents. It was easy since I'd done it all before, but it was different with Pyrus—different because he was a piece of the old Izzy that wasn't so lost after all.

"I cannot say that was the most gripping of tales," Pyrus said when I was finished. "But it does take the cake."

I stuck out my tongue. "Cake," I drawled.

Pyrus gave a full-bellied laugh, but then we both sobered quickly. He was used to my jokes, and maybe even found me less annoying than most, but we were still not in a place to be so carefree. I knew it. He knew it. Which is why he took me by shoulders and squeezed gently.

"I should be dead," he told me. "By Dal's hand or my own, I should be dead, but something told me to stick around."

"Was it Pax?"

He smiled. "No. It was the sun rising outside of my room. It was the promise of spring, and knowing you were alive."

I am well. Do not write back. Those had been the last words I'd said to Pyrus, written in a note and sent over the mountains by Pax. A wave of sadness curled over me. Pyrus had deserved more than seven words. Without him, I wouldn't be here right now.

"None of that now," Pyrus said, as he released my shoulders. "You've come back to take the throne, and if the position of wizened, potbellied fool hasn't been filled, I'll gladly apply."

I choked out something between a laugh and a sob. "Pyrus, we can cure all of those Voiceless, can't we?"

The old healer nodded. "That was the plan, after all, was it not?"

Oh, my friend. I'd be lost without him.

Wargrave's door eased open, and Tyron fit through the gap. "I may not have full use of my words, but I know the feeling of the press of time." I let him lead both Pyrus and I back into the shop. "Show us the wolf."

Now that I knew Tyron was cured, his power hummed as if it were taking hold of the air around us. Had he used it yet? No, that would be too risky, but so was this.

Wargrave looked on, impatience etched across his gaunt face. We all had something to lose. He couldn't fool me. Aquarius meant more to him than he let on. The favor he'd done for the Gwylis king was not done without sacrifice. If ever there was a more important piece to this game, it would be Wargrave.

I led our guests down into the cellar. The air grew thick as we descended, as if it were feeding off the anticipation. And it wasn't because of the Gwylis magic. There was doubt and tension crawling on every person there.

They wanted a wolf. A king.

I opened the door and gave them one.

Part of me hoped Aquarius would say nothing, for what the old wolf had to say now could not be a grand speech made to rally allies. I feared it would be nothing more than disappointment in the range of, "You're wasting your time," or "Last night's beef was overcooked."

I had faith where faith thrived. It did not exist in that room.

But he did raise his head from the floor and fixed a yellow-eyed stare at Tyron, who stood behind me. I stood aside and gazed at the former Voiceless boy, realizing he would probably be old enough to have fought with Aquarius. Even when the gigantic wolf stood, towering over all of us, Tyron held the older wolf's stare in a show of defiance. A show of *dominance*.

This wasn't going as planned.

But what had I planned? That they would fall to his feet? I thought maybe just a glance that he was alive would be enough to rally them to fight back. The cure was one thing, but having a leader was another.

There were murmurs amongst the Voiceless who had regained their voices. The others signed back and forth, but I also heard their whispers along with it, as if they were not comfortable speaking yet. All the while, Tyron stood facing his king. I could almost feel the wave of his magic as it pulsated in the air. It sucked the breath from my very lungs. "Tyron..."

He shook his head adamantly. "That's not Aquarius."

My heart plummeted into my stomach. Did he truly not recognize this own king? "I assure you, it is—"

"I assure you it is not," Tyron cut in. He tore his eyes away and fixed them to me. I did not expect the hardness in his eyes. It came from a person who had to move through the darkness of war, but now had a different darkness running through them. It ran through us all.

"I remember the king," Tyron continued, now addressing the Gwylis, who took turns coming into the room. "Sure, he looks like him, and he may even speak like him, but this is a dog with his tail between his legs. This is a coward."

Tyron pushed through the onlookers, and I followed him into the corridor outside. He stood near my room in the west end of the cellar, placed one palm against the wall, and bent at the waist. With the top of his head touching the wall, he gasped for breath.

"Hey, are you all right?" I approached him slowly and softly laid my hand onto his shoulder. Broken things needed a gentle touch.

Tyron flinched, his eyes wide. "I can feel it in you," he said, straightening. "Not in that sad excuse for wolf. But in you. You should be the one to lead. We don't need him. Not anymore."

I swallowed hard and removed my hand from Tyron's shoulder. But before I could, he snatched it up and held it firmly. His fingers were calloused, hard, of someone who had worked to survive. He reminded me of someone I left behind.

"It's true, then," he said, examining my palm. "We're all going to become demons."

I wanted to pull away—I should have—but I had been without the touch of another person's skin on my own for so long. I had forgotten how good it truly felt. Even coming from a friend.

I cleared my throat. "Tyron, you misunderstand my role in this," I said. "The only way to take back Stormwall is to take down the king, but we cannot have the Greatwolf Pack warring with us. If we can sow the seeds of dissent within the pack, we can increase our numbers so when the time comes to fight, we have a chance."

Tyron quirked an eyebrow. "Sounds rehearsed."

"Your voice is soft and intelligent. You must know I was never meant to lead the Gwylis. Pick someone else."

"Have you heard the rumors? The Uncanny have manifested into something more ferocious than the Gwylis? Monsters, Isabelle. Monsters beyond our imagination. Dal Paratheon is bringing the monsters of the underworld to Mirosa."

Monsters like me. "Yes, I have heard the rumors."

"There is nobody else, Isabelle."

Commotion behind us turned both our heads. One of the Gwylis, a woman around my mother's age with fine blonde hair and light blue eyes, approached us. She looked first to Tyron and then to me, noticing Tyron still held my hand.

"I will follow you," she said. "Daughter of Aquarius."

Her words barely registered. I still looked at Tyron, who finally released my hand and embraced the woman, who had begun to weep. There was a lot of that going on now. The sight of Aquarius and the fact that they had their voices and could defend themselves again, was such an emotional upheaval that the only logical way to deal was to cry.

There is nobody else.

Tyron was wrong. From the looks of the Gwylis here in Wargrave's, there were some sturdy contenders for the right to lead. Whether we failed at Stormwall or not, I was to go west to Hassara, where I feared I would meet my end. I was but a princess without a kingdom. A wolf without a soul. *They must pick someone else.*

"Mala," Tyron said, pulling me from my raging thoughts. "I trust your opinion over all others. What do you make of our king?"

The blonde woman—Mala—stepped back and took stock of Tyron. More and more people filed out of Aquarius's room and began to take notice of me and Tyron at the end of the corridor.

"Mala," Tyron pressed. "What do you make of our king?"

Mala blinked once and shook her head, as if coming out of a stupor. "My apologies, but I do not recognize a king."

I shook my head. As much I expected Aquarius to let me down, I did not expect this. "Tyron—"

Tyron fixed his gaze on me. The fierceness behind his eyes pulsated with magic. "There is no one else," he said. "If you do not accept this, I do not understand why you're here."

"I am here to take back my throne."

"And once this is over, when you break the curse, will we not also be your people?"

When I break the curse. Not *if.* I looked away. "Yes," I decided. "If the Gwylis choose to stay, I will be their queen. I will fight."

Tyron's mouth quirked upward. "Then fight."

I looked over the heads of the crowd packed tightly in Wargrave's cellar and swore I saw a flash of white and grey from the Gwylis king's room.

~

I DREAMED OF BLOOD. BUT FIRST, THERE WERE GHOSTS.

I stood in a world of blackness. In the distance appeared a group of things so diaphanous, they could have been sheets of silk tulle. But they widened and stretched into shapes of men as they grew closer. They were all different heights and ages.

They all wore crowns atop their heads.

The world around me shifted into something that resembled color. Shades of grey and layers of white. Something like the sky rose above, but it was blue and purple like a bruise. The kings before me became more substantial, taking on human features. They were all wore identical clothes. The Bear of Mirosa, reared for battle.

They were my grandfathers.

I walked the line of them, and at each turn, I watched how they died. One was impaled by a long sword, while the other mimicked signs of a heart attack. One by one, they fell, and by the time I got to the last, it was finally the one I recognized. With pride my heart, I watched as my father's belly opened to spill his insides until I was alone with nothing but a heap of gold crowns at my feet.

The ancient gods of the Old Kingdom abandoned them, and they would abandon me too.

Just then, a sound echoed from all around me. No, not one sound. Many, voices overlapping, male, female, and animal inlaid in one another. I clapped my hands to my ears at the shrillness as a figure appeared before me. It wore a black cloak and held a staff of fire. There was nothing to suggest it was human. Blackness curled from beneath the cloak like tendrils of smoke.

"Demon," I said, recognizing it at once. I kept my feet planted, daring it to think me weak. I moved my hand to my dagger before realizing I did not have it. Nor did I wear the necklace. Both items I'd taken off when I'd laid down to sleep.

The Uncanny stayed silent. Its staff of flames burned so bright, tears pricked my eyes. Still, I did not move.

"Isabelle Rowan, I can feel the racing of your heart and the fear of dying that you cannot hide," the many-toned voice said. At the end of the last word, a strange clicking sound emanated from its throat, much like the territorial sound of a raven. The sound unnerved me, and I feared I'd never look at a bird the same way again.

"You can't touch me," I said, with all the haughtiness of a spoiled child. I had nothing to fear of these demons. Fear was a distraction, time wasted.

"Why did you come home, child?" the demon asked. "You have everything you need. You will be the Queen of the Uncanny."

"I was made for more."

"You aim too high and you fall so low."

The last word dragged out until it was an echo in my skull.

I gritted my teeth against it. "You're only here because the gods allow it. When they return, you will run."

The demon laughed, and the staff grew brighter. "We like humans because they are weak."

"Then leave us be if we are so weak."

"We cannot, because we like chaos. Do you think it is only wolves we can change your bodies to? We can do far more, child. Give the right desperation; we can create new gods of claw and wings. Of rot and fury. We can ravage your world until it is nothing but ruin. You test me."

My mind wanted to focus on the phrase, 'gods of claw and wings,' but had to push the words away. "I test you?"

My voice was booming thunder. The fire staff flickered.

The demon smiled, a cold and grotesque thing. "I like you, Isabelle Rowan, but you are cursed twice over, and your heart is dead. Love for the Gwylis simply cannot be. It's an illusion. As you know. You cling to the remnants, perhaps, but nobody will ever love you. Nobody ever has."

I faced forward, meeting the Uncanny head-on, refusing to admit it was right. My hands shook, and I grabbed the hem of my tunic to steady them.

The Uncanny hissed, "The Paratheon king's growing an army for me, whether he knows it or not."

"An army?" I nearly choked out the words. *I am growing fearful.*

"To the west, where wicked things rule. Children of the fire."

Children? These demons lied. It was how they led men to their clutches: with promises of power. The Uncanny were right. Men were weak. But it wasn't men I truly relied on any longer. It was the strength inside of me to bring the gods back to our side. To grant us the small magic, as it was once called, and restore the kingdoms to their original majesty. I did not need golden thrones and lavish parties. What my soul begged for was the talents of the Old Kingdom, the artistry their culture was built upon. Of cities built with love and not those postured of nobility, bent upon a show of power and built from the hands of the fearful. I yearned for the moments of knowing where I came from: a world of gods, and not of demons.

"You didn't know," the demon said, and snickered. "Have you not noticed the missing?"

The terrible reality of the demon's words crept in. "The children...

Dal Paratheon is stealing children to turn them into Gwylis?" I asked, not quite believing it. Such a thing was evil. It was...

Everything Dal Paratheon was. It was everything I should have expected from men. I had briefly suspected such a thing during the attack at the Den. But never children.

Where have you been?

In those four words, Flea had asked the question I may never have an answer to. Where was I when Dal Paratheon sat upon my throne? Where was I when the children of Mirosa were stolen from their beds and forced to become monsters?

I was not here. I was not. I was not.

"And so, finally, you understand," the demon said. "You cannot win. Men were never destined to win."

My breath left me in a gasp as I sat up to wake, my heart pounding. I crawled from bed and stuck my hands beneath the mattress where my necklace lay. I clutched it to my chest, drew strength from it before slipping the chain around my neck. I laid back, grasping the jewels so hard, they left indentations in my palms. I could not see the stars from the small room in the cellar, but I feared they still would not help me. I had two of the three that I needed to break the curse, I had potential allies, and I had hope. But all that died out like a fire doused in rain. "It's not enough," I whispered.

I'm not enough.

CHAPTER FIVE

I had experienced sadness, fury, and desire many times throughout my life. But never fear. Not like this.

My servants dressed me in black and silver—the colors of the Peek Islands—with pressed pants and a jacket tailored precisely for the shortcoming of my missing forearm. The buttons were an engraved silver, and the cloak heavy and black as a starless sky, fastened with a clasp made of bone. When I moved, I felt every inch the prince I was supposed to be. The prince I used to be.

They placed a crown on my head. I'd seen the gold and iron thing before, atop the head of once-Prince of the New Kingdom, Henry Yuel Rowan.

I flinched when I looked at myself reflected in the mirror. I did not recognize the man staring back at me. It might as well have been a ghost.

You are half a man.

When the servants left me, I took a moment to compose myself. I dropped my face into a basin of water, letting my crown fall to the floor of the washroom, and only came up when my lungs screamed for air.

I was alive. I might as well act like it.

A knock on my door startled me. I grabbed the crown and shoved it onto my head in time to see Isabelle's former guard, Crimson, standing at the open doorway with a large sword in his hands. He stood, waiting, as I dried my face and motioned for him to enter.

Since my father's violent takeover, a lot had changed within the castle. New servants and cooks were brought in, while others stayed and took on different roles. For Crimson, it was working in the weapons room, assigning swords and other gear to soldiers. I'd only spoken to him once. I'd asked for a one-handed sword when I'd first begun training. Since, he'd watched me in the training yard, nodding with my victories and my defeats.

Now, he held out a sword far different from the one I expected. For a prince being presented at any sort of ceremony, I was expected to carry the sword of my kingdom, which so happened to be a heavy two-handed sword. I wasn't expected to wield it. Only show it off there on my hip. Crimson offered the one-handed short hunting sword I'd practiced with all these weeks.

At his urging, I took it from his hands, allowing him to sign to me, but I did not understand sign language, not really. But one hand gesture did give me pause. The large man took one finger and jabbed it toward his open palm.

Kill.

I took the sword and threw it toward my bed. It missed by an inch and clanged to the floor. "You can't be here," I urged. "You can't be seen giving this to me."

Crimson signed, faster now. Even if I knew the language, I wouldn't be able to keep up.

"Stop," I snapped. "I can't understand you."

Crimson's face fell. For such a big and powerful man, he sure looked very small.

"Can you write?" I asked him.

He shook his head.

"All right, let me—"

Crimson held up a hand to stop me from speaking. He reached into his pants pocket and withdrew a small piece of parchment, wrinkled as if it'd been folded over far too many times. He shoved it at my chest.

The ink had run, but I could still make out the words: *The Wolf-Princess and the rebellion will attack when both the traitor king and the prince are present. There will be no survivors. Fight or run.*

I let the letter fall. She thought I turned against her. *She's going to kill me.*

And with good reason. Crimson found a way to receive letters. I had not tried hard enough to ensure her that I was still on her side. I was nothing to her now, nothing but something akin to my own father.

I did not blame her.

I blew out a long breath and retrieved the short sword. A perfectly timed strike would sink the single-edged blade straight through my father's back and into his heart. And after, I'd die by the hands of my father's men. Surely.

Or I could wait with my weapon sheathed and let Isabelle finish us both.

My hand trembled. My heart crashed against my chest. I'd come to terms with dying when I reached the Den and came face to face with hundreds of Gwylis. I was sick and weak. Death would have been a reprieve. But after all of that, when I found that hunting lodge and laid in wait for winter to end, I found myself considering a future that was not only uncertain, but imminent. I saw something beyond my own loneliness. It looked something like hope.

When I left Isabelle that night at Rixon's cave, I found my gods.

On the islands, we prayed to the old gods who once bestowed us with small magic. But as I grew, the old gods began to vanish as my father took up idolatry that focused on mortal men, such as himself. A statue of the sun god was pulled down to erect one of the King of the Peek Islands. The moon god was broken into rubble to extend the length of my father's palace. Prayers were empty, uttered only by habit.

The gods left us as they did long ago. They might have disappeared long before we even took notice.

There in the Old Kingdom, I felt them like I felt the wind. They pressed against me, begging for attention, tired of the anonymity. I spoke to them more than I ever had before. In turn, they directed me which ways to travel, where to hunt, and even how to fashion the hook I used to shoot my bow. Some may call it mere survival instincts, and some may even call it luck.

I called it for what it was. The gods cared for their children. They did not want to see us suffer.

That night talking to Isabelle opened everything I felt I knew: that the Uncanny wanted to rule beyond their own station, and they did not fear the gods because the gods abandoned us long ago. Henry's plan of evocation seemed plausible.

The only way we were going to defeat the Uncanny was with the gods by our side.

My heart panged with the thought of the Old Kingdom. When I wasn't busy dying, I'd come to terms with the peacefulness of the land. But I knew I did not belong there.

My life had taken me down a different path than I ever imagined. The choices I made broke hearts and shattered lives. But what I had always done was let my heart take over and affect my decisions. My heart filled with fear that only death would cure.

Crimson whistled to get my attention. I looked up as he signed. He crossed both hands over the center of his chest. This gesture, I knew.

It meant love.

Abiyaya told me many things when she visited me. I was going to kill the very thing I loved and hated most in the world. Now, looking at the sword, I knew what had to be done, and to do it, I had to have nerves of pure iron. I sheathed the sword and straightened Henry's crown.

Whatever I did tomorrow, I was going to die. I might as well make it a good death.

Crimson ran a hand across his bald head and frowned before gesturing for me to follow him. He kept his eyes diverted and his pace slow. I knew this could only mean one thing.

My father wished to see me.

It'd been almost two weeks since the soothsayer appeared in my bedroom. Since then, I'd taken care to how I behaved around my father. During swordplay—where I'd been learning to use only my right hand, which was not my dominant hand, as fate would choose it—I'd made sure he watched me as I feigned fury and determination. And once, he even nodded in approval as I beat my two-handed opponent. I pretended not to see it, but it was there.

Now I stood outside his chambers, where he'd called me not ten minutes earlier. There was a meeting going on inside, and my father was in no rush to attend to his son.

I thought about Abiyaya and what she'd told me. "You must not show weakness," she'd said. "Dal Paratheon hates the weak, as you know. If he is to trust you, you must show how ruthless you can really be."

I rubbed at my calloused fingers and smarted when I stretched out my sore arm. I knew by experience that pain was the path to success, and my father loved to dole that out in bucket loads. If I showed him how hard I'd been training and how hard I could be, maybe he'd allow me into his meetings, and I could fulfill my promise to Isabelle.

Abiyaya's last words haunted my nights.

The door to my father's chambers swung open before the words could surface, and a group of men paraded out into the hallway, walking past me without a glance. I stepped inside.

"I'm sorry," I said, noticing the other person in the room. "Am I interrupting?"

The Gwylis my father called Katka stood from her seat at my father's desk and bowed at the waist. "It is a pleasure to see you again, Prince Asheton Paratheon."

I made a point to scowl. "Nobody calls me that, not even my father."

She drew back, a bemused smile on her face. "As you will."

"Katka is here to oversee a few things, and I thought you'd be interested in them, seeing as you've impressed me as of late." My father sat at his desk, leaving me to stand, as there were no empty seats. I shifted my weight. "What do you think of that?"

"I think you can trust me, Father." I paled at my own words. Nobody who tells you to trust them, truly meant it.

The king wants to break you.

Katka made a sound in her throat. Even seated, she was tall, with broad shoulders and a battle-experienced sharpness in her eyes. Her clothes were finely made—a gift from my father, I assumed—and seeing as she had the use of her voice, she was not part of the group of Gwylis who had become the Voiceless. Had she defected from the Den?

"You have seen my old home," Katka said, willing her way into my thoughts. "How are they?"

"Broken."

The lie slid smoothly.

There was nothing broken about the Gwylis at the Den. From what I'd seen, they would die defending their home and their people. From what little I'd experienced, I knew why Isabelle wanted to call it her home. She found love there, a sense of belonging, and a reason to live. This Katka had none of that. Nor my father or anyone who sided with him.

They wanted nothing but power.

"They wither away," I continued, pacing the room. "They are weak."

"If they are so weak, why did they defeat our soldiers?"

My father's eyes turned to fire as he looked to Katka. He had not spoken of such a defeat. As far as I knew, they'd overcome the Den and killed everyone in it. If Abiyaya hadn't told me that Isabelle was here, I'd assumed she was dead too.

"That is news to me," I said. "But we will not again be defeated."

This shook my father from his fury, and something softened inside of him. "Yes, the city still stands, but we will throttle it until I killed every traitor, and then I will raze it to the ground."

I nodded. "Defeat and destroy."

"Shall we bring your son up to date with what we've discussed so far?" Katka asked.

"Yes." My father clasped his long fingers in front of him and kept his eyes on me. His stare licked my skin like a candle's flame, bringing an uncomfortable itching at the stump of my arm and, most shockingly, the scar along my abdomen. A bead of sweat ran down the back of my neck, but I did my best to keep my cool demeanor.

My father lived for causing pain. Although he appeared a gentle and fair king to the islands, behind closed doors, he was a monster unleashed. I had the scar to prove it.

But I was not a boy any longer. I was a man, and I would not be afraid.

"I am building an army," my father said. "An army the kingdom has never seen before. An army of Gwylis."

"Gwylis?" I asked, genuinely surprised.

"Yes, people willingly volunteering to change."

Dryness crept into my throat. "I don't understand."

Katka laughed. "Your citizens will find honor, giving themselves over to the Gwylis. They will find life as wolves much more enjoyable. Much more powerful."

"You're changing people into wolves, and they are choosing such a thing?" I asked.

"Yes," my father said, drawing out the word, as if I were a child asking foolish questions.

I locked eyes with my father. "And enough have volunteered to build such an army?"

The king shared a look with Katka and spoke as he dragged his eyes away. "We have discovered certain crimes in the kingdom have different punishments than the Rowans have instilled."

"You've changed the laws?"

"Entire families will be punished," Katka said. "Children included."

"Children," I said, not quite believing what I was hearing. "You're turning children into Gwylis?"

The king sat back in his chair. "What I am doing, I am doing for you and your children, son. Gwylis, as you know, live for many years longer than humans. In doing what I am doing, I have given you an immortal army that will thrive for generations. For your children's children and so on and so on. Do you not find that agreeable?"

I should not have been surprised. The fact that my father took up arms against Stormwall and planned to obliterate the entire Rowan family should have been my first clue to the lengths the man would go to achieve greatness in his eyes.

My father was turning children into monsters.

"*I* find it agreeable," Katka said.

I sneered at the Gwylis and wondered what empty promises my father had made to lure her into his circle. She appeared loyal: She was in his chambers, after all, and this wasn't the first time I'd seen them together. It made me question what ever happened to Queen Chelsea. Did my father cast her aside after getting what he wanted? Was she dead, or imprisoned in the dungeons wishing she were?

"I think it sounds grand," I said, plastering on my best smile. "In fact, I wish to see the progress you've made."

"Unfortunately, we do not house the children in Stormwall, but a little further west in the city of Essex," my father said.

My father, pretending his horrifying deeds did not exist, was very much in character.

"But shall we show him something else?" Katka asked, her eyes turning wild with anticipation. "I've been itching to see the look on the boy's face."

My father threw his head back and howled with laughter. "Katka, my dear, you are positively terrible."

We didn't speak as we walked through the castle, and ultimately came to the entrance to the dungeons. I remembered the first time I'd come here. It was after I had brought Fray Castor back from the forest, after I'd seen Isabelle covered in his blood awaiting news of his condition. I'd told her about the scar my father had given me. She'd seemed so vulnerable then. I'd wanted nothing more than to hold her and never let her go. But she'd never allow it. She'd told me she didn't know him. I didn't blame her for lying. She'd seen too much death in her short life. She couldn't have borne to lose him too.

The vision of Isabelle sitting knees to chest faded quickly as we moved through the dimly-lit corridors. The place some called the catacombs was more than just infirmary rooms. The deeper you went, the darker and mustier it became. There were tunnels that led to the cemetery outside, wide enough to haul dead bodies to their final resting places.

It'd been quiet before, but our presence had ignited something cold and terrible. A howl like a wounded animal sounded and continued as we walked closer. I held my arms to my chest, allowing my father and Katka to lead the way. It smelled like old blood and rotting flesh—a smell I'd known well from when my amputated arm had become infected.

"Just over here," Katka said. The howling had ceased, but I still could hear the faint sound of someone breathing heavily, panting heavily. We stopped in front of a cell, and I watched with bated breath as Katka unlocked it and let the door swing open. They stepped aside to let me look.

I peered into...whatever it occupied the cell. It huddled against the wall in a mass larger than any man I'd ever met. It breathed raggedly, as if its chest were filled with phlegm. As I adjusted my eyes, I saw it was not wearing clothes, but was cloaked in fur. A Gwylis? No, this thing was misshapen, not like a wolf at all. When it moved, chains clanged. I took a step back as the creature rose, higher on its back legs than on its front. Almost human-like, but far removed.

I stared at it for a long time without speaking. The face was like a canine's, but wider, and its eyes were red as if they were filled with blood. Its lips peeled back, and something burst forth from its throat. Not words, but something akin to it. A sound like agony.

I backed away from it, bumping into Katka's chest. "The queen says hello," she whispered into my ear.

The queen?

I blinked and faltered, casting a look to my father. But I had to compose myself. If I let myself think about what this creature was, I would lose everything I'd worked so hard to obtain. If I let the shock and disgust push through, I would break. Gritting my teeth, I let myself smile. "She's a wonder. How did you achieve this?"

"The Gywlis are vessels for all sorts of monstrosities," Katka answered. "The Uncanny presents itself in all its dark beauty when humans are weak. Isn't she wondrous?"

Behind closed doors, I felt brave. I could imagine destroying my father from behind these castle walls. I could even tell myself that I would survive it. But looking at what the queen had become, I knew now I was too weak and far too human to do what needed to be done.

Even if I summoned enough bravery to kill him, I would get struck down soon after. This was a suicide mission. I could not deny it any further. From the moment I woke up this morning, I knew. Death would come for me, and it would be soon.

But I made my choices. This was my choice.

I stared at the queen. She'd once invited me in her home and fawned over me as if I were the object of all her admirations. The Queen of Mirosa was as cruel as she was beautiful, and if I were a weaker man, I would have let her flirtations lead elsewhere, as they once did for my father. But for all her wrongdoings, the queen did not deserve this fate. "Yes," I said finally. "She is."

At that moment, the queen fell into a crouch and widened her ruby-red eyes. "Help," she begged, her voice coming out in a wet rasp. Something thick fell from her mouth. It smelled so badly, I held a hand to my nose. "Please, help me."

The sight raised the hair on my skin. Never in my life had I seen such a thing. Never in my life would I ever forget the consequences of my actions.

If I'd only let her go.

I turned away, slapped a palm against the stone wall, and vomited. My eyesight blurred from the world around me to black as pitch. I couldn't look at the queen, not again. Instead, I leaned against the wall and curled into myself like an injured wolf.

Isabelle's face appeared. Bright as the sun, and coming closer and closer. I could almost reach out and touch her. The memory of a friend was almost enough to drown out the voice of my father.

Almost.

I still heard him there next to me. "You've always had a weak stomach. Never could stand the sight of blood."

Katka's voice came next. "Does it shame you to have such a disappointment for a son? We'd have drowned him in the river long ago."

Half a man. Half a man. Half a— Bile rose in my throat.

"The weak ones can be broken. We will build him up. It may take time, but have patience."

I looked at my father. His smile was so small, it might have been a trick of the light.

I shook my head. "I am not a disappointment."

He came close, his lips near my ear and whispered, "You've always been weak. Have you ever taken a life? You could never do it. You'd lie in your bed and weep rather do what needs to be done."

I wiped my mouth and said nothing until my father and Katka's retreating footsteps faded, and I was left alone with the thing that was once the Queen of Stormwall. If I had any courage up until this point, it was now gone.

I'd never felt so alone.

CHAPTER SIX

Two weeks after my last meeting with Flea, Derwin, and Tyron, a full moon waned above the city of Stormwall. The skies knew what tomorrow would bring, and I felt as prepared as I'd ever be. While we may not have the numbers, and the former Voiceless may not have full control over their powers, I still had mine. The same protective shield I used over Fray and then again at the Den would protect us. It was all I had. Was it enough?

Wargrave closed the shop early. I could hear him pacing upstairs as I packed my bag. It didn't hold much except Henry's journal, some food, some extra clothing, the vial of poison, my necklace, and waterskins. I would have to stash Henry's sword, my dagger, and the bag at the docks tonight as well. The only thing I would take with me tomorrow morning would be my bow. The one the Prince of the Peeks had given me. The same prince I would have to kill.

If I had to abandon the weapon, so be it. It was now something I could do without.

I fell asleep. No demons came to me. No ghosts. My dreams were nothing but a slate of blackness, and I'd never felt so alone in my entire life.

I woke when the moon sat high in the starless sky. I made my way upstairs, rubbing sleep from my eyes. There were still candles lit, which meant Wargrave was still awake. I found him sitting by the front window, muttering something about *time* and *fate*.

"What are you doing?" I asked.

"Watching the night one last time." He tapped the empty chair beside him. "Sit. I would like to talk to you about something I should have talked to you about a long time ago."

I sat and slumped back in the chair, crossing a leg over my knee. "You don't owe me anything, Wargrave."

"Yet I think I do," the shopkeeper said, and hacked into the cloth he held between his knees.

"You're dying, aren't you?"

"Yes, so let me get this out," he said, still looking out the front window. It was strange to see Wargrave so composed, so...normal. I knew he couldn't have been a ragged, high-strung shopkeeper his whole life. I wondered too late how much humanity the man had, and what had happened to strip it away.

"Go on," I said.

"Your cousin." Wargrave stopped and shoved one hand into the ripped pair of trousers he wore. He closed his fist over something, but didn't withdraw it. "I knew it wasn't you when she came to settle your debt. But it didn't matter. She had the money I wanted."

"You couldn't have done anything to stop her," I told him. "When Lulu wanted something, she got it."

"I could have. I saw the men outside the shop, in the streets, watching her as she entered and following as she left. I closed the shop and did the same."

A breath got stuck in my throat. "You saw?"

Wargrave refused to meet my eyes, staring only through the window. "They stood in that alley there. I knew they were Gwylis. I could smell their magic, and so did everyone in the Barge. The streets cleared out and the girl—your cousin—did not notice a thing. She started toward the steps back into the brightness of Stormwall and fell before she could reach the first step."

My mind raced, but I settled on the details. "You saw them kill her."

Wargrave closed his eyes briefly, and nodded. "They left her there, bleeding on the steps. I don't know if she feigned death, but she was still for so long that they left her there. She tried to stand. I watched her.

She crawled as far as she could until one of your guards found her. I ran."

I ran.

Like a crack of lightning, the scene brightened before me. Lulu paying my debt and leaving the Barge with a sense of accomplishment in her heart. Wargrave standing there, doing nothing as she bled out and tried to move, tried to survive. Did she cry out? Would she have had to? No. Wargrave was there. He knew what happened. I leaped from my seat as the first pricks of fire tickled the hairs on the back of my neck.

I blinked at him. "You did nothing."

"I couldn't, and I wouldn't. Do you know what they would do? They would have accused me. They would find Aquarius, and what do you think they would do?"

My stomach lurched. "Who cares? He's useless."

"Not useless," Wargrave said, finally meeting my eyes. There was nothing there but a cloudy look of regret. "He made you."

"You sound like the soothsayer," I said, forcing my magic down. I gripped the jewels at my breast and felt my body relax. "Everybody is a piece in this game. Meant to be in a certain place at a certain time. It's ludicrous. I hate it." I breathed slowly, letting my anger dissipate. "Why are you telling me this now?"

"Because come tomorrow, a lot of things are going to change," Wargrave said. He withdrew whatever he had in his pocket and held it out to me. I wanted to slap it out of his hand, but instead, I took it. "This will get you to Hassara, and beyond if need be."

I looked down at the familiar pouch in my hand. The velvety material itched my palm and forced me think of such times when I'd wear such things as clothing. I emptied the contents, recognizing the jewelry I'd taken from my mother. I'd stolen it, giving it to Wargrave for payment. The others, I did not recognize, but assumed they were the ones Lulu took to pay my debt. I inhaled and exhaled. This was too much.

"Do you see now, how things have all been playing how they were supposed to be played?"

"I was wrong about you," I said softly. "I thought you were a crook. I thought you were mad. But now I understand the bigger part you played in my story, so I thank you. You could not have done anything for my cousin. She made her choice. As we all did."

Talking about Lulu should have hurt. It should had felt horrible. But Wargrave was right. Things had played out, and the pieces were moving. They always had been.

I lowered myself back into the chair and poured the jewelry back into the pouch. We both said nothing for a long time, only sat and watched the night together.

"I'm sorry," he said finally.

I nodded. "I am too."

"If I hadn't plucked out my eye, I wondered if I'd have lived longer, being a wolf."

I couldn't see Wargrave as a Gwylis, but he was right. He probably would have lived longer. This was why Aquarius stayed in wolf-form, as the shopkeeper had told me, to stave off death. It made me wonder how old Aquarius truly was, and if he'd die in that cellar eventually.

Aquarius wasn't useless. I wanted to be angry at him for abandoning his pack, and abandoning me, but he'd created me, and I could not hate him. No matter how hard I tried.

Morning came. Wargrave stirred fresh porridge on the stove and scooped me a bowl. He topped it with some fresh fruit, imported I assumed, but I didn't question it. I ate it quickly, along with black tea and bread. It had to be the best breakfast I'd had in weeks. The silence was deafening. A calm before the storm.

After eating, I made my way downstairs to retrieve my bow. Last night, I'd gone to the docks to stow away my pack and sword. I felt naked without them. Vulnerable, almost. I sat on the edge of the hard mattress I'd called my bed for the past few weeks and stared at the wall. I never truly gave the room a hard look, but looking now, I saw small indentations, scratches from when I'd turned from human to Gwylis. Even the bedpost bore the results of my thrashing with gouges of their own. I laughed aloud. Here I was at the beginning, when I felt more alive than I ever had. When I had a new family, a new father to guide me, to help me through it. I had hope.

Now, there was nothing but war and death. Henry, Lulu, Ghetee. All main characters who'd met their end too soon. Their faces haunted me.

I kept calm until I couldn't keep calm any longer, and made my way to Aquarius's room.

He got to hide this way while the rest of us fought for our lives against the curse he helped create. But he gave up. He retreated. He stopped fighting.

When my eyes adjusted to the darkness of the room, I immediately locked onto the glow of the old wolf's eyes. Pale yellow eyes warning to stay away. Beacons signaling danger ahead. "You're a coward," I told him. "I could stand here and beg for you to help me, but even if you did want to, you wouldn't. Because a cowardly man does not change. You're cursed in more ways than one, but guess what? We don't need you. I thought we did, but we don't. So, die. Alone, without anybody left in the world. You utter piece of shit."

I would kill Dal Paratheon and his traitorous son and anyone who stood in my way. I didn't care any longer. I thought I came here to save Aquarius, and maybe I could have if I were a better woman. But he deserved to die for doing nothing, just as the ones who would die for standing against me. The thought burned my mind, as I turned my back to the King of the Gwylis for the last time. The burning sensation crawled up my throat until I thought I would faint. But instead, I lit the torches in the cellar with a flick of my finger until, one by one, I was surrounded by a path of flames as I moved down the corridor and upstairs to where Tyron waited.

"They're all in their places," he said. His hair was tied back, slick against his head. He wore a bow slung over this back and several knives at his hip. When I said nothing, he took a step toward me and took my hand the way he'd done after showing Aquarius to him and the Voiceless. It wasn't a romantic gesture. It was deeper. Much more important.

"I lost last time I fought here," I said.

"You have to fight a battle many times before you win," Tyron replied. "Thus, is the game of life, and if I die today, so be it. I lived long enough to see humanity fall, and that's enough for me."

I started. "You want humans to die? There won't be anything left in the world."

Tyron released my hand. "Would that be so bad? The gods will not help us. We die here in this hell, and then again for eternity."

I shook my head. Tyron had it all wrong. I didn't plan on dying today, and I sure as hell didn't plan on spending my afterlife with the Uncanny. We were still human, at least a small part of us, and that part wanted to survive.

We weren't doomed. Not all of us.

"I'm ready," I told the shopkeeper. "If things go bad, don't stay for him. Save yourself."

I clapped Wargrave on the shoulder and turned to leave. I swore I heard a howl as I left the shop. A mournful one.

CHAPTER SEVEN

Truth be told, when I'd first met Ashe Paratheon, I thought he was charming despite his smirking problem. If our paths had merged at another time, we may have come together differently. After the events at Stormwall, and when he had been banished from the Den for good, it was a relief to be rid of him. He stirred up memories and made me feel weak for how much I did not want to see him harmed, despite the things he'd done.

Maybe I trusted people far too soon.

There was no weakness to be found now. I trudged through the city I once loved, unsurprised at how many people filled the streets. After all they'd been through—their king murdered and a foreign ruler stepping in—I would have thought they cared little for their new king. But I recalled the crowds when Fray was to be executed. Death draws an audience whether they knew death was near or not.

Our best archer could shoot an impressive shot at nine-hundred feet. I'd never tested my own ability in this field, but I knew how good I was. Tyron led me past the main square, down a few maze-like alleyways that eventually poured us into a quiet area where a temple stood. I gazed up as we moved up the front steps. The bell tower was the tallest structure in all the city. But it wasn't where we'd make our stand. I waited outside as Tyron went in to check the archers stationed above. He gave a thumbs-up as he emerged, and we were on our way again.

I'd been on many rooftops in the past few weeks, so breaking into a few houses, climbing through windows, and ending up on one via a lot of precarious drainpipes and rails was nothing new. These houses though were like the ones in Abiyaya's neighborhood, stacked upon one another like crates. We were up high. The next roofs were a short jump away and perfectly aligned. I bet I could race across them in one good straight line. Up there, we could see the main square where a stage was set up. It looked like the one they'd tied Fray to. Although I lacked a straight line of sight, I would be able to see exactly where Ashe would appear.

Where my arrow would be. Or someone's arrow. Hopefully not mine.

The space within the main square grew tighter. It had not been built to hold Stormwall's population; so many people filed onto balconies or observed from their windows. I watched as people streamed down the many connected streets, trying to get closer.

My heart beat furiously as I crouched in position. I watched the people milling below. There were so many soldiers, but I sensed no Gwylis besides the ones on the towers and rooftops around me. But I didn't have time to wonder where the wolves were.

I squeezed my eyes closed and tried to imagine I was somewhere else, but in my mind, everything played out just as surreal. I saw the face of my father before I killed him. *Please*, he'd begged, *I am ashamed of what I've done. Have mercy*. I imagined my teeth sinking into his flesh and his screams ever fading as his life bled out from his body. I made that choice again—to kill someone I may have once loved. My choices molded me into what I was.

They'd called me a monster. I'd give them one.

I lost track of how long I'd stayed there drowning in my thoughts, but by the time I opened my eyes again, a tall man stood in the center of the stage, addressing the crowd. If it weren't for his cloak, adorned with the silver fish of the Peek Islands, or the gold crown on his head, I'd thought he were just another man.

Dal Paratheon was just another man. I bet he bled like one too.

"It is time for a new beginning and a new world," the traitor king intoned. "I know you mourn the loss of your dear king and queen and their children, but I can, with great honesty, tell you I will give you a new royal family to adore."

The usurper king talked with his hands. Every word was a sweeping gesture, long fingers cutting the space between him and the crowd. The people responded, clearly distracted at how charming the Paratheon men can be, and started to cheer.

"I will assure Mirosa forgets the generations of bloodshed the Rowans have given your kingdom, and usher you into a future bigger and brighter. No longer will we fight the Old Kingdom. No longer will we waste our efforts and human lives searching for something that's always been in front of our eyes."

Something stirred inside of me. I recognized it as envy. Dal Paratheon wore my father's crown. He sat on my family's throne. He ate at their table and slept in their beds. He walked the halls where Lulu and I once roamed, feeding our late night cake addictions. Where Henry once stood, the best of the Rowan name.

I closed my eyes and sighed. *What a waste.*

My eyes opened to the sky where I said a quick prayer to whatever gods decided to listen to a young girl with demon magic coursing through her veins.

It did not matter what my family had done. This kingdom was mine, and I would not let him run it into the ground.

The demons snickered, and I gave a full-body shake to shut them up.

I nocked an arrow.

My hands trembled.

Breathe. One, two, three.

"Mirosa is stronger with a Paratheon on the throne, for a long time to come," Dal continued, his voice surpassingly baritone for how skinny he appeared. I released a little trickle of magic and light the end of my arrow. From the other rooftops, Tyron stared back. *The gods will not help us. We die here in this hell, and then again for eternity.*

I watched him touch his fingers to his lips and wave—a sign of farewell. I held up my hand to signal him to hold, and he relayed the message down the line. We had to wait for Ashe to appear, or all of this would be for naught.

Amid it all, Ashe Paratheon came into view, taking up beside his father. From this vantage point, I could see his hair had grown, but he'd trimmed his beard into a shadow. He wore a sword at his hip in the finest clothes Mirosa could buy. He didn't turn to look my way, but stayed facing the crowd.

Rage surged through me, fierce like a firestorm. *I trusted you.*

Still, I held my hand to Tyron. For what, I did not know. A shred of hope, perhaps? A wish that somehow, I did not have to see Ashe fall? He'd come so far to die here. Why?

His father continued talking, but I drowned him out. Words meant nothing now. I stood from my crouch, impervious of the danger I put myself into by doing so, willing the prince to look my way. I thought I saw it. A tick of his jaw. My scent, maybe hitting his nostrils. But I decided there was nothing, and set to aiming again. I lined it up, right into the side of his head. I gave Tyron a sidelong glance and prepared to give him the go-ahead when something happened.

A look. A glance, barely there, but seen by only those who were looking.

The scene went deathly quiet as I watched Ashe unsheathe his sword and, in one quick motion, brought it toward his father's back. The sword did not cut cleanly through, but it'd been enough to kill the king. His body stood still before crumpling into itself.

The world stopped.

The crowd, still confused as they watched the blood pour from their king's neck, and Ashe, oh Ashe, still wielding his sword with one arm whirled toward me. The entire world held a collective breath. In one swift move, he dropped the sword and spread his arms open, awaiting the barrage of arrows soon to come his way.

I sucked in a breath.

And finally came to life.

Something tore open inside of me. The world snapped back into place, and the screams began as I called on my demon magic to protect Ashe. A light, unlike all the darkness I'd come to know, pitched forward and encircled the prince just as the first arrows flew. Screams thundered through the air as the people's stupor finally broke. Chaos erupted.

Run, my mind told me.

Run, it screamed.

I surged to my feet and bounded across the roof. I leapt onto the next roof, where Tyron whirled toward me with his bow in one hand, dagger in the other. I looked past him, to the others, who still tried to penetrate the magic I'd given to Ashe.

"We were wrong," I croaked. "Call them off the prince."

But Tyron made no move. *He must be in shock.*

I slapped him good and hard. "Wake up! Get to the ground. Lift your swords!"

The crowds below were already in turmoil. They streamed every which way, making it difficult for the soldiers, who had only arrived, to get to Ashe. But nobody focused on them. They were all still trying to bring down the prince.

The sky growled, a warning of a storm coming through.

"Stop!" I screamed, and ran past Tyron to the next roof and then the other. My heart crashed against my ribs, threatening to tear itself from my body. I skidded to a stop at each archer we had stationed, telling them to direct their arrows west to the soldiers streaming through into the main square. More and more of them. Not Gwylis, but men armed to the teeth.

A sudden sense of a hope erupted inside of me. We could do this. We could win.

But first, I had to get to Ashe.

My chant was a match for the thunder cracks above. I tore my clothes off as the sky opened to drench my human skin. A fierce burn traveled through my blood. The wolf came quickly, and I raised my head into the crashing rain and howled, long and hard.

Time for battle.

The roof threatened to break under my weight. I dashed to the next roof as the once Voiceless began chants of their own. One by one, they became wolves. I didn't slow until my four paws finally hit solid ground. I shook the rain from my fur in a full-body shiver and howled again. This time, others answered.

I'd landed in an alleyway barely wide enough for my massive form. But I knew I'd have an easier time getting to the prince than the soldiers. People parted for me, fear rampant and thick in the air. The rain came down so viciously, I could hardly see, but it didn't matter. My other senses were sharpened to fine points. Fire burned under my skin, igniting the space around me. The world was mine.

The battle was already raging when I made my way into the main square. Emptied of spectators, it now showcased both humans and wolves, steel against teeth and claw. The scent of blood laid heavy. I followed it toward the stage, toward Ashe, hoping my barrier magic had stayed.

The bells chimed. Soon, more enemies would come. I hoped the former Voiceless knew enough of their magic to stave them off.

The familiar scent of him took me not to the stage, but behind a shop. A strange buzzing interrupted my senses. *My magic must be gone,* I thought. *He's vulnerable.* He huddled behind a stack of pallets. The sounds of battle edged out in the distance as I moved.

"Ashe, it's Isabelle. You must go to the docks. The Queen Isabelle. Are you listening?"

Are you listening? My body shuddered with shame. I'd pegged him a traitor, when all the while he'd been orchestrating the biggest move of all. I'd been wrong, but there wasn't time to lament. Not yet.

I casted a glance behind me to make sure nobody had followed. I'd have to return soon. I couldn't leave my allies alone to fight without me. I took myself into a sitting position beside the pallets as Ashe stepped out.

Without warning, his arms encircled me, clutching my fur tight and burying his face into my ruff. Ashe's frail body took a staggered breath.

"Ashe." My voice was deep, and vibrated through him.

He pulled back. His hair wet and matted against his forehead. Weary eyes sat behind dark circles. "Isabelle."

I felt nothing but fear. He had to get to safety before his father's soldiers came for him. But I couldn't go with him. I had to go back.

Eyes wide, Ashe took a step back and nodded, his face dotted with blood.

Adrenaline pumped through my body as I turned away from him, setting my sights on the task at hand. *Take back Stormwall.*

I slipped out of the alley and back into the thrall. The Gwylis sympathizers were still on the rooftops. Arrows whizzed by sporadically. Most of them missed entirely, impeded by the wall of rain. The Voiceless, now Gwylis, roared into the square like the massive drums at the Den. There were hundreds of us, at least. More than I thought. Our bodies filled the square, daring any soldiers to enter. The enemy did dare, creeping out from the streets bracing out every highway, and one by one, they went.

It was an unceremonious affair, and my teeth were still clean.

So, I bounded up the stage where Dal Paratheon's body still lay and took up the crown in my teeth. "Listen up, people of Stormwall," I roared. "I am Princess Isabelle Victoria Rowan. I hereby take back my crown by blood and by right. Bow or die."

The soldiers halted their efforts and listened as the rain beat down on their heads. I had their attention, but not their allegiance. That was all right. I didn't need it. I smelled their fear, and that was enough for me.

I opened my jaw for another rousing speech.

And then the screams began.

CHAPTER EIGHT

The bells alarming Stormwall of war.

The clang of swords on swords and teeth on teeth.

The smell of blood in the air.

The sight of a girl on a rooftop, her face pale with shock, arm outstretched toward me.

I killed my father.

When I walked out onto that stage, I saw not only the man I hated, but the crowds. It was almost as if all Mirosa had come to stand before me.

It couldn't breathe. I wasn't sure how my feet made it across the stage to where my father stood. I pressed my fingers into the hilt of my sword as my father rattled on. I stood tall, spine straight, chin raised, like a prince. Like he taught me.

The crowds cheered at their king's every word. How quickly their allegiance swayed. It angered me to the point where I felt nothing when I unsheathed my sword.

Everything rushed at me as I stumbled through the streets of Stormwall. Get to the docks. Find the Queen Isabelle. She said I'd be safe there. But first, I had to survive.

As I ran, my mind shifted back to when my sword sunk into my father's flesh. I hadn't a single second thought. One moment, the king was speaking, gesturing toward me, and the next, I'd killed him.

I should have died.

But Isabelle was there, and she stayed her arrow.

All around me, women and children ran. The streets pulsed with frantic energy. They ran into homes and locked and barred their doors. But I knew that wouldn't keep the Gwylis out for long.

I killed my father.

I shouldered my way through toward an armory. Thankfully, the doors were still open. I rushed in, elbowing a man who came out from my left. He tried to shove me back, but I got a good grip on his collar and managed to throw him into a wall of daggers.

"I'm human, you idiot," I growled. I eyed the weapon on his hip. "Give me your sword."

The man relented, but eyed my missing arm with wariness. "You're the prince."

I straightened my spine and took the word in hand. "Your city is gone, and if you don't plan on becoming a demon, you should run now. As far as you can go. Find the symbol of the moon and sun merging with stars above. That's your best way to survive."

The man shook his head, his eyes widening. He started when I laid on hand on his shoulder.

"The stars are bright tonight. Remember that or die."

I did not know my way around the city. I followed only the scent of the ocean and the tips of ships I could see in the distance. When the earth sloped and the buildings rose, I found myself panicked. I felt like a mouse in a maze. I tripped on a cobblestone and nearly fell into my sword.

Stop. Breathe.

The battle was far behind me, but I knew I would not outrun it today.

"This way."

I drew in a sharp breath and turned to see the soothsayer's teal robe disappearing around a bend. My boots echoed in the quiet. I held out my sword, and my arm ached.

Down another left and then a right, and I found myself in a court-yard. Stacked housing all around me. Abiyaya beckoned me across the yard with a whistle like a songbird. I double stepped, taking a moment to walk backward to see behind. I ran. The ocean cut between two buildings. I was close. Abiyaya waited for me to catch up to her.

Our eyes met—my green to her dark. And in that moment, I felt peace. I felt hope.

Pain stabbed my skull, and I fell forward. I caught myself before I hit my knees and whirled, sword in hand, toward my attacker. This sword was meant for two hands, and it took a great deal of strength to wield. A raging storm of emotions ran through me—anger, unadulterated fear, but mostly shock. The man wore the silver fish of my island home. This was my kin.

It had been a monstrous thing, killing my father, and I would never seek forgiveness, because it wasn't a thing so easily forgiven. Still, it was a thing I did not regret. It should have brought me down, but only made me stronger. A taste of power. A sense of the control I never had. The control he took from me. But I not only did it for myself; I did it for my home, and my friends. For my family.

Instead of gutting the soldier, I merely kicked and shoved. I raged like a beast unleashed. The world had broken me, and I raged and raged until he lost his balance and did not know what to do with me.

"You think you are a man?" My arm ached from holding the heavy sword steady, and it took everything in me not to give into the lightheadedness threatening to overtake me.

The man dropped his sword and scurried backwards, dragging his backside across the dirt. He trembled violently at the sight of me. Suddenly, I saw what exactly he saw: my father. I could deny it all I wanted, but I was Dal Paratheon's son. I was violent, deceptive. Killing him had been my one act of proving everybody right. But the difference between us was that my father never regretted anything cruel he'd ever done. He would never let his actions make him sick. He'd have a party over it instead of wanting to vomit all over this poor soldier who had only been following his orders.

"There's no time for grieving, boy," the soothsayer called out.

Somewhere between that courtyard and the Queen Isabelle, I'd dropped the heavy sword and stumbled up the ramp onto the ship. A man with a scarred face and missing eye threw out one arm and knocked it against my throat, throwing me onto the deck. I landed hard on my backside. A searing pain shot up my spine.

"Where's the princess?"

I choked and struggled for breath. I hit my chest with my fist, as if to start up my lungs once again. "She's coming," I said. "I'm Ashe Paratheon. She told me to come here. She said I'd be safe. The stars are bright—"

"What happened to your arm?"

I opened my mouth, but nothing came out. The missing part of my limb twisted and burned painfully. I gritted my teeth against it.

"Aye, yeah," the scarred man said, holding out a hand. I took it and climbed to my feet. He narrowed his eyes as he looked at me. "Did you do the thing?"

"Do the thing?"

The man laughed a with his whole body and threw an arm around me. He gazed out into the distance, to the smoke rising from the city. "I'm Derwin. Looks like we lost the city."

The words hit me harder than I thought they would, seeing as I'd been thinking the same thing this whole time. But hearing them was different. There was a finality to it.

I couldn't speak to it. I wasn't sure how.

I killed my father.

I shivered at the memory. I walked out of Derwin's arm and retched over the side of the ship. When I finished, I hung my head over the railing and threw out a prayer to the gods.

"You're pale as a ghost," Derwin said. "You're in shock. You need to lie down."

"No, I shouldn't be here. I should go back for her."

Derwin laughed again. "Aye, she can take care of herself, boy, don't you worry. Besides, you'll only get yourself killed walking around out there looking the way you do."

As the battle for Stormwall raged on, I let Derwin lead me beneath the ship to a room with a single cot. He left me there, in the dark, but even then, the vivid images playing out behind my closed eyes.

I waited for Isabelle to return so we could leave this nightmare behind.

CHAPTER NINE

"Gwylis, coming from the east!" someone hollered from the rooftops. "Retreat!"

I had not sensed another Gwylis in the weeks I'd been in Stormwall, but now, with those words, things have changed.

I'd won the day, hadn't I?

Ashe killed Dal, and I took the throne for myself, and I declared it in the city streets. I had taken Stormwall.

I'd been wrong.

I leapt from the stage and approached Tyron, who stood, legs spread and ears pinned back. "We have to run. There's a Gwylis army coming from the rear."

A muscle in his snout twitched. "We will not run."

"This cannot be where we fight this army, Tyron. We will hurt too many innocents."

Tyron huffed. "We knew we would die today. This is nothing new."

The other wolves dipped their heads in assent, looks of determination set into their eyes and into the cage of their teeth.

Tyron wanted to win—I knew this—but we had to win smarter, and the only victory we would take from this was running and assembling a new plan.

Tyron turned and address the rebels. "We knew victory would come with our own bloodshed. We stand here, and we fight! Today, we will stand beside the gods with honor. Today, we will have their favor!"

A chant grew within the wolves now, growing louder and louder. The first of the marching feet as the Gwylis army grew nearer. "They'd have to come through the forest surrounding the city, which would ultimately slow them down," Tyron said. "We could pick them off as they came, funneling them through the city gates and into the narrow streets. Innocent people would die, but such is the way of war."

I chose to believe it could be done, and it was better than the insurmountable sense of defeat.

"Bring me the white wolf's head," Tyron roared.

"Tyron!" I roared. He and the rebels charged from the square toward the King's Road. The earth shook beneath their paws. Past the first of the trees, they met Katka's head-on in a violent slam of bodies and teeth.

Wolves snarled and fell around me, by claw, by magic. Before I finished shifting, even before the first wave of demon-filled flames lit my skin. I charged toward the nearest enemy, tearing through the thick mass of bodies beginning to block the road into the city, staying close to Tyron as we led the army through the city gates in an attempt to funnel the army through and pick them off one by one.

Fury built up inside of me at the thought.

It rose to greet me, scorching fire that would be my namesake.

I found myself knocked to the ground, the breath leaving my lungs by a slam to my ribcage, and I lay there momentarily stunned, unable to breathe. A crow passed overhead, circling above me as the clouds moved to block the sun.

Teeth came bit into my back leg, clamping shut until I howled in pain.

But something slammed my attacker off its feet. The pain subsided enough for me to regain my footing and watch my attacker choke on its own blood, stabbed through the heart by a soldier's sword.

"Isabelle." My savior, a young soldier, pulled his sword free and turned to me. It was Aliper, Lulu's suitor—the one who'd carried her dying body back to the castle.

I shook my body and bared my teeth. "There is no winning this," I told him as the battle raged before us. The stench of blood filled my nostrils, causing a frenzy amongst the Gwylis. We backed away until we stood on a sidewalk in front of the Old Hen tavern. "This is no place for a human."

Aliper swung his sword at an advancing Peek Island soldier and cut him down swiftly. I saw what my cousin had seen in him. He was handsome, strong, and brave. But he was also going to die today.

"Is Tamir with you?" I inquired about the old captain of the guard.

Aliper nodded. "We played sides, as most did, but when we saw you on that stage, we knew what side to take without question."

"Thank you, my friend."

Aliper bowed his head. "It was what she would have wanted." With that, he charged forward, bloody sword in hand.

I began to follow when an explosion shook the ground beneath me. I looked up in time to see a building collapsing on itself, sending a cloud of dust into the sky. Then another, and another, until building after building was leveled and Gwylis came through. They were tearing the city apart.

My world became a haze of violence. I couldn't see the fight ensuing around me. I gnashed my teeth, claws used like steel swords. Fighting through the fog, the ringing in my ears, I carved through the enemy with the ease of a god. Nothing could touch me. I was burning embers.

I called out to Tyron only to find him amongst a tangle of both Gwylis and human bodies sprawled in the city square. The fog thinned, and I saw allied soldiers made a wall against the advancing Gwylis, which gave me time to get Tyron to his feet.

"It's over." Tyron tipped over and fell onto his side. Blood gushed from a severe wound to his abdomen, spilling the intestines from inside. He coughed blood. The spatters hit my face. "I've honored the gods."

The line of soldiers fell away. Soon we'd be exposed to the enemy. I took up guard in front of Tyron's body and called upon my magic to puddle the ground with fires. But ice-magic froze them away. I tried again, but fear surpassed my power.

Gwylis rebels to my right clashed with the oncoming enemy. A wolf fell to my right, and two soldiers battled off to my left. Flame-tipped arrows shot down from the roofs of buildings.

"Isabelle," Tyron said, shifting into human form. His injuries looked so grave, I almost had to turn away. The color slipped from his eyes. "Our queen, you have to live."

I called upon my power to shield Tyron and myself. It took everything out of me to do so. I laid on my belly and set my muzzle atop the man's body. "I will live, but not because you told me to."

Tyron laughed as he turned to look at me. His eyes, once pale blue, looked almost clear as glass as his life swept away from him. Grief poured into me; tears pooled in my eyes. I licked away the blood, but the rebel would not last much longer. The battle continued around me, only as close as my shield would allow.

"Do something for me." Tyron tried to sit up on his elbows, but failed. He swallowed and asked again. "Break the curse. Set us free."

Tyron looked at me expectantly.

I laid still, hearing the world as though I were underwater. Muffled screams of the dying. I could stay in here forever if I wanted to. But I stood and finally let the shield drop.

My roar shook the world around me.

I'm sorry, Tyron.

Abandoning my friend, I raced again toward war.

I focused back on the battle to find a trio of wolves charging toward me. I sidestepped out of their path and sunk my teeth into the closest one. I tasted its soft belly before throwing it away. The other—a reddish-brown wolf with an ugly gash on its snout—came at me. But it was injured in more places than one, and I knocked it aside easily enough.

"Stormwall is ours," it roared, saliva mixed with blood dripping from its jaw. One of its lower canines had been knocked out. "You are no queen. You are nothing."

Rage burned like a fierce firestorm. Shadows spun around in my vision, and with it came my magic. My entire body buzzed with it. When the red wolf ran at me, it found my fire, hot as the seven hells. It burned into ash in less than a minute. It never had time to cry.

I slipped through the thrall like the wind, leaving battered bodies and abandoned swords in my wake, the cries of the dying like a chorus from the underworld. The city drowning in red.

"Leave now!" I cried out as I went. "Retreat, or you will all die!"

The rubble of fallen buildings moved under my feet. I set my fire onto everything I encountered. Houses. Enemy Gwylis and Peek soldiers. I aided a few rebels before moving on, sniffing out the one wolf I knew would end this: Katka.

Through the thick curtain of the burning city, I kept moving. I staggered over bodies, my legs weakening and my body exhausted. I wound my way through the streets, blowing out windows with the force of my magic.

The further I went from the battle, the stronger Katka's scent became. Was she running? Or was she hunting me, as I hunted her?

Finally, I reached the entrance to the Barge, where innocents were fleeing. Pain made me stumble as I walked past them toward the outskirts of the city, where the less fortunate lived. I padded down the streets, encountering a barrage of arrows and makeshift traps. I broke them with my own heavy paws.

"Katka!"

My deep and scorching roar shook the earth. People screamed at the sight of me now. Bows were abandoned on rooftops. Children huddled into corners.

When they looked at me, they saw a monster, but I felt every inch a god.

At the height of my magic, I found her.

I recognized her immediately. How could I not? Standing fifty meters down a straight, dimly-lit street stood the wolf I had not bet on, the wolf who I'd seen once before in the forest outside of the Den. Fifty meters away was Katka.

She was the thing in stories made to frighten children, and Dal's secret weapon. How could we not have seen this? Tyron mentioned her only in passing, and did not feel concerned. He had been wrong.

"Bow to your new queen," the great white wolf snarled. She moved slowly, calculating. Every step in tandem with my heart, in tandem with the demons hissing their joy and writhing for release.

"I don't see a queen," I growled. "I see nothing more than a dog. A big one. But honestly, I'm a little underwhelmed by you."

Katka laughed, her giant paws lifting daintily as she walked toward me at a snail's pace. She was white as a ghost, but certainly not as friendly as any I'd met. "Where is Aquarius?"

"This again? I thought we'd gone over this. I don't know."

Katka licked her lips. As she neared, I noted a shimmering all around her. Had she cast a shield as I had? I didn't know other Gwylis could do that, unless...

"You made a deal with the Uncanny."

Katka stopped, not ten feet between us. I lowered my head, snarling under my breath. I brought one paw down onto the ground, the equivalent of slamming a human fist onto a table, and let loose the quake magic. But it split the ground beneath my feet and snacked toward Katka only to stop short. I tried again, but the battle and my own personal wrath had drained my magic.

Panic seized my body. I thought tracking Katka and finished her would end this war—a quick and sudden plan that felt all too easy. All I had to do was kill her, and I'd have control over the Greatwolf Pack. But I thought the same about killing Dal Paratheon, and look where that ended.

It took everything in me to start backing away from the white wolf. *Our queen*, Tyron had said, *you have to live*. It seemed easy enough.

But there was nothing easy about this.

Katka attacked. Despite the fatigue in my body, my mind was alert and reacted, but not in time for Katka to land a blow. My body landed on the ground, the air leaving my lungs. A blow to my head, leaving me unconscious would be a welcome relief, its own form of escape. But the adrenaline pumped in me so hard and so fast. A spark of flames hit Katka's thick white coat, setting it ablaze.

My body sagged with exhaustion. I felt depleted. Empty.

"You stupid shits!" I snarled, pushing to my feet. "We had a deal!"

And we have only a limited source of power. Work with what you have.

What I had was nothing. Branch taught me to harness and control my magic and how to fight as a human. Such a small amount of time was spent on how to take down a monstrous bitch on a power trip.

But either way, if I were to die, I would die standing.

The world does not bend for you.

I vaulted toward Katka, taking her by surprise. Once on her back, I pinned down the white wolf and held her there with all the strength I had left. She pushed me off, and we tumbled and spun, lips peeled back, whining and growling simultaneously.

Katka took hold of my already injured leg and sent fire into her teeth. It seared my skin, sending shocks of pain forking through me.

My magic waned from my body. My heart beat with every step the white wolf called Katka took, as if counting down the moments before it stopped.

I managed a small burst of fire. It spiraled from my snout into the air between us. It made me feel more dangerous. Less trapped. The tears slid from my eyes as my body shifted back into human form. I slumped there on the cobblestone, allowing myself at least one more moment to look at the sky and how the clouds had parted, revealing the sun. The sky turned from black to blue. Had the sky always been this blue? Why had I not stopped to notice it before?

"Henry," I said. "Lulu. Ghetee."

Katka was more than twenty steps away, but she stopped to admire my frail body shivering not with cold, but anticipation. I saw the people I lost not just in my mind, but in front of me as living, breathing things. I recalled a moment like this when I was shot in my shoulder by the arrow, before I lost consciousness. I had seen Henry then, but that was before I sold my soul. I closed my eyes, feeling in my heart and in my bones, this may be the last time I would see them. As memories, as ghosts, as pieces of my heart I had lost.

A bubbling of laughter erupted from Katka. "Such a sad, sad girl. It's almost a shame to kill you. You'd be great entertainment for my court."

"A Gwylis will never sit atop the throne," I rasped.

"They will, oh, they will. The lords of Essex are making sure of that."

I choked out the words, "What's in Essex?"

Katka howled a laugh. "My children."

I don't know how long I sat there, watching the Gwylis's jaws come to open above my head. The saliva came like rain, and I shivered at her breath on my skin. I didn't even lift my head to watch my death. I couldn't. My vision clouded, and my body iced over. I felt the world tilting out of my control, and I was a mere pawn on its axis.

Footfalls and a growl sounded. Something was coming behind me.

My vision slipped in and out as I turned. A shadow came bounding up the street, first on two legs and then on four, and all at once, the shadow leapt into the air and became a storm.

Katka reeled back as the storm hit her. A roar unlike anything I'd ever heard took the world into its grasp. Katka whined, and the storm ate up her voice, cutting her off. The skirmish was enough to bring me back from the edge of fainting. I saw snippets of what was happening. A white blur. A thrashing of teeth on flesh. The way the wind shifted and the sun blinked. The strong scent of blood in the air.

"Aquarius," I tried to say, but the blackness was coming again.

The world grew silent. The storm stood over me. Waiting. Watching. Blood slid down his smooth white teeth and dropped onto my slick skin. "You've mourned for too long," he said. "Get up."

The voice was so familiar—one I'd heard just after the Gwylis king had bitten me. After, he'd become just as voiceless as the results of my father's poison. Now...now, his words were as patient as the trees, but as ruthless as an earthquake. I stood up on shaky legs, naked as the day I was born, and set my spine straight as an arrow. The King of the Gwylis considered me once and then turned away, his tail nearly knocking me off my feet.

"Let's go," he grumbled.

I took one glance back, expecting a heap of white and red fur, but Katka was not there. I shifted back into wolf form and dashed to catch up to Aquarius.

The city was lost; that much was clear. The fires were spreading. We dodged flaming timber and frantic townsfolk as we moved toward the docks. I limped behind Aquarius to the south end of the city and down the steps to the Barge, where the chaos of battle felt less frantic. We pushed through until we came to Wargrave's, where a handful of soldiers emerged.

"Go," Aquarius told me, shoving his head into my side.

"No, I won't leave you here—"

Aquarius cast his pale-yellow eyes to me. "You have no choice. You either stay and die in this city, or you do what came to do." His eyes searched mine.

I nodded. He was right, and I could not refute it. I was too weak now to fight; the shadows had yet to return, and my body refused to summon even a trickle of magic.

I grazed my muzzle across the old wolf's neck. "Thank you."

"Go now." He pushed me away. My feet found purchase and took me down the dark streets.

Steady, Izzy. Count to three.

I ran. I ran so fast the world blurred around me. There may have been enemies coming my way, but I was already gone. By the time I made it to the docks, I was near ready to collapse.

Shift back.

Someone was screaming. My belly hit the ground. I had to shift back, or I would not make it onto the ship. I'd fall through the docks with my weight.

A wave of disquiet rolled through me. My eyes shuttered closed. Exhaustion rolled over me like a wave, my muscles weak, my heart slowing to a dull thud. I felt like a legless thing, ready to succumb. Ready to sleep.

A smell hit my nose, and my eyes cracked open to find the shape of a man standing over me.

He had sandy blond hair and light green eyes. A handsome face.

"I'm sorry I didn't trust you," I said, shifting back into a human. My words were barely there, like whispers.

"Isabelle, stop." His arms wrapped around me, lifting me from the ground, and he was warm like a blanket. I buried my face into his chest.

The tears came swiftly. I thought my heart was destroyed, but I was too numb now to feel it. "We lost the city. We lost."

His arms tightened around me as he moved, his pace quickening as his boots hit wood instead of cobblestone. He stumbled once, but kept going. He was weak. My own strength drained. How could we make it now?

Aquarius was gone. The city, burned. It may not have a ruler, but one would step up. To keep composed, I imagined instead the things I loved, the things I missed. A boy with startling blue eyes and sun-kissed skin. Would he be the last thing I saw before I died? I hoped so, but his face faded, gone like the memory of a sound.

"Don't leave me too." My words choked me up, and I coughed until my chest ached. Spots danced behind my eyes. "Don't leave me like everyone else does. Please don't, Fray."

"I'm not going to leave you."

With that, I finally closed my eyes and drifted into darkness.

CHAPTER TEN

I hung my head into the basin of water and let myself drown.

My head was leaden. My arms hung uselessly at my sides. My grief swept through me, fatal as the fang of a venomous snake. I closed my eyes against the sting, willing it to stop.

Will it ever stop?

I remembered the last time I felt so...downtrodden. It had been after I drank the poisoned water and went to speak, only to hear nothing. After I'd been broken and beaten and had everything a man should have taken away from him: family, strength of both heart and body, and faith most of all. Faith that things would work out, even though you'd done things all wrong.

It was after I stood amongst my pack and saw that we had lost everything.

I could not resist the roar and the intake of water it sucked into my lungs as I lifted my head. I spat it out. Olio looked on. He'd watched me do this more than once. He probably understood why.

He knew not to mention it.

My house at the Den was quiet, save for the dribbles of water falling from the tips of my hair onto the floor. Quiet was my worst enemy. In the stillness, I thought too much, and thinking too much never led to anything good.

It led to broken furniture and the entire pack giving me a wide berth.

In the days following Izzy's departure, the world had gone still. Roiling with hurt, our separation felt almost too much to bear at times, often keeping me up at night. When I did sleep, I saw her, and I'd wake up reaching for her, but only finding an empty space.

Why didn't you tell me you were leaving? Why didn't you trust me? I loved you. I did not fault you for what happened to my mother. You must know that.

Forcing away the urge to shift into a wolf, run through the mountain and past the Archway to find her, I turned instead to watch Olio shift in his chair. He crossed one leg over the other, and sighed. "It's exhausting, watching you do the things you do."

I scowled at him. "Then leave."

"What, and miss the great character arc I know is coming?" He tipped his head and grinned. "The down-on-himself young man, seemingly lost in the world with only a handsome man as his friend, who finds his place in the world after much turmoil. I wouldn't miss this story for the world."

I shook out my wet hair and frowned. "Let me guess, you're the handsome friend."

"In the flesh."

This house, in the Den, was going to tear me apart. Although I wasn't currently alone, it wasn't always like this. I should be used to being alone; I'd been alone for a long time before. But now, solitude was a pressing thing, and sometimes I woke as though I'd been underwater. I dreamt of a person who was made of fire, who I'd given my heart to.

The thing was, it still felt as though a big chunk of it was missing from my chest, and I almost always slumped over as if the rest were going to fall out too.

I must be in shock. I didn't think we'd win. The odds were stacked against us. The Den should have fallen, and I should not have been alive. But weeks had passed. Weeks and weeks, and still I woke with breath in my lungs and with a very real thought: Something much bigger was about to happen.

My world was slowly breaking apart. Only losing her would shatter it completely.

Whether the blame lay on Izzy alone was not up for debate. Rixon left her no choice. She saw the vulnerability and the loyalty in Izzy. Anyone could. Which was why, when I woke up to find her gone all those weeks ago, it did not surprise me. Not one bit.

I dreamed of her voice. *I love you. Don't come after me.*

So, I waited. And waited. But there had been no crows, no word of anything happening beyond the Archway. And the vulnerability I once saw in Izzy, I felt every day since.

Something had to be done. Olio knew it too.

"She won't forgive you if you go after her," he said, reading my thoughts. I slumped down at the table and ran a hand through my hair, tugging at the knots. "And she wouldn't want you moping around like some sad case, either."

"We've been doing nothing since we won," I said. "We've rebuilt parts of the wall, but other than that..." I looked Olio dead in the eyes and said, "Nothing."

Olio narrowed his eyes. "If you want to go, I won't stop you. I think that Izzy has a bigger plan than you and I think. I also think she's mad as a goose, but she's not my mate."

I rapped my knuckles on the table. My left knee bounced incessantly. Men needed a purpose. And wolves needed to feel that bond to another. We were not meant to stay in one place.

We were not meant to be alone.

Sometimes I wondered which traits were mine, and which were those of the Gwylis.

So, I stood up and headed out to the one place I knew would help; a place where I could release what burned inside.

Olio called after me, "Wait! We need to go see Branch. He said—"

The words cut off the faster I went. I didn't need to hear them. I needed a release.

~

THE DEN HAD IMPLEMENTED THE PITS AS THEIR OFFICIAL training ground. Without Kester around, we were free to fight and train whoever wanted to be trained. Sometimes it felt like pulling teeth, the way we had to recruit people. But reminding them of what happened and what we lost during the battle deemed enough. Especially after Ghetee's funeral.

Spring came, and when the snow melted and the sun warmed, we set out to bury the young wolf the way his mother, Rini, intended. She'd found a spot in the gardens to the north side of the city: a quiet space just for him. One of our woodworkers created a coffin fit for the small boy, and in it, we laid the first flowers of the season. Burying Ghetee felt like the end of something. But also, the beginning of something else.

Branch was elected leader of the pack with not much fanfare. He refused the title of king, something we all agreed was not fitting at the time. But the votes were unanimous, and he accepted with modesty.

I wondered what Izzy would say if she were there. Part of me thought the Den would cast her name into the ballot. But Izzy was not anyone. I knew that was something she would not have wanted. Branch was her teacher, and her friend. She would be happy for him.

So now, we were a pack of fighters, and not only in secret, but out in the open again. Gone were the days of sneaking out to battle each other in our Gwylis forms. Gone were the days when weapons were no longer forged and magic no longer practiced. We would no longer be caught off-guard when the enemy came. We would be prepared to defend ourselves, and if Izzy did manage to break the curse, we'd have to look to man-made weapons once again. We had to be ready.

Olio trailed behind me, whistling tunelessly. It had rained this morning, the earthy smell still strong on the grass and leaves. Our ancestors called rain *echor*, tears of the gods, and here I was with it soaking my boots and dripping from leaves. The gods should be crying for what we'd done.

The thought of Aquarius making a deal with the Uncanny and ultimately trading away our lives fuels the fury inside. Before, I had sided with him. To fight someone with power, you must have power in return. Or so I'd thought. But now, I wished I'd died a soldier's death rather than let a demon take hold of my body.

Powerless yet again.

The first time I'd shifted into a wolf, my mother watched with a smile on her face. It was painful, and I was sure I would die. Still, she watched, doing nothing, and when her child was no longer human, she opened her arms and cooed, "Come here, my little pup."

Naked and afraid, unaware of the enormity of my affliction, I crawled to her. Rixon taught me the ways of being a wolf, and each time I changed, it grew less painful. She said everything would be all right.

It would never be all right. Gods, it was never all right.

I stalked through the forest now, only slowing when I reached the Pit. Overcome by the scent of wolves, my magic stirred. Whispering the chant under my breath, I stripped off my clothing, tugged my tunic over my head, and undid my belt. I'd only kicked off the remaining leg of my pants when I dropped to all fours.

I roared once as a human, and then loud like thunder as the demon magic took hold in furious waves, turning my human body into something taut with muscles and thick tawny brown fur. When I was done, I joined the other Gwylis at the Pits.

I could hear their breaths and the beating of their hearts, as if we were one. My senses sharpened to points. I could hear birds rustling in their nests; the steady stream of another wolf pissing nearby; scurrying of animals in the underbrush. The world felt alive.

A large white wolf named Shaine was there, calling out the names of two young wolves who were facing off in the center of the crowd. They fought clumsily, as young wolves did. After some time, they were called to take a break. The pups were taken aside and informed them of what they'd done wrong, and how to better themselves for their next bout. After, they turned and announced free-fighting time.

I dug my claws into the soft earth. My fur rippled with the anticipation. I curled my lips as the young wolves practically tripped over themselves to get out of my way. I smelled fear on them, rank and vile. "I will fight."

Shaine rose his massive muzzle into the air, taking in my scent from across the fighting grounds. "Fray Castor, that's what, the third time this week?"

"Fourth," I corrected, and shook out my fur. "Who will take me on?"

The Gwylis murmured amongst themselves. Since arriving at the Den, my popularity had slowly increased, but not without sacrifice. They no longer saw me as a traitor, but one of them. But when Izzy left, I had taken on a new role. My presence at the Pit as of late nearly solidified their feelings toward me. I was powerful, and I wasn't going anywhere.

I looked around, but nobody offered themselves up. I strode out into the center and dipped my head low, letting out a deafening roar, hoping to rope in a serious contender. My teeth gnashed. Several wolves retreated, but none volunteered.

All except one skinny mound of black and white fur attached to long, spindly legs.

The flash of amusement in the wolf's eyes as it approached nearly had me lunging without the go-ahead. "I'll have a go." A female.

"Neera Vano," Shaine announced. "Fray Castor. Play nice, now."

Neera Vano. The name sounded familiar, but I could not place a face to it. There wasn't time anyhow. She fell into an attack stance and darted toward me before Shaine finished speaking. I sidestepped and grabbed her by the ruff, hard enough for her to bow. But her legs did not buckle, not even as I tasted her blood on my tongue.

My whole body tensed as I dropped all control, opening myself for the magic flooding through me.

I lifted her slight body and threw her.

Neera landed with all four paws on the ground. She tossed her head back, sleek black fur shining like obsidian against the afternoon sun, and howled. The Gwylis returned the action, as did I. We, as a pack, wanted the other to succeed, even in battle with each other.

Neera bared her teeth and leapt. I sank to my haunches and used my forepaws to knock her away. She rolled to the side and was up an instant, teeth clamping down on my throat; my snarl was cut off into a weak gurgle. I threw myself onto the ground and rolled my body onto hers, pinning her body beneath me. She released me immediately. I stood over her, four paws trapping her in, and lowered my muzzle so all she could see was the inside of my mouth as she stared past my gaping maw.

Neera grinned. "So, you like to be on top, Fray Castor?"

A muscle in my jaw ticked. The hesitation lasted only a second, but it was enough for Neera.

She took all four paws and shoved them against my belly. I stumbled back, trying to find purchase. In a split second, she got hold of my ruff and clamped down as I had done to her. The pain ripped through me. A pathetic whimper escaped me, despite my attempt to disguise it. My knees buckled, and I bowed.

The fight was over.

I found relief when Neera let go. She stood near me, head tilted and teeth red with my blood. If she were human, she'd lend a hand for me to stand, but all she could offer was a lick to my wound and a gentle tug on the skin between my shoulder blades.

The Gwylis all howled in response and greeted Neera back into their ranks. I shook myself off and lumbered to where Shaine stood. He lowered his head in respect and allowed me to stand beside him.

"Undefeated until today, Castor," he said. "What happened? Where did you go?"

Where did you go? I'd asked Izzy those same words when she returned from killing Rixon. Something else happened, wherever she went; something she didn't want to tell me about. Why couldn't she tell me?

Where did you go?

Olio cleared his throat at my back, and I let a feral snarl escape me.

"All right," he said. "Now that you've gotten that out of your system, how about we go see Branch?"

I brushed past Olio without a glance. "I don't want to see Branch."

"You and I both, but you know we can't avoid that pretty scowling face, can we? As a matter of fact, your face kind of reminds me—"

"No, I'm good."

"But a crow arrived just this morning."

I froze midstride, nostrils flaring. "A crow from where?"

Olio stiffened at my growl, but released the tension by slapping me on the shoulder. "From a little place called Stormwall."

CHAPTER ELEVEN

It felt like nothing, being dead.

I thought it would be more dramatic. There was nothing but darkness and the sensation of swaying. I gripped the air for anything to give me hold as I sat up. Death was uneventful and terribly boring. But the sudden pain from somewhere in my lower half told me I was far from gone.

My eyes adjusted to the dark, and I found myself on a cot, covered by a nicely knitted blanket. It felt soft and pretty. I clutched it to my chest. My chest, where the two jewels rested. Someone must have put them on. My dagger laid beside me. My pack, on the floor within arm's reach.

The room tilted, and I found purchase to the wall to my right. I knew where I was. This was the Queen Isabelle.

I'm alive. But still I wanted to stay there under that blanket where it felt safe and warm. My leg ached, healing slowly but surely. I kicked off the blanket and swung my legs over the bed, without a bit of teeth gritting to go with it.

"Don't move too much. You're not fully healed yet." A figure moved into view. His hair fell into his eyes as he leaned over from the shadows in the corner of the small room.

"Look at you." My voice cracked despite the humor I put forth. Ashe handed me a cup of water, which I drank too fast. I sputtered a cough as he stood.

"You've looked bad before, Isabelle." He paced the short length of the room and ran a hand through his hair. "But this cuts the cake."

"Cake sounds really good right now." But it didn't sound good. Not when the small amount of water I'd drunk churned in my stomach uneasily. I counted to three, over and over, willing it to stay down. "You made it."

Ashe stopped pacing, and hesitated before responding. "What happened back there?"

I watched him closely. Ashe, the boy who played this game better than anyone, knew better than to ask me what happened. "You knew we'd lose the city. You knew."

His brow scrunched together. "It was a chance I took."

"A chance you—" I stopped mid-sentence, struggling to find reasoning in all of this. "You were supposed to contact me. I didn't hear from you at all."

"I tried. Believe me, I did, Isabelle."

I didn't know what I expected, but it wasn't for Ashe to be so passive. But wasn't that the way he'd always been? He never combated me. Before today, I'd never seen him do a truly violent thing in his entire life. "I had to act."

"I expected you to. I didn't think you'd leave me there."

I dared to meet his eyes, but I could not bear it a second longer. He was smart enough to know what conclusion I'd come to when he didn't send a crow. He still was not absolved, in my eyes. In fact, I wanted to punch him. I tried to stand, but grunted in pain.

Ashe placed a hand to my shoulder and eased me back to sitting. "There'll be time to beat me up later. Right now, you must rest. Aquarius is doing the same in the next room."

I must have heard wrong. "What?"

"That old wolf who came leaping onto the ship as we sailed away. He shifted back to human. Said his name and who he was."

I held my head in my hands. "Everyone else is dead. The city is destroyed."

Ashe didn't respond. Instead, he sat beside me, his weight creaking the cot. His presence felt nice. I forgotten what it was like to have a friend, someone who knew me from...before. With Ashe, he was there for almost everything. Did he still think I was the same feisty princess? No, he would never think that now, not after what I'd done. *I am a monster.*

After a few minutes of drowning in my thoughts, he broke the silence. "My father was creating Gwylis."

My lips trembled.

"To the west, outside of the city of Essex."

Essex. The name sounded familiar, and not because it was a place on a map or because Katka had uttered them. "So, it's true? Your father was—"

Ashe cut me off, thank the gods. "Yes."

I swallowed a great lump in my throat. Dal Paratheon was turning children into wolves. "Add that to the list of things I'm incapable of handling right now."

Ashe smiled and took my hand, adding pressure. "When I decided to do it, I knew I would die."

By my own hand, I thought. But I didn't say it aloud. "You were very brave, Ashe."

His eyes widened, staring at me, an eternity of grief within them. It was almost as if he'd seen his entire world burn. Maybe it had. Or maybe killing his father broke him in a way he could never ever be fixed.

The silence drew on for so long that I started to think none of this was real. That I'd pinch myself and wake up in my warm bed in the Den.

Ashe released my hand and left my skin feeling cold and naked, but I felt more awake than ever. "You saved my life," he said.

"You saved mine. I'm glad we're together."

I was too. I look at Ashe, but he'd turned away, so all I got was his profile. His straight nose, his strong jaw. I almost forgot the way his face looked without all that hair on it. A familiar one. Yet the horrible feeling of loss weighed heavy on my body.

There was a place I'd go when I felt like this. A place I never told anyone about. I'd found it after Henry's death, when the loneliness threatened to swallow me whole. A space in my mind where it wasn't so cold and so restless. I went there now. I'd been in there so long that if it were a real place, it'd be covered in cobwebs and dust. But despite that, I let my mind ease into a dream I once had, a dream Pyrus once told me Henry had dreamt of. A small house on the edge of a beach on the ocean. A place always warm. Always happy. Henry had mentioned such a place even before Pyrus told me about it. I feared now such a place would never exist for me, but only in my head.

If I closed my eyes, I could almost convince myself I was there.

I lost the crown. I lost my kingdom. I might lose everything else if I didn't keep my head straight.

I sat with Ashe until my heart stopped hammering, and my thoughts became less of a jumbled mess. Maybe after a minute, or maybe an eternity, Ashe stood. I started after him, but the lurching in my stomach kept me bent forward on the cot. I hated this. I hated feeling so weak.

"Flea said it would take a little while for your magic to return and to heal," Ashe said, inching his way toward the door. He opened it and light splashed in. Not sunlight, since we were beneath the ship, but torches. Fire.

A tingle danced beneath my skin, the hairs on my arm standing on end. I clutched my necklace as Ashe looked on in confusion. *No, no.* No more magic.

It was too late to say that. I didn't need to hear the Uncanny say it to know it to be true.

I'd taken from the Uncanny something wild and dangerous. But until today, I had no idea how untamed my magic was. Was I the one controlling it all, or was I merely a vessel for the demons? I knew the answers. Yes, to all. To get further now, I had to harden up, and so did Ashe.

"I can't take back what I did."

Ashe frowned, but he didn't ask what I meant. He probably thought I meant everything stupid I'd ever done, which wouldn't have been wrong.

"I'll bring you some food in a little while," Ashe said. He opened his mouth to say more, but brought the door behind him.

"Ashe."

He turned to look into the room.

"How does it feel, knowing you killed your own father?"

Ashe pulled in his lips and turned a hard gaze to mine. "I don't feel anything."

I nodded. "Good."

∽

I COULDN'T SLEEP, EVEN THOUGH MY BODY BEGGED FOR IT. THE ship creaked as I stood. My left leg still ached, but it wasn't as bad as when I'd regained consciousness. Someone had dressed me in loose linen pants and a beige tunic. I found a piece of rope in my room to cinch my waist and gathered the end of my shirt together to tie a knot. My hair was knotted, and my skin felt gritty. Ashe had left a bucket with a shallow amount of water. I bent down to it and washed away the memories of the day. I'd have enough time to wallow later, and it was time to get myself together.

Ashe had said Aquarius was staying in the room beside mine, so it wasn't hard to find. Finding my sea legs was another ordeal altogether. But the corridors down here were so tight, I could brace my hands on either side to stay upright. I groaned at the twist in my belly. A wolf should not be on water.

I hesitated in front of the cabin door. I smelled the wolf behind it, though I knew he was in human form. Questions formed in my mind. *How did you escape? Why did you come to begin with? Why were your first words to me in months a simple set of orders?*

Get up.

I steeled myself and edged the door open. Unlike my room, there were torches lit here. A dresser, most likely bolted to the floor, sat in one corner. The old man sitting on the edge on the cot in the center of the small room told me to come closer.

I didn't know what I expected, but it wasn't a skeletal man with dark spots on his bony hands. He stood, taller than me by at least five inches. He bent forward anyway. The hunch in his back looked permanent, and not because he didn't want his head to hit the ceiling above him.

"Izzy," he said, his voice worn and tearing at the seams.

Haunting.

Wargrave had said Aquarius was dying, but I didn't expect him so soon a ghost.

His eyes met mine.

Open, unguarded, watery with unshed tears.

"Isabelle," I said flatly, keeping eye contact, reminding him that I had not yet forgiven his silence. "You're alive. It's a day of miracles."

Sarcasm wasn't the old man's strong suit. Aquarius made a move to approach, one hand reaching out as if to hold me. I stepped back.

"I don't trust you," I said. "This could have been different, but you refused to speak. You weren't like the Voiceless. You had your voice. You had words and you did not use them. Why? Why?"

Aquarius, this frail old man who was just a shadow of the Gwylis I'd seen back in Stormwall, merely bowed his head again, saying nothing. His arms hung loosely at the floor as if he wanted to shift back into a wolf and stop talking to me once again.

I tasted salt on my lips as the tears came, fast and heavy. "How dare you come now, when everything has fallen apart!"

To my amazement, he retreated back a step and seemed to fold in on himself. My anger festered. The torches on the wall flickered and rose in height.

My jaw ticked as I took the fire and stretched it out so that it looked like a tendril floating in the air. I could burn this man alive. I could do it now. But I would also burn down the ship and everyone on it, so the risk was too much. I let my magic retreat and immediately felt a lightness in my head. Too soon.

Trying to breathe out the anger, I leaned against the wall. "Just answer me one question: Why did you come?"

Aquarius looked up, his yellow eyes flashing. "To teach you, now that I know you to be the one to save us."

"You crazy old man." A thought sputtered to life. A memory, rather. One of Rixon, the Gwylis queen stepping out of Abiyaya's hearth. *She said you could, but I have my doubts.* "I alone cannot do everything."

"You are right, daughter. You cannot, but along the way, you forged alliances, and they will come to your aid when it is most detrimental."

He thought I was still going to break the Gwylis curse. I snorted. "Dal Paratheon was turning children into Gwylis."

Aquarius's eyes widened. "No."

"Yes, so that's where your grand plan has taken us. You used me. So did Abiyaya, and so did Rixon. The city is gone, probably taken over by the Greatwolf Pack and whoever else decided to stay. It's in ruin, and by the looks of it, so are you."

Aquarius stared at me long and hard. "They tried to cage you, but they failed."

I swallowed the dryness in my throat. "You said you didn't have time to teach me everything and to find someone who would, and I found that person in a man named Branch. But I did something terrible to save the people I'd grown to love, and now I don't understand it anymore. So, if you're here, truly here, prove it."

Aquarius straightened his spine and winced. How badly did it hurt being such an old fool?

"I never left you," he said. "You only needed time to see for yourself who you were."

I scoffed. He was making excuses for being a useless bag of bones. "Sure, okay, let's pretend that's true," I said. "Let's pretend all of this was part of the game. It still doesn't explain why we lost. Everything is gone. If I do break the curse, there's nothing to go home to. Nothing at all."

A smile formed on the old man's face. "Is finding a home everything to you? Is there a point where a little is simply enough?"

"That doesn't make any sense."

"Home is where you feel safe. Stormwall would have never been that place for you. The Den will never be that place. There are too many memories there to haunt you, and the continent is large."

I didn't miss the gleam in the old man's eyes. "If this is one of those fatherly advice speeches, you're failing miserably."

Aquarius smiled, but his head hung low.

"Are you all right?" I found myself rushing over, but the old man waved me off.

"There's nothing to be done," he said.

I took his hands in mine. "Stop wiggling and let me look." Now, his hands shook so violently, I feared he could not stop even if he wanted to. "It cannot be healed?"

Aquarius shook his head, the lines of his mouth tensing. "The end comes when the end comes. No magic can stop death."

I dropped his hands and stood, curling my fists at my side. "This is your fault. You made the gods turn away from us."

Aquarius frowned and pulled his cloak tight against his chest. "The gods turned their back on us the moment the New Kingdom was established. Mirosa's people forgot who they were, and their small magic dwindled into nothing. They became enraged and blamed the gods just as you're blaming me now. They sought out new gods. They erected statues of mortal men to fawn over, and the gods watched with indignance. Hundreds of years and still, the damage they'd caused was not enough. For those who stayed beyond the Archway and kept to the old ways, they were met with war. Those who still cherished the ancient gods, they were punished by war and poisons. Do you see how one could see that as a betrayal?"

My hands shook and fluttered. Gods, I wished Wargrave had killed him while he had the chance. Hells, maybe I had the chance now...

My vision clouded over like a black storm cloud. I clutched my temples and bit down on my tongue. No, too many thoughts that were not mine, too many things I could not control. It felt like I was only a visitor in my own mind; that I could be shown the door at any moment.

These demons would never let me go.

"Do you want to hear my part in this story or not?"

I teetered on the word "not," but nodded anyway.

"When your grandfathers came into the Old Kingdom, we thought they were coming home. Or, in the very least, coming to relearn the ways of their ancestors. But history was skewed. They came seeking the power they forgot they once had. Magic. Although they did not shout it to the people, they knew deep inside what they had lost when they renounced the ancient gods and passed through the mountains. They wanted it back."

They grew bitter at the gods and vowed to destroy magic altogether.

I drew in a deep, controlled breath as I turned this over in my harrowed mind. "I don't understand. I was told something different. Did my father and grandfathers come back to the Old Kingdom to reclaim magic or to destroy it?"

Aquarius took me in. "I have lived a hundred years, Isabelle Rowan. The Uncanny's magic, especially in Gwylis form, extends my life. I know better than anyone what your father came to the Old Kingdom for. He wanted magic just as his father did, and his father before him. They wanted it back! But the gods would not allow it."

"But it did not stop him from trying," I whispered.

"Then the Paratheon king comes, and his thirst for power far outweighed that of the Rowan line. He did the thing your father never thought to do."

Take sides with the Gwylis, I thought. "Instead of beating them, he joined them."

Aquarius nodded. "So, we've come to the part about the Uncanny."

Something dark crossed his yellow eyes. I clutched my necklace in response.

"Do you know what the Uncanny are?" Aquarius asked.

"Demons."

"Yes, but demons were not always demons, you see. The Uncanny were gods banished from the heavens. They want nothing more than to destroy the things they helped create."

I sighed. This cycle of rage and revenge was endless.

But there was one thing I had to know.

"Why did you do it?"

"Desperation."

"Do you regret it?"

"Every day."

I eyed him with disbelief. "That was why you hid away all these years."

"I wanted nothing to do with war or anything ever again," Aquarius said. His hands weren't trembling so much anymore, but he did fold them over quite a bit. A nervous tick.

I laid a hand on his once again. "But you changed me. Why?"

"Because I saw that same desperation in your eyes, and through you, I could live another life: a life I had wasted."

We sat in silence with nothing but the creaking of the ship to fill the empty spaces. I saw an old grief in Aquarius. I knew sadness and pain; I understood it in others, but I'd been so consumed and bitter that I could not see it in Aquarius until now. Grief was a man who changed me into a wolf because he wanted to leave something good behind.

"Aquarius," I pressed on. "Do you think I can finish what Henry started? Can I break the curse?"

"I think you can do anything you believe to be true, but if I told you give up this journey, would you?"

"No," I said, thinking first of the missing children, the people I left behind at the Den, the people whose lives I'd ruined back at Stormwall.

So many lives were relying on me. I took the emerald and the ruby and turned them over in my fingers. "I'm going to save as many as I can."

A smile spread across the old man's face. "I chose right in making you my daughter."

For a moment, I saw the man Aquarius once was: fierce and wild, ruthless and loyal. A man who wanted nothing more than to protect his people. He began to cough, and the great king disappeared, replaced by a dying old man.

"Will you—" I took a deep breath, steeling myself. "Will you teach me the old ways? I learned a little about who you were back at the Den, and about the magic the gods bestowed to us long ago. Teach it to me."

He shook his head. "It's impossible now. Our souls are drowning in darkness."

Thoughts of a blue-eyed boy cropped up, sending an ache through me. His perpetual frown. His hands. His deep and lovely voice.

How much I loved him.

"That's not true," I told Aquarius. "I know of love and loyalty. I could not feel those things if we were soulless. We still have free will. I know it."

"If I don't?"

"I'll leave you on this ship, eating hardtack and sardines until you die. Imagine dying with fish breath."

Aquarius's hand pulled back. He clutched it to his chest. "You're well on your way to escaping this. You could easily run away now and leave it all behind."

"No." I pulled my lips into a thin line. "I don't want to become you."

Aquarius finally stood. He went to the little window and gazed out. "You're a part of me now. My magic is yours, but you've got a little more, didn't you?"

I shuddered at the memory of speaking with the Uncanny for the first time. Before I could respond, Aquarius's arm shot out and grabbed my wrist.

"I know what you did, and if you're not careful, it will consume you." His eyes darted to my necklace. "Even charms will not protect you now."

Tears slid down my cheeks. "I did what I had to do for my people, so you're right. We are alike, aren't we? Nothing but pawns in a game."

"No, you're more. You are every person who wanted to fight and felt as though they were too weak to do so. You are every person who did not have a voice. You are every person who could not make the hard choices. You are not nothing. You are everything."

I swiped at my tears and held my chin higher than before. If I found the celestite, I could break the Gwylis curse. The gods of old would return to us, and Mirosa would again be wholly equal. It was a lot to hope for, and I knew it would not be without hardship. But I had allies again. Friends.

I was the story of Rydell, but instead of falling to my death when I leapt from the mountain, I flew.

CHAPTER TWELVE

"Why didn't you say so before?"

I'd nearly shifted to get back to the city faster, but in the end, I ran as a human with Olio huffing and puffing behind me. I hadn't heard a word from Izzy in weeks, and although I trusted that she was still alive, I wanted proof. Maybe not proof of life, but proof that she cared for the people she left behind.

"I did, but you only wanted to go play fighting games. You don't ever really listen to me."

I ignored the whiney tone of Olio's words and shoved the doors of the Den open. In a rush, I bolted to the meeting hall where I found Branch standing, one hand on his hip. He barely gave me a glance and opted to stare down Olio, who appeared behind me.

"It took you an hour to locate Castor?" Branch growled. He flexed his arms, his corded muscles thick. He cracked his neck and cast a questioning glance my way.

"He was without reason," Olio replied, conveniently standing behind me to avoid our leader's glare. "He opted instead to go get beat up by Neera."

"My brother got beat up by a girl?"

Sonia walked out from a side room, her face twisted with amusement. Although our relationship had softened, my sister still took the chance to tease me whenever possible.

I bristled and turned to Branch. "Can we forget about that and tell me what the letter said?"

If there was anyone Branch tolerated, it was me. He'd never let anyone get so snippy around him. I thought Izzy might have softened him up.

Branch nodded and pulled a small piece of parchment from his pocket. "The pieces are moving, and so should you. The king is dead, but Stormwall has fallen once again. Isabelle is alive and accompanied by Ashe Paratheon. If you value your lives, you will leave the Den before Katka's army comes. You will find aid where your ancestors lie."

Shock ripped through me as my teeth ground against one another, and I took a slow step forward, reaching out for the letter. I read it, backing up until my back hit the wall behind me.

The power I'd contained for years threatened to unleash here and now. The urge to shift and let the magic overwhelm me surged up like a powerful wave.

"What does that mean?" Sonia asked.

It meant Izzy took off with Ashe Paratheon. That was what it meant.

"Sounds to me like the princess has let loose her arrow," Olio said. "Do you think she could have done it all on her own?"

"Kill Dal Paratheon and reclaimed the throne in Stormwall?" Sonia asked, eyebrow raised. "Izzy is a lot of things, but she's certainly not foolish."

I grew still as clarity reclaimed me.

"She wasn't alone."

My voice was too soft, a grumble at most. Only Olio coked his head. "Say again?"

"I said she wasn't alone. Obviously." My hand shot out, gesturing to the letter. Pain clenched in my heart, my throat, my eyes. "*She was with the prince.*"

The room stilled. They all stared at me, except Olio, who looked uncomfortable. Branch folded up the letter and shoved it into his pocket. Nobody wanted to talk about the exiled Prince of the Peek Islands. Nobody more than myself.

Izzy rescued the prince.

What did she give to accomplish such a feat? Certainly, she took a risk, and it appeared to have paid off. But she could have returned. We could have regrouped and gone together, if the prince had been her only conquest. Why did they go off alone? What was the big hurry?

I rubbed at my eyes to reaffirm what I'd just learned.

Izzy wasn't coming back. Maybe not ever.

"How can we trust this?" Sonia asked. "It could be a trick to get us out of the Den so they can destroy it."

Olio groaned long and hard. "Sonia, your distrusting bit is getting stale. Somebody needs to chase away that storm cloud that follows you around."

Sonia's lips twitched. "So what, Olio? You want to pack up and head on down to some imaginary place where the gods will say, 'All right, we'll help, all you had to do was say so?'"

"The gods don't care for us," I said.

Sonia widened her eyes. "We agree for once, brother."

Olio swept across the hall, holding his hand to his head. "We let her go off on her own so we could stand around and argue as if we know anything that's going on beyond the Archway. We will not be complacent again. Branch, we've sat around for too long."

"It's only been two weeks," Sonia cut in.

"Two weeks too many!"

Branch, who'd been quiet, finally chimed in. "Every day, I think of Izzy and wonder if I had made a mistake in letting her go alone. But I believe we have our own parts to play. It doesn't end with the princess. It will end with us.

I watched Sonia's face grow pensive. "What are you proposing?"

"I propose we take a group and head east. There, we will find the others."

"The others?" I asked.

"A different people in a different land, who escaped Aquarius's curse. The gods may have abandoned us, but they live with them. I know it."

"How do you know this?"

Branch stood, unblinking. "I don't."

I shook my head. "The gods no longer exist."

"Another attack on the Den is imminent," Olio said. "If this isn't a warning, then I don't know what is. Let's get our tails moving."

I balled my hands into fists. "You told me to stay put," I said, directing my finger to Branch. "You told me to stay. You told us all to stay. I should not have listened to you. I will not run again."

"I don't think this is running," Olio said, facing me.

"I think we should find out what else had happened in Stormwall."

Olio *tsked*. "Boring. Let's do Branch's thing."

"It's a fool's errand. We'd do no good chasing something we don't even know exists."

Olio wasn't even listening. I swear his eyes glazed over.

I pushed off the wall, fury thick and potent in my blood. "We should direct our efforts toward Stormwall, and preventing another attack. We should be running toward Izzy, not further away from her."

"She's got Ashe with her," Branch stated. "That's something."

The Uncanny's magic was terrible. But I'd never felt it the way I felt it when I heard the prince's name. The name triggered rage in me so raw, I might have turned this entire building to ice and all within it.

I swallowed back the bile in my throat. "Don't ever say his name around me."

"Fray," Branch said with an edged calm as he moved toward me. "There is no room for this right now."

I threw up a hand to stop him. "I should be with her," I said, my teeth clenched in a snarl. "It wasn't supposed to be like this. The prince showed up, leading his father's army right to us. Tell me you don't agree. Tell me she was wrong to leave here without us. *Without me.*"

Branch's gaze was as fierce as my own. "I won't speak of things that could have been. Would we have died in Stormwall? Captured?"

I blinked rapidly, adjusting to Branch's words. I could sense him holding back something else—an admission, perhaps, that I was right. Maybe even sadness for not following Izzy. "You know we wouldn't have died in Stormwall. We are stronger than that."

"Are we?" Branch asked, his voice steel.

I looked away, overcome by self-doubt. We could be killed like any human. Losing Ghetee, as well as several pack members only weeks ago, proved that. Not even the Uncanny could stop death—only delay it for a while.

"I...I don't know," I forced out, misery thick in my throat.

Olio sighed heavily. "We understand the bond you have with Izzy, and we understand how much it pains you to be apart from her, but Izzy, she can hold her own."

Sonia nodded. "Her brother was as confident as his sister."

All eyes flicked to her.

A shudder ran through my body, but I had to hold it together. I could not be the storm I'd been these past few weeks, snarling around the Den like a wild beast. "What does that mean?"

"It means Henry talked about breaking the curse all the time, but calling on the gods using three gems; well, it sounded foolish even to him. What I'm saying is, if Izzy fails, then it's up to us to take on that weight. We must find the gods and beg them to return favor."

"How do we know if Izzy fails?" Olio asked. "What if we let her go off for nothing?"

"Sonia, why didn't you tell us this before?" Branch asked in an even tone. His face betrayed him, twisted up with tension.

"Because who am I to dash hopes? I don't even think this thing we're discussing will work." She bit her inner cheek and looked away again. "Besides, I knew she had something going with the prince."

Slowly, I said, "What?"

"Calm down, brother. I meant that night I heard them outside talking the night before the prince was taken. I didn't hear much, but I saw the looks on both their faces when the soldier came for him. They were scheming. I just know it."

Olio snorted. "I knew it!"

I opened my mouth to speak. My mind set into a full-blown battle with itself, running through the options: Destroy this building; kill Sonia right here, or maybe later when she's sleeping. Or running away during the night, far into the Old Kingdom and forget all of this had ever happened. Forget Aquarius. Forget Izzy. Forget Stormwall. Everything.

But I couldn't get the words out. Not a threat to Sonia, not even a sigh. I was caught in an agonizing frozen state as Sonia's words blared through my mind. *They were scheming. I just know it.*

The last nail in the coffin. *I'm going to kill that prince next time I see him.*

"Shut your mouth," Branch growled at Sonia. "You don't know anything."

"Maybe that's why she didn't let us go with her," Sonia said. "Maybe our parts in this story lie elsewhere."

I cocked my head, my mind astonishingly empty for the moment. "Which is?"

Sonia gave me an all-knowing look, one brow raised. "Not here."

~

I COULDN'T SLEEP. I SAT AGAINST THE WALL, IN THE BED I ONCE shared with Izzy, lost in thought.

If Sonia was right, Izzy and the prince had been scheming, even before she killed Rixon. Had she meant to go after Aquarius? Take Stormwall from within? From that letter, it appeared her plan had gone awry. But Dal Paratheon was dead. The Greatwolf Pack, now led by Katka, had taken the city. And Izzy...where was she now? Was she hurt? Was she safe?

I propped my elbows on my knees and leaned forward, head in my hands. The nighttime chill blew in from the open window above the bed. There was no light, the moon blocked by clouds and the stars likewise cloaked. The darkness curled around me. These sleepless nights reminded me of when I was younger, fighting in Aquarius's army. Those days, I felt no different than a starless night.

I thought of Izzy traveling with the prince. The muscles in my back tightened. I might never sleep again. I kept hearing her telling me not to follow, her dreamlike voice like a curse.

Izzy was my curse.

If she wanted to stay in Stormwall, she should have told me before we crossed the Archway. But she let me go on as if I was taking her away from a life she hated. She let me think I was saving her. I took her to the Den, a place I had betrayed, and suffered for my actions, for her. For *her*. And she made her plans with the prince to retake the kingdom she abdicated. She took Branch's training and harnessed it to reclaim her crown. Her cunning could put Aquarius to shame.

But I found my muscles loosening.

I remembered her face when she killed her father. She hated him. But she never truly fit in Mirosa. Or the Den. But I'd kissed her, and assured her life would get better. My words now tasted bitter in my mouth.

Stillness did nothing to clear my head. I pushed myself off the bed and stood. My shoulders ached. How long had I sat there, tight as a knot? I paced the room from one end to the other. Moving gave me clarity.

What happened with Izzy was as much my own doing. I hadn't let her in, and it destroyed us.

Finally, sometime during the night, I'd fallen asleep, only to be woken up violently by someone lifting me by the shoulders. I fumbled in their hold, but they were stronger than me. They pressed my chest into the bed, hard enough to make it feel like my heart was stuffed into a vice, and hissed into my ear, "The time for wallowing is done."

The weight disappeared and I sucked air into my lungs, sputtering a cough and checking myself for blood. I knew I should have locked my door. It would have kept out those trying to knock sense into me.

Which is what Branch thought I needed.

Stupid old man.

"Get up," he growled, pulling me up by my tunic. He was twice my size and at least two feet taller, and in the darkness, he felt like a shadow; except shadows didn't try to lift you off your feet in the dead of night.

Not that I knew of.

I bared my teeth anyway, unafraid of Branch's punishments. Nothing he could do would ever compare to what I'd already been through. A boy, raised to be a soldier, forced into being a Gwylis, amusingly almost killed by one, and surviving a stint in a dungeon in Stormwall while they beat and starved me until they decided I was ready to be tied to a pole in the center of town and shot with arrows until I was dead.

I had nothing left to lose. No dignity. No pride. No love. Nothing. And everyone knew it.

A flash of worry drew in the lines of Branch's face. Why should he care? I was not his son. I was not even the strongest Gwylis in the Den. Or the smartest. If he wanted anyone to go east, he'd have to pick someone better.

He finally released me and stepped back, his foot hitting one of the chairs at the table I never ate on anymore. It was full of weapons, knives, daggers, arrows I'd been carving, and one simple broadsword. I'd had Jovi, the blacksmith, fashion me armor. A chest piece, greaves, gauntlets, the works. With them, I'd go into the forest and practice. Listening to the *woosh* of my sword and the sound of metal unsheathing from leather, I'd spend my days there, preparing for the day we would no longer rely on claws and fang. Was I smart, wasting my days that way? Probably not.

The others had freely used the Pits, and some had even begun practicing the old ways again. The elders, now unrestrained by my mother, unlocked the city library. I'd even seen them doing a dance involving an excess of arm flailing in the large space of the meeting hall. Not my kind of dance, to say the least. *But who am I to talk?*

The meeting hall was where Branch led me, practically pinching my ear as we walked. I knew the moments where I could get away with acting like an insubordinate mule. Tonight was not one of those moments.

"You want to say the gods do not exist?" the old man grumbled. The Den was quiet, but I knew the wolves prowled, nocturnal as they were. "I'll show you the gods."

We'd stopped in front of the meeting hall. I could hear voices inside. Lights emanated from the windows. "Why do you care what I think about the gods?" I held his dark stare. "I'm not going on your little pilgrimage."

Branch looked about ready to pummel me, but instead of throwing a punch, he stepped back and clasped his hands behind his back. "You're so eager to be hated," he said. "For what? So you could feel as if your loneliness is justified? You're a lone wolf of your own making, and if you don't wise up, it's all you'll ever be."

Belief was a deeply terrible thing. It preyed upon the kind and openhearted, as fragile as a bird bone. Able to take flight, but easily broken. I'd spent years alone, fending for myself after Aquarius threw away the war. In my solitude, I'd shattered all the trust I had in everyone. But now, I felt like those pieces were slowly gathering again. And despite my doubt, I hung my head in submission.

Branch rubbed the bridge of his nose, exhausted by having to deal with me, and opened the doors.

CHAPTER THIRTEEN

My dreams were of fire and death.

I choked on it, the ashes of the dead. They burned in the houses I'd set alight. Children cried for their mothers. Horses screamed in terror and bolted any direction they could go. Fire filled the sky with red and orange and yellow and black as the smoke burned down, turning the sky to dust. I dreamed of my own mistakes. *The princess with stars in her eyes and darkness in her heart; you will bring nothing but death.*

Terror slashed through me as I woke. Sweat slicked my forehead and dampened my neck, as if I'd been in the center of it all. The city of fire.

I sat up, disoriented at first. I shook off the remnants of the nightmare. No need dwelling on dreams when reality was so much more terrifying. I made my way up to the deck. I spotted Flea first, munching on some hardtack and what smelled strongly of sardines on one of the benches near the hull. *Breakfast of the gods*, I deadpanned to myself.

But the sky was a bright blue without a cloud in sight.

"Saved you some tea." Ashe appeared at my side, holding a luke-warm mug. I emptied it to the last dregs of bitterness. It wasn't the best tea. I wondered if good tea ever existed outside of Stormwall castle. *Small price to pay*, I thought.

"Is Aquarius awake?" I asked. I looked around the deck for the first time. It really wasn't as large as it appeared when docked. But it was still a magnificent ship. The only ship I'd ever been on. It wasn't the oak build or the elaborate engravings along the rails, but the figurehead at the bow snatched my attention. With a gaping jaw of ivory teeth, a wolf head stared out at the ocean. Its eyes were black as night, with pointed ears rising to the heavens.

"Not yet," Ashe said. I'd forgotten the question by the time I turned back to him. Seeing the prince now in the daylight shed a whole new light on him. While the sun shone, igniting his blond hair into gold, his eyes held a hardness that could only have come from killing someone he once loved. Not regret for doing it, but sadness for having had to do it at all.

But the weakened Ashe I'd encountered in the Old Kingdom was no more. He now wore a tunic with the sleeves shorn off, revealing an arm and a half of corded muscle. The arm Fray had bitten, long gone by Archibald's ax, left just a bicep. It had healed nicely. The stump even bore new hair growth. Small victories. But the remnants of Ashe's choices stood as a reminder to me that scars never truly healed. And that some things could never be replaced.

"We're going to Essex, then." Ashe's voice startled me from my thoughts. I nodded as we started to walk. We stopped at the railing and I peered over, watching the waves as they slammed against the ship, my thoughts geared toward Stormwall and the city I'd left behind.

I closed my eyes and envisioned the chaos, the fires, the dying. It all flooded through me. The risk I was taking for the survival of my people and for those of the Old Kingdom. They too were my people. And they were in danger if I failed.

The entire world would fall into flames.

"I can't let it go," I whispered, meeting Ashe's eyes. "Could you?"

His gaze was steady on me. "No." He shifted his weight to his right leg. "Never. Would you think so lowly of me, even now?"

"No, I wanted to know what you would do, since you used to be a prince."

Ashe's jade eyes looked past me. "I'm still one, to a degree. I think after all this, the Peek Islands may be wanting to see me home."

"You don't think they all sided with your father?" What I really wanted to ask was if he saw himself having any rights to Mirosa's throne. *A monster for another day.*

Ashe shook his head. A breeze blew strands of hair into his eyes. "No. There are still good people out there, Isabelle. They're harder to find than the bad ones."

My blood pounded in my ears at the thought. Allies would be nice.

"Will you tell me what happened after?" Ashe's expectant gaze now locked onto mine. They mirrored the twinkling of the water. "Please."

I nodded in assent. "We won, but I lost someone dear to me."

He rubbed the back of his neck. His voice grew small, quiet. "Who was it?"

I swallowed the dryness in my throat. A sour taste replaced the bitter tea on my tongue. "It wasn't...him, if that's what you're wondering."

Ashe's jaw ticked, and he took a step back, finding his footing on the swaying deck. "I would never celebrate such a thing, Isabelle." He pawed furiously at his eyes. "Why is he not with you?"

I could see more questions in Ashe's eyes. Why did you come alone? Where are the others? What did you do?

I bit the inside of my cheek. "I killed Rixon."

"Rixon was—"

"Fray's mother."

Ashe blew out a breath and ran a hand down his face, as if he understood the extent of what I'd done. He could never understand. "I'm sorry."

He didn't have to be. "It wasn't your fault. I made my choices, so here I am."

"Here you are."

I closed my eyes, letting the salty smell fill me up. After a long moment, I opened my eyes to find Ashe watching me. His mouth turned in a frown, and his eyes squinted against the rushing of the wind.

"Why did you leave the Den alone?" he asked. "They would have come if you asked."

I turned fully to face him. "They would have died, and I've had enough of that to last me a lifetime."

Ashe's gaze bore into mine. For a moment, I thought he'd died, and it took a moment for his body to keel over. But he blinked, and a dark look crossed his face. "There's something different about you, Isabelle. It's in your eyes. I can see it."

The words reminded of something he'd said while on our way to meet Rixon beyond the Archway: *You're different. Your eyes, your face, the way you walk. You're different.*

I tilted my chin skyward. Ashe always had a way of seeing me as nobody else did. But it wasn't enough for me to spill my secrets.

Besides, thinking of the Uncanny made me want to vomit.

Or maybe that was the ship and its ever-sloping decks.

I blew out a breath and turned back to Ashe as he pulled a wrapped bundle from his pants pocket. He held it out to me, the frown on his face twitching. "I had it before it all started, so it might be a little squished."

I took the bundle. Before I even unwrapped it, I could smell what it was. Cheesecake. My stomach grumbled as I unfolded the parchment and threw my head back to shovel the crumbs and bits into my mouth. Shameless.

Ashe cracked a smile and looked away. "I wish it was more, but I did what I could."

Something in his voice filled the words with truth. Something in the way he looked at me with soft, sad eyes made my heart full.

I looked past the smile forming on his lips to where Derwin stood up near the bridge of the ship. I frowned and crumpled the cake wrappings in my fist. There would not be enough time to catch up on anything. There was only the now.

Aquarius and I had left things incomplete last night. Now, in the rays of the morning sun, I felt a pressing against my chest to see things right. I could not go with such uncertainty weighing down my bones.

Ashe took his leave. "I'll be in the hull if you need me, Isabelle."

"Ashe?"

He turned, squinting against the sun.

"What do we do when this is all over?"

That smirk I'd come to adore spread across the prince's face. "We eat cake."

It was midafternoon by the time Derwin, Flea, and I hashed out the details of our trip. Derwin had a dozen crew members on the Queen Isabelle, and every now and then, I'd look up from the map we were poring over to see them working the pulleys and other riggings of the sails. With their captain tied up with me, the quartermaster doled out orders. They looked like ants down there, scurrying back and forth.

Although I didn't know them, I did not want them to die too.

We planned to land on the southern coast near the port city of Alaster, where I would procure horses and supplies for the weeklong journey to Essex. Weather dependent, of course. I still had the jewelry Wargrave had returned to me, so provisions would not be an issue.

Derwin and his crew would stay in Alaster for a time, or if things looked rough, they'd sail along the peninsulas to avoid a skirmish. Sailing back to Stormwall was out of the question for now. I'd offered some of the jewelry for food and housing, but Derwin refused it, saying it was better spent on the children when we found them.

We'd find them if it was the last thing I ever did. Curses be damned.

But there was more thing to do before then.

OF ALL THE BAD IDEAS, THIS WAS ONE OF THE WORST ONES.

Magic sparked from my fingertips, like tiny shooting stars. "Branch had already tried to teach me," I said, "and it felt like it worked until I messed it all up and made that deal."

"You are not a lost cause," Aquarius said, bracing himself over the rocking of the ship. He'd almost fallen more than once. The old man was liable to fall and break a hip before I learned anything of value.

Aquarius had at least said something more than my parents ever would. They'd tell me to give up. I wasn't worth the time.

"The Uncanny will never respect you if you don't give them a reason to."

I stilled. The Uncanny did not respect anything but their own evil deeds. How would they respect a mortal woman?

"They control me," I said. "Even from the very beginning, I felt it. Even before—"

Aquarius cut me off. "Think of their magic as blood. It flows through our veins, keeps us alive, but we only spill it when we choose to."

"Or accidentally, like that one time I got shot by an arrow in the forest."

"Because you have my power," Aquarius said, "you have little control. Your body is too small to hold such a burden. Now, your magic is the equivalent of smashing a dam. Raging waters. No escape."

I clicked my tongue. "If my magic is water, then yours is an ax. I saw what you did to Katka."

"Yes, but if you release too much, you will drown, Little Wolf."

I pinched my lips together. Aquarius might be right. The Uncanny's magic grew every day. Would I be a danger to myself? To others? "How can I ration it if they won't let me?"

"Fight them. Every step of the damn way."

I shook my head. "It's more than fighting them, Aquarius. You'd know that if you'd only spoken to me these past weeks."

"You did not need my words to execute your plan. War is here whether I was present or not."

"You told me not to start war, but I fear I have."

"You did not start it," Aquarius said, putting a hand on her shoulder. I relaxed. "But I told you to end it, and you listened."

I said nothing. I only stared.

"I am going to tell you something you may not want to hear." Aquarius removed his hand and heaved a heavy breath. "You do not need demon magic to win this war."

The old man's words made sense. If I were to break the curse, the enemy Gwylis would lose their power in this world. There'd be no need for magic to fight them any longer. They'd be equal in strength.

But what would happen after? Would the gods once again side with us and restore the small magic? Or would they still find us unworthy?

I rubbed my tired eyes. I thought of every person whose lives I'd affected by not stopping my father sooner. Every person who died because I had been too cowardly. Too tied up in mourning Henry and fretting over suitors and towing the line of rebellious princess. I took no notice of things that sat right under my nose. But not this time.

I locked eyes with the old wolf and gave a deep breath. "You're not coming with me, are you?"

"No," the old man replied.

My lips parted in some sort of response, but it died as I caught movement to my right. Ashe approached, his footsteps loud and conspicuous.

He stopped in front of Aquarius and looked down his nose at the Gwylis king. "What do you mean, you're not coming?"

Aquarius regarded the prince. "If you are to gather an army, so am I."

"You're going to the Old Kingdom." I took a staggering breath, my heart racing. "You're going to them."

Ashe shot me a worried look. "Izzy..."

My rational mind was clear. I knew Aquarius and I would not have a bonding period. We'd allied together as father and daughter. As friends. But I was unable to escape the tide of disappointment as it caught me in its undertow.

It would be Ashe and myself for as far as this journey would take us.

My heart felt like it was shrinking. I closed my eyes and struggled not to cry.

I wanted to go home. But when I pictured a place resembling somewhere cozy and safe, I could not see it. But my mind yearned for a place I could call home, and it materialized to a face I recognized. A face I knew all too well.

Could home be a person and not a place?

I heard Aquarius shift. "I will see you as far I can, but they need me more than you do. You have love at your back. Never let that go."

I made a point to swallow my sadness and make my body straight as a rod, but Ashe didn't miss a beat. He turned to me and gave a slight bow. "I won't let you down."

"Does that mean you'll go with me to Essex?" I asked.

Please say yes. I don't want to go alone. I don't want to be alone anymore. I anguished at the very thought.

Ashe's eyes took on a dark glint. "I didn't survive months in the middle of winter, in the mountains, may I remind you—*with one arm*—to turn tail and hide now."

He held out his hand. I clasped it and pulled it tightly against my chest. We were fated, Ashe and me. Not to be together, but to become allies. Together, we could break the curse and set all Mirosa free.

Free against the Uncanny.

My grip around Ashe's hand tightened, and he responded with a firm nod.

We were going to survive.

CHAPTER FOURTEEN

When evening came, I descended into my cabin to pack. I'd spent the day with Derwin, mulling over maps for so long that I started seeing double. After a dinner of some sort of fish stew and hardtack, I decided that I'd had enough. We'd be landing in Alaster in a few hours, so I might as well get some sleep in while I could. But after a fitful hour, I sat up and shoved my fist into my pillow.

Sleep would not come so easily.

A gentle knock on my door. It eased open to reveal an arm and attached to it, a hand holding a steaming cup. "I managed to find some lemon on board," the familiar voice said.

Lemon in my tea! "Come in, Isabelle."

I took the mug from her hands and cradled it against my chest. It smelled semi-decent. Isabelle stood by the door, unsure of whether to take the two steps over to me. "I take it you're not hoarding any cake between those sheets, are you?"

I suppressed a smile. "Unfortunately, my magic of conjuring cake from thin air is depleted."

There was awkward pause as I met her gaze. Her brown eyes reflected the light of the single torch by the doorway. "Would you like to walk?"

The corridor was quiet as we made our way up to deck. Cool air filled my lungs the moment I inhaled. The night sky was blanketed in stars, shining brightly and greeting me like long-lost friends. The smell of the ocean filled my nostrils, and my tiredness crept away. It was unlike anything I'd ever known. It felt freeing. I felt so alive.

I wished being on a ship on the vast ocean did not remind me of the Peek Islands.

Wood and rope and canvas. I could almost smell the fishing boats of the island, see the wherry's as they transported goods on the main island. All Peek Island children were taught two things when they reached a certain age: how to fight and how to sail. Sailing, my father had once said, was in our blood, and we had a kindship to the waters. A bond stronger than anything. Chalot, the god of water, blessed my people and set us apart from the continent. We would pray to his likeness at the docks, and hung on our front doors. He guided us on his seas and lulled our hearts.

I'd been away from the ocean for so long, I'd forgotten its song.

"You should be resting." Isabelle stood beside me, a hand to her chest. "We won't see land until morning, but there are no other ships pursuing us. So rest easy."

Rest easy. Was that a thing people did? "I'll sleep when you do."

She matched my smirk, but it fell away quickly. I thought briefly about Stormwall and how easily my sword had felled my father. I'd never forget the sight, closed eyes or not.

Isabelle leaned over the rail. A cool wind swept through her short hair. I liked it. It made her face appear shaper, more focused. She'd always been beautiful, but now her beauty felt raw. She was no longer the girl in the tacky gowns. She looked a great deal more like the woman who killed her own father, and then did dear old dad one more by joining his mortal enemies.

She met my gaze as I took her in, and then she looked way. "I don't care if it's dangerous. I don't care if there's a threat of death. I don't care—"

The taste of the tea turned in my mouth. "You're not going to die, Isabelle. It's me who should be worried."

She turned to face me, her mouth turned down. "You didn't seem worried before."

"That's because I made up my mind."

I knew I would die the instant my father fell, and I'd opened my arms to greet it, only to feel Isabelle's magic surround me not a few seconds after. I thought...I don't know what I thought, but it wasn't that we'd lose Stormwall.

Looking at Isabelle now, looking at my friend, I was not so sure I'd give my life so soon. I had more to live for.

Valuing your life, and believing you are capable of more, was not something I learned so easily. But I was learning now.

I leaned over the railing and looked out to the infinite water. "The thing is, with my father gone, I have never felt such freedom. I've lived in shadow for so long, I'm not sure what sort of man I really am, but I want to find out. I want to fight. With you. Wherever that leads us, I will go."

"You killed your father, holding a sword with one hand, Ashe. You are fully capable. I have no fears for you."

I looked away, unconvinced.

"I hope you're not going to ask me to change you into a Gwylis again. I'd have to shove you overboard if you did.

"How long will it take us to get to Essex?" I asked. "When we dock, I mean."

"A week. We should get a few horses and supplies and head north. There's a couple towns in between and a really big forest."

"No mountains?"

She snorted. "No, not this time."

I finished my tea in silence. The gentle rocking of the boat should have made me sleepy, but I'd never felt so awake. Here with the full moon and a friend by my side, I felt like I could conquer the world.

Was it the moon that ate away at all my dark emotions, or was it something else entirely?

"What do you think it's like out there?" I peered out into the black ocean, not looking at Isabelle.

"From what I saw on Derwin's map, it's not much different than Stormwall."

"I don't mean the terrain, Isabelle."

She hung her head and sighed. "I don't know, Ashe. Your father did a lot of damage in a few months, and he did manage to turn himself a Gwylis-maker, so there's that for you."

My face flushed. "If I could kill him again, I would."

"I would too."

She stood there, saying nothing, and finally, "Do you still—"

She never finished her sentence. Her eyes glazed over as she looked at something behind me. What appeared to be a ball of fire streaked across the sky. A falling star. I'd never seen one so big. I stood, frozen, staring at the thing until it grew larger as it fell.

The crew burst out from their cabins. Derwin stood high up on the captain's roost, gazing at the sky in wonder.

Isabelle clawed at her chest, her eyes wild and frantic. "Gods, what is it?"

"Turn the ship!" I shouted, darting for Derwin. "Turn the ship. It's going to hit us!"

But Derwin couldn't get us out of the way in time. The massive falling star approached and hit the water just at the wolf figurehead. It dropped like a cannonball. The ocean to shot upward, flooding the deck and knocking me to my knees.

I shot to my feet, boots sliding on the slippery deck, praying to whatever gods were listening that this was a rare occurrence. But after years spent on the oceans, I had never seen something like this. The sky lit up with a dozen of the same feverish stars. Were they stars? What else could they be?

"Hold on!" Derwin shouted as the ship lurched. "Bearing away!"

I grabbed hold of the nearest railing and tried to set my feet. "Stay here," I ordered.

Isabelle went to protest, but I was already running. I got down below, to the cabins where I grabbed Isabelle's pack, making sure her dagger and necklace were safely inside, and breathlessly rushed back onto the deck.

Chaos erupted above where the crew were up on the riggings. A man in the crow's nest called down to Derwin saying, "Incoming!"

Without so much as a second thought, I grabbed Isabelle by the waist and hauled her toward the longboats. I heaved the ropes on one side. "You have to get out of here."

I shoved her pack into her arms.

"What are those?"

"Gwylis magic." Aquarius bounded forward, in wolf form, nearly losing purchase on the flooded deck. One of the falling stars hit the right side, causing the ship to lean. Ocean water drenched us from head to toe.

"Where are they?" Isabelle shouted over the commotion. If Gwylis were causing stars to fall, they had to be close by—on a ship, I assumed. I swore.

I worked on the other side of the longboats lines until the boat plopped into the water. "Get in, Isabelle."

But she didn't. She stood dead still, as if paralyzed. I grabbed for her arms, but hissed. Her skin was smoldering, like burning coals.

"Isabelle, what is happening to you?"

She staggered back, glancing at the sky and then back to me, her eyes terrified. "This can't be happening. Not now." She bent forward. "The Uncanny are trying to use me, Ashe!"

I still didn't understand until she started to scream.

"No! I have Gwylis magic too. I could protect the ship. Derwin's crew should be the ones abandoning ship now. Not me. I'll use my shield."

She shoved the heels of her hands into her eyes and tried to summon the same protective magic she'd used on me, presumably. But the magic flickered from her hands like a dying light. She thrust out her hands, expecting to see the bubble of protection, but nothing came.

"You'd said you'd help me," she cried out. "This wasn't the deal!"

As if sensing her weakness, the shadows detached from her body and took up space between us. I cried out, attempting to get to her, but the demons blocked my path, knocking me backward on the tilting deck until I almost lost my footing.

They looked like smoke, but were as solid as stone. They took shape, almost. I could make out a human-like head, a body with arms and legs. A mouth filled with fire opened and a voice spewed forth saying, *"Demons lie."*

I drew my dagger and swiped at the shape, but it billowed away like fog, appearing again behind me. A heavy hand smacked me in the chest, and I fell onto my backside. My dagger clanged on the deck, out of arm's reach.

Isabelle rushed to my aid, but she stopped, her body leaning back as if pulled by an invisible tether. Her back arched and her head fell back.

A sound emanated from her throat, low and guttural. My body went cold.

She lunged, shoving me so hard square in the chest that I nearly went overboard. I caught myself, quick on my feet, and retrieved my dagger.

The demon cackled from a few feet away. It pointed a long finger toward me. *He is the enemy. He always will be.*

I shook my head as another fireball crashed into the ocean, spraying me with salt water. "Stop! Isabelle, this isn't you!"

The demons, still coming in and out of their human shapes, laughed at my expense.

Her hands shook. Bright red spots shone on her palms. Blood. *She's digging her nails into her skin, trying anything to stop the Uncanny.* My heart pumped in waves against my ears.

She clutched at her face, screaming in agony.

But even she could not fight what was overtaking her.

She clawed at her face and crumpled. She let out a roar that was like a beast four times her size. She bared her teeth. When did they become so sharp?

She lunged toward me like a wild animal, screaming, "That was my throne, and you took it from me!"

I stepped out of her path, and even through the commotion around me, a soft cry escaped her lips as the breath left her lungs.

"I didn't take anything!" I shouted, dodging her again. What was happening? Would I have to fight her?

I won't hurt her again. I won't.

She kicked me in the leg. I staggered and bent forward for a moment. She drew back, ready to go for a more vulnerable part of me. Fully aware of it, I sidestepped, nearly tumbling over my feet.

Something black seeped into the whites of her eyes.

He is the enemy. The demons screamed the words.

"No!" I screamed. She lunged, and my reluctance to hurt Isabelle became my downfall. We fell onto the deck, entangled in a scuffle. Her nails felt like claws as they sunk into the flesh of my neck. Her grip was strong, strong enough to crush my windpipe before I could utter a last word. Air fled my lungs, my brain. My throat squeezed down on a scream.

A coppery taste of blood filled my mouth. The shouts of alarms and all other sounds drowned away. She pressed a knee into my chest. Her eyes darkened until there was no white left. My pulse slowed beneath her fingertips.

The darkness was everywhere, seeping off her, and part of me screamed for it to stop. I screamed inwardly, *What you're doing is wrong, Isabelle. Stop!*

Her grip on my neck suddenly loosened, and while I was still seeing stars, her weight vanished, and my body curled into itself.

A falling star hit the quarterdeck, behind where Derwin stood wrangling the steering wheel. It burned a hole straight down to the hull, and it must have hit the keel. The ship tilted, liable to take on water.

"Be gone, demons!"

I sputtered a cough and eased my lungs to take on air. Aquarius repeated the words. At the same moment, I found my strength, grabbed Isabelle's forgotten pack, and threw it toward the demon shape. A useless action, but somehow, it seemed effective. The demon cackled once more before shrinking in size and vanishing altogether.

Isabelle fell forward, her body looking brittle and small. Terror marred her gaze. The dark force within her made her hurt—made her suffer. It wasn't her. The demons had made her do it. And I heard her soft weeping. Her legs gave out at the weight of it. Aquarius caught her before her knees hit the deck.

She nearly killed me.

I got to my feet as another star fell, drenching the deck where I stood. I wiped ocean water from my eyes and stared at Isabelle in disbelief, my hands wrapped protectively against my throat, as if I expected her to come at me once again.

Derwin, who had not seen what happened, began to yell at us for standing there doing nothing when I could not move a muscle, too terrified to do anything.

"Come with me," Aquarius said to the captain. "We can use the other boat to steer them away from Isabelle." He looked to me. "Prince, take her from here."

Flea approached and conversed with Derwin, and quickly, a decision was made. The remaining crew looked at me, bowed, and turned away.

They weren't coming with me. They were going to sink with the ship.

I set my eyes on the bow as it lit up in flames. We would sink in no time if another one of those fire balls hit us now. There was no time to argue.

"Isabelle," I ventured. It hurt to swallow. It hurt to breathe. "We have to go."

She flinched, as if the sound of her own name shocked her. "I'm not sure—"

I watched Aquarius draw Isabelle into his arms, whispering something into her ear. It was a quick embrace, and before she could reciprocate, he was gone, and so was Derwin.

"In you go," I said. I wondered if she felt the shaking of my hand as I took hold of hers and helped her down into the boat. She said nothing, positioning herself, looking almost infantile. Her wide eyes were bloodshot, lined with red zigzags like lightning strikes, and her wet hair clung to her forehead. She bent forward, putting her head in her hands.

Gods, what are you doing to her?

I climbed atop the railing and leapt down into the longboat. We took oars and pumped our arms. The further away we got, the more terrifying the sinking ship looked. She dropped my oar and clapped a hand over her mouth to stop the sobs.

"Isabelle, I need you to row!"

She ignored me, and stood up on shaky legs as the burning ship dipped below the water. Above, the flaming stars met storms clouds—conjured by Aquarius, no doubt. Rain fell in violent streams. The fiery stars sizzled as they fell.

She collapsed back into the boat. Rain lashed her face; the wind came in heavy gusts. They threatened to capsize our boat if she didn't help me row. I urged her on, nudging her with my sopping wet boot. She lifted the oar weakly.

We rowed until our arms burned, and the Queen Isabelle was nothing more than a small fleck of orange on the horizon. No more stars fell. The rain stopped. From afar, lightning bursts lit the sky, and the further away they got, the more I knew that we were safe.

Safe because of the sacrifice of Aquarius, Derwin, and his crew.

I stopped rowing. I sat on the bench of the longboat with my arms over my head, my breath coming out in rapid bursts. Isabelle dropped the oars, slid over on the bench, and said my name.

I lowered my arms and looked at her. The terror in her lit against the glowing moon.

"This wasn't supposed to happen," she said, breathing deeply through her nose. "None of it."

"But it did, and we have to go on."

There was a brief silence, then she nodded. "The more you move, the faster your body temperature will return."

"How far were we from the coast?" Derwin had said only three hours, and that was over an hour ago now, so we couldn't be far.

"Not long now. Look for the lights."

I forced my mind toward happier thoughts. Rescuing the children. Obtaining the celestite. Seeing both Isabelle and me live through it all—anything to distract myself from the pressure building in my chest. But I was running out of hopeful things.

How long could Isabelle fight her demons before they succeeded?

I did not know what the future held. So instead of wondering, I prayed the gods were listening, and we'd see the sun rise again.

CHAPTER FIFTEEN

Every head turned toward me as Branch and I entered the hall. Torches lined the walls, making the tapestries hung there come alive. There weren't many pack members present: two dozen or so sitting in a circle, but it was the elders in the center of the room demanded my attention.

They were both women, hunched and deeply wrinkled, wearing long robes cinched at the waists. Their hair, like the fluff of a baby chick, was white as snow. The taller of the two held a torch in both hands. She stole its fire with a flick of her wrist and made it dance into the center of the room. The other elder sucked the flame toward her as though she were taking a deep breath, but as soon as the flame came close to her lips, she captured it in her hands and palmed it tightly in her shriveled fist.

I'd seen magic like this in human form, but only from the oldest of the pack. And from Izzy. The latter did not make sense. The older generations held onto their small magic, somehow. But Izzy, she'd come upon it so soon after becoming a Gwylis. Her protective magic had saved me from death. Was it because of Aquarius?

Amid this show, Branch pulled out a book from the back of his pants and approached the center of the room.

"This is only but a taste of what the gods had given us." Branch's voice resounded, and the room watched intently.

I stood against a wall and folded my arms across my chest. "I feel a story coming on," I muttered. It wasn't like Branch was well known for quick and straight to the point speeches. He'd keep you all night talking about who knows what unless you dozed off. Even then...

"A long time ago," Branch began, "the gods decided the land below was too empty, and so they gave it life. Tyvasi, the god of all life, created the trees and insects, the creatures and the fish. She gave the land water and soil to house the new life. Peratil gave the world light and dark, to make things grow and give them rest.

"But something happened in the heavens they did not expect. Some of the gods saw the new life and sought to control it. A betrayal. An uprising. And the gods above banished the traitors to the depths below, to live in darkness and never to see light. For the gods did not control every living thing they created. That was our freedom."

For the room, this information was intriguing. But although I knew nothing of the gods' history, this was more of a bedtime story. My eyes began to droop. I pinched myself to stay awake.

"Feeling guilty of the way things in heaven had proceeded, the gods touched the humans of the earths below, giving them but a little of their power. So they would know the gods loved them and would never let corruption take them. But magic placed in the hands of living beings with freedom was a dangerous thing. They wanted more than the gods could give them. They killed each other. Fought for land. For control. And so the gods took away their magic, and the people were angry."

Angry was an understatement. When the New Kingdom was established, the gods all but abandoned them, and when they weren't looking, the Old Kingdom, weary from war, turned their backs just the same. Making deals with fractured gods who still craved the power they felt entitled to.

"Aquarius," Branch continued, "turned to the Uncanny with the hopes of saving his people. But his grave mistake cost us our souls and kept us locked away from the heavens forever. Monsters."

The room shifted uneasily, and Branch took his pause before continuing. "What happens outside these walls, outside these mountains, concerns all of us. The gods gave us freedom to choose. This, right now, is irreversible, and there's a woman out there beyond the Archway who is fighting for that freedom once again."

I stood up a little straighter. Now I knew what this was. Scanning the room, I spotted Olio and Sonia and behind them, Neera. I hissed through my teeth.

This wasn't story time. Branch was recruiting.

My lips pressed into a thin line, determined to storm out and make the biggest scene possible, but I made the grave mistake of looking at Sonia as my heels turned. Her look, disappointed and pleading, rooted me to the spot. I gave a slow shake of my head, and she responded with an eyebrow raise that said, *please, just hear him out. Just this once.*

My sister, just as petulant as myself, here listening to Branch preach, was something else. Olio leaned forward and met my eyes, waving his hand furiously as if to say, *I saved you a seat!*

I splayed out my fingers and touched the tip of my thumb to my chest. *Fine.*

But I wasn't sitting with them.

Branch paced the room, reminding me a little of Kester, the self-appointed caretaker of my mother, whom we'd exiled. But Branch was a better leader by far. Even better than my mother.

Besides, he loved Izzy more than he'd ever let on.

During my ruminations, I did not notice Branch had stopped talking briefly. He smiled at me, which was more of a sneer, but a smile just the same. "But enough about the gods," he said. "Let's talk about us."

THE NIGHT PASSED SO QUICKLY THAT BEFORE LONG, THE SUN HAD risen, the Den was alive, and I was not tired.

I listened to Branch talk about the war that we had lost. He spoke about Aquarius, and the Lonely Fields, where Henry Rowan had died. He recalled the sounds and the screams—much like those of the battle we'd fought only a few weeks prior—that haunted him.

Once the hall had cleared, he took me aside. Weary from standing with my muscles in a constant state of tension, I followed him into what was once Kester's workspace and sunk into one of the chairs. Olio followed close behind.

"If talking burned calories, you'd be tiny as a mouse," he quipped, plopping down onto the floor in what he called a "good morning stretch." Flat on his back with his limbs splayed. "Castor, I spied your eyes glazing over more than once."

I groaned. "Didn't anyone tell you to shut up when you were younger?"

"Yes. Many times."

"How about we practice?"

Olio sat up and deadpanned, "Your life will amount to nothing but crushed dreams."

Branch slammed a fist onto the desk. "Enough. Olio, you're not needed."

Olio threw a hand to his chest in mock astonishment. "You get to talk about questing without me? Rounding up the gods? Visiting old friends? This is what I live for!"

I closed my eyes. "Let him stay if it gets this over with quicker."

"I've gone over it with the others already," Branch said. "So, I will keep it brief. We will follow the river north as far as it will go, cross, and head north. You are all strong wolves—humans—so I have the greatest faith we will make this journey without incident."

I opened my eyes in time to catch Branch's gaze. "What incidents would there be?"

Olio answered. "Oh, you know, ancient monsters, the like. I hear the gods loved to experiment, and the things they created..." He shuddered. "What? You don't believe me?"

My lips curled. "This is irrelevant."

Olio snorted. "Is it? We're about to walk into a land we've never been to seek out allies we've never met. What do you think lives in the land of nevers?" He didn't wait for an answer. "Anything."

"Enough!" Branch interrupted. "Do you think my stories about the gods tonight were for nothing? We need to learn how to be people again if we are to seek their help. We have demons living inside of us. Demons! We must be cautious with our hearts and our minds."

My stomach kicked. "I never said I was coming."

A long pause, and then Branch asked, "But didn't you?"

Olio clapped and hopped to his feet. "All right, how about we get a few hours of sleep and head out bright-eyed into the unknown."

I glowered at him.

"No sleep," Branch said, rounding the desk and heading out of the room. "We leave in an hour."

Olio pouted, but said nothing.

I wanted to protest, but in the end, I opted for going home and falling into bed.

What a waste of time. If the letter from Stormwall taught me anything, it was that we should have stayed at the Den and defended it. Not run away on some fool's errand while pretending to know how to pray to the gods who did not listen.

A trickle of unease ran down my spine. All feelings aside, Izzy was out there risking her life for my people. Her people. And what was I doing? Lying here, staring at the ceiling, wallowing in my own self-pity.

Hey, Mr. Grumpy-Pants, a familiar voice echoed through my mind. *Why don't you try smiling for a change? You look pretty when you smile.*

My scowl deepened. *Izzy, you're not as funny as you think you are.*

Her voice said nothing to this. Good. The last thing I needed while trekking through uncharted territory was the ghost of my former lover chiding me every step of the way.

I sat up. Who said I was going?

A knock on the door, and Sonia entered without waiting. She looked around the room, hands on her hips, and sighed. She shrugged off the pack she'd thrown over her shoulder and clicked her tongue. "If you don't come," she said, blinking the exhaustion from her eyes, "you're going to regret it. I lost my brother once. I won't have it again."

"I made a mistake once," I replied. "I won't do it again."

"You made a mistake in following a power-hungry leader who also made a mistake. Mistakes happen because we're human, and the gods gave us the freedom to make bad decisions and to live with the consequences. You, my brother...you are not a mistake. And I will be with you."

I got off the bed, pulled out my pack from under it, and held it out to my sister. "You have the best food. Throw some in there for me."

Sonia took it gratefully. "I love you, Fray," she said, her eyes watery. "I know what you went through with mother and then with Aquarius was not easy. But if we ever want to live in peace, you have to trust Branch and everyone." She clutched my pack to her chest. "I need to know if you trust me too."

A fire lit in the depths of my gut. Not just from Sonia's words, but from the thought of Aquarius abandoning his people. Abandoning me.

Revenge was a monster, and I let it eat me alive.

~

THE WHOLE OF THE CITY HAD COME TO SEE US OFF. BY BRANCH'S calculations, we should only be hiking through the mountains for a week. If all went to plan. The way he said this, though, was not comforting. He knew as well as I did that this was all a chance we were taking. Allies may not exist. Not anymore.

Upon spotting me, Olio smiled in my direction. I side-stepped his awaiting arms in time to knock into another body, who grunted in protest.

"Watch it, Castor." Neera threw back her crimson hair, braided tight against her head. She batted her eyelashes at my sneer. "You're accompanying this sad little group?"

My lips curled, remembering her victory over me yesterday. Her gloating and posturing grated my nerves.

Olio snorted at our interaction. "I can cut the tension with a dagger."

"Neera!"

Three young girls with flaming red hair bounded through the crowd. Triplets. Neera's sisters. They all gathered around Neera, practically shoving me out of the way. I shrugged. I'd rather not speak with her longer than necessary.

"Can you believe Branch is letting us come?" one of the sisters exclaimed.

"I packed Mama's dagger, and she even let me take her cloak, see?" another squeaked.

I grunted loudly in my head. Their voices were so...high-pitched. My ears started to ring.

Wait. They were coming with us?

Olio threw his arms around me, peering at the girls. "Children are so fun," he mused.

"Yeah, when they're quiet." I said the words low enough, under my breath, but Olio heard anyway. "Aren't they a little too young for this?"

He nudged me in the side. "Oh, my grumpy wolf, perk up. Kids are great."

Neera's sisters weren't kids, per se. Sixteen was young, but old enough to know right from wrong. We wouldn't have to chase them around, asking them to spit out whatever they shoved in their mouths. Unless they were anything like Neera. She seemed...unpredictable.

Neera approached us, her sisters in tow. Together, they all looked like firecrackers about to explode. "Castor, Moore, meet Cas, Mack, and Desi."

The triplets smiled widely, but said nothing. One of them tilted her head to Neera and muttered. "He looks like he wants to bury us alive."

I scowled.

Olio snorted. "Not you girls. Maybe just Neera. Did you know that she..."

Branch approached, looking none too happy. "We're about to visit our ancestors," he snarled. "At least try to represent our people to the best of your abilities."

With the last of our goodbyes spoken, we left through the main gates of the Den. I'd been expecting to feel something the moment the gates closed behind us, but there was nothing but determination. The last of the winter snow melted under the morning sun, making puddles shimmer. The mountain path led south and then broke east or west. We'd take the east road toward the Lonely Fields, where the largest battle in the Old Kingdom occurred. The battle that killed Izzy's brother, Henry.

Sonia adjusted her pack and fell into step beside me. We hung back from the rest of the group, finding solace in the quiet. "You could at least look like you're having fun," she quipped.

"How much do you know of the gods?" I asked. "How much besides what Kester and the elders taught us?"

Sonia frowned. "Not much, I suppose. We were born after everything had happened."

Everything included the years when the New Kingdom was established, when the gods took back their magic, when we went to war.

When the Rowans sought to rid the world of an entire race and find the magic they themselves had squandered.

"Knowing what you know," I said. "Do you find them cruel?"

Sonia's hesitation was answer enough.

I tipped my head back to the warm sun. "I think they are cruel, maybe as cruel as the Uncanny. Think about it, Sonia. They stripped their creations of the magic they gifted us because we did not follow their unspoken rules. They wanted piety, and sure, Aquarius was wrong in what he did, but have you ever thought that maybe he wasn't? The Uncanny were gods once, cast away, much as the humans were."

Sonia stopped walking and looked at me. "Fray, what are you saying?"

"I'm saying I hate Aquarius for abandoning us when we needed him the most, but I do not fault him for giving us the powers the gods stripped from us."

"Fray, you always hated being a Gwylis. It was a means to an end for you."

I crossed my arms over my chest. "All I'm saying is, the Uncanny were there when the gods weren't."

Sonia shook her head. "They turned into monsters."

I thought of the small magic we'd been taught. How we'd use it to enhance weapons and to grow seeds. We'd had magic long ago, even when the New Kingdom was established. Power hungry kings and war. Maybe we just lost our way with no clear path on how to return. The gods should have shown us. They should have been there to help.

But they weren't there. They didn't help.

Sonia thought the Uncanny turned us into monsters. But didn't the gods do us the same favor?

CHAPTER SIXTEEN

The night wore on as we rowed. We might as well have been the last two people left in the world. I counted stars. I watched Ashe, even though he still refused to look at me. I didn't dare offer a vocal apology. It wouldn't be enough.

I'm sorry for trying to kill you. I didn't mean it. I don't know what I would have done if I had—if I lost you. Please, forgive me. Please. Please.

The words wouldn't form on my lips. All I could do was put my energy into rowing, over and over, with the hopes that he'd see the pleading behind it.

How could Ashe ever trust me?

I should have let the demon take me then and there.

Ashe did not hear the battle of thoughts in my mind. He was rowing too hard and too fast to meet my eyes. I wanted him to look my way, so he could see the apology in them. So he could see that I wasn't the monster the Uncanny made me into. But he wouldn't. He may never.

I focused on the ocean, trying to banish all thoughts until my mind was a blank piece of parchment. The silence became a pressing thing. I opened my mouth to say something, anything, but as I did, I spotted a light on the horizon, and the sun began to rise.

Land.

"There it is," I croaked. My mouth was dry, and my throat scratchy like sand. But my words had an impact. Ashe finally looked my way.

He smiled. I knew it hurt him to do so, and I knew he was doing it for my sake. My heart broke all over again. Still, I had a duty. Ashe was still here, and that was enough for me to row on until the lights grew closer.

The beach was inside of a harbor, surrounded by breakwater, but exposed to the open ocean on one side. Ashe's expertise on anything to do with the ocean had me trusting in his words. If we kept to the break-water, we would be safe. But as we approached, we noticed the waves coming very close to the shore, which, as Ashe informed me, would give us less time to set the oars before we'd come crashing against them. But we didn't have a choice.

"Get your pack on," Ashe said. "Hold on."

Everything seemed to be going all right until a large wave took us up. There was nothing to be done now. The longboat's nose dipped under the ocean before it lurched violently. I screamed as it flipped end over end. For a startling moment, I felt suspended in the air, and then I fell feet-first into the cold ocean water.

I didn't go under at first. When I looked up, I saw nothing. No stars. No rising sun. The hollowness of my screams told me the boat had pearled and sat floating upside down above my head. I gathered air into my lungs and dove under, pushing my arms and legs until I felt as though I were free of the boat. I coughed and sputtered as I came to the surface.

But I wasn't clear yet.

A wave crested over me, and I had only a moment before the water closed in over my head. Swimming was not my specialty, so I assumed the deeper I went, the more I would escape the wave as it crashed down. When my lungs swelled for breath, I kicked for the surface. I dove back under a few more times before finally swallowing water and screaming. I couldn't see Ashe anywhere, but a figure crawled onto shore ahead.

I kicked toward the beach until I felt the sand under my fingertips. The boat was there, awash, along with Ashe, who was lying on his back, gasping for breath.

I got to my feet and fought against the waves as I made my way onto the beach. My knees buckled, and I fell onto the sand.

"That wasn't my greatest beaching." Ashe sat up and coughed up a bit of water before standing. "But the result is the same. We made it."

I laid there a moment before jumping into action. "We need to get you changed, or you'll fall ill," I said. I set my hands on my hips and looked toward Alaster.

From my standpoint, it didn't seem like much of a city, but we seemed to land directly near a beachside inn. It looked inviting enough, with torches set outside of a very large deck where several tables sat. It had an impractical straw-like roof, but it held a certain charm.

We'd look like a pair of fools coming into such a place soaking wet, but what other choice did we have?

I gathered my pack on my shoulder and trudged through the sand. Ashe fell into step beside me. I could practically hear his teeth clacking against one another.

Inside the entrance of the inn was a huge fireplace with two sofas. Ashe took residence on one and proceeded to warm his hands as his clothes dripped onto the plush-looking carpet beneath his feet. The innkeeper at the front counter watched him with worried eyes before turning her attention to me.

"Oh," she said, surprised. "You too, huh? Did you fall in?"

A tried to smile, but it probably came off like a sneer the way the innkeeper's face darkened. She was older with snow-white hair pulled back smooth against her head and gathered in a small knot at the nape of her neck. Her apple red cheeks brightened at the sight of me and Ashe, and her blue eyes took on a glazed-over look.

"You two aren't going to be any trouble, are you?" she asked warily. She probably thought we were criminals on the run. She wouldn't be wrong, I supposed.

"No," I said. "We had a problem with our ship and had to disembark. We came into some vicious waves that overturned our boat. Suffice it to say, we're pretty shaken up and in need of some dry clothes and warmth."

The woman took me in another moment, considering my story. "The cost is sixty coin a night."

"We only need a few hours."

"Sixty coin, either way."

I sighed and rummaged through my wet bag. I produced the pouch of jewelry, chose one, and set it on the counter. "I expect it's too early to trade, so will this do until the shops open?"

The woman's eyes widened at the sight of the gold chain. "This will do," she said, sliding it into her palm. "Are you sure you aren't going to be trouble?"

I cast a look over my shoulder to Ashe, who had fallen onto the couch, eyes closed, chest gently rising and falling. His head rolled to the side, mouth open with the beginnings of a snore. I looked back at the woman, whose look had softened. "No," I said. "No trouble at all."

Our room was small, but cozy. Though I hadn't asked for a single bed, a single bed was what I got. Although it was big enough for us both, I had no qualms either way. The innkeeper had brought us some old clothes that we'd have to return once we were fit to leave. I laid them out on the bed and watched Ashe light the fireplace.

The food in my pack was ruined, so I dumped it into a wastebasket by the door. I hung the change of clothes inside on a chair by the fire and addressed the prince, who'd taken a seat on wooden chair, slouched down with his legs spread wide.

"You have to get out of those clothes." No amount of fire was going to warm him up if he stayed in soaked clothing. I watch his head slump onto his shoulder. "Ashe?"

I rushed over to him to see his eyes were closed, but his chest was heavy with breath. Gently, I tugged off his boots and socks to find his toes cold as ice. I cupped a hand to my mouth.

"Ashe, wake up," I urged. "Undress now."

Ashe groaned, but stood up on his own, which was a good sign. He unbuttoned his jacket and slid it off. He peered at me through hooded eyes as he lifted his tunic over his head, only for it to get stuck on the one side where he had a hand.

"Here, let me." I helped him the rest of the way, my eyes snagging on the scar on his abdomen where his father has slashed him when he was younger. I prompted him to remove his pants as I went and pulled off the blankets on the bed and set them in front of the fireplace. "Lie back."

I tore at my own clothes, letting every bit peel away. Ashe had lain down, but had yet to remove his pants. I threw the second blanket over us and leaned over the prince. His eyes fluttered closed, and his breathing slowed once again.

I exhaled one big breath and then went to undo his pants. I shoved them down until I could feel his chilled skin against my naked legs. I rolled him on his side and fit myself against his back.

Ashe needed body warmth. It would be the quickest way to help him now. I couldn't think about our nakedness, only Ashe's survival. I draped my arm over him and use my hand to rub warmth into his chest. His slow heart rate picked up speed. A good sign.

"Ashe?"

No answer.

I curled my legs over his, massaged his arm. I worked my way to the flat of his toned stomach to the raised scar there. Awareness crept into the prince's body, and he flinched away unknowingly.

"Don't touch me." He was sleeping, and possibly delirious, but I couldn't help the way my belly lurched at his words.

He hated me. He must. Every part him rejected me.

Just like...

My throat closed, and swallowing became a feat. Never had I been in such a position with a man, or with anyone. I'd thought it would be with someone was conscious, for one. But also, someone I loved and who loved me back. I imagined that someone and came up with sharp blue eyes and a consistent pouty frown and pushed them away with such force that I nearly choked on my own contained sob.

Love did not belong in war.

Now was not the time for this. I shoved my body flush against his and tugged the blankets higher against us. Ashe's body stayed motionless. I counted the beats of his heart against my palm. With my cheek on his shoulder, I nearly fell asleep with him.

I wished I could erase the tightness in his face; the way he didn't trust me and never would again. I laid there, a little angry, a lot miserable, and filled with regret.

I closed my eyes. I shouldn't have let him come with me. I should have seen him somewhere safe to hide while I took care of things. But no, I couldn't blame his presence for doing what I did. There was only blame for myself.

Ashe shifted onto his back, and I pulled my legs back as to not touch certain parts of him I shouldn't be touching. His eyes peeled open, albeit slowly.

"What's happening?" he groaned.

"Your body temperature was too low," I replied, keeping my arm draped around him.

"I...I'm still cold."

"I know." An idea occurred to me. "Do you mind if I shift? It would be the only way, just until you feel better."

To my surprise, Ashe nodded. His throat bobbed as he swallowed. "I'm n-naked."

"Sure as rain. Let me rearrange the room. Hold on."

I stood and fit the blanket back around Ashe. I felt his eyes on me, and his sharp intake of breath. Such scenes, I supposed, were not common in the Peek Islands. I turned to meet his gaze, but he'd already looked away. Such a gentleman.

I shoved aside the wooden chair and a small table and surveyed the room. It would be tight, but it would work.

"I-Isabelle."

I'd crouched and had begun my chant when Ashe spoke my name. I stopped, but stayed low to the ground.

"T-thank you," he said.

I averted my gaze. "Don't thank me, Ashe. Don't thank me ever again."

He sat up on his elbows and turned to look me in the eyes. "I...I know that wasn't you b-back there. I-I-I know it was something e-else. I s-saw it."

Ashe's words dug into me. They made sense in theory, but I knew everything that happened was my doing. I'd made Aquarius change me. I'd made a deal with the Uncanny. I'd returned to Stormwall. I burned my city to the ground and got innocent people killed. But here was a prince, laden with apologies I did not deserve.

But he spoke lies. Maybe he wanted to believe all of that was true. But his subconscious knew what I was. His skin recoiled at my touch when his mind wasn't fully aware of what was happening. This was this equivalent of the "drunk men tell no lies." He was afraid of me, and with good reason.

I continued my chant to shift into a wolf and fell atop the blankets beside Ashe before he could lie back down. After a moment, I felt him slide closer to me. I moved my head and rested it atop Ashe like a protective mother to her cub.

Ashe stirred, his heart picking up rhythm. "I tried to protect you," he whispered.

My chest rose and fell with a measured breath. I felt truth in his words, but I answered him only in my mind. *You can't protect me, Ashe. As much as you wanted to, you never truly could.*

"You weren't like this before."

My breath hitched. How little the prince knew me. In the weeks he spent at Stormwall awaiting my engagement to him, I'd been sneaking out through the cemetery walls like an assassin hells-bent on revenge. While he preened, and watched from a safe distance, I discovered the treachery of my parents and aligned myself with the Gwylis. What a surprise it must have been to see me that day on the cliff before he lost his arm. Did he truly think of me as a different person?

I didn't mean to close my eyes, but I did. Feeling the rise and fall of Ashe's chest lulled me into a dreamless sleep.

~

I woke when the sun was high and the rumble of my stomach was too much to bear. Ashe was breathing steadily in his sleep. His body temperature was normal, but I shifted and stoked the fire anyway. He'd need at least another few hours' rest before we set out again. Maybe even another night.

But first, I'd need money.

I dressed in the clothes the innkeeper gave us and stuck my feet into my damp boots. I shouldered my pack and locked the door behind me. The inn was quiet, save for a few stragglers in the front entrance. I dipped my head as I passed and exited back onto the beach.

Following a path up the hill, away from the beach, I came to large stone building hosting vendors selling right outside its windows. The street was covered in sand from the beach. I followed the flow of the crowed between the two structures where the road inclined. The buildings on either side jutted toward the sky. People hung on balconies above, calling down to friends or merely sitting with drinks. The salty smell of the ocean permeated the air.

My heart swelled. Henry would have loved it here.

The road opened to the main square. Vendors congregated in the center. Along the inner circle, businesses such as restaurants and other shops took residence. I kept close to the buildings. Somehow, avoiding the openness of the square made me feel safe.

A tall man wearing a strange straw hat ambled past and bumped my shoulder. We both turned to apologize, but his came out first. I couldn't believe the likeness he had of Henry. He was the same height and even the same build. He even had the same smile lines as Henry. He was decidedly handsome and kind, and it made my heart ache.

For the first time in what seemed like forever, I felt far from home.

As the man turned to leave, I felt cemented in place. I hadn't spoken to Henry, not even in a prayer before bedtime. I didn't have a grave to visit. Would he find me here? Here, with a girl without a home to call her own.

Henry would have liked Alaster. I imagined what he would say if he were here.

"Look. Izzy, that woman is wearing feathers on her head!" he'd exclaim. "Try this shellfish. What sort of instrument is that, do you think? It sounds heavenly! Should we try this eatery? It has some sort of fish stew that sounds good right about now. Izzy, have you seen this sea glass?"

I swallowed down the swelling in my throat and focused on the task at hand. A trading post stood at the corner of the square and happened to be right beside a bakery. There was no door, just a window with an awning above it. A grizzled man sat on the other side, a sweet-smelling cigar hanging from his mouth.

"Afternoon," the man said by way of greeting. "What do you have for me?"

I considered walking away. Would I draw too much attention with this jewelry? This town didn't seem worse for wear, and I couldn't imagine being thieved on my way back to the beach, but looks could be deceiving.

"Just a few things to trade." I took only two necklaces from the pouch, leaving the rest. The shopkeep finished his cigar and put it out on an ashtray there on the counter. The sickening smell of ashes filled my nose.

He eyed the jewelry greedily. "Unloading before you go?" he asked, holding a looking glass and examining them closely.

"Before I go where?"

"Up north there to Essex." The man took one of the jeweled necklaces between his teeth. "The king is offering lots of coin to anyone willing to relocate and offer their services."

The phrase *offer their services* made me shudder. But I didn't say a word. Alaster was not aware of what happened in Stormwall yet, and bringing attention to how I knew would not be in my best interest. Better to get coin and some horses and get out.

"No, sir, I'm not going to Essex," I lied. "I'm going far west. As far as I can go."

The man nodded and turned to retrieve his coin box. He counted more coin on the counter than I expected. "That's for the best," he said, sliding the money over to me. "There's no good out there." He leaned over the counter, as if letting me in on a secret. "I hear there's demons out there. You look like a good girl. You don't want none of that. You're not traveling alone, are you?"

"Yes, I am," I lied. "Thanks for the advice."

As I walked away, my body sagged. To the tradesman, to everyone here, I looked like just a normal person. What would they think of me if they could see the rot in my heart? Or all the things I'd done to make it that way?

But I was danger wearing a human skin. I was nothing now but fury, panic, and fear.

I was not a good girl. I was the very worst.

CHAPTER SEVENTEEN

I'm naked.

Pulled from a nightmarish dream cycle of thrusting a sword into my father, I woke to find myself alone, without clothes, under a thick blanket in front of a fire. I had no recollection of anything after washing up on the shore after our boat capsized. No memories except that of committing murder.

I squeezed my eyes closed and then opened them again with a renewed vigor. I sat up, letting the blanket fall from my chest, and looked around. This room was an inn. Now I remembered vaguely of Isabelle checking in and holding me upright as she led me here. I moved the blanket aside and frowned. She'd taken off all my clothes and warmed me back to life. There was some animal fur stuck to the blanket. She'd shifted to keep me alive. The loose hairs told me she'd been here for hours.

"Gods." I pressed the heels of my hand into my eyes. "Oh, gods."

It had been so long since I had trusted someone. It had always been me, on my own, depending on no one. Nobody put my needs first. Having Isabelle here dissolved the edges of my loneliness, like finding your way home after being gone for so long.

I tried to focus. I was alive. I slipped on my dry clothes and looked around for Isabelle's pack, but she must have taken it with her when she went into town. My stomach grumbled, but I ignored it. I had much more pressing things to worry about than food.

I shook the remaining bits of sleep from my body and left the inn, making my way into the city. I knew Isabelle would probably head toward the market square, where she'd find somewhere to trade her jewelry. My destination would not be so obvious.

Look for the sun and moon.

The rebellion hid within towns like this, and if I were to gather them, I had to start somewhere. Alaster boasted a place you could get lost in. It reminded me a lot of home with its ocean scent and palms lining every street. The streets were tight, built only for a single horse to come or go. I could reach out and touch the walls on either side of me—if I had both hands, of course.

If my father had done his job a little better, he'd send his Gwylis into cities and towns across Mirosa. Instead of building his army, he should have looked at eradicating the one that was built right under his very nose. Maybe he would have, had he had enough time on the throne.

Isabelle tried to kill me.

The moment had come at breakneck speed. Now that I had a moment to reflect, I knew what dangers I'd put myself in. I knew what she was—a cursed human, a wolf. I knew from what I'd seen in her mother, the queen, what the Uncanny could do to a human body given the right situation. Isabelle was strong, and I had no doubt she would fight off whatever the demons had for her, but for how long? A moment of weakness was all they needed for her to turn her back on her allies and upend her.

For all of this to fall apart.

Behind me, a rustle of fabric breathed across the stone walls and turned a corner.

I darted toward it and peered out, watching a woman glide away from me. She stopped once to glance my way before disappearing into a what appeared to be a shop of some kind. Being off the beaten path, it wasn't busy, but there was a bell on the door alerting the owner to my presence. I caught the door before it closed and looked at the flyer fixed to the door.

A sun and a moon.

"The stars are bright tonight," I said, letting the door close. The woman I'd seen now stood in front of me, two pale hands cupped to her mouth. She was younger than me, but only by a few years, I'd assumed. Her hair fell in long amber strands, and she wore a robe of deep violet.

The woman did not respond, and my heart fell into my belly. I was prepared to leave the shop before she dropped her hands from her lips.

"A crow came at dawn," she said. Eyes the color of honey peered back at me. "They told of a great battle at Stormwall and the death of the usurper king. Is it true?"

I let out a breath and nearly lurched forward with relief. "It is true."

"And you are the prince?"

I shook my head. "No, not a prince. I'm am just Ashe."

"Asheton Paratheon of the Peek Islands."

I nodded. "Yes, but just Ashe."

The woman smiled. "All right, Just Ashe, you are here for a very important reason."

"A soothsayer named—"

The woman held up a hand to cut me off, turned and swept away deeper into the shop. I finally got a good look at it, and it was rather pleasing. The walls were filled with weapons of every kind. From swords, to daggers, to bows. I stopped at the bows, admiring the workmanship. Isabelle had come without the bow I'd given her, and it would be nice to hold one again.

"You require something to accommodate your situation?"

I glanced up at the woman. She locked eyes with me. She was beautiful, I had to admit, but it wasn't her appearance that warmed my core, but her tone. I'd spent so many weeks surrounded by vicious and cruel people. To hear someone gentle speak to me was a welcome relief.

Someone who hadn't known what I'd done.

I instinctively moved aside my cloak, peering down at the sleeve folded at the elbow and cast a wary look at the woman. "I require more than you can offer. Unless you are a god."

The woman's lips pressed into a tight grimace. She moved behind a counter and produced a box. She rummaged through it, biting her lip until she found what she was looking for. "There are beasts in the waters," she told me. "Sometimes our men come back with missing limbs, and I came up with this."

She holds out a replica of a person's arm, made to look like a glove of iron. It was surprisingly light, and the fingers were curled, as it were in a constant state of grabbing hold of something. Leather straps fell at the end, assumingly used to tighten the thing to a person's arm. I looked at the woman, impressed. "You made this?"

She nodded. "My name is Moora."

This false arm would not be strong enough to hold a weapon, so why would she make something like this? Were people so vain that they needed things like this to pretend they still had all their parts?

Was I so vain?

I shifted from foot to foot. "Are you giving this to me?"

She lifted one shoulder. "You do not have to pay me. I know you've come a long way and seen many terrible things."

My breath stalled, and I nearly dropped the steel arm. Had I come to the wrong place? The sinking feeling in my gut told me to run, but was I running from the truth of Moora's words or the denial of them?

I handed the metal arm to Moora. "I can't take it. Not after what I'd done."

Moora gasped a laugh. "Ashe, you've done the greatest thing you could ever do at this moment in time. Do you not understand what you are? You are important. Don't let the ghost of your father tell you otherwise."

Moora took the arm from me and moved to uncuff my sleeve. I flinched away. Hurt crossed her face.

"Are you ashamed of it?" she asked.

"It almost killed me." I swallowed at the memory. "Gwylis healed it and took away the infection."

Moora's eyes brightened. "Gwylis? Are you sure?"

I laughed, remembering the sharp-eyed Sonia, who wanted to cut off the rest to save us the trouble. "Yes, I'm sure."

Moora sucked on her teeth, looking more like a child than a woman in her twenties. "May I?"

"Do you have interest in Gwylis magic? It wasn't magic, per se. Just good medicine. Herbs of some sort and a badly tasting tea."

Moora ignored me. "May I?" She nodded in assurance and then gazed at my place where I used to be whole.

I sighed and relented.

She pushed up my tunic sleeve to expose the stump. I looked away, eyes on the ceiling, the walls—anywhere but on Moora. I'd seen the pity on people's faces more often than I liked, but it didn't mean I had to subject myself to it again.

I felt her finger, light as a feather's touch, graze the healed skin. My body tensed at the touch. A gentle touch. Something so foreign.

"It healed beautifully." She paused. "Ashe, would you look at me, please? I cannot speak to another unless I can see their eyes. Otherwise, I feel like I'm talking to a brick wall."

I squeezed my eyes shut and then opened them, meeting Moora's gaze.

"You know I've learned a great deal about what it's like to lose a limb," she said. "Be it arm, leg, finger, or a toe, and do you want to know something that I've found common amongst those who've suffered these injuries? They've all seen themselves as less of a person. Can you imagine that? Seeing yourself as inferior...it's absurd. There's a great deal of love and courage and strength inside a person that perhaps the outside does not matter as much as we think it does."

Overwhelmed by her words, I moved to step away, but Moora caught my wrist.

"You are more than this," she said, turning my hand palm up. Her touch was like tiny sparks under my skin, and she stared down at it as if trying to read something written there. "I know you are."

"Why?" I cautioned, my heart hammering as if bracing myself from jumping off the side of a cliff.

Moora released my hand and narrowed her eyes questionably. "Because you did what you needed to do for the good of the kingdom."

Anxiety tightened my chest. "I did what I did because I wanted it to end, even if it meant sacrificing my own life."

"That's what I mean." Moora held up the false limb and tilted her head. "Life is precious; we must do what we have to. Sacrifice is love, and this limb here—this is my labor of love, so how about we quit the inspirational speeches and get this thing on you?"

I rubbed at the back of my neck, unsure.

"Look here." Moora held the arm at eye level. "See these tiny gears? Turn them, and they clench the fingers so you can hold onto things. Not heavy things, mind you, but simple things like clothes or a mug." She bit her lower lip cautiously. "May I try it on you?"

I furrowed my brow, saying nothing.

"I know you are under a great deal of pressure, but let me help you."

I loosed a breath. What harm could it do? I was already here, and since it was made for me...

I nodded finally, and Moora's eyes lit up. She wasted no time, tugging the leather cuff over my stump and gently buckling the strap so it fit properly. The metal half of the false arm was cold and chilled my skin, but soon, my body accepted the foreign thing. It fit perfectly.

Had it only been months since I lost my arm? So short a time to forget what it felt like to feel the weight of it on my body. Balancing it. The inanimate hand hung awkwardly, but in time, I supposed it would not feel so foolish.

For the first time in many months, I felt like the me I was when I'd first stepped foot in Stormwall castle. The stronger, more confident me.

I admired my new arm with sudden hesitance. "How does this fit so well?"

Moora stood back. "The Rowans had ordered it back when you'd lost your arm initially," she told me. "But nobody ever called to retrieve it."

The Rowans, meaning both Chelsea and Hugo had sent a crow requesting a metal arm made for their future son-in-law. They could not bear to see me weak. I removed the metal thing and handed it back to Moora.

"I don't want it," I said, letting Moora's work dangle in my hand. "But I do want to know what I must do. Abiyaya sent me to find you."

Moora took the arm, her brows lowered over her eyes. "You don't like it," she said softly.

"It makes me feel weak."

"You are not weak."

"I am."

She held my gaze. "You want to be worthy?"

I shook my head. "I only want to be good."

Moora considered this and handed back the iron arm. "The wheels are turning, Ashe Paratheon, and things are in motion. You cannot stop it. From the moment you killed your father, a sun rose in the minds of the New Kingdom. A truth. We learned of what your father had done to the Gwylis. We learned of where she had gone and what she did there.

We rose up." At my furrowed brow, she smiled. "Word travels fast on the wings of crows."

A maelstrom of emotions swirled through me. "Unbelievable."

Moora nodded, her jaw tense. "Every city, every town, every village, you will find us. But we need a leader, and we need to convince more and more if we wish to retake Stormwall."

"Aquarius is gone. Back into the Old Kingdom." Maybe dead, for all I knew.

Moora's eyes brightened. "Yes, the wheels are turning," she mused. "But I mean you. You are going west with the princess?"

"She's the queen."

Moora's lips pulled into a thin line. She said nothing.

"First to Essex," I continued. "My father has been kidnapping children to build his army."

Moora paled. "Oh my."

"Yes, I know."

Moora nibbled her lower lip. "We need a face for the rebellion, and I know how much she must mean to you, but can she go without you? What will it take to keep you here?"

"Everything."

Moora nodded, looking disappointed. "I thought so. In that case, here." She went over to the front counter and produced a box. She poured the contents onto the counter and pursed her lips. "Responses, from all the lords of all the cities across Mirosa. Well, maybe not all of them, but the ones that count. Will you—"

I was at the counter in two big strides, a sense of trepidation weighing in my gut.

Moora had, what appeared to be, the letters Abiyaya had me write back at Stormwall, begging lords to unite against my father and the Greatwolf Pack. "Where did you get these?"

"Abiyaya."

"Help me read them?"

Moora nodded without hesitation. She peeled open the first, breaking the wax seal, and read it aloud. "Yes."

My chest felt suddenly painful. "The next one."

Moora obliged. "Yes. This one also says yes."

I blew my breath out in a slow stream and picked up a letter of my own. Again, the same word. Onto the next. *Yes. Yes.* They all said yes.

"Ashe, what does it mean?"

I read the next letter and then the next. The last one held the signature of Kine's lord—the one I'd spoken to briefly in Stormwall. I opened it slowly, wondering if I'd been worthy enough for him.

"Ashe?"

I mouthed the word in the Lord of Kine's letter. *Yes.* So, I'd been enough after all. "I asked them to take up arms my father, and whoever came after, had Isabelle and I failed."

Moora sucked in a breath. "They all said yes," she said softly, looking at the discarded letters. Then, with a snap, her head came up and her eyes widened. "Ashe, we have an army!"

I carved a hand through my hair, held it back, and then released it. I couldn't help but feel disbelief. At the thought of all these lords and ladies calling to arms with me—it was too much to bear. "All my life, I've been beaten down." A heavy, dull pain radiated throughout my body. I looked at my feet, struggling with my emotions. "Up until I killed my father did I believe that I was meant for nothing in this world other than to serve him. To shadow him. To carry on his ideals and his legacy. I was nothing."

"Your father made you feel so low?"

I said nothing.

Moora tapped her chin. "I imagine we have more to discuss."

She was avoiding the subject of my father, and for that, I was grateful.

I gave a single shake of my head. "I don't have time to talk." At her sudden frown, I added, "Although I'd certainly like to."

She smiled, but it didn't quite reach her eyes. "I see that we did not receive a missive from Essex. Did you write to them?"

"Yes, but you already know why they did not respond." Certainly. They threw my letter into the fire and killed the crow that delivered it. "I do not expect to hear from them."

"I will send a crow to Alder. He lives in a squat part of the city. Look for the sun and moon symbol above a window covered in a red curtain."

She shoved the false arm into my chest, staring at my throat, where

I'm sure the bruises from Isabelle's hands were ugly by now. "Take it. To protect yourself. Two hands are better than one."

I slouched. She was as bad with jokes as Isabelle.

"Whether you use it or not makes no difference, but take the damn thing before my arm falls off."

I tilted my head to the side, and she broke into laughter.

"What is life if we can't laugh through tragedy?"

I stood, unmoving.

Moora poked me again with the arm.

I took it finally and twisted my body to leave. At the last second, I looked over my shoulder to Moora. "Will I see you again?"

Moora's smile grew wider. She stuck out her tongue as she dipped her head in a small bow. "Yes, Ashe, you will see me again."

With the arm and this new information, I made my way back to the beachside inn. I echoed back what Moora had told me, regarding the rebellion and needing a leader. I hadn't responded to it, and I wondered if she took that as a rejection. I shook my head. No, she didn't need a reply. She knew I'd bring them together, even if I had to die to do it.

I breathed a laugh though my nose as I looked down at the iron arm. It was funny that as a child, I dreamed of being a warrior clad in iron. Now, I felt I had to make metal encasing my entire being. To help Isabelle, I had to push back every emotion weakening me and focus on what had to be done.

I had to become a ruler. But what a ruler do when faced with such challenges?

One part of me was false, but I wondered which part.

CHAPTER EIGHTEEN

They sliced the skin under my eye and watched it heal.

"Abomination!" they called me.

I smelled blood and fear.

They'd taken Izzy and imprisoned me. But I'd nearly bitten the arm off the prince. I thought of that with a smile as they starved and beat me to an inch of my life. I felt pain, but then it was gone, and it started all over again.

I wanted to save her.

Did I save her?

I'd die thinking I did. It'd be easier that way.

A sharp and cutting voice: 'You will always be hunted. You will always be hated. You are nothing.'

Was I nothing?

"Fray, it's time to get up."

The female voice lifted me from my dream and to a small copse of trees where I'd fallen asleep. I sat up slowly and ran a hand through my mussed hair.

I rubbed my eyes and cracked the tightness from my bones. The camp had been packed up and the fire doused. They all looked ready to go. "Why didn't you wake me earlier?" I asked.

"You were sleeping so deep, I was afraid to."

I hunched over, recalling the dream. It hadn't been the first that had haunted my sleep. Before all of this, I saw a lot of Aquarius and war and death. Now, my mind wanted me back in Stormwall's dungeons. I'd rather have been in battle.

Branch stood over the remnants of last night's fire, fitting his belt and sheathing the daggers he held there. The chilled morning air would give way to warm afternoons as spring pushed its way through. I wondered how it would feel to be cold. I shook the thought away.

Despite the ache of hiking all day yesterday with little to no breaks and the fact that I almost missed the meals at the mess hall, all I wanted to do was get moving. We still had days of traveling left, and my bones were already aching. My discussion yesterday with Sonia got me thinking more about how Branch's plan of winning over the gods and asking our allies how to go about that and how foolish it sounded. If they truly were to listen, they would need more a reason to do so.

And whatever the reason, I would do it. I'd be a better person than Aquarius. Maybe even a better leader.

I stifled a yawn and approached Branch. "Give me more responsibility."

The large man turned, slowly at first, as if he hadn't heard me correctly. "What do you wish to do?"

I hadn't a clue. Maybe oversee provisions. The map. Scouting. Anything.

"Scouting," I said, without much thought. Scouting was dangerous, but also quiet. I could think better without two dozen voices drowning out my thoughts.

"Scouting?" Branch made a face and then nodded. "All right. Neera!"

My heart plummeted into my belly as the red-haired female jogged over. She gave a wide-eyed grin full of white teeth. Her braids had been tied back, showing off the sharp angles of her face. She gave a slight bow at the neck. "Branch?"

"Castor wants to scout. Teach him?"

Neera tacked on a look of astonishment. "Teach him? I'll teach him anything you want me to, boss."

I rubbed my jaw, regretting I even said anything.

"I'm not one for conversation," I said. "Keep it short."

Neera gave a low whistle. "He's going to be trouble," she said with a short laugh. Branch rolled his eyes and stalked away. Neera stayed put. "What are you *really* up to, Castor? Looking to gain some points to become a member?" She scratched her chin. "I'm not sure who's keeping tally, but I'm sure you don't have many."

Desperate to get moving, I brushed past her and retrieved my pack and sword. My dagger was still sheathed on my hip when I fell asleep last night. Once I shouldered my pack, I waited for Neera's instructions. She stood with her arms on her hips, probably still waiting for my retort. I wasn't giving her one. After a moment, she sighed and trotted forward through the trees. With a heaving sigh, I followed.

My boots crunched the earth beneath me, kicking aside fallen branches and stepping over logs as I worked my way through the forest. I could hear the group behind me, their voices traveling on the wind. I squinted against the bright sun and brushed my fingers against the hilt of the dagger at my hip. The Gwylis relied on elemental magic and teeth and claws. I'd never felt safer than when I was holding a piece of sharpened steel.

I'd been broken long before gaining employment in Stormwall, built back up to the kind of soldier Aquarius wanted me to be. The kind he wanted all the Gwylis to be. After, I'd been broken in a new way, only finding myself again when I'd hunted Izzy's attackers, and was slowly becoming that soldier once again. But that wasn't who I was.

Who was I?

Coming back to the Den had not answered my question or me. I felt more lost than ever. I could speak again. I had a woman who loved me. But it wasn't enough. There was a voice buried deep inside, calling out for rescue, but trampled by demon magic. Suppressed.

I'd been leashed like a guard dog. I'd be damned if I ever let myself feel that trapped again.

The memory of my time imprisoned in Stormwall slammed into me. Hugo Rowan, once a king, smiling over my battered body. The cruelty in his eyes, knowing that he had beat the Gwylis once again.

I hissed through a cage of teeth, and picked up the pace. Despite what the rest of the pack thought, I was not so submissive. I'd gone through hell and back, and I wasn't about to cower to the likes of Neera.

I'll show them who I really am.

I fell into step beside Neera as we left the forest and edged out into the Lonely Fields. "Stop and listen," she told me, closing her eyes and letting the sudden harsh wind blow the strands of hair that had come free from her braids. She was lithe, like a deer, but the wind did not move her. "There are ghosts here."

There are ghosts everywhere, I wanted to say, but held my tongue.

"We're okay," Neera said, opening her eyes and training them to the distance. She gave a birdcall and descended the hill.

"That's all this is?" I asked, taking my steps slow and calculating. No use twisting an ankle trying to show off.

"All this is? We're the first to find danger. We're protecting our family, Castor."

I snorted. "Protecting your family? You let your little sisters come along."

Neera narrowed her eyes. "They're sixteen, old enough to make choices for themselves."

"Do you truly think that?"

Neera jutted out a bony hip. "Yes, I do. If I had it my way, they'd be locked away somewhere where nothing could ever hurt them, but we all sacrifice in different ways."

"That's not sacrifice."

Neera clacked her teeth together. "Have you ever heard of a blaht ritual?"

I shook my head. I hadn't heard of any rituals, to be honest.

"It's when our people used to talk animals and sacrifice them for the gods."

I frowned. "Seems like a waste."

Neera's face turned stony. "It's a deep honor to be part of one."

I brushed past her. "Maybe that's why I hadn't heard of it. Lack of honor and all."

Neera gave a loud huff. "Gods save us," she muttered. "I don't see you as a traitor, Castor." I turned and she pursed her lips. "Not anymore, at least."

"Sure," I muttered. "So, this ritual?"

Neera nodded. "Yes, so it entails making a sacrifice to the gods for their goodwill and protection. I read all of this and more when they reopened the library. I told Branch of it and he confirmed with the elders. We're going to have one tonight."

"And you truly think the gods care about us holding a dead deer in our hands and doing some dance in their honor?"

Neera frowned. "It is our culture. It *was* who we were."

I walked on, my boots soft against the wet ground. "It may be who we were. But it's not who we are now."

Neera growled as she caught up, grabbing me by my shoulder and twisting me to face her. We were eye to eye. Scowl to scowl. My muscles immediately tensed. I clamped down on my teeth to stop myself from lashing out. "Branch wanted you with us for a reason. He wanted you to be part of history." She gestured to the old battlefield ahead of us. "This is a bloody part of our history; fighting for our survival, making deals with demons. But what we're doing now...they will talk about for ages. We're reuniting heavens and earth."

A strangled-sounding laugh escaped me. History would not be kind to the Gwylis. They'd paint us as monsters who deserved to die. We made deals with the underworld and expected the future to speak highly of our people? No, never. They would not see the way the past twisted us, separated us, massacred us. We were magicless because we forgot the gods.

No, history would not be kind to my people.

"Yoo-hoooo!"

Olio appeared at the top of the hill and waved frantically before deciding to do a head over toe flip down the hill. I shook my head. *He's going to break his neck someday.*

As Olio smoothed his clothes, one of his sleeves rode up, and I spotted a dark spot on his upper arm. A bruise?

Olio yanked his sleeve down. "It appeared a week ago," he told me and scratched the back of his head. "It's not a bruise or anything. It feels scaly, though. Like lizard skin."

I wrinkled my nose. A rash. Leave it to Olio to go rolling around poisonous shrubs. But still, a rash would fade in a few hours' time with our healing abilities. "What do you think it is?"

Olio gave a tiny shrug. Behind us, the rest of the group was descending the hill. "It's nothing to worry about," he said. "Maybe—" He paused, a flash of worry crossing his eyes as though he'd stopped himself from saying too much. He bounced on his toes and shook out his shoulders. "I'll be fine, Mother," he jested.

Neera dipped her chin as Olio sashayed past us. She turned her gaze to me. "He says he's all right, but he's not. We'll ask the gods for answers tonight."

I sighed as Neera walked away, her words ringing in my ears. Something discomforting slithered in the pit of my belly. I looked up at the clear sky, wondering why people prayed there for answers to the questions they were too helpless to formulate on their own. There was death all around me, and if none of this worked—if Izzy and the prince failed, and if we failed—I'd be a ghost along with them.

Nobody was going to save us.

CHAPTER NINETEEN

When I returned to the room, I found Ashe sitting on the single wooden chair with his head flopped backwards.

"I have the biggest headache," he drawled. The fire burned bright. He sipped his glass of water as if it were wine. He was fully dressed, which was a relief. He crossed an ankle over his knee and bobbed his foot.

It was a warm moment, interrupted only by the rumble in my stomach. "Here." I held out a bag of oddly shaped cakes I found at the bakery in the square.

All the comfort drained from Ashe's face when he turned to look at me. I felt myself pale. Could he have remembered the way we'd lain together as I tried to rub warmth back into his body? Or was he recalling that one time I tried to kill him?

He took the bag as I willed color back into my face. I averted my gaze and rubbed at my arms.

"Are you all right?"

I perched on the armchair and turned to him warily. "I bought two horses, provisions, and a new map. Also, some clothes, with a lot of coin leftover. If we moved now, we'd make it to the town of Rahr. Although it wouldn't be a lot of miles, it's better to keep moving. We could make it by nightfall." The thought of a good night's sleep was all the motivation I needed.

Ashe's laugh made me look up. "How can we fail to address the big naked issue?"

I jerked from the armchair, mortified.

I slapped a hand to my forehead, realizing how foolish I was being. "Listen here, I didn't want to do it, but I couldn't have you dying on the floor of some inn before you even got the chance to tell you how sorry I was for doing what I did on the ship. But I'm not sorry for stripping you and keeping you alive, even if I did get a good show out of it."

"Can you imagine what your cousin would say if she knew?"

My frown softened at the fierce smile Ashe gave me. "I wouldn't tell her, of course. She had a bigger mouth than a river carp."

Ashe closed his eyes; they crinkled in the corners like starbursts. His shoulders shook with contained laughter. "Henry would have killed me then and there. No questions asked."

I never got to experience a protective older brother, but the image was amusing. "Your skin's real soft," I purred. "Like a baby."

A cake shot out from Ashe's hand and hit me square on the side of the head, dissolving into crumbles. I reached into my bag for one to throw, but thought better of it. Cake was to be preserved. Not wasted.

Soon, the moment passed, and the weight of everything came crashing back down upon our shoulders. I changed back into my now-dry clothes and left the ones the innkeeper gave me there on the bed. Ashe had done the same. He munched on one of the cakes, making noises of approval.

"Aquarius is going to find us, isn't he?" Ashe said, staring at his half-eaten pastry.

I snatched the bag from his hands and stuffed a cake into my mouth, although remaining silent was just as bad as an "I don't know."

I felt his eyes on me. "We need him, Isabelle."

I choked down the cake and brushed the crumbs from my lips. The weight of those words laid heavy in my stomach. Of course, we needed him. We needed his power, his protection, his guidance. I unstuck my tongue from the roof of my mouth and told Ashe about Aquarius, and how he would die quicker if he were still human.

"He'd never be able to swim as a wolf," I said. "But I supposed he could control the winds to push them to Alaster. That being if any of them—"

"You don't have to say it."

"No, it's all right. If I don't talk about those I lost, it doesn't feel as though they lived to begin with. I have to make them real."

"Like Henry?"

I nodded.

"Lucy?"

My shoulders rose and fell with a deep breath. "I don't think you've ever said her name before."

Ashe shrugged on his coat, buckled on his belt, and shoved his daggers into their sheaths. He took one last look at the room before turning back to me.

"Before we get to Rahr, you're going to tell me what you did between the time I let myself get taken and when I saw you on that rooftop in Stormwall," he said.

I narrowed my eyes. "What?"

Ashe frowned. "You know what I'm talking about, Isabelle." He eyed my necklace and frowned. "You know damn well."

He rubbed a hand across his neck, and I finally saw what I'd been subconsciously ignoring. There were bruises from where my fingers squeezed into his skin, breaking blood vessels and making them an angry mix of red and purple.

I did that to him. My friend.

He deserved it.

I pawed at my ears, willing the cruel voices away.

"What do you think happened to me?" I snapped. "Are you dense? I'm cursed!"

I retracted the words immediately, stunned at how much hatred poured into them. That wasn't me talking. Those weren't my thoughts. When my hands had pried from Ashe's throat, they stayed sore and aching for hours. I'd choked him. The pain and fear in his eyes. He felt so fragile.

"It wasn't you. I know it wasn't. It's all right."

No. It wasn't all right. I had a feeling it was only going to get worse.

"Isabelle, tell me." His voice was gentle and pleading.

"I couldn't use my magic because it terrified me, and the Den was in danger." I swallowed and fixed my eyes to a spot on the ceiling. "We were going to lose the city if I did not act. After I killed Rixon, I sought out the Uncanny."

His brow furrowed. "What do you mean by 'sought out?'"

I clutched the two jewels at my neck so hard, I felt the indentations on my skin. I could still hear the sickening sound my dagger made as it slid through Rixon's flesh; felt the victory soaring in my heart. Perhaps even then, I'd been depraved. Seeking revenge by any means. Taking lives without remorse.

I let out a long, shuddering breath. "At first, I didn't plan on doing much but maybe trying to kill them, which was foolish. But they make you feel things. It's like all of your fears and vulnerabilities are right in front of you, staring you in the face."

Ashe studied me, his expression uncertain. "On the Peek Islands, we were taught never to converse with demons."

I snorted. "Oh, believe me, it's not something I do every day."

Ashe let out a long breath. "It can't be helped. We can only move past it."

It was strange to see him this way; his whole demeanor strangely accepting. He'd grown into it when we'd brought an injured Sonia to his hunting cabin. The furs on his back. The beard. Although he seemed at peace, there'd been something eating away at the prince. Something had been missing from his life. Something significant within him had changed.

"I know it was foolish and I know it was dangerous, but I did it," I continued. "I made a deal with Uncanny to give me magic to protect the Den, and in turn, I would give them my soul and stand over the damned in the underworld."

Ashe blinked, his expression unreadable. "Your soul?"

My heart rattled against my ribs. "Yes," I whispered.

The realization slowly dawned on him. He slid a hand down his face. "Is that what happened back there on the ship? Were they trying to control you?"

"It happened in Stormwall, as well. Or maybe I lost control. It's hard to tell anymore."

"Do you feel them now?"

My hand instinctively went to my necklace. I fisted the jewels to my heart and shook my head. "I always feel them. It's like they're swimming around under my skin, but it's not like before. It feels contained."

"That's good, right?"

"I think it may be when my emotions are piqued. When I'm scared, maybe?"

"I expect locating celestite will be grueling."

I lowered my eyebrows. "Why do you say that?"

His hand reached my shoulders. I winced as it came down near the scar from the poisoned arrow. "Because nothing is ever easy, not when it comes to you. But I won't let the Uncanny hurt you."

I choked out a laugh. "Big words for a human."

Ashe smirked, and it lessened the taut tension in my belly. "Demons were once gods who got knocked down a peg, Isabelle. They can be beaten."

"Sorry for trying to kill you."

His mouth twitched. "No, you're not."

I raised my eyebrows. "You're right, I'm not. I forgot how annoying you are."

My throat still held a bitter taste, but I could feel it slowly ebbing away. I placed a hand to Ashe's chest, and his heartbeat kicked against my palm. I closed the distance until Ashe's body aligned with mine. He lowered his head so our foreheads rested against one another. "We have to stick together," he said softly.

I closed my eyes. "Together."

~

WE SADDLED UP AND PACKED, AND AN HOUR LATER, WE LEFT THE town of Alaster behind. We followed the directions on my map, which took us through some farmland and up miles of rolling hills that looked as if they'd go on forever. The lack of cover made my heart speed up. It wasn't until we hit a patch of trees that I finally stopped grasping my horse's reins until my knuckles turned white.

Night fell, but we couldn't risk lighting lanterns. We used my heightened eyesight to guide us. More hills greeted us. My horse snorted, its breath steaming in the chilly night.

"Are you cold, Ashe?" I asked, looking over my shoulder.

He reined in his horse to stop and slid off the saddle. His boots made a *thump* as he landed. "I think we should camp instead of finding an inn."

I chewed on my lip, imagining the innocent lives that would suffer if we were attacked within the city. Would I burn it down too?

"Good idea," I said, and craned my neck. "Rahr is north, but there to the east a little is some woods that we can hunker down in. Better trees than people."

Ashe didn't need me to elaborate. He stretched his limbs, cracked his back, and led his horse on foot.

The woods turned out to be a dense forest, little triangles on my map scattered for the equivalent miles on the piece of parchment. "You know, we could get there quicker if I shifted and you rode on my back."

Ashe stopped walking and fell back against the trunk of a great tree. Amusement glistened in his eyes. "There would be paintings dedicated to us. Imagine it. It would be titled: Hero Atop a Great Beast."

I snorted. "I kind of like: Great Beast Saves Humanity."

Ashe smiled softly and looked up at the stars in the patch of sky between the canopy of treetops. The moonlight reflected off the sharp angles of his face, reminding me how much weight he'd lost when he ventured past the Archway, all alone. He tied his horse and sat with his back against the tree. "Just a few hours."

We had to keep moving, of course.

I sat opposite Ashe and unpacked the hardtack and dried meat I bought in Alaster. I plucked out two apples and rolled one to Ashe. He ate it in silence and then stood up.

"I'd kill for those animal furs I had back in the Old Kingdom," he said, with a shiver of his shoulders.

I listened to the heartbeat of the forest. From the rustling leaves in the night wind, to the chittering of animals in their burrows. I trained my ears to anything threatening, but there was nothing. "Lay with me," I finally said. Before he could say anything, I stripped down to nothing and shifted into a wolf.

A demon took shape in front of me. Not a shape, no, that was a solid idea, and the Uncanny were not solid. They were both formed and see-through, stayed still and snaked around me, tall and short, human shaped and beast shaped. With every blink, they were something else. A thousand things all at once.

The horses sputtered with alarm, but Ashe's words hushed them. He was too busy readying for bed to notice the shadows playing out behind him.

My hackles rose, but I was not scared. They could not hurt me any more than they already had. But then again, I was scared, for Ashe and his frail human body. What would they do to someone like him? I could not bear the thought. I slid my pile of clothes with my necklace and dagger on top and brought them nearer. The demons slunk away; harder to see, but still present.

"I don't think I'll ever get used to seeing you this way," he said, pulling a blanket from his saddlebag.

I laid down, my muzzle resting on my paws. "You think I'm a monster."

"I think you're beautiful."

My chest rumbled, but no words came. Ashe rolled out the blanket and fit himself atop it and fit the rest over his body. Ashe's sigh rustled the fur on my face. I turned slightly, as to not knock him over with my large head.

"Back on the islands, we were taught that women needed our protection," he said. "They were the bearers of our children. We held them on great pedestals. Men became the hunters and the soldiers, and women stayed back to raise our heirs."

"You didn't let them hunt or fight?" I asked.

"No."

Idiots. They should have died on those islands, treating their women that way.

I groaned, and the thoughts faded.

"It was the same in Mirosa. My mother hated that I had a bow, so I had to hide it in the stables where she couldn't find it. She would have taken away Henry's dagger had he not given it to me as a gift."

Ashe blew out a puff of air. "I miss him."

"Lulu wanted it, though—the family, the dresses, the children. She would have made a great mother, you know."

"Henry wanted daughters. Many of them."

My breath hitched and my voice felt small. "Henry wanted children?"

"Yes, we talked about it often."

I tried to imagine my brother and Ashe taking water breaks after swordplay, dirty with sweat and grime talking about...children? Henry was a dreamer, so I could see him discussing his future family in detail, but Ashe? "Do you like kids, Ashe?"

"Not the gross ones with snot running their noses, but yes, some sort of offspring would have been nice."

My chest rumbled with a laugh. "All kids have snot running down their noses at some point."

"Mine won't."

The humor in his voice was betrayed by the serious look on his face. "There's still time, Ashe. You're young."

Ashe let the silence go on so long that I thought he'd fallen asleep. "I sometimes think of what would have happened if I never came to Stormwall. My father would still have attacked your father. But if I hadn't known you, where would I be?"

"Dead by my arrow."

Ashe laughed and positioned his body to face me. "What were you like as a child?"

"Defiant to the core. I would not have made it on your islands."

"If I were king, I would have taken you into my army."

"If you were king." My words drifted away, lost in the meaning behind them. He was next in line, after his father. Who ruled the islands now? Katka? My mother?

I released a long sigh. "You would have been a good king, Ashe."

"I would have been a fearful king," he said, quietly. "Scared that my father would haunt my every move, even in death."

I stopped breathing. "Does he haunt you now?"

His voice was soft, barely there. "Every moment of the day."

I looked at Ashe and spoke slowly, as though unsure of what to say. "When I am queen, I will free the islands of Mirosa's rule once again. You can make up your mind whether you want to be part of the kingdom."

Ashe smiled, and a burst of hope fluttered in my chest, like a little bird. "Thank you."

As I drifted into sleep, I could still see the moment Ashe drove his sword into his father's chest and threw my world into chaos. I'd almost killed him. Twice. We had a long journey ahead of us, and we might be hunted by enemy Gwylis. But I had a friend again, and I slept more soundly than I had in weeks.

Once, during the night, Ashe woke me with a sneeze, and I used my muzzle to roll his head away from burrowing into my fur. He snorted, but didn't wake. I waited for him to sneeze again, but he was quiet. I fell back asleep beneath the stars.

CHAPTER TWENTY

We kept a steady pace over the next few days, finding camp not far from either a small village or a city. We'd taken turns buying food and whatever else we needed. On our fourth day, I tore my pants on my horse's saddle. Exhaustion rode through me in waves. I could feel it in my bones.

Most of our days were uneventful, and the terrain just as monotonous. I found myself missing the mountains and the snow and the thick forests. We did spot the occasional herd of wild horses or cluster of sheep from nearby farms. I got lost in the countryside, trying to shake my own sense of fear. I couldn't help but feel as though our detour to Essex was a waste of time. I only wanted Isabelle's fight to be over, and to start her life with Fray, should they reunite. I wanted all of this over as fast as we could.

My thoughts drifted to Moora and her promise of a gathering army. Never had I felt as though I wanted to be in two places at once. Aiding Isabelle, but also helping the rebellion in any way possible. There wasn't enough of me to go around, and there wasn't enough time.

I awoke at sunrise on the fifth day just before the first slivers of light could slice through the trees. There was a wrongness in the air, something almost sweet, and it may have had something to do with Isabelle having shifted back into a human sometime during the night. I yawned and closed my eyes, missing her big furry body and earthy scent. *Five more minutes, and I'll face the day.*

I slowly unpeeled my eyes. The position of the sun told me that it was late morning, almost afternoon. I sat up and saw Isabelle tending to the horses, lifting their hooves to make sure they were still acceptable to travel. We'd have to trade out our horses soon. We didn't have time to wait until a groomer to trim and maintain them. "Why didn't you wake me?"

Isabelle stood and brushed herself off. "Why would I? You looked like a baby. Snore like one too."

"If I murder you here, nobody would know."

"Just promise not to eat me. I'm pretty gamey." She grinned despite my irritated look and added, "I might get stuck in your teeth."

There was a brief silence where the memory of her hands squeezing the life out of me flashed before my eyes. The skin on my arms goose pimpled, and my heart crashed against my ribcage. The Uncanny darkened the ground beneath Isabelle's feet, swarming together like insects. She retrieved her necklace from her pack and looped it over her head. The shadows dissipated, hissing like angry wildcats peering from dark corners.

"You weren't wearing that when you attacked me," I said, warily inspecting the ground, expecting to find one crawling up from between the earth.

She bit her lower lip. "I wasn't wearing it when I burned the city either. Do you think it truly protects me, then?"

I nodded. "I think it does, but not by much."

"If Henry was correct, if I did get the last jewel, maybe the curse would truly be broken. This is going to work."

Only if we both stayed alive to see it through.

～

IT WAS MIDAFTERNOON WHEN WE STOPPED. ESSEX DREW NEARER, and with it, a sense of hesitation. What would we encounter here? This was no mere village. It was a city with its own lord and lady. We had to tread carefully.

The weather grew warmer as spring solidified itself across Mirosa. I forced myself to bite down on the memories of swimming in the ocean during the hotter days on the islands. I recalled Henry didn't like it much. If he could have lived there in the forest, he would have. He'd bring food for lunches and spend his days sunning himself against a palm tree in patches of warmth. I wondered now if he remembered those days when he was off at war, and that was why he dreamed of quieter days. Maybe it was the Rowan way of coping. They dreamed of what little light they could find in the darkness.

I looked back at Isabelle, and her red-rimmed eyes and disheveled hair, and felt a pang of guilt. What were her biggest regrets? What did she see when she closed her eyes? Did she dream of a better life? Did she see Fray Castor?

None of those questions were simple. Isabelle was like me—broken, with scars inside and out. Our edges were singed and burnt, and fear weighed us down. She no longer smiled. I wondered if she even knew how. Determination set her eyes into something hard and unreadable. I wondered if she saw the same in me.

She glanced at me as she packed her horse. There was a strand of hair in her eyes. I wanted to brush it out of the way, but stopped myself.

Her silence didn't help things. I wanted to know what she was feeling, and what her life had been like for the past few months. But when I attempted conversation, she shut me down, only answering direct questions or pretending not to hear me at all. Was she worried that she wouldn't save the children? Or was she thinking about the celestite? I worried about it all too, but mostly, I worried that she wouldn't have the strength to make it that far.

~

FROM OUR STANDPOINT, ESSEX BOASTED A SUBSTANTIAL WALL surrounding the city—ten feet high, at least. The tops of spire-like structures pointed toward the sky like gleaming canines.

We measured the mood of the city from outside the gates, where groups of vendors parked their carts in drifts and heaps. Circling the wall, we split up and visited food carts and made small talk with potion makers and artists. Tables laid out with weapons, skins from hunted animals, and pottery dominated the west side, while homemade stews and pastries and picked fruits and vegetables took up the east.

It took two hours to circle the wall, and by the time I met back where we began, my throat was dry and my stomach rumbled.

Isabelle hid her head within her hood, just like me. The crowds outside the wall were thick and loud enough to mask our conversation. "You should stay back while I go into the city," I told her. "There's lots of people coming and going, but we can't risk it."

"I can't let you go alone." She shook her head. "In a city this size, I wouldn't even know where to begin."

Nor I, I thought.

"They'd hide a place like that," I said. "Most likely in plain sight."

Isabelle considered this. "An orphanage, maybe? A school."

"A prison?"

Her lips drew together in a thin line. The thought of children being held against their will in a prison-like setting was enough to set my nerves on edge, but I could sense the despair coming off the princess. She cared as much as I. She wanted to see them free.

She eyed a table of fabrics, toying with the scarves and sashes distractedly. I moved on to a seller of belts. I fingered through them until I found one, made of thick leather with several compartments for weapons and such. The belt was made to wrap around twice before buckling, but I couldn't do it. Not with only one hand.

The seller looked at me with pity, and my body flushed with heat.

"Let me."

Isabelle took the belt from my hand and wound the leather, once and then twice. "I saw that thing in your pack," she said. "I wasn't trying to look. I needed a small knife and happened upon it."

My eyes flashed to hers, but she looked away. She worked the belt with deft fingers, careful not to let it buckle too tight.

A myriad of emotions rolled through me. Stripped down. Bare. As if the entire city was watching me, pointing at the man with one arm who couldn't even try on his own belt. My knees locked together, and my pulse raced in my ears.

"Isabelle," I began. "I don't—"

She met my fraught expression with one of defiance. "If you don't make it, I don't make it."

"It's not that easy," I said, my humiliation making way for self-loathing. "It hasn't been that long."

Pain flashed in Isabelle's face, a storm of emotion raging in my own.

"You're so brave," she stated simply.

My lips parted. I closed my eyes and compulsively nodded. *Leave it to her to raise me up.* I had no reason to feel emasculated. Not with a woman like her by my side.

I paid the seller for the belt, and we headed back to where we tied our horses and began to reorganize our weapons, securing them to my new belt.

"It is because I'm telling you to and you have to listen to me. I'm your queen."

I started to smile, but her seriousness stopped me.

"If I don't get through this, you have to fight for Mirosa," she said. "You must. Promise me."

I looked at her, sadness etching every line on her face. She hated asking it, I could tell. She may have given up the throne when she initially left Stormwall, but before that, before all of this, she would have been queen, and she would have been a gods damn good one at that.

"Promise me," she repeated. She straightened, set her jaw, and drew her mouth into a grim line.

"I promise," I croaked.

She sighed and slowly removed her tunic, stretching out her muscles. I caught sight of her scar, and images of that night danced before me. I'd stayed up through the night, searching and then worrying that the poison in her arrow had killed her. It still hurt her. She winced when she thought I wasn't looking, and I had the very strange thought that perhaps it hurt because it reminded her of when she was human. Gwylis healed their wounds, and they did not scar. She would always have that reminder of being so close to death's cold grip.

Dwelling on the things you cannot change didn't do anyone any good. But I could not help but wonder if I had not driven her from that dinner table as I assumed I did, she would not have been attacked. And perhaps a ripple effect would have occurred, and I'd still have both my arms.

I shook my head. No, it did not do me any favors to think of such things.

But a realization came to be with stark clarity.
Some wounds never truly healed. We were all scars to one another.

CHAPTER TWENTY-ONE

We found camp near a gurgling stream, bordered by tall tree with twisting trunks. Their leaves had not fallen during the winter and blunt to the branches and swayed in the breeze.

Neera and I scouted the area before returning to the others. They'd already started a fire, and several had gone out to hunt, I assumed. But the area was still, and I doubted they'd find much of anything out there.

Moonlight filtered through the trees, casting its glow on the group, which was busy preparing for dinner and unpacking bedrolls. Not all the Gwylis shifted into wolves to sleep, and some took that form for guard duty. It was fine by me except for the fact that wolves snored louder than humans. But I wasn't sleeping much anyway. Who could?

I collapsed by the fire and watched the leaping flames cast shadows all around. A sweet aroma wafted to my nostrils.

"Honey nut cake," Olio said, handing over a piece to me. He'd found a seat beside me. I hadn't even heard him sit. "Rini makes hers with apples. Try it."

I shook my head. "I'm fine."

Olio moved closer into my personal space. "It's good because it keeps for a long time. Even stale, it tastes good."

"I'm sure."

Olio ate in silence, mesmerized by the fire. "I bet Izzy would have tried it."

If the words came from anyone else, I'd have snapped my teeth. But from Olio, my temper only rose slightly.

"You have first watch tonight."

Olio groaned. "I know it's better to have first watch, but gods, I wanna fall over and die," he drawled.

I gave a long sigh. The air filled with Gwylis chomping away and rustles of sleep positions. But nobody laid down to rest. Everyone gathered around the fire. Waiting.

"I smell a doe!" Olio suddenly exclaimed.

The smell had reached me. I turned and watched the hunter return. One, in wolf form, was carrying the lifeless body of a large female deer. Accompanying this was someone throwing more wood into the fire until it reached over six feet.

A wall of fire.

Thunder broke overhead, like the roar of a beast, and sent strips of light across the sky. Flits of surprised sounds came from the group. Someone laughed, and another growled.

I saw you jump, Izzy's voice chided. *Who would have thought the great Fray Castor startled at the sound of a thunderstorm?*

The scent of blood filled my senses. Behind me, someone was slicing the deer's middle, dumping its stomach contents onto the ground and separating the ribs. The cracking, like the lightning, grated my bones.

Are you listening to me?

Lightning flashed again. Without it, the world went darker than usual until the next strike. I closed my eyes, remembering how I used to run into storms, chasing them as though they were rabbits. My mother would get so angry, having to chase me in the dark of night in the pouring rain. Storms never scared me, because I knew they would never stay. They always passed.

My pulse quickened as my emotions churned.

I braced myself for the effects of the dredged memories of my mother. But my body did not react, and my mind remained clear.

My mother is gone. She is dead. Izzy killed her.

So the nerves I felt now had nothing to do with the storm and everything to do with tonight's ritual. But why? They were doing nothing but offering up a dead animal to the gods, who wouldn't eat it. Chant some prayers to the gods who weren't listening. Maybe even dance for the gods who weren't watching. It was all absurd.

Someone was carrying the deer toward the fire, and my nerves fired. What if the thunder was the gods trying to communicate with us? I shook the thought free. *That's absurd.*

Neera approached the offering, a punch slung over her shoulder, something cupped in her hands. I stood back, recognizing the scent of various herbs and crushed flowers. She breathed into her closed fists, and with a burst, propelled the contents into the fire. One hand and then the other; each time, the fire burst higher, animating colors of blue and green. Impossible. What was in those herbs?

"Let your minds go free," Neera said. "Remove all your doubts and all your worries."

She walked over to each person in our group, giving them a handful of herbs from her pouch. They all took it, even Sonia and Branch. "Breathe into it and let it free."

When she arrived in front of me, I did not hold out my hands. "What are you doing?"

Neera winked. "Always the sour puss. Just take it, would you?"

Sighing, I took the herbs, cupped in my palm, and blew them into the fire like one would a dandelion. The fire flared golden and bright, and for a moment, I thought it took shape of a woman. I blinked and it was gone.

Using a knife, Branch slit the deer's throat, letting the blood fall, and swung it toward the fire. Thunder crashed again, alongside my heart. I was aware of the time passing, people laughing, and Neera chanting something or another. And the flames danced higher and higher.

And the drums began to beat.

I blinked again. Someone brought drums? Along with the steady beat came the sound of clicking, and then the melodious sound of a woman singing in a language I did not understand. In a daze, I walked the circle forming around the fire to find Neera and her three sisters singing, taking turns with their own verses. The faster the drums, the faster they swayed with the beat. While her three younger sisters stretched their tune, Neera came out front, her hips moving, her hands pawing the air. Her voice was like a feather, like breeze. Her sisters, when they harmonized with Neera, formed a song both haunting and exciting.

I paused to listen. The words were peculiar, but familiar. The old language. The sisters sang the words like mournful bell. The air crackled with energy. The entire group turned their heads to watch, as transfixed as myself. Branch stood with his eyes pointed at the night sky.

The flames rose.

But the sight of Neera's red braids as they flew like tendrils as she twirled took my attention away from the fire and snagged on the way her body moved. I gave a long exhale as the singing and the drumming continued. The deer had all but been consumed by the flames.

Neera made her way around the fire in a flourish. Her breathless singing grew even more rhythmic. When she came my way, it was all I could do not to run. The air grew thick. Lightning flashed as she wound her arms around my neck, her singing growing softer, brushing my ears.

She kept a hand on my chest as she curled me, her vocals pitching high enough to make the hairs on my skin rise. Time slowed until she came around to face me again. She lowered herself and rose, her hips swaying with the drums and the triplets crying out in song like seabirds. I met her gaze. I could not see the color, but her eyes burned something raw and animalistic. "Let go, Fray Castor," she whispered. "Let go of all your worries."

"No."

Neera lowered herself again and as she rose, captured my bottom lip in her teeth. They scraped gently, and I pulled back instantly. Neera grinned wickedly and swayed back like a wave in the sea as the drums slowed.

My control snapped in half. I bared my teeth, letting out a low growl, absorbing the weight of the monster inside of me, and smashed my teeth together. My body trembled like a caged animal shaking at the bars of its prison.

"Let it go," she told me, her feet carrying her away, toward the fire, where she reached into her pouch and blew another handful of herbs. "The demons do not control us. The gods are with us."

As soon as the music stopped, a tiredness washed over me. Nobody paid any mind to me as I forced my legs to move back to where I'd dropped my pack. I bent over it, letting air fill my lungs, slowing my heart. That song, the tower of fire, Neera's body so warm and so close to mine—it was enough to shred all my intentions and run. Run far away. This was all too much. All too bizarre.

Did they truly think resurrecting an age-old ceremony would garner the gods' favor? The gods didn't want dead deer. They didn't want our prayers. They certainly didn't care whether a man like me lost my burdens. They wanted our shoulders heavy, so they could laugh at our insurrection.

The gods were dead, and soon, we would be too.

I shouldered my pack, prepared to find Olio and offer to take first watch, when my gaze locked onto the fire again. The colors were gone now, leaving it red and orange, but the flames rose high, presenting me with images of the woman standing amongst the flames.

Panic assailed me, fueled by my recognition of the vision within the flames.

It can't be, I thought, stepping toward the fire, unable to hold myself back.

A single word formed on my tongue.

Izzy.

She looked different from the last time I saw her. Her once-long black hair was cut short. Her bright eyes were now dark and shadowed beneath them. Her skin took on an unhealthy pallor, and she was screaming. Crying out, her voice muffled as though she were underwater.

Crying out. For me.

Gods, no. No, no, no.

I neared the fire, reaching out. "Impossible," I whispered, creeping as close as I could get without singing my hair. The camp faded around me—all the figures, all the voices, gone. I was there with her, standing over her body as it writhed on the ground in the alley of some city I did not recognize. Izzy, my Izzy. I reached out, but I couldn't touch her. My fingers went right through.

Where are you? I silently railed. *Tell me so I can come.*

A strong wind blew, catching the fire, and blasted the image of Izzy into nothing.

Grief took hold. Suffocating, inconsolable grief. I was barely aware that I'd taken to one knee. That a hand had come down onto my shoulder as I stared at the dancing flames.

"What did you see, brother?" Sonia's presence brought me back to camp. The air returned, along with the voices, the smells of other Gwylis, and the thunder above. "Fray, talk to me. You look like you've seen a ghost."

The thought sent a chill down my spine. Was she a ghost? No, it couldn't be.

She looked so real.

I fell onto my haunches and clasped my hands behind my head, rocking back and forth to try to get myself grounded. Sonia did the same, dropping her head to my shoulder. Around us, conversation continued, and even some of the drums began to beat. As if Izzy had not just been here. As if she weren't crying out for me.

"I saw her," I told my sister, not mincing words. "She was there, in the fire."

Sonia slipped a hand into mine, and I dropped my arms. "That concoction Neera made was a hallucinogenic. It was used in rituals in the past. It's supposed to open your mind to the things you've suppressed. You saw Izzy because you haven't wanted yourself to see her. Even in your memory."

"But she was crying. She was—" *Screaming in agony.*

"I understand, brother."

I stared at her, my chest having, my pulse pumping wildly in my veins. "Did the gods do that?"

Sonia blinked. "Perhaps."

I let go of her hand and stood. "The gods are as cruel as I imagined."

With that, I stripped my clothes and shifted into a wolf. With a roar matching the thunder, I bolted into the forest.

CHAPTER TWENTY-TWO

The next day, I waited until the sun dipped below the horizon, turning the sky red as blood. I left camp with only one idea on where to find information on the missing children: the taverns.

Approaching the city, my clothes suddenly felt tight; it was hard to breathe, and my shoulders were tensed so much that when I relaxed them, my entire back ached. This wasn't going to be easy. It was hard enough leaving Isabelle behind. She was chomping at the bit until good sense finally overcame her. If there were Gwylis in Essex, they would catch her scent straight away.

We also knew that we could not waste our days here. The impalpable presence of time crushed against us, with no way around. It was tonight, or it was nothing.

The city shifted as soon as night fell. The vendors outside the walls had all packed and gone home, replaced by women in scandalous clothing. Guards gave them sidelong glances as wealthy men wearing furs and shining jewels gave them a once-over. It felt as though the city were wearing a mask, replacing the humdrum facade with something much more sinister and dangerous.

The guards gave me no notice as I entered through the gates. Torches blazed overhead, along the outer wall, giving my heart a lurch. It reminded me a lot of the Den, from what little I'd seen of it, but without the drunken laughter of men and women pouring in and out taverns. Smoke from burning meat and the scent of ale hung heavy in the air.

I kept close to the crowds, tucking my missing arm beneath my cloak. Gratefully, nobody paid me any mind. They were too busy with their lives to notice an interloper in their midst.

I thought of Moora and had a decision to make. If things did not go as planned here in Essex, it would be in my best interests to find my next contact before any missteps could be made. I ran a hand down my mouth. These were the types of decisions a king had to make. Prepare for the future while possibly sacrificing your present.

I moved away from crowds and into quieter streets with a feeling of trepidation.

The squats weren't far from the main square, though I had to go a bit further than I had planned. I walked briskly, but slow enough not to draw attention.

The poorer part of the city reminded me much of Stormwall. Although we did not have such place on the islands, there were homes that were not as large or as sturdily made. But here in Essex, the poor were housed in whatever they could find. Pallets stacked and draped with tarps. Blankets and curtains stitched together to create tents. People milled about fires in the center of the streets, burning in barrels. Children in torn clothes begged me for food. I did not think to carry any, and my heart broke as I denied them one by one.

Isabelle would raise the hells if she saw how they were living.

Past a cluster of tents, I found structures resembling homes. I kept a close eye for the red curtain, but the further I went, the more my stomach seized with dread. Izzy and I had agreed I'd do nothing but get a sense of the city. Listen for anything unusual. But as I slipped into every alley, backtracking several times, nothing looked familiar. Worst of all, no curtain and no symbol.

The night sky was blanketed in stars. Away from the main part of the city, it was easy to see them without the light pollution, and I took this rare moment to settle my heart and breathe.

I need to find the rebels. I need to find help.

Filthy and tired, I was seized by a memory of traveling through the Archway after the battle at Stormwall. I'd brought nothing but the clothes on my back and a few weapons. My arm had been wrapped in cloth I did not have to spare. I'd survived on making small traps for animals and tree bark while my wound festered. I didn't know how I got through those long nights, in agonizing pain.

I was dying, and still I kept walking.

I let out a long breath and oriented myself. "Let's go, Paratheon."

The air changed suddenly, the thickness carrying with it something wrong.

I froze mid-turn, my hand hovering over the sword beneath my cloak.

Arms grabbed me from behind, eliciting a cry of shock from my throat. Quickly, I felt for my assailant's fingers, grabbed two, and bent them backward. My attacker leapt away, groaning in pain, but in a fighting stance.

A jolt of confusion rushed through me as I set my sights on a young boy, thirteen or fourteen perhaps, his eyes swirling with anger, fists balled tightly at face level.

He reminded me of Isabelle when she'd tried to outrun her parents after their plan of marriage to me. She'd looked like a cornered animal, scared and desperate. Apt to do anything to survive.

The boy raised his fists and I held out a hand to stop him. "I'm not here to hurt you," I told him. "I promise."

The boy uttered a bitter laugh. "I'm not afraid of robbers."

"Then what are you afraid—"

The boy's fierce expression stopped me from pressing further.

I raised my hands in mock surrender. "I'm not going to kidnap you," I said. "I'm from the Peek Islands. I'm here to help."

The boy straightened, but only slightly. He took note of my missing hand and frowned. Did my reputation precede me, I wondered? Or was he merely calculating how to escape me?

The sudden caw of a crow sounded above me and briefly took away my attention. When my eyes flicked back to the boy, he was gone. Apprehension filled me. Would he return with others? Was I in danger here?

My gaze landed on the dark alley where the boy had stood not a minute earlier. Someone had emptied a large container of steaming water. My boots sloshed through it. The sight of the steam rising before me like a curtain made my heart pound a little faster. It smelled unusual and gave the alley an eerie look.

It had rained the day my father told me that I was to gain the hand of the Princess of Stormwall and unite the kingdoms. We'd stood, the two of us, on a beach where the waves came in hard and heavy. If we stayed any longer, we'd have been swept up and washed away.

At first, the news struck me as odd. Father never wanted the islands unified with Mirosa. When I'd questioned him, he struck me across the face and threw me against a stone wall, bruising my arm.

An apology slipped my lips.

An apology he did not deserve.

The rain had lashed at my burning cheek as my father explained. I'd grown too old and too arrogant, and settling down what at the best of my interests. He'd given me a guilt trip, using Henry and reminding me of my duty and loyalty to my friend.

I wondered now if Henry would have approved. We'd been so young, and the world had not yet settled its heavy hands on our shoulders. *Yes,* I thought now. *He loved me and wanted the best for both me and for Isabelle.*

But what happened when your best was not good enough?

The wind had howled and tore at my skin as I agreed to my father's plan. The trees had swayed nearer to the coast, and the storm blanketed the sky in grey, blocking the sight of our smaller neighboring islands. I'd felt the weather that day like I'd felt my own storm within my own self. I'd thought that I could calm the squall if I gave in to what my father wanted.

I felt that storm now—a raging squall threatening to drown me if I did not keep moving. The breeze was like whispers in my ear, telling me I was not good enough.

But then they were gone, replaced by only the sound of a curtain billowing in a breeze.

A red curtain.

A crow sat on the ledge of the window, watching me as I knocked on the door. It appeared slightly ajar. I nudged it open to find the house empty and abandoned. Cobwebs stretched in the corners, and a dusty, creaky floor was void of any furniture. A musty scent caught my sense. I sneezed and pawed at my face.

I'd have turned away if not for the mural of sun and the moon painted across a wall.

"The crows have already been sent, Prince. Alder has left the city."

I whirled around to find Abiyaya standing in the doorway, hands on her hips. She did not look as though she'd endured the journey to Essex. She wore the same teal robe, and her eyes were bright as ever to see me.

"You didn't trust me to make it here?" I asked, eyes glued to the mural.

"I did, but things are moving faster than expected. Fray Castor and company have moved to seek allies far across the Old Kingdom. Aquarius is with them. They wish to prove that they are deserving."

"Deserving?"

"Of the gods."

The pieces were moving, and Fray Castor had a hand in this after all. I smiled despite all the bad blood I'd had with the Voiceless servant.

"Something is happening to Isabelle."

I faced her now. "What?"

"Darkness is consuming her, slowly."

A mounting alarm swelled. "What do you mean?"

"She's not going to wait for you to return."

I swallowed hard. Isabelle would never go into the city unprotected, without a real plan of action. "I'll return to her," I insisted, my voice shaking. "I have to go—"

"She's going now. You'll never get to her in time."

"No, she wouldn't."

Abiyaya only shook her head before handing me a piece of parchment and an ink feather. "Write to your family in the islands. It's time they choose a side."

I stared at her. "You don't trust me to do what needs to be done?"

Abiyaya set the feather and parchment at her feet and turned away. "I do trust you, Prince, because I've seen it."

CHAPTER TWENTY-THREE

I spotted a gutter and began to climb it. The roof was flat and high enough to get a good view of the city. I squatted there, taking deep breaths, counting in my head. I stood and surveyed my surroundings.

Below, I could see the square, but I forced myself to look away from the glowing fires and set my sights on the tallest structure in Essex: a tower, silhouetted black against the golden sky.

My heart leapt into my throat.

Pedoma had told me that Henry knew a woman from Essex—the daughter of the lord. Upon hearing the news of Henry's death, she'd killed herself. He was going to marry her.

She'd died from a fall from the highest tower of her estate.

"What was her name?" I asked aloud. I closed my eyes against the throng of emotion. Heat coursed through my veins; monsters of darkness whispering lies into my ears.

She had no name.

Your brother never loved you.

He wanted to die to get away from you forever.

I clawed at my hair beneath my hood. "Stop. Stop."

We will never stop. You are with us forever.

I sensed, with a staggering horror, that it wasn't only a few voices in my head now, but what sounded like many more; an entire army of shadow creatures slithering around in me.

They were growing stronger, lurking in the hollows of my bones, awaiting release.

Tears burned in my eyes as I clung to the memory of Henry. As I told myself the Uncanny were liars. He loved me. He loved me.

"Her name was Delia."

My skin prickled, and I looked up as a ghostly figure came into being, gradually taking on a more corporeal form. I released my necklace and swiped at my eyes. I hated him seeing me here like this.

But Henry did not care for such things.

The ghost of my brother watched me for a moment before turning and looking over the city. "This place isn't the way it used to be. But that tower has not changed."

"Is that where they are?" The children.

Henry nodded. "There in the estate. Not the tower."

The Uncanny rose from my skin and seethed at Henry's presence. But he was unafraid and paid them no mind. "You have to fight a little harder, Izzy. You can't let your feelings overtake you."

My fingers went to my chest, grasping for my necklace. "More human than wolf."

Henry grinned. "Become more wolf than human." His eyes followed the shadows puddling across the rooftops. "At times," he added. "Find a balance."

"Easy for you to say. You're dead."

There was no retort. The shadows leapt toward the space Henry had been, but had since vanished. Gathering myself, I took one last look at the tower before leaping from the roof.

Claws raked against my skin. Stabbing pain that left me feeling sore and tired. I stumbled through the city streets, snaked down alleys, and pushed through crowds, keeping the tower in view and the Uncanny from making me turn back from my objective. They wanted the children; of course they did, and they'd do anything to stop me.

But they did not have the upper hand. Not yet. Strength coursed through me, and Henry's words echoed in my mind. Did his spirit come into me? If so, it'd be the thing I needed tonight.

The tower came upon me like a beastly monolith. But it was behind a short wall, well-guarded with a palace-like estate flanking it. I took refuge behind one of the trees lining the road.

I smelled Gwylis.

And the demons laughed. They roared with wicked glee.

I scaled the wall when the guards were not looking and landed softly on the other side. With my nose to the sky, I tracked the scent. It took me past the tower, which was in fact a singular structure. Henry crouched with his back to me, his face angled toward a single gravestone. I turned away, leaving him to grieve as he saw fit.

The lawn was spacious, but there were several large trees and fountains to duck behind if any of the roaming guards caught sight of me. The Gwylis scent grew stronger the nearer to the house I came. It gave me a dizzying effect, and I stood a moment, hand to my head against a large tree trunk.

Pain. Gods, it hurt from my jaw to the base of my skull. Dark clouds danced before my eyes. Elongated teeth; a sudden pull.

Bones snapping, stretching, pushing.

No. This wasn't possible. I couldn't be changing into a wolf, not without the chant.

Over time, the Uncanny would gain its power and turn humans into something worse than wolves. I'd seen it Katka's duplicate tail...the way her eyes flared like wildfires.

I was no longer a wolf. I was becoming something far more terrible.

But there was still a part of me raging against it. I contracted my muscles, pulling my stomach in, taking all the breath in my lungs and bearing down on this...thing. The pain stabbed like a thousand knives on my skin. I smashed my teeth together to hold in the worst of it. If I were discovered now, there would be no telling if I could hold the demons back.

I have to save them.

I spread my fingers and curled my toes. The pain subsided, but only enough to think straight. I was still human. My teeth were sharp in my mouth, but I still stood upright. No fur coated my skin. No long canines.

I continued across the lawn.

By now, my senses felt so keen, I could smell everything as if it were set right in front of me. The sweat of the guards mere feet away, tobacco, a woman lying with a man somewhere within the dozens of rooms.

And I smelled fear. Sweet as honey. My mouth grew dry with need. I thought of the frenzy, the bloodlust of wolves. But this was a different sort of madness. I wasn't lusting out of hunger, but pure unadulterated savagery.

A roar rose in my throat.

I flinched back from the feeling, my mind at war with itself. A violent and dark side surged into my conscience being. I bucked and trembled at the mercy of the Uncanny's power, and I was helpless to stop it.

I closed my eyes tight as red flickered behind my lids. *Think of them. Don't let them stop you.*

A small swoop of air as a bird soared overhead. Dark wings against the stars.

I stopped, right there in the middle of a courtyard, guarded by nothing but the darkening sky. I needed to calm myself, count to three... several times, but my feet would not stop moving. All I could think of were those innocent children on the missing posters. All I could think of was killing those responsible.

Suddenly, I wasn't alone. The scraping of iron and a stomping of boots told me I'd been spotted.

Four guards. All men with young souls.

It would have been smart to turn and run, to disappear and regroup back at that old abandoned hut with Ashe. Coming here alone was a mistake. That hadn't been the plan. What had been the plan?

"Stop!"

"Turn around and put your hands in the air!"

An arrow shot through the air, whistling past the tip of my ear. Another came, but I tilted just right to dodge it.

I felt the world again as if it were made for me. I crouched as the first guard ran up. He brandished a double-edged sword that shone in the moonlight. I sprung over him like a rabbit as the iron bore down on the earth. He stumbled forward. I shoved him, jammed my boot into his spine, and rammed his own sword into his back.

The second guard charged. I met him, angling my body from his dagger, and grabbed his arm and twisted it back until I heard the snap. He slammed down hard on his back, fear rolling off him in waves. I stood over him, bared my teeth, and screamed until the sound drowned out every demon voice inside my head, its force driving out the two remaining men as they fled across the courtyard. More would come. If there were Gwylis—and I knew there were—they would smell the blood. Instinct told me to run. Good sense regretted coming here to begin with. But I felt full inside; vulnerable, yet strong. The Uncanny were playing with me, tricking me into thinking I needed this feeling.

If we could always feel like this, why would we ever look to the skies?

If I surged forward now, it would be a mistake. This city would become like Stormwall and turn to ash beneath my feet. There were still people here who still saw the good in the world.

That cannot be.

I won't let it.

I willed the demons to grant me their protection, but instead, they gave me nothing but fire.

Demons were liars.

Movement in the estate. Figures running by open windows. Lights flickering on and off. I threw off my hood and stalked forward. Somewhere within that building, there were terrified children.

Everyone I loved was either dead or gone. I had nothing left to lose.

CHAPTER TWENTY-FOUR

I stepped through the courtyard and into another world.

At least, it looked like another world through the shades of red fogging my vision. I pushed through toward the front doors of the estate, my chest heaving in agony.

The darkness grew inside of me.

It led me here, where the scent of people filled my nostrils.

And I did not feel the least bit guilty for wanting to rip them apart bit by bit.

I took a deep breath—a breath meant to give me courage and strength instead of air—and entered the estate, knife poised to kill. Guards were already waiting in the foyer, armed to the teeth. Two dozen. Maybe more.

"Drop your weapon." A large man in a silver helmet stepped forward, longsword polished and poised.

Heavy footfalls knocked against the marble floors. I glanced behind me as a man barred the front door with an ax. No way out. I let a growl escape my lips. "Where are the children?"

"There are no children here," the axman replied. He drew a dagger from his belt. "Drop your weapon."

I cracked a smile and sheathed my knife. But I did not relax my fighting stance. Regardless, the guards advanced, grabbing me by my forearms and locking them behind my back. Shadows swam behind my eyes and a tear slipped down my face. One of the men wiped it away.

"What is this?" He brought his finger to his face and examined the streak of black. "How are you doing that?"

More black tears warmed my cheek, slipping down my face and dropping with a soft pit-pat to the shiny marble floor, like a puddle of spilled paint. It ran from my nostrils and ears.

What was happening to me?

I whispered as the black tears began to take shape. They thickened and rose like bread in an oven. I knew what they were, and I laughed.

The guards backed away, perplexed. Little did they know, they invited the demons in all on their own. Their bodies had already been claimed the moment they took the children. The moment they stood by and did nothing.

The demons took them.

"Magic!"

The guard pulled me backwards as the Uncanny advanced. Blackness, like sheets in the wind floating about the room, encasing everyone within distance. By the time the foyer had descended into chaos, I had completed my chant.

My limbs grew longer and longer.

When I opened my mouth, I felt as though my jaw unhinged.

My screams were guttural, filled with bloodlust.

The shift was so violent that the armored man holding me captive had been thrown backwards against the door he'd barred, his back snapping with a sickening *crack*. The rest of the guards were screaming and running in a way I'd never seen. The same black ooze seeped from my pores, filling their eyes until there was no white left.

I turned away from the foyer and padded into a hallway lined with thick red carpet and golden trim. I let my nose guide me. The children were here. There was no question about it. I descended a set of stairs and then another until I found myself in a dark, slippery dungeon. I shivered from tail to nose, anticipation vibrating in every limb. They were close. I could feel it.

The dungeons were larger than I expected. They must have spaced the entire length of the estate grounds. The deeper I went, the further the scent of Gwylis went. It was like I were in a game, but I was no closer to finding my objective than I was minutes before. This game was not fair.

Corridor after corridor was empty. I used magic to light the torches along the walls as I went. The further I moved, the more my anxiety rose into a near debilitation. There was nobody here. What if I were too late?

A realization hit me. What if they'd moved them? Two guards outside had vanished when I turned away. Did they alert the captors? *Keep running.*

Garbled voices sounded from around the next corner. I pushed forward, slow and tentative on my paws. I passed a row of cells reeking of human waste and rotting food. But they were empty.

"Let me go!" a little girl's voice called out.

I rounded the corner to see not one, but dozens of little girls being herded down an even deeper tunnel. One of the guards with them nocked and arrow and shot the tip of my right ear. Pain seized my body, but it passed quick enough for me to charge forward.

"Mama!"

The little girl's scream nearly stopped me in my tracks. I saw myself in her, pleading for help from a parent who was not there. Her eyes, large and brown, her hair black and dirty. She was cursed. Her parents would no longer love her. They'd cast her out like an invading spider. Frightened. Disgusted.

"Please, help!"

I snarled.

No. Her parents were alive. She had someone looking for her.

She was not like me.

She had a future.

In an enclosed space, a Gwylis of my size did not have the advantage of proper lupine combat. But I did have my teeth. The men pushed back, funneling me forward. I snapped at the captors, trying my best to block out the sobs of the girls being wrangled further and further from me.

Let them die, the demons said. *They will play with us in the underworld.*

"You will never have them!" I roared, at both the men and the Uncanny. But the guard did not respond. He took a girl, and snapped her head back by her hair. He drew a dagger and held it to her throat.

Torch light flickered across the planes of his face. He looked frightened. "We'll kill them."

I opened my jaw and roared. Saliva shot forward into the men's faces. The girls behind them screamed again, a cacophony of sobs and horror.

Don't be scared, I wanted to tell them. *Don't fear me, please.*

The guard stumbled back, his eyes wide with terror. But still, his dagger did not lower from the girl's throat. I focused on him, pawing the ground like an angry bull. It was the sound of a heavy iron door closing that snapped me from my stupor.

I was too fixed on the girl to notice the rest of them had disappeared into the darkness.

The guard, an apparent sacrifice for the rest of them, noticed the betrayal and pressed the dagger further. I smelled blood now.

"Let her go," I said. "Let her go, and I will let you live."

The demons living inside of me said otherwise. *Lies*, they hissed. *Pretty, pretty lies.* The guard thought the very same. He stepped back, dragging the girl around a corner I did not see.

She whimpered quietly, her eyes wide and pleading as she disappeared.

The sudden scent of freshly spilled blood filled the dungeons.

NO!

I threw my head back in an enraged howl and threw my body forward. I ran past the iron door, and the lifeless little girl, careful not to look lest I lose myself. I took the guard as he attempted to flee. I took him into my jaws and threw him against the wall.

"Where does the door go?"

The guard whimpered as I pressed a paw into his ribs. Part of me begged for the Uncanny to come and take this man for their own. He needed to suffer for what he'd done.

But the Uncanny only applauded.

"To the incinerators!" the man wailed, making no attempt to keep me waiting for an answer. "The door is locked from within. You'll never get through in time."

I let my full weight press against the man's chest until his fragile bones threatened to snap. "Is there another way in?"

The man had the audacity to laugh. "No."

My mind told me to go, find another way in, and save those girls. I searched my mind for ideas. I could use fire and try to melt the door, but how long would that take? Every second I stood here was a second too long.

"Next time…" the man said, choking on his own blood. "Next time, try not making such a spectacle of yourself." Then he spat blood at my feet. "Wolf scum."

I bore down on the man, two paws crushing his chest until his heartbeat thumping on my paw pads stopped. Heat sizzled and sparked off my fur, and caught onto the guard's body, incinerating it.

The air split with horrid screams.

Dozens of them, from behind that iron door. I threw my body against it. I let loose a shock of heat, but instantaneous fire would not melt such a metal.

The fire caught the dingy carpet beneath my feet, rising alongside my own agony.

I could smell the girls now. I could smell their burning fl—

Bile rose in my throat.

My body arched as I fell to the ground, the breath gone from my lungs, my whole body wracked with agony.

I'd failed.

An unmoored fury roared through me, heat flooding every inch of my body from claws to the points of my ears. The urge to draw up every bit of power I had left and burn this entire city to the ground took hold with such force that I knew; I knew I could do it if I wanted to.

I rose to my feet and fled the dungeons.

Guards and soldiers alike poured into the corridors, but the flames were trailing me like a cloak, and they retreated or else met their end by being burned alive. My grief stretched to all-new heights as I entered the main floor of the estate once again. It was there. I could hear the bells of Essex ringing loud, assaulting my hearing like thunder. Men in nice clothes stopped on the mezzanine above, watching me with curiosity. They smelled like Gwylis, but only because they had a hand in forcing children into this curse.

I crashed through a window, avoiding a group of soldiers coming down the winding staircase, and rolled into a heap on the estate's front lawn.

Next time, try not making such a spectacle of yourself.

Flames shot out like arrows, igniting the grass. I pushed to my feet and bore down on my magic until the lawn was blanketed with yellows and reds and oranges—the colors of my rage.

It looked lovely against the black sky.

Archers came from the balconies, releasing a barrage of arrows in my direction, spearing the ground around me.

I recalled what happened during the scuffle with soldiers in the Old Kingdom; when I'd rescued Sonia and brought the avalanche down onto the camp. I summoned that strength now and turned toward the estate. Those innocent girls would not die in vain.

If they die, they will all die with them.

The ground trembled. My limbs felt heavy. All at once, the entire estate's windows shattered, and with a roar, I sent all the magic I had into sinking the foundation beneath it. The earth cracked and the building snapped in two as it sunk beneath the crater the quake had created.

Shadows rose and seized my lungs. I sucked in air when I could as the demons took me deeper and deeper within my own fury. If I was a better swimmer, could I have resurfaced? Could I be what Ashe said I could be? *The Izzy I remember.*

Ash coated my throat. The world came into focus as if flipping the page of a book. I could hear the terrified and the dying from within the estate. I smelled death. Everywhere.

I stumbled away, racing as fast as my legs could carry me. I shifted back into a human, bare skin slick with sweat. I met the chaos of the city head-on, but managed to get lost in the crowd. I swept down an alley and snatched an old blanket from a trash bin. I wrapped myself with it and fell to my knees.

"You were wrong," I cried, thinking of Ashe. "You were wrong about me."

The bells kept on ringing. I closed my eyes and covered my ears against the sound.

Fray, help me.

I opened my eyes and drew in a lungful of air. It was dark, so I could not see exactly where I was. There was a great pounding in my head and centralized pain near my right ear.

My other senses returned. But instead of smelling garbage and rot, I smelled the familiar scent of sweet root. "Fray."

But a different face came into focus. Dark brows over green eyes, a wide mouth and straight nose. He stood over me, one arm against my side, his chest hovering above my own. *Ashe Paratheon.*

The sweet root, nothing but the lingering effects of a dream.

"Sorry," Ashe said, his mouth in a grim line. "I'm not him."

I let him lift me to my feet. "That's all right," I said, and then we ran.

I ACHED EVERYWHERE. HESITANTLY, I REACHED UP TO TOUCH MY right ear, where the arrow had sliced. I shook my head. Sonia and I now had something else in common.

"What happened, Isabelle?"

A question I could not answer.

We'd escaped the city by the skin of our teeth, evading detection. Essex had more to worry about than two thieves in the night. Their operation was blown. The city close to burning.

Burning.

Fire and darkness everywhere.

I went into the fog of my memory and saw the girls who were alive, and then...

"They're dead," I said, grief making a play to tear me apart. There'd be time for grieving, but not now. "Are you all right?"

Ashe nodded. He wanted to chastise me, but he knew it wouldn't change anything. The children were dead.

I sat up, still dizzy from the magic I'd expelled. Ashe was at my side in an instant, allowing me to use his shoulder to stand. There was nothing left in me. Even the demons must have been tired of my antics. They did not make the smallest of efforts to speak to me.

They'd gotten what they wanted.

"I killed them." The agony of what had happened crashed into me with the weight of a mountain. My body lost all its strength, and I fell into dead weight, too quickly for Ashe to catch me with only one hand. I let the tears come, the real tears. I sobbed there on the ground, as if crying would drain all the darkness out of me.

It didn't.

I let those children die. The thought exploded into my mind, and a kind of paralysis took over. I tried counting. I tried breathing, but nothing helped. My lungs squeezed. My chest ached. I couldn't take much more. I tried to save them, but I was too weak, too fraught with anger. I'd let it consume me. Pyrus's vial of poison was a welcome release.

But before the thought could turn into an action, a reprieve.

"Isabelle." Ashe's voice cut through my heaving breaths. He bent down and wrapped his arms around my trembling body. Wordlessly, he held me, his body shivering in sync with my own grief.

At least he is safe, I thought. If I had lost Ashe, I did not know what I would have done.

"Isabelle," he said. "We have to go. There is no time to grieve."

I sniffed, and in doing so, caught the fear on Ashe's skin. Guilt made me flush with heat liable to burn me alive. But I would not burn, would I? I would endure the heat forever more.

What hope was there for me?

You will bring nothing but death.

Abiyaya had been right all along.

"I was too brash," I told him. "The guards saw me before I had a chance. They alerted the captors and took the girls down into the dungeons, where they—"

"I don't need to know." Although Ashe's words were cold and final, I sensed a slight shiver beneath them. I'd let him down.

Shame collected in my stomach and twisted in my throat. I shoved Ashe away and let myself be sick.

I emptied my stomach until there was nothing left. After, I tucked my legs beneath me and bent forward with my forehead in the soil.

Somewhere far away, I could still hear the tolling of the bells. The sobbing of the little girls. The screams of the men as they caught fire. The shaking of the earth as I split it apart.

I wished the entire city had burned.

Wicked girl with wicked thoughts.

Burn, burn, watch the world burn.

I wiped my mouth and straightened. Although my body continued to tremble, my mind relayed one thought:

Survive.

The word was a ghost in my mind, a whisper on a breeze. I'd done nothing but survive all these months, and people had died.

Survive.

Surviving is not living, I thought. Surviving was losing people I loved. Family. Friends. Survival was making the hard choices that put people in danger. It was shattering the dreams of the living.

But I had to figure out how.

Ashe watched me, his look distant. What was he seeing? The girl who ruined everything? Would he leave now, finally realizing this entire thing was foolish? I almost gave him the necklace, ordering him to go to Hassara on his own. Call down the gods. Take back our world.

But I knew, deep down I knew, it had to be me. Or maybe it had to be us. Together. I watched Ashe's face change as my own thoughts shifted. He stood and offered a hand. I took it and pushed to my feet.

"We won't let this stop us, Isabelle," he said, his jaw jutting in defiance. "I made mistakes. I will bear yours if you let me. If it gets you through."

My face was hot and flaked with dried blood and grime that wiped off black. I could taste the ashes of the people that burned. But even now, I knew I would endure more, much more.

Because this was my fight. *Our* fight. I would face judgment for my actions when the time was right. But for now...

Survive.

~

AT DAWN, WHILE ASHE GOT IN A FEW HOURS' SLEEP, I MADE MY way out of the bedroll and into my pack, where I found Henry's journal tucked safely away. The mist sat heavy in the trees. To me, it looked like ghosts. But very, very quiet ones.

Henry had written nothing much about Hassara, only that it was a city built into the side of a mountain. I set down the journal, disappointed. Although I'd already read the journal back to front, I'd hoped for a clue maybe I missed. No such luck. But according to our map, Hassara was not far, so I should have been able to see the mountains from here.

I found a tree with a copious number of footholds and began to climb it.

The sun was a ball of orange in the misty dawn, cutting through the fog and banishing it, albeit slowly. From atop a perilously springy branch, I hoisted myself up and over, cresting the top of the tree and finding a spot on a larger, much safer branch. I found the heavens.

The distant mountains illuminated a reddish glow like something out of a lovely dream. The sky painted itself into layers of red, orange, and purplish blue. I sat there in awe. The birds called out and greeted the sight.

People used to worship the gods in the sky, and now I understood why.

I thought of all the things the Uncanny had taken from me, and all the things they hadn't. I still had the ability to feel, to love, and to know that my time in this world would move the stars. I would not be forgotten.

I guaranteed it.

The sun appeared and lifted, calling the start of the day. I heard Ashe calling for me, so I ambled myself down the tree, careful not to lose my footing and fall. I was halfway to the ground when I looked down over my shoulder to Ashe, shielding his eyes and staring up at me. "Human, wolf...bird?"

I went to smile, but squashed it. It didn't feel right, not yet.

"Something is coming," he said in a harsh whisper. "Did you not sense it?"

I hadn't, but now that I was closer to the ground, a smell hit my nose. Gwylis. I quickened my pace, slipped on the last foothold, and nearly broke my ankle landing harder than I planned.

"How many?" Ashe asked as I ran past him toward the horses. It was hard to tell. A dozen. Maybe more. I hadn't smelled it that high up in the tree. I cursed to myself and packed up our things. If we were to outrun this many Gwylis, we had to make haste.

I scanned the forest. The trees no longer looked like valiant guards, but more like an army closing in on us. Ashe mounted his horse and gripped the reins. Just as I went to do the same, my chant lying in wait on my lips, a whimper sounded, high-pitched like a lost dog, echoing through the trees. I halted, one foot on my horse's stirrup, and listened.

"Is it them?" Ashe whispered.

I couldn't answer. I smelled Gwylis, but it was...different. I rubbed at my ears, ignoring the pain in the injured one and stepped away from Ashe, much to his protest. But I knew the sound. A whimper, like the one Ghetee uttered during his fight at the Pits with Branch. The whimper before he died.

The shapes came from the trees, hesitant at first. Through the dawn's haze, they looked like little specters, come back from the dead. But they weren't ghosts.

They were little boys.

Pups.

One by one, they came into focus. None of them younger than twelve, they held each other's hands and kept close. Safety in numbers, even from me. I swallowed and lifted my hands as a show of greeting, but inside, my heart was bursting. I wanted to run to them, lift them in the air, and kiss their cheeks.

But I couldn't. Their looks were distant, faces dirtied and clothes tattered. One taller boy—the oldest of the group—came forward, unsticking his hand from a smaller, much frailer looking child.

"The girls," he said, his voice cracking. "They didn't get away."

I laced my hands behind my head and squeezed my eyes closed. Tears squeezed out in fat droplets. I felt Ashe behind me, strong hands wrapping around my waist. I turned to meet him, and he lifted me from my feet, his hands clutching my back, his laughter buried in my chest. He knew this moment was a miracle. He knew the gods were with us.

I approached the taller boy and bent down to his height. Ashe crouched beside me. I could tell he was itching to comfort these boys, but first they needed assurance.

"What is your name?" I asked the tall one.

"Lile." He scuffed the toe of his boot into the dirt. "But they called me Scruff."

I nodded. "Did you track us?"

Lile sucked in his lower lip and nodded. "They took the girls first and left us unguarded. They said they'd return, but they never did." He met my eyes, and something familiar passed between us. "I'd heard about you, back in Stormwall. I saw what you did that day when you saved that man."

I steadied my breath. "You were there."

"In a wolf mask, of all things."

My chest tightened. "I'm sorry this happened to you." I looked past him, to the others. "Are they all right?"

"Yes, but we lost a few escaping the city."

I bit down on my lip, willing myself not to cry. These boys needed someone brave right now.

"I miss my mom."

The voice came from the smallest, maybe five years old. He smelled like a Gwylis, but I doubted he had the memory to recite the chant they'd fed to him.

Ashe took in a sharp breath.

"I know," I said softly. "I know."

"This is a miracle," he said as the rest of the children neared us, their hesitance slowly ebbing. "You did something good, Isabelle."

I looked at the prince and watched his smile bloom. It'd been so long since I'd seen it that it felt surreal, like this were a dream I'd wake from at any moment. I returned the action, but it didn't feel right, and Ashe knew. As he gathered the children to him, he watched me with a furrowed brow, but I kept it. That smile.

I'd just have to keep trying until I got it right.

CHAPTER TWENTY-FIVE

Our days trekking through the Old Kingdom fell into a routine. The entire group took hour-long shifts as lookouts so the rest could sleep. Neera and I scouted, sometimes falling into long lapses of silence, which was fine by me. But also a double-edged sword. Too much quiet made my thoughts run mad. Too much talking irritated me. At half-day, we'd eat and rest and then start again until nightfall, where we'd take our hourly shifts and I'd fall into a restless sleep for a few hours before starting all over again.

"How about a game?" Neera asked one early morning after hours of scouting in silence.

It was day four of our journey. Most of our group lapsed into quiet after the initial excitement wore off, soothed by the uneventful trek through the Old Kingdom. For the past two days, we'd tramped across miles of flatland spying nothing but sporadic houses, weathered with time. The mountains that split the old with the new became nothing but tiny shadows along the horizon. We headed into a deep forested valley Branch named, but I'd since forgotten. This was the furthest I'd ever been in the Old Kingdom. Judging from the brooding from the group, it was the same for most of them.

Every now and then, I'd hear Izzy crying out for me, but her voice withered like an old leaf, gone so soon.

"All right, pack grump," Neera said, skipping ahead. "I'd like to know who I'm traveling with. So I know who has my back."

"Are you familiar with everyone in our group?" I looked over my shoulder. Branch and the rest had stopped a few hundred feet behind us. Someone must have needed water.

Neera snorted. "Do you?"

I lifted a shoulder. "Don't need to. I don't need anyone to watch my back."

Neera threw her head back and laughed. "Sounds to me like you're afraid."

"Sounds to me like you're bored."

Neera shrugged. Out of everyone, she seemed the most eager, besides Olio of course. Brach had developed dark shadows under his eyes that may have matched my own. Neera made sure to stare at them and give me a look of disapproval every morning.

Up ahead, the forest grew thick with tall trees that touched the clouds. It'd be a welcome respite to be in a forest again. This open land was not good cover. Not that we needed it. We'd seen nothing for miles, save for small rodents and the occasional deer. Birds were scarce, even. It would put my nerves on edge, but I did not know this landscape. Maybe it was normal. Why worry for nothing?

"Question one," Neera said, flipping her braids over her shoulder and walking backwards. "What was it like working in Stormwall?"

A strange feeling that someone or something was watching me quickened my pulse. But when I turned, sniffed the air, and listened, nothing was there. I put distance between me and Neera, maintaining an erratic pace. "It was work. That's all."

"But you met the princess there."

I struggle through a hard swallow. "Yes, I did."

"Would have come back to the Den if it weren't for her?"

The sound of wings distracted me, and I looked up to see a black shape soaring across the clear blue sky. An eagle? No, it was stark black; I was sure of it. Too big to be a raven.

Neera appeared in front of me. Or maybe I'd been walking and ran straight into her. "You didn't answer the question."

She batted her lashes at me, and I stared at her, jaw set hard. "No, I wouldn't have," I said. "I'd have died serving royals tea for the rest of my damn life. Without a voice. Without much of anything. Izzy, she got me out of that. She saved me."

Neera considered this. "And here I thought it was the other way around."

I growled low in my throat. I'd said more than I intended. "What do you care?"

Neera began walking, her arms flapping at her sides like bird wings. "Oh, I don't know. Who wouldn't I want to get to know the moody young wolf with the striking blue eyes who is emotionally unavailable and prone to temper tantrums?"

I rolled my eyes and walked after her. "Give it up, Neera."

"What? Asking questions?"

We continued hiking, letting the silence stretch. I got the feeling of being watched once again. I scanned the area, the trees, the group following behind, but there was nothing out of sorts. Neera did not break pace. The air was still.

But you know there's something there, Izzy's voice drawled. *Trust your instincts. You're the best hunter there is. You saved my backside more than once.*

I grabbed at my temples and dug my nails into my skin, shaking the voice from my head.

"What's wrong?" Neera asked.

Grimacing, I shook my head. I could still hear her voice as if she were right beside me, nipping at my heel like she used to all those months ago. I could feel the speed of my heart whenever she came close enough to share breath, the stiffness of my back, the way I knew even then what would become of us. I knew the depths of her feelings for me, and I tried to stay away.

I tried and I failed.

Grimacing, I stalked away from Neera. I was as damaged as a broken promise, an unanswered question, and there was nothing I could say to make it any better.

I put distance between myself and the rest of the pack, and even though the silence surrounded me, a certain numbness overtook me, and it sunk into me like fear. Fear that I would never forget the pain of loving, and losing her.

Fear that I would never stop remembering.

~

By nightfall, I'd all but given up talking at all, reverting to my Voiceless days. Shame crawled over me by the time dinner was done. Izzy had risked her life to give me back my voice, and I was squandering it by brooding. What was wrong with me?

I watched Sonia and Olio with the group—how they got along, and found myself envious of the lives they'd led before Izzy and I showed up. They'd been a pack. They were bonded.

What had she even seen in me?

"You realize you're doing this to punish yourself."

I looked up from my roost on a fallen log to see Sonia. The sky had gone from bright blue to a dusky orange and red, illuminating a halo around my sister's head. Her black hair was braided over her shoulder. Her skeptical look gave away the jesting of her words. She was worried about me. And maybe even reluctant to speak to me at all.

I gave a deep, weighted sigh. "Doing what?"

"Secluding yourself." Sonia put her hands on her hips. "Not speaking. This self-loathing is not becoming of you, brother. You were born for so much more than this."

My muscles strained against my skin, and I closed my eyes. "You're not any better, you know," I pointed out. "The Castor curse runs deep in us. Rage is second nature."

Sonia pursed her lips. "Why are you deflecting?"

I blew out a breath that rolled my lips. "I put up enough with Neera asking a thousand questions a day. I don't need you doing this too."

"Olio is sick."

My eyes widened. "Say again?"

"He's sick." Sonia turned her gaze to the sky and bit her inner cheek. "He won't admit it, but there's something off. You've seen that black mark on his skin, right?"

I nodded, feeling suddenly ill.

Sonia blinked and met my gaze. "I have one too."

She untucked her tunic and lifted it high enough for me to see the bruised skin around her ribcage. No, not bruised. Stained.

I pressed the heels of my hands into my eyes. "What does it mean?"

"Something is happening to us. Something bad."

I thought back to what Izzy had told me about the Uncanny, and how they were going to overtake our souls and use our bodies to reign terror on the land. I knew it was true. We were cursed. The demons lived inside of us. What would stop them from taking the outside, as well?

But the thought was too much to bear.

I slumped over and dropped my face into my hands. Was that why I was hearing Izzy's voice? Seeing her? Was it the demons playing with me? I'd taken a small bit of comfort hearing her voice, but now I felt a sort of devastation, a gaping hole widening inside of my belly.

I was going to lose my family.

Moving slowly, I drew Sonia to me. For a moment, I did not feel the in and out of her chest, and then all at once, her chest heaved as if she'd forgotten to breathe at all. "We're going to stop this. I'm going to do my best to make sure the Uncanny do not win."

Sonia buried her face into my neck. "That's the most heroic thing you've ever said to me."

I pushed her back within arm's reach and held her shoulders with cautious hope. "And hopefully it won't be the last."

Something shifted within me. A fear, yes. Not suppressed and buried as it had been. But something else, something wild.

I'd do anything for my pack.

CHAPTER TWENTY-SIX

I found myself drowning in a sea of relief.

I watched Isabelle with the children. She learned their names and where they were from. She spoke to them like a mother, like a sister, like someone they could look to for guidance. I watched her with a smile. She needed it, this victory. She needed it more than she knew.

"Fourteen boys; all but three are from Stormwall," she said when she left them to eat. I sat up against a tree with my waterskin to my lips. "There's more out there, I know there are."

I sipped my water and offered it to Izzy. "I know."

She looked taken aback. "How do you know?"

I pulled in my knees and pushed to stand. "Because I'm the new leader of the rebellion, didn't you know?"

Izzy frowned. "Now is not the time to joke around, Ashe."

I snorted. "I'm serious. The stars are bright tonight, Izzy."

She lurched back as if she'd been punched. "You knew about them? How long?"

"Since Stormwall, when Abiyaya visited me."

At this, she nearly lost all the bones in her legs. "The soothsayer."

I nodded. "She gave me the task of uniting them. I wrote letters and—"

Isabelle blew out a gust of air.

"Will they be at Stormwall?" she asked. Her voice sounded child-like and full of hope. "With Aquarius and Fray?"

I lifted a shoulder. I could not make promises I could not keep.

"I don't know about the old man or your boyfriend." That last word didn't mean to come out with edges, but it was too late to take it back. *Irrelevant.* "But it's all going to come together, Izzy."

She bowed and her head and said in a low voice, "You didn't tell me. Why?"

I opened my mouth, but nothing came out.

"You knew how worried I was," she continued. "You knew, and you said nothing. Were you scared of me?"

I shook my head. Why would I have feared her?

"Izzy, that's not it." I swept my hands down my face. "I didn't want you to worry about more. I wanted you to leave that burden to me for once."

She pinched her lips together. "How many are willing to fight?"

"Thousands."

She'd let out a gust of air as if she'd been holding her breath. "I cannot fail."

I did not react. What good would it do to agree with her? It would only weigh her down more.

What I'd seen when I found Isabelle in Essex had an uncanny resemblance to what Abiyaya had explained would happen if Isabelle's body was taken by the Uncanny. She'd rain down a destruction on Mirosa. The earth would burn and crack and turn to ash. Nothing would survive after she was done with it.

She would rule over a land of ruin.

I looked to the sky and said a prayer to myself that it would not come to that.

"These kids," she said, looking back at the boys. "They are going to need us. What do we do?"

I licked my lips. "We give it everything we can."

Isabelle looked away. A breeze swept through her hair, tangling the short strands. "I called out to Fray because—" She paused and never finished.

I finished for her.

"Because you love him." I moved my hand and felt for my missing arm, the ghost of it suddenly burning. Part of me hated everything I was about to say next, but after everything, I only wanted the best for Isabelle. The last thing I wanted was to see her sad. "I want you to be happy, and I want you to realize you deserve happiness. You've punished yourself for far too long. Part of you didn't care what would have happened to you back there in Essex. Part of you probably thought you deserved to die."

"I didn't want to die." Her voice broke, and it shattered my heart.

Because I knew it was a lie.

Perhaps she didn't mean to die tonight, but she did mean it. Eventually.

"I hope you remember everything from before," I said. "When you were at the Den, when you were almost...joyful because you thought you'd finally broken free and found a home. But you came back to Stormwall. You left him, and you are miserable for it. You should have let Castor come with you."

She started. "I could not—"

"You should have let him come with you." My interruption made her shoulders slump. "Because home is wherever he is."

She tugged on the back of her neck and let out a heavy exhale.

"You think I don't know that?" She scrubbed her hand across her eyes. "You think I don't look at you sometimes and wish you were him?"

I tilted my head and suppressed a smirk. "Should I feel offended?"

She sniffed and shook her head. "No. I never liked royals. You knew this already. Don't look so shocked."

I looked up at the flat blue sky, no cloud in sight. "Tell me a good memory."

She loosed a breath. "It's so hard to think of one right now."

"Try."

"All right. Henry was always trying to get me to learn how to swim, but I always seemed to sink like a stone. I used to flail and panic even when my feet could touch the bottom."

"That's why you almost drowned when our boat flipped?"

"Water and I don't get along. Anyway, so this one time, I got so mad that Henry was pushing me—he was always pushing me—so I took his boots and threw them into the springs. He dove in after them and didn't resurface for some time. I paced, and then decided I had to go in after him. I jumped into the water and held my nose and went under, only for Henry to pop up as though nothing had happened. I was under for so long, I'd swallowed water in a panic. I coughed it up all over him as he laughed."

I cocked an eyebrow. "This is a good memory?"

She snorted. "Yeah, he scared me on purpose, to get me back into the water. To show me that I could do it. He always saw the potential in me, even when I couldn't, and that was the first day I saw it."

"Henry had a way of showing you that you were more. He used to wake me up before the sun to practice the sword. I didn't have any siblings, so I looked up to him as though he were my brother. When he died, I felt the loss for a long time, so when my father proposed the idea of wedding his sister, I only agreed because I wanted to protect you. It had nothing to do with how you looked or your wealth or title. You were Henry's sister, and I had a duty."

A flash of stark pain passed over Isabelle's expression. "I never needed protecting, Ashe."

"I know that now. Believe me."

She scuffed the toe of her boot on the ground. "You never told me how much Henry meant to you."

I used to believe that doing what my father told me would lead to happiness. Marry. Rule. Sire children. But I was so scared to do any of that with my father's shadow looking behind me.

Learning to see my worth was a voyage I wanted to keep sailing on.

"Everyone has their secrets, Isabelle," I said. "I felt my memories of him were kept locked away, in a place only I knew."

Noise from the boys at camp took our attention from each other. We ate breakfast—fruit and some meat from a caught rabbit the night before. Some of the boys marveled over my missing arm, asking what it was like and if I had a hard time dressing myself. I had no problem answering their queries. For the first time in a long time, my injury felt like something awe-inspiring, and not something shameful.

When we finished, Isabelle walked up to me as I stretched my muscles. "Do you feel anything?"

I nearly dropped the half-eaten apple in my hands. I caught it before it hit the ground. "What did you say?"

"Your missing arm." She gestured to the pinned-up sleeve. "Do you still feel as though your arm were there? I've heard stories."

"Sometimes, I'll go to fold my hands and realize there's no other fingers to fold into, but that's mere habit of having a hand for over twenty years of your life to suddenly not."

"You use a sword rather well, despite it."

"Well, your brother taught me well. It's not easy."

"Will you teach me?"

"I—" A disturbance in the forest coming from behind me cut my answer short. I turned to find the boys peering at the two of us, half hidden by tree trunks.

"I don't know," I told Isabelle. "Your arms are kind of scrawny."

I said the words without a smile, though she caught the teasing tone. "Branch would tell you otherwise."

An image of a massive bald man with a scowl appeared in my mind. "He was the one who looked like he wanted to eat me, right?"

"We all wanted to eat you, Ashe."

My eyes widened. "Really?"

She slapped me on the shoulder. "Yes, and I'm sure these boys would love to see you in action, Ashe Paratheon. Isn't that right?"

There was a murmuring amongst the children, and then finally Lile, who spoke for the group, came forward. "We'd like to see the prince fight."

"Fine," I said. "Pick up my sword."

She obeyed, unsheathing the weapon from his horse's saddle. "What is this one called?"

"I don't always name my weapons, as you do."

She looked at me.

I sighed. "I named her Faithkeeper."

"A good name!" one of the boys called out. "Though I'd probably name mine Deathslayer."

I cocked a brow and shook my head.

Isabelle looked over the blade, double-edged and longer than my torso. "The hilt," she mused. "Is that a tooth?"

I measured my words. "It's a Gwylis canine."

She grunted. "A fancy use of a tooth."

With expert fingers, she took the hilt and gripped it. "Hold it like you're shaking someone's hand. With a sword like this, it's all in muscle strength, so there is no real correct way to hold it. It depends on the situation and proximity of your opponent. Also, your personal methods."

Isabelle nodded. "Branch and I had covered swords during training, but we focused mainly on close combat such as my dagger and knives."

"This one is likely to tip you over. Let's use a stick or something."

She moved Faithkeeper from my reach. "No. Teach me."

I searched the ground for a stick long enough to spar with. With one in hand, I readied my stance. She copied it.

"Don't clench your fingers. Keep your thumb and first two fingers and keep the rest loose. Do you understand?"

She nodded. She knew all of this. Keeping your fingers tightly around the hilt would tire you out quicker.

"Now, the one good thing about one-handed swords is that your other is free to do whatever you please," I said. "Bring your sword down, but lock your elbow before you hit the branch. See, now watch."

With the sword stopped in midair, I made my branch to look as though it had parried with the sword. "Now, grab my wrist and take my sword." I rocked back on my heels and puffed out my chest. "Or at least try."

She bent forward, keeping her sword still lined with my branch and went to grab my arm, as instructed.

"Come on, Isabelle!" Lile cried out.

I rolled my eyes. "With this move, you can either break your opponent's arm, or perhaps steal their sword if their grip is weak. But it must be done quick, and only if you're one on one. If you do so in a battle, you risk hurting others when you push both swords."

We went through a couple more moves before deciding to break camp.

"I didn't kill a Gwylis for it. Just so you know."

She locked eyes with me. "What?"

"I didn't kill a Gwylis for the sword's hilt."

"Oh."

It must have been difficult to be torn between two worlds. Unease wrote itself on every line on her face. I knew in my heart that she would never become the kind of ruler her father was. Anyone who knew her could see she loved her people. She would do anything for them.

But as would I.

I thought of the boys and how they marveled over how I got along with a missing hand, and how Isabelle wanted me to teach her one-handed sword fighting.

Before then, I'd felt broken, stuck in a past where my father had me by a leash and hardly looking toward the future where I'd take up leading an army and aiding a queen. My former self would never have imagined the pride I now I felt inside. The courage.

Isabelle clearing her throat interrupted my thoughts, and we spoke at the same time. Her voice overshadowed mine. "I'm scared of what awaits us. What if it's too much?"

What she meant to say what the thing I'd been thinking, and successfully pushing from the forefront of my mind for these past few weeks. What if we weren't strong enough for what we'd encounter in Hassara?

The blunder in Essex taught us that we, as two people, did not have the capacity to make a difference, and if presented with an enemy, I might be the first to fall. Isabelle had her magic, demons or not. But she was losing control.

But I couldn't tell her any of that, not with the demons listening to everything. "What do we do?" I asked, repeating her question. "The sun will rise, and we will try again."

She drew a long inhale and spoke, "I think you would make an excellent king."

A fluttery feeling took flight in my belly. I opened my mouth, closed it. I could think of nothing to say. It was entirely possible that Isabelle was possessed by the demons and had no control over the lies they made her tell. "What are you talking about?"

Isabelle smiled, her eyes shining bright. "Mirosa would follow you. I know they would."

I shook my head, but she continued. "Our families have both done unspeakable things, but Ashe, what you did, leaving home, injured and dying, risking your life coming to the Den and then again letting yourself get captured, only to live under the same roof as your insane father... Ashe, you killed him to save the kingdom, and now you're here, with me, on what may be a fool's errand, but still you're here and you're seeing it through to whatever end. You're raising an army. This story is as much yours as it is mine. As it is Henry's. As it is—"

The pain was written on her face so clearly. It was like she was already there, living in a world where I had a crown and she was with—

"Fray," I finished for her. "Fray's story."

Isabelle's smile faded. "Yes."

I could feel the emotion warring on my face. "Your seal of approval means everything to me, but I did not do any of those things for a throne. That is not my birthright. Mirosa is not mine to take."

"Maybe," she said, her look serene. Genuinely considering this could be a viable option for the kingdom. "Maybe I'm too tired to be queen. Maybe this is all meant to kill me."

My heart gave a twist. To hear her like this reminded me of myself when I thought I deserved punishment. When I slogged through the Archway with one thought in my head: *Die somewhere far, where he can't get you.* But I hadn't died, and I was stronger for it. "Some things break us down, just to build us back up."

"I don't know, Ashe. I lie at night, and all I can see is a beach with waves and gulls and blue skies. I see quiet. I see a place where I can think and find out who I really am."

My heart gave another devastating twist. "It sounds like a good place."

"It does," she said quietly, looking at her necklace. She straightened her spine and set her jaw, the defiant and brave Isabelle I'd come to know came to be, leaving no trace of the vulnerability she'd shown me moments before. She nodded to me and turned to walk away, but not before I saw that her eyes were bright with tears.

CHAPTER TWENTY-SEVEN

The plan did not change, even with fourteen extra bodies to feed.

We'd kept moving long into the day, through the thick forest until we came out into a field of long grass. Ashe led the way, with the children and me trailing behind. We were tense and alert. But this was our choice.

We knew we could not send the children home. Stormwall was overrun with Gwylis, and having them go back there was like sending them back to slaughter. The only thing we could do was either find them a safe place to hide until this was done, or take them with us.

Ashe wanted them with us.

As the days wore on, so did the heat. We'd abandoned much of our clothes and traded them for lighter wares and food. I still had a good amount of money left over, so providing the children with food and clothes was not a problem. What became a problem was having to answer the hard questions that came when the days were done.

My bones ached. I'd gnashed my teeth together so much that they felt filed down. Urges, barely swallowed, overcame me at times. I could easily kill everything in this camp right now, and they wouldn't know their lives had been in danger until they woke up as ghosts.

My blood turned to ice. Those were not my thoughts. I kept hearing them, over and over again. I pulled at my hair and raked my skin, but they would not subside.

"I can't do it," I told Ashe, after the boys were bedded down against a cropping of woods along a narrow ridge. It allowed a good view of anyone coming from ahead, and protected us from behind. "Having them here is not safe. What if I try to kill them in their sleep?"

"I'll stay awake and watch over you."

My lungs cinched tightly. "Ashe, you have to sleep sometimes. I can't lose you."

Ashe stuffed his hand into his pocket. His beard was coming in quickly, shadowing his jaw. He stole a glance to where the children slept and sighed. When he turned back to me, I saw something there—something paternal, and it made my heart pang.

He saw a future in those boys. Hope.

I rubbed at my eyes and wiped away the stinging. My thoughts ran like wild horses until they slowed their canter. Sometimes when I breathed, my lungs felt heavy. The near constant snickering of the demons filled my ears. Inside, I was rotting, dying like an apple left spoiling in the summer heat.

I threw up nearly all the time. I made sure I was out of hearing range, so nobody asked questions. But it wasn't food or even stomach acid. A thick, black mucus exited my body. I buried it in the dirt and leaves.

But the worst of it, oh the worst of it, was seeing Fray's face in my mind and begging for him to help me.

I clung to his image—the only thing keeping me going now. As awful as it felt to think of him, to remember what we had, I welcomed the hurt. It made me feel human.

After all I'd done, all I'd given up, it still came around to him.

"I've looked over the map, and there's a village east of Hassara, a half day's journey," Ashe said, cutting in my monologue. "We will take them there, give them money, find them housing, and instruct them to wait until we return."

I hung my head. The prince sure had enough hope for the both of us. "Ashe."

"We'll return for them, Isabelle." He looked at me expectedly. "Say it."

"You will return, Ashe."

He held a finger, preparing to scold me, but instead, lowered it and wagged it around furiously, hardtack falling in bits at his feet.

I shook my head, feeling as though it was going to topple from my neck. "Don't do that thing."

"What thing?"

"That thing you do when you want to say something and don't and let it fester around in there. I know you."

Ashe gave a shake of his head. "How do you know me?"

I raised my eyebrows. "Because you snore like a baby bird, and have this weird thing where you stick your finger in your mouth when you're thinking, and you also smell. Badly. I've come to know that stink. I won't know any different."

The hardtack flew, and flew fast. I caught it before it hit my face, and chucked it right back at the prince. Before I knew it, we were having a good, old-fashioned food fight right there in the middle of nowhere Mirosa, and for a moment, everything felt like it would be all right.

And then the demons of the seven hells would press their clawed fingers onto my bones and remind me of who I was. And who'd I'd always be.

No matter how much I tried to smile and tell myself that at least I'd saved fourteen lives, I would still feel weighed down by my choices. No amount of food fights with my friend would change that.

Nothing changed. Nothing was enough.

"We should leave at first light," Ashe said, brushing crumbs from his clothes. His manner was looser, his eyes less wary. I straightened and brushed the hardtack crumbs from my shirt. This hope, I wished I could bottle it up for myself.

"What are you thinking?" he asked. Gods, if this man were a Gwylis, he'd be able to sense me from across the entirety of the New Kingdom. That was how keen his senses were. "Isabelle."

"Call me Izzy."

Ashe's breath left his lungs in a big rush. He backed up, bumped into a tree, and sat. I chuckled at his shocked expression. Of all the things we'd been through, of all the things we'd said to one another, this was the one that surprised him the most.

"You have no idea," he croaked. "You don't know how long I've been waiting for you to say that."

"I shouldn't have revoked it from you," I said, feeling suddenly guilty. I used my nickname for those whom I kept close, those I loved. Taking that from Ashe had made me feel powerful, as if I'd taken his other arm. He hadn't deserved my wrath. It hadn't been entirely misdirected, but he deserved an apology nonetheless. "I'm sorry, Ashe. I'm so sorry."

He shot to his feet and grabbed me around the waist, nearly lifting my feet from the ground. I melted into his embrace, soft and warm, and slid my arms around his neck.

"No more apologies," he said, righting me onto the ground. "I love you, Izzy. Nothing will that happened or will happen will ever change that."

A strange merge of emotions flowed through me. Gratitude. Love. Happiness...

Hope.

Ashe dropped his hand from my waist. "I've wanted to tell you, from the moment I saw you in front of those thrones beside your mother, you looked like a queen. You would have thought I was currying favor." His gaze dropped to the ground. "I wish I'd known what my father was planning. I could have warned you."

I did not know if I would have put those two things together—the Gwylis hunting down my family and Dal Paratheon planning to usurp the throne. I was too wrapped up in Fray, getting his voice back, and thwarting my parent's plans of marriage. I couldn't even save Lulu.

I closed my eyes so tightly that they ached for the things I had lost.

With sad sigh, I confessed. "I wouldn't have believed you."

~

I WAITED UNTIL ASHE'S BREATHING GREW SLOWER BEFORE slipping from camp.

I packed only what I needed. My dagger and my pack with Henry's journal and the vial of poison, along with some food and a waterskin. I cast a protective bubble over the group of children and stepped away.

I'd only made it a dozen steps before a small voice called my name. I turned to find Lile standing outside of my magic, his eyebrows knitted together tightly. "You're leaving us." Not a question. A statement of fact.

"Ashe will take care of you, I have no doubts," I replied, softly. "But I cannot risk your lives any further than I have."

"You saved our lives," Lile said softly, the memories of it playing over in his mind. "If it wasn't for you, we'd all be dead."

I shifted my shoulders uncomfortably. I considered this young boy. He was lanky, arms and legs grown too fast for the poor boy to adapt. But he had the makings of a valiant young man. I could tell by the hardness in his eyes, it would not be an easy road for him, not by far.

"I will try and stall the prince," Lile said. "To give you a bigger head start."

My heart paused for a beat. "You're not angry?"

Lile grinned. I wondered if he and Ghetee would have gotten along. I loosened the image of the young wolf dying in my arms and backed away from Lile.

"Stay safe," I told him. "When this is all over, your lives will begin."

"I know what's inside of me. I do not fear it."

Tears caught up behind my eyes. "Be brave, little wolf," I said as I turned away. "The worst is yet to come."

～

Once outside the immediate area of our camp, I let the weight of what I'd done settle over me.

Before I'd chosen to become a Gwylis, I'd never once felt as though my future was so grey. I thought, at the very least, I'd be married with children, with a crown and several ugly dresses at my disposal. Even then, I knew I had little choice in what I did.

But now, my choices were entirely my own. I would not let those children down.

I won't.

The cool night air prickled my lungs as I picked up my pace. I kept to my human form, fearful of encountering opposition. In my skin, I could slip through quietly, without a giant wolf head to give me away. If I hurried, I could make it to Hassara in just under two hours. I could make it before Ashe even woke up.

I could break the curse tonight and end this war.

As I walked, the press of loneliness replaced my fears. Before, I had Lulu, and I had Henry, and Pyrus and Crim. And after, Fray, Branch, Olio, and Ghetee. I missed the girl who wanted the people who knew her worth, and loved herself unconditionally. But my arrogance turned to selfishness, and I was not strong enough to go back. I was nothing but another casualty. That girl was a ghost.

It didn't seem real to me. None of it. I had allies back at the Den and still some scattered across Mirosa. But the thought of anyone coming to my aid now was a dream long erased. It had to be me. It had to be.

"Thanks," I said to the night sky. "For nothing."

There were still things to remember.

Even if I did manage to break the Gwylis curse, Stormwall would still be overrun. Would the Greatwolf Pack surrender? They had no king or queen to lead them. Would the Peek Island soldiers sail back to their own kingdom? Again, without a ruler, would anyone look to me; the traitor of both wolf and human?

You do not need a crown here, the Uncanny hissed. *We have one waiting down below. A crown of fire.*

I pawed at my ears and slashed my dagger through underbrush scratching my arms. "I don't want a crown. Not anywhere."

The words were considered long before I spoke them aloud. Now, they were absolute. They'd been there all along.

Liar.

I bared my teeth and hissed at the demons. I was tired. So, so tired. I imagined somewhere quiet, where the waves crashed to the shore and gulls called overhead. Where I could watch the sun come up over water. And in all the visions, I was not alone.

Fray would be with me.

I came upon the path through the mountains as tears pricked my eyes. I allowed myself to think of him, wholly and completely and not just in fragments. I allowed myself to hear the way he spoke and how he breathed words into me as we kissed.

I blew out a gust of air. *Not yet.*

I was so close. Just a little further.

Traveling through the canyon took all my strength. The wind was fierce and the night long. I felt so utterly small between the vast rock.

Vast, empty, littered with bare trees and dried shrubs. It looked how I felt. But beyond this, I would find the place Henry needed me to be.

"I'm going to finish it," I said, my voice echoing. I shouldered my pack further onto my shoulder. *I am going to finish it.*

Not long after, I closed in around the area of Hassara. Using the light of the moon, I looked over my map. With the canyon behind me, I felt a bit more exposed. I came to a river that, according to the map, sliced between Hassara and the untouched land where I currently stood.

"Just over here," I whispered, crossing the river by way of a stony arched bridge. The construction was quaint, a far cry from Essex, but as the night sky brightened into dawn, I saw the basin I'd come into and the mountains that curved in front of me.

Hassara showed itself with a ball of fire.

Dawn looked upon the city, carving hard lines upon the rock face. The valleys spread out before me, sprinkled with poppies on one side and wildflowers on the other. The staggering sight took my breath away.

I walked forward through the knee-high grass. I felt like I came out of a nightmare, straight into a dream of the loveliest kind.

But I was old enough to know that even the prettiest things can have the deadliest bites.

I kept my guard up, even as my fingers brushed the poppies springing up on either side of me.

The celestite was here. The end of my journey.

When the poppies ended, a wall began. It came to my waist; short enough to leap and surely not high enough to mount weapons of any kind, or even guards. But I didn't have to leap. I walked straight through an opening as if I were walking directly into a garden. There, horses grazed in the pasture between me and the city. I approached a grey roan and stroked its nose. "Hello, girl," I said. "Where are your masters?"

The horse didn't respond, as expected, but the sky appeared to take my question as a cue. A fierce wind, sudden and impulsive, swept through me. The clouds moved in, making the sky dark and deep as night. Thunder rolled like a caged beast raging against the bars of its prison. I moved against the coming storm, quick to get under cover before the deluge began, but as I neared the city of Hassara, I quickly realized how wrong I'd been.

A sudden sense of fear ran through my nerves.

This was not a city.

This was a temple.

Four gargantuan structures with a set of stairs between them were all that greeted me. The sculptures were carved to look like people. They stood at least twenty meters high, all holding swords pointing downward at their feet. They wore blank expressions, or at least I thought they did. Time had weathered the faces, rendering them almost featureless as well as genderless. I'd never seen something so imposing, not since the Archway.

Tentatively, I took the first step. I swallowed hard and noticed the way the humans held their swords. They clasped the hilt at their abdomens, the sharp tip pointing straight into the earth below them, as if destroying whatever lay at their feet. The younger part of me wanted to imagine these beings coming to life, rocks crumbling as they heaved their heavy feet, swords scraping across stone as they lifted them poised to fight whatever enemies I'd pronounced.

Magic existed, and sometimes, it was not so friendly.

I looked away, suddenly feeling dizzy, and slowly took another step. The sky opened as I reached the entrance into the mountain.

Inside was nothing but darkness. I summoned my fire and lit what sparse torches I could find. I found myself in a damp hallway. Before me was a door, but it wasn't the darkness or the statues that set my anxiety free. It was the complete and utter silence.

Barring the thunderclaps and the rain, there were no other sounds. Sometimes, I had trouble hearing others if they were behind thick walls or picking up their scent if they were too far away. But this was different. There was nothing to sense. There was nobody here.

I rummaged through my pack for the map and spread it out there on the damp stone floor. I took one of the torches from the wall and crouched. The mountains cutting off the New Kingdom from the old ran off the page, the further west you looked. Hassara sat in the western-most corner, where the mountains had disappeared from the paper. Was this not part of the New Kingdom at all?

The thought came to be short lived, for something pricked my senses. I stood, leaving the map there on the floor, and turned to face the stone doors before me. Something was beyond them. The celestite, maybe. Or perhaps something else.

I went to the doors and pushed them open.

And nearly lost my breath.

The doors opened to a vast circular room with a pool of water in its center. My footsteps echoed on the stone as I walked, and a low hum rose and fell, as though someone were playing an instrument very softly.

But none of that interested me. What truly stood out was the old woman standing at the end of the room.

"You've come so far," she said, projecting her voice. When she approached, I realized the telltale jangle of the soothsayer's jewelry was missing. She wore nothing but a simple tan woolen robe. "How about a little further?"

"How are you here?" There was no way the old woman could have ridden or even sailed this far. Unless she'd gone before I'd left Stormwall, but even that felt far-fetched. I shook my head, walking the curve of the room. "Are you a ghost?"

Abiyaya now stood before me, but she didn't seem like a ghost. But I couldn't trust myself. The soothsayer had said so.

"Not a ghost," she said.

"What is this place?"

Abiyaya glanced around as though she'd just arrived. "A temple. Did you see those men and women there out front? Guardians of the old. This was not the first time humans have had to fight demons."

"Will this story be long?" I looked around, itching to keep going. To find the celestite.

Abiyaya clicked her tongue. "So impatient."

I looked at her.

She gave a world-weary sigh. "I've only come to meet you at your journey's end," she said. With those words came a touch on my shoulder, right where the poisoned arrow had scarred me.

In the blink of my eyes, I wasn't in the temple any longer.

I was in the center of a large stretch of grassland. Plains. The sky was layered in black and orange and red. The grass was burnt and crunched beneath my boots. In the far distance, the silhouette of a city. The setting looked like a garish painting, except the city was real, and it was on fire.

At once, the sounds of scraping filled the air, so loud I pressed my palms to my ears to block it out. Two hands on mine forced them away.

"It is the sound of a dying world," Abiyaya said, standing before me. Her hair blew around her shoulders. Her face pulled tight as she gazed at me. "Rixon said that you'd be the one to change all of this."

I wanted to ask what she meant, but my eyes stayed fixed to the fire all around me. This was the future of Mirosa if I failed. I would become a beast and turn the land into ash.

Suddenly, I was back in the temple. I could still feel the ash in my nostrils, taste it on my tongue.

Abiyaya withdrew her other hand from her robe and pressed something into my palm. "You were looking for this."

My heart beat furiously as I uncurled my fist.

It looked so...ordinary; something you'd find in a place like Wargrave's shop. It shone in shades of a pale sky, layers of delicate blue over harsh edges. It could have been mistaken for a normal stone, if one hadn't looked closely. I couldn't look away.

I felt Abiyaya's eyes on me as I unhooked my neckline and set all three stones in my hand. The celestite emitted a soft glow, growing brighter with its companions now side by side. Something like a lightning bolt shot up my arm and into every space in my body.

I closed my hand over them, as tightly as I could.

Emerald for loyalty. Ruby for purity. Celestite for clarity.

The Uncanny screamed.

I pressed my fists into my ears and nearly bit my tongue clean from my mouth. The demons were angry, and they had every right to be. I was about to banish them from my kingdom forever.

Let them cry.

I turned away from the soothsayer, ignoring her calls to me, and returned to the hallway where I'd left my pack. Rain still beat down outside. I withdrew Henry's journal and flipped it to the page about the stones.

"Present them to sunlight," I murmured. "And recite the lines: I call upon the gods of old, a mortal under your skies. I call for your power, that you may bless it upon me. I reject all evil, although I am made of darkness. I accept your love, although I am not worthy. Of this, I beg of you, oh gods." I paused, and then, "Here goes nothing."

I spoke the lines, but with slip-ups. On the third and most desperate try, I echoed the lines word for word.

I glanced toward the rain, forlorn. Images of Fray marching into battle, bloodied and bruised, flashed before me. I knew he would not succumb to the Uncanny without a fight. What of Olio and Branch? Would they survive such an assault?

I groaned and slammed the journal closed. Look at how far I'd come. Look at everything I'd lost, only to stand with everything I needed, waiting for the clouds to part just right. The world was cruel.

The world does not bend for you.

My eyes searched the sky to see black wings soaring above, through the fall of rain.

I slumped down at the top of the steps, covered by the archway. From this vantage point, I could see the feet of the giant sentinels. The longer I waited, the more I wished Abiyaya would come, but she seemed to have vanished away from this place, because she never emerged from the circular room.

The Uncanny were strangely quiet, although I still felt their presence. Were they put off by the stones? I laughed inwardly at my victory.

It will not be enough. Ashe's words forced their way into my mind, barraging me with doubts. I banished them as quickly as they came, but the feeling lingered. I held the three stones, moved them around in my palms, and listened to them clinking together. They reminded me of the massive amounts of jewelry Abiyaya wore—something mainly for show, to look pretty.

A fine tremble began in my fingers. *Please let this work. Please let me become something other someone who ran away. I don't want to run anymore. Not from anything. Not from—*

Unbidden, the memories of Fray came into the forefront of my mind. I'd been gone for almost two months. For the first time in what felt like forever, his absence stung like a hole carved into my chest. Had he thought of me? Had he missed me? What had become of his place in the Den?

And Henry. Strong and brave, Henry. He became a martyr, killed for standing up to his beliefs. I'd felt his loss every day since he died. Rixon was right. As much as my heart belonged to Fray, it was Henry who I'd dedicated this part of my life to avenging. It was because of Henry I'd discovered what my father had done, poisoning all those people. It was because of Henry I'd come to the Den and learned about what he'd been doing there. It was because of Henry that I returned home to reclaim what was ours, and to break the Gwylis curse, ending these wars forever. Henry lived in me. He ran through the blood in my veins.

You love too strongly, too fiercely, and it will be your downfall.

No. That was not correct at all. Love, as it would be, would always be worth fighting for; worth sacrificing; worth everything.

I'd been so deep in thought that I hadn't noticed the rain had let up to a light drizzle. I sniffed and wiped at my cheeks to find them wet, and not from rain. I blinked away the tears and took a deep breath before pushing to my feet.

It was time.

I waited only a few minutes, and from the gloom, the sun peered through, as though the gods were opening their eyes.

"I call upon the gods of old, a mortal under your skies. I call for your power, that you may bless it upon me. I reject all evil, although I am made of darkness. I accept your love, although I am not worthy. Of this, I beg of you, oh gods."

I was trembling, but I thrust my hand containing the stones into the sky and repeated the words, again and again until my voice grew hoarse and my shoulder ached. The clouds moved to block out the sun once more, and I lowered my arm.

And waited.

A memory pushed its way into my mind. Of screaming in joy, racing down the halls of Stormwall castle, and leaping into my returning brother's arms, my laughter mixing with my tears that he'd returned from training safely.

"I'll always come back to you, Izzy," he'd told me. "Why are you crying?"

I squeezed my eyes closed, letting loose a solitary tear.

Nothing happened.

I blinked away the rising thrall of emotion and raised my hand again, as the clouds moved, revealing the sun once more. I repeated the chant. My entire body shivered. It had to work. Why wasn't it working?

Perhaps I did not have enough sunlight.

The clouds shifted, and soon after, the horses below me were bathed in light. This was it—the finale. I repeated the chant, this time with fervor. Hope strengthened me, propelled me forward, down the steps and into the warm sun. I smiled through the last of the words, "I beg of you, oh gods."

I lowered my arm and tipped my head upward, closing my eyes. No more would the dark overtake my body. I would be made of sunlight.

Foolish girl, the demons snapped. *Did you think it would be that easy?*

I opened my eyes to see shadows pooling around me, circling like buzzards. I felt the thick slime running from my nostrils, creating shapes as it fell to the earth.

My legs gave way. I hit the ground on my knees, my hand opening, letting the stones roll from my palm and fall to the dirt. A scream tore through me, wounded and broken.

Voices spoke to me—not demons, but those who were the living and long dead alike.

He believed in an ancient tale of three stones meant for evocation. He thought that this would break the deal with the Uncanny and make us human again.

We must reverse what our ancestors pushed them to do. We must make them whole again. It is our duty.

Olio and Henry were wrong.

It is not enough.

The sobs shook me tiny quakes, and the demons laughed at my misery. "Why," I wailed. "Why would you do this to me?"

I wasted this time chasing after something that I felt would exonerate everything my family had done. But I tried. I tried for a long time and now, I didn't want it anymore. I wanted a warm bed, beside someone who understood me and loved me despite the person I'd become. I wanted a future. I wanted that now. But it was too late. I'd traveled a path that would ultimately be my end. I would not have another chance. It was over.

No, I couldn't give up now.

Maybe it took time. What was I expecting? A group of celestial beings to come floating down from the clouds to give me a pat on the back for a job well done?

I came this far. I had to go a little further.

I kept repeating the words in a feverish flurry until my head grew light and my body sunk down to my knees. *It's not over. It's not over.* There was nothing else for me to do. I failed in taking Stormwall; I failed at saving all the children in Essex.

I couldn't save Lulu.

I couldn't save Ghetee.

I could not fail at this.

I laid on the ground right there at the foot of the temple stairs and curled into myself. Exhaustion took over, and when the tears were dried, I closed my eyes and drifted into blackness.

CHAPTER TWENTY-EIGHT

A storm blew in the following day, reducing the world to a hazy grey. Torrents of rain battered our skin. Branch considered stopping and finding shelter. But Olio refuted.

"It's just a bit of rain," he said, turning his back to the ferocious wind. He was soaked through, as were we all. I blinked through the strands of wet hair falling into my eyes and decided to side with my friend.

"Olio's right," I said, thinking of his blackened skin and what terrifying thing it could turn into. Granted, we were already massive wolves with the magic of the elements. What could be worse?

We'd been traveling through the barrens for the past three days, with nothing but straggly trees that offered no shelter. We had to keep going. Especially when I felt the presence of something out here; something I could not explain even if I tried.

Neera's sisters jumped to agree. Cas first, with Mack and Des close behind.

"If we stop, we waste time," Cas said, blading her eyes from the rain.

Mac nodded and shouted over the wind's howling. "Besides, it's making it hard to pick up any scents in this storm. We'd be leaving ourselves open to prey."

Without another word, Olio charged past, brushing shoulders with mine. Over the past few days, he'd appeared to lost have most of his manic energy. His eyes were hooded, his shoulders slumped when you weren't looking. Squared if you were, as if he were pretending.

We all knew what was happening to us. But nobody discussed it. Could I blame them?

Sonia put her hand on my shoulder and dashed the rain from her lashes. My knee buckled and my body tilted under her hand. "You good, brother?"

I nodded and watched her leave with the others. Neera called me ahead, but I took my time catching up. My mind was too focused on the place where Sonia had placed her hand. The skin beneath my tunic seared as if it were burned. When the others were out of sight, I unbuttoned my shirt and moved it aside.

And drew in a sharp intake of breath.

My entire shoulder was blackened. The skin felt leathery, like that of a lizard, and it hurt. Gods, it hurt when I touched it. I hissed and raked a hand through my wet hair. Time was a physical thing, twisting at my heart, ticking away and killing me bit by bit.

THE LONGER THE STORM STRETCHED, THE MORE THE GROUP LOST hope. The entire day felt like night, which should have put us feeling right at home since wolves were nocturnal, but I wondered if more of them bore the same stained skin as Olio, Sonia, and myself. If they did, we were putting not only ourselves at risk, but the others. The Uncanny were unpredictable. But mostly, they were dangerous.

We stopped in a tiny copse of trees that swayed in the fierce winds. Although it was early afternoon, the sky was layered in greys. I approached Sonia. "We're turning into monsters."

Sonia's eyes darted back to the group and then to me. "A softer tone, brother," she chided. "Do you want to cause a panic?"

I stared at her. "We should be panicking. We should be addressing this."

Sonia bared her teeth and leaned into me. "There's nothing to address. There's nothing to be done about it, so why waste our breath?"

An uncomfortable silence stretched between us. The rain had lessened, but the wind took up my sister's hair. She pushed it from her eyes. "Don't you think I would have brought it up to Branch?" she said, her voice softer. "Don't you think I haven't thought about what this could mean if we all fail? Izzy, Ashe, all of us? This isn't a game. You think I'm avoiding it. I'm not. It keeps me up at night." She looked away toward the dark horizon. "I regret meeting Henry Rowan every day."

"You don't mean that."

Sonia sighed dejectedly. "I do, and you want to know why? Because I don't only fear for our people, Fray. I fear for everyone in Mirosa. Every man, woman, and child. Gywlis or not. Old Kingdom, New Kingdom. Henry taught me that, and I'd only just remembered."

I smoothed a hand over my shoulder. "I know what you mean."

Sonia met my gaze, holding back her hair from the storm. "Fray..."

She said my name as though it were an apology.

I shook my head, willing the thought of Izzy as far away as I could manage. It was for the best. Love had no place in war.

"Listen," Sonia said. "I don't know what we're going to encounter when we get to where we're going. But I need to say this so stop making that face and listen to me." I screwed my face into something resembling normalcy. "We have to protect each other. No lone wolf act, Fray. We're a pack. We need to act like it."

"And when we're not wolves any longer?" *What are we then?*

In a rare moment for the Castor family, my sister smiled. "We're family."

I let loose a gust of air and went to smile when a scream cut the air.

CHAPTER TWENTY-NINE

I took the boys and set a clear path to a small town called Fellholt. We arrived within six hours and set forth finding a place for the kids to stay. Lile stayed by me like an obedient pup. I caught him glancing at what was exposed of my iron half-arm, questions in his eyes.

"A story for another time."

Lile nodded in assent. I trusted the boy. He was good with the others. How long they'd been in this horror? *But at least they had each other.*

We found a boarding house to accommodate the children. I paid the woman in charge for a month and slipped the rest to Lile when nobody was looking. "This is in case I don't come back."

I didn't know what I expected, but it wasn't for Lile to understand, at least not this quickly.

"I will keep it safe," he said. "For when you return."

Not *if*, but *when*.

I clapped a hand to the boy's shoulder. There was nothing else to say, so I left them there.

But then the crow appeared.

It soared overhead at first, gauging me from afar as I walked. I felt a solid regret in leaving the kids behind. But gods, I had a duty. I was doing it for them. *Your people need you.*

The crow landed on a nearby wagon and began to preen itself. I walked past it and heard clanging jewelry.

"Do you remember what I'd show you?" the familiar voice asked.

A group of women bustled toward me, baskets in their hands. I watched the stemmed flowers bob as they ambled past. Roses.

I'd once brought Izzy a tulip, thinking it'd been her favorite. But it was roses. This after I'd been up all night searching for her after she'd disappeared from the castle. She'd gotten attacked by the Gwylis and sent her world into a spiral. What if I'd been different that evening at dinner? What if I hadn't caused her to run away?

The memory echoed in my head. *What if. What if. What if.*

I replaced it with the second meeting with Abiyaya in my room in Stormwall. She'd asked me to write letters, requesting aid from Mirosa. But after that was done, I gave her a drop of my blood, and she told me my future.

But not before she told me Izzy's.

"She will bring nothing but death," the soothsayer had said. "I told her this long ago, but it did not stop her from seeking out Aquarius."

I'd shaken my head in disbelief. "Do you realize what you're saying? You're practically blaming Izzy for what has transpired. She didn't make my father attack Stormwall. That would have happened whether she changed into a Gwylis or not." I gestured into the air around us. "All of this would have happened, but by killing Commander Ivo, she showed him he has something to fear."

Abiyaya had lowered her head. "I know this, but it did not stop me from trying to prevent it. Rixon knew what had to be done. The Gwylis would not follow her or Aquarius in the state he is in. We took a chance, and by doing so, it still did not change the future I saw for Isabelle. She will become something bigger and more monstrous than Mirosa had ever seen. The Uncanny, they want her. Her bravery and ruthlessness has made her open. She is the perfect vessel for destruction."

A vessel for destruction. "What does that mean?"

"It means her brother was wrong. No three jewels will call upon the gods. It is a farce."

I nearly choked on my words. "No, it's not."

She stirred the blood in the silver tray and frowned. There were no words to describe the feeling washing over me.

I had thought of the look of my father's face as I sailed away toward Stormwall, my own blood as my arm was severed, the saltwater on my skin, the feel of the wind through my air. I never thought I would crave home so much. I didn't think I had it in me to consider anything besides following what my father had ordered on any given day. Going after Izzy had yielded me back there. In a prison of my own making.

I had closed my eyes briefly, and when I opened them, Abiyaya was arranging the letters I'd written and shoving them into her cloak. "You don't believe me," she had said. "I'll see you when the time comes."

I shook my head in frustration, feeling horribly daunted. It may still be possible to take Stormwall and win even if Izzy failed. Even if she became something I could not reach.

But I was powerless, yet again.

Maybe I always was.

"Prince..." Abiyaya reached out to touch my arm, but I moved away.

I did not want her comfort. "There's got to be another way."

"There isn't."

"I don't want to kill anyone!" The words ripped from my throat as I pushed the heels of my hands into my eyes to stop the tears from flowing where anyone could see them.

"Mirosa needs you." Abiyaya's words were certain. Iron-hard.

Defiance sparked as I laughed bitterly.

But she was right.

Mirosa was waiting for me, their leader.

I straightened and took a long look at my surroundings. At its people. I was so far from home. Not where I belonged. Yet...a myriad of feelings inside of my sprung to life. Survival. Duty. Courage. Teeth gritted, I looked past Abiyaya, to an uncertain future, but the wings I'd kept furled against my back now began to flutter.

The gods were watching me.

And they wanted to me to fly.

~

HASSARA WASN'T FAR ACCORDING TO MY MAP. I TOOK MY HORSE and rode without rest. By now, Izzy would have arrived. Would she have found the celestite by then? I glowered at the sky. Rain clouds, dark and ominous, rolled overhead.

A storm signaling a battle about to be lost.

I bent over my horse as we ran, my stomach squeezing in on itself. The landscape blurred in colors, shadowed by the incoming rain. I prayed to whatever gods were listening that the evocation would work. That they would find us worthy and return to end this war once and for all.

But I knew as well as anyone that this would not end so easily.

A canyon gave way to grass, which took me through a field of flowers, and before I knew it, I was less than a half mile from the largest temple I'd ever seen. I took my horse into a flat-foot walk as I took in what appeared to be four massive statues, and between them, a large set of stairs.

And at the base lay a woman.

I gasped at the sight of Izzy and quickly dismounted. She was a fetal position and appeared to be sleeping. In her hands were two jewels hanging from a chain and another close by. The celestite.

I stepped back and looked around. Did it work? I shook my head. What was I expecting? The world to be somewhat changed? No, the only way to know was to—

"You knew it wouldn't be so simple, didn't you?" Unsurprisingly, Abiyaya descended the steps of the temple. She looked so small between those colossal statues. "Prince, you know what you have to do."

I set my jaw. My fingers twitched as I eyed Izzy's dagger, right there sheathed on her hip. "There has to be another way."

"It's the only way."

A chill snaked down my spine. "I can't do it."

Abiyaya was close enough now that I smelled her perfumed scent. "It's the only way to free her," she reminded me. "You are doing her a favor. It's all she's ever wanted, to be free."

Are you listening?

That day Abiyaya had come to me back in Stormwall, she laid a burden upon my shoulders that was only slightly loosened when I ended my father's reign of terror. The only other task would relieve me of my promises, but it would also destroy me.

"Do you want Mirosa to fall?"

If I said yes, what would that make me? A traitor? A coward? Could I watch my best friend rage an unholy fire on the entire land? I had a chance to end this now. If I took myself out of my head the way I'd done when I killed my father, I could get it done.

The choice was clear.

I had to do what the gods asked of me.

Izzy was my friend. More than a friend, for I loved her. She was a symbol for everything I wanted in my life. Happiness. Peace. Bravery.

I could never erase my past. All I could do was come to terms with the present, carve out my future, and live it. I made up my mind.

CHAPTER THIRTY

A noise rose, like something from a deep and dark nightmare. It wasn't human. It wasn't wolf.

Olio.

He writhed on the ground, a living nightmare. A wolf that had somehow gotten stuck mid-shift with patches of fur mixed with blackened skin. Large talons replaced his toes and fingers, too big to be wolf. His face, human but with a snout disproportioned to his face and his eyes, red as dawn.

My tongue stuck in my mouth.

"It's happening," Sonia said. "The Uncanny are taking us." She bent to me, her face a mask of fear. "I felt it too. The voices, whispering in my ear."

To my left, Neera and her sisters looked on. She had all three of them against her chest, holding them with a tight grip.

Olio sat up, turning his blood-red eyes to me. His back was split open in two places below his shoulder blades, and growing from each of those cuts were two folded wings, crumpled like paper and bent at odd angles.

To my right, Sonia gasped.

Olio launched himself into the air, dirt lifting with the beat of his black wings. He flew only for a moment before banking and tumbling to the earth.

His body landed with a sickening *crunch.*

A beat of silence, and then one of Neera's sisters began to cry. The world froze. Nobody moved. Nobody breathed.

Shakily, I ran to where Olio had fallen. I looked over this body, now smooth with human skin. There were no visible wounds but the marks from where the wings had sprung, bleeding freely into the mud below him. I wanted to lift him, but fearing he'd broken his back, I left him be until the rest of pack approached.

"What do we do?" Sonia asked. She wasn't looking at Branch. She was looking at me.

I returned my attention to Olio. He looked deathly pale, blood forming in a pool at his back.

He opened his eyes and gave me a smile.

"Nothing like a demon trying to take over your body to make someone's day," he croaked.

I pressed Olio's limp hand to my chest and closed my eyes.

Aquarius had once promised me safety and peace. But after that shattered, I'd found my own peace in Stormwall castle. But even mundane things had their secrets. After arriving at the Den, I had my doubts whether Izzy and I would truly be safe anywhere. But I tried, for her, and mostly for me, to rebuild what I'd had missed out on.

To find the life I had lost.

But we weren't safe. Every step I took was a step toward another battle, another nightmare.

I took a staggering breath, the veins in my neck pulsing with my heart. Magic inched its way up my arms until I could see the faint gleam of ice on the tips of my fingers.

We were losing control.

"Can you move at all?" Neera asked. "Come, Cas, help him."

Cas, presently the most composed out of everyone, bent over Olio and carefully began to lift his arms and legs. "Wiggle your toes for me? Good, now your fingers."

"I'll get his clothes," Mack said and bounded off, Des hot on her heels.

Olio didn't move at first, but finally his foot bobbed and his hand squeezed mine. "I don't feel any pain."

"That's good," Cas said, running her hands over Olio's ribs and chest. "But also, not. You could be numb. I'm going to need you to try and sit up, all right?"

Mack and Des returned with Olio's clothes, and I dressed him carefully. I'd neglected my own bareness until Neera pushed my own gear into my arms.

"Not that you aren't a pretty sight," she said with a wink. She was trying to lighten the mood. It wasn't working.

Olio unpeeled his sticky back from the ground and sat up. He turned his pain-clenched face to me, as if begging for answers I did not have. My heart clenched. Seeing Olio, fun-loving, always optimistic Olio this way forced a wavering breath from my lungs.

I don't want him to die. I don't want to die. I anguished with every beat of my terrified heart.

Cas reached out and placed a reassuring hand on my arm. "Nothing is broken that I can tell, but he still may have a fracture," she said. "Can you try to walk?"

Olio's expression pulled into anguish as he tried to stand. He nearly fell, but I caught him before he toppled. He took one step and then another. The blood from his back soaked through his tunic as Cas held onto his arm to keep him from swaying.

He was walking, but it wasn't enough to quell my almost debilitating fear.

"He can't go," I said, pulling at my hair. "He has to stay or go back."

Branch bowed his head. "He can't go back, not when we're so close."

I turned, my eyes flashing to his. "So close to what? We've traveled for days with nothing in sight, Branch. You can't even give us a name. No marker on the map. We're walking on blind faith alone!"

"We don't need to fight," came Neera's soft voice. "Let Olio make that decision for himself."

"I can stay with him," Sonia spoke up. "I can stay. You guys go ahead."

My pulse roared in my ears. Leaving Sonia behind with an injured packmate was not in the plan, not if there were more soldiers out here. She'd be fighting alone. She wouldn't make it.

My sister. My friend.

But before I could speak up, Olio answered for us.

"I'm not staying here," he said as Cas lowered him into a sitting position. "I won't stay, and you can't make me."

"You'll heal within a day or two," Sonia said. "We can catch up after."

"No," Olio forced out. "I won't stay."

Tears streamed down Sonia's cheeks, but she dashed them away quickly. "All right," she said. "Branch?"

Branch, who'd been quiet since I'd exploded on him, nodded.

I sat beside Olio while the others made their preparations. He angled an arm over my neck. "Thank you," he whispered, pulling me in. "If I'm going to die, it's going to be on my feet."

Taking turns carrying Olio on our wolf backs would have been easier had we not begun to hike at a gradual incline, heading higher into what appeared to be a mountain range. The little straggly trees had disappeared completely, leaving us surrounded by jagged rock formations that rose high like stone guardians on either side of our path. I second-guessed my decision to come on this journey. This place set my nerves on edge.

The terrain grew difficult the higher we went. Loose rocks threatened to sprain ankles, or worse, cause a fall that would severely injure us; if we didn't die, of course. The larger pack members had the most trouble; their larger fames were not built for such balance. They stopped often, catching their breath before continuing. Even Branch was having a hard time.

The winds were determined to blow us off-course. We fought against it, ducking our heads as we pushed our bodies to their breaking points. Night had fallen, and the grumbling of the group finally pulled Branch to a stop.

"We have to get to the top!" he called out over the wind. He was in human form, his pack overloaded with Sonia's clothing for when her shift carrying Olio ended. "Then we can rest!"

Lightning streaked across the sky like the swipe of a snake's tongue. I thought the more we inclined, the less the wind would bother us, but I was wrong. One more hour of walking, and we finally came to a narrow flat terrain. Not at the top, but a good spot to breathe.

I wiped the water from my eyes. The wind kicked up dust and made them sting. "We need to stop, or this wind is going to knock us over!"

"We can wait it out," Sonia said, heaving her load to my right. She sunk to her belly; her tongue lolled from her mouth in exhaustion. I'd kept close to her side, making sure the straps we tied around Olio hadn't come undone to make him fall and hurt himself worse. He looked bad. Tired mostly, but bad.

The rest of the group huddled on the flat earth, taking every second of rest they could afford. They held strong against the battering wind.

We'd gone through too much today. The soldiers hadn't been too much of a bother. But Olio...the way I'd almost lost control. We could use a breather—time to process it all.

Branch sneered against the elements, as if showing his teeth would scare it off. "No, let's keep moving," he ordered.

Neera and her sisters came up to my left and dropped to their knees. They wrapped their arms around each other. What was it like to feel safe and protected?

Neera met my eyes and nodded at me, as if to say they would give it their all no matter what. For the first time, I noticed a large cut traversing from the back of her ear, down her neck, and ending somewhere beneath the shoulder of her tunic.

My heart beat a furious rhythm in my chest.

You were born for so much more than this.

"No," I said. "We need to rest. We're not moving."

Sonia's lips parted in a moan. "Thank the gods."

Branch, who'd been no more than six feet away, crossed the distance in two strides, his breath hot in my face. "Who made you pack leader, Castor?" he snarled. Even in the darkness, I could see the way his eyes burned with a mix of something like fear and desperation.

Two things we did not need right now.

"Stupid wolf," I muttered. "I'm not even part of the pack, yet you dragged me along."

Branch sneered. "You made that choice!"

My eyes widened as I spoke. "I did, and now I'm making the choice not to move an inch until I know we can all make it through the night alive and not dead at the bottom of this ridge."

Branch hissed. His large fists furled and unfurled at his sides. "They won't be dead. They have me. They trust me."

I snorted. "I bet they do."

Branch was a huge male, three times my size and able to punch a hole straight through my stomach and out the other side. And his fury pulsed between us.

"Back off, Castor." He turned around, but my hand shot out and forced him back. In an instant, his fist connected with my jaw. I absorbed the punch, but swayed on my feet. Pain lit beneath my skin, on top of the raging urge to hit him back. But the jab had turned my head, and now, I faced the group. They looked on in wide-eyed shock, fearing a fight right there on the ridge. It'd be suicide. Everybody knew it. Which was why I cracked my jaw back into place and faced Branch.

"I can forgive you," I said, my voice throbbing, "because you are a brother, but if you kill these wolves because of your overconfidence, I will throw you from this mountain."

Someone gasped. Neera, maybe?

Branch drew in a long breath, and on the exhale let out a tremendous roar. I planted my feet the ground, fearing a rockslide. The sound bounced off my skull, prickled my skin. But as much as I made ready for another punch to my face, my shoulders sagged in relief when Branch retreated, stepping back and seeming to fold in on himself.

I sucked in a gulp of air and jerked my head sharply to the rest of the group, hoping they hadn't noted the brief glimpse of weakness in their leader. But my worry shifted into anger. "No," I said in an uneven voice, my tone strained and hoarse. My ribs tightened and my hands quaked. *You cannot afford to be weak. Not now. Not ever.* "We can't be weak. The strength lies in the pack. If we are not one, we will not survive."

As if in response, the mountain began to shake. I nearly lost my footing. Someone cried out. One of Neera's sisters? I started my chant, quickly thinking I could use my ice to freeze fallen rocks if this were an avalanche, but I barely got past the first few words before the mountain fought against my will to survive and gave a terrible roar, boulders knocking together and trees cracking.

In the darkness, it was only the sound and the feel of dust and pebbles raining on our heads. Quick-thinking Neera, who was already a wolf, called upon her magic and lit up the sky, her strikes of lightning filling the eerie dark. Rocks fell at rapid speed. A boulder surged to my right, tumbling down the way we'd come.

"Grab onto something!" I shouted, falling to my belly and grabbing at the nearest impeded rock. I felt Branch beside me doing the same before he thought better of it, and managed to stumble this way to Sonia and Olio and cover them both.

I hung on, breathing ceased as the world around me quaked. *I'm going to die here. On a damn mountain!*

I managed to make my way toward the rest of the group, slowly crawling on my belly, throwing my hands over my head as more of the mountain fell. I had to wait between quakes to start up again, but it didn't take long before I was inching toward Neera, who was folded in on her side with her head beneath her elbows.

I caught a moment to breathe. But then the ground gave out beneath me.

I fell, suspended in air right over the ridge.

I rolled, head over knees and upright again as I skidded against the rocks. Pain and terror surged through my body. I threw out my arms, desperate to grab onto something. My nails dug into the dirt and rocks, somehow managing to get hold of something. I hung there, my boots scrabbling for a foothold until they found purchase. My muscles strained as I pulled myself up, but I slipped and lost my handhold.

My own gasping breath filled my ears, knowing I wasn't going to come out of it unscathed.

That's because you're not trying hard enough! Izzy had said when I'd scoffed at the idea of making the pack my family. Had I done enough? Who was I against a trembling mountain?

I hit something, and my body lurched. No time. I headed upward again, the wind whipping at my face, whistling past my ears. What was happening? Was I dead? *Am I ascending to the gods?*

I found myself on solid ground, lying face-up. A falling star streaked across the black sky. Everything was quiet and still.

I laid there for a long time before I trusted myself to move. I sat up, wondering who'd I'd sold my soul to this time to find myself aching, but very alive. The mountain had quit its tantrum, but my legs still shook as

I stood. I'd bitten my tongue at some point, and blood had filled my mouth. I spat it out and pressed the palms of my hands to my eyes. *I should have died.* "That shouldn't have happened."

"If it weren't for your squabbling, it wouldn't have."

I froze.

A large figure moved in the shadow of the mountain. Pacing on four legs, like a predator. Finally, it stopped and inched closer, dissolving its shape into something much more...human.

I hesitated, struggling to find the right words. "Aquarius?" The word felt strange, as if it shouldn't exist. Not anymore.

But he was there. A tangible thing, right there in front of me.

My knees gave way. I dropped to one knee, gaping at the old man in disbelief. Seeing him alive and on this mountain brought back every memory of battle I'd ever had with the former king. The gnashing teeth. The clanging iron. Waking up on the eve of battle to find him gone. Feeling lost. Betrayed.

"You're not here," I whispered, unable to tear my eyes away from Aquarius as he approached. His eyes fixed on mine. I couldn't look at him. I couldn't. I wanted to embrace him. And kill him all at the same time. "You saved my life."

"So it seems." He took another step, but stopped when he saw me flinch. I finally looked at him. I searched his eyes for something, anything. An apology, maybe?

The shock of the past few minutes drained away. Instead of feeling numb, I succumbed to a boiling fury. "You left me." I hated the how small my voice sounded. I hated how much I wanted to trust him even after everything he'd done to me. I hated him.

"It took me a long time to finally see," he said. I heard voices from somewhere up above, but they faded into the background. "We have much to talk about. Let's find your friends."

I narrowed my eyes, uncomprehending, and took a slow, deep breath, counting to three and then, "What?"

Aquarius dared a step forward, his eyes painted with anguish. Wrinkles sagged his eyes and his mouth. Dark spots littered his entire body. This was not the same king I knew. He was thin and sickly. A pang of pity hit me. For one heart-wrenching moment, I gave in.

I took a deep breath, feeling a sense of peace rush through me.

Sometimes the world worked in strange ways, and somehow paths met just to split and converge once again. Somewhere out there, Izzy and the prince were risking their lives, and after all this time, so was Aquarius. That deep pit of sorrow that always dragged me under shrunk.

My family. The missing piece to my broken world was here.

"All right," I said with a heavy sigh. "Let's go, Father."

CHAPTER THIRTY-ONE

I dreamed that Fray and I were walking along a white sandy beach, our bodies only a breath apart, our fingers grazing one another's. The sky was a bright blue, and the ocean just as lovely. Fray looked at me, and I remembered that this was the first time he'd looked at me this way for so long, but I couldn't remember what I'd done to make it stop. His eyes were so depthless that they might as well have been the ocean itself. He took my face in his hands and leaned in for a kiss. He smelled like sweet root and all things wild.

Fray.

My Fray.

But before his lips could touch mine, I felt myself being pulled away, as though I were tied to a tether and suddenly yanked back. Fray and the beach became smaller and smaller, and I closed my eyes and screamed.

When I opened them again, I was not on a beach, but in the court-yard back in Stormwall, and I was not eighteen; I was seven, and begging my brother not to leave. I slammed my fists on his legs, but he did not budge. He turned to march along with the rest of my father's army, and I fell to my knees and wept.

All at once, a scene appeared below me. Thousands upon thousands of shapes, clashing into one another in a massive flurry of teeth and steel. Screams. Blood. A world of darkness.

~

I gasped awake, eyes opening to a cloudless sky. It was morning, by the position of the sun, and I lay on my back, the three jewels in my clenched fist. If this was the underworld, it was a very cruel trick.

I stood, letting the weight of my body balance on shaky legs. I turned to where the temple of Hassara stood, unchanged behind me, and wiped the sleep from my eyes.

My throat was dry and hoarse. My eyes felt puffy and my bones weary. I stood for a moment, unsure of where to go from there. I could go into that temple and beg the gods to listen. But if they hadn't by now, they weren't about to start.

Instinctively, my hand groped for the vial in my pocket. Pyrus had given it to me in case things went awry with Ashe, had we been married. But now I knew that really wasn't what he was thinking all along. Did he know things would play out the way they had? He'd concocted the Voiceless poison for my father. He had to have known a thing like that would never go away.

And he'd given me a way out.

I clutched the vial, as tears streamed down my face. Something so tiny, so seemingly insignificant could do such damage. But my fingers couldn't move to unscrew the top. How could I bring myself to do such a thing?

With a cry, I flung the vial as far as my arm could throw it. It catapulted through the air and landed on the steps of the temple, shattering.

Something moved from behind one of the statues. A figure cloaked in darkness cut against the marble and the dawn. I stepped backward. Never had the Uncanny taken shape as a human before, but I had failed, and they grew stronger by the day. If this were so, there was no hope for Mirosa. They'd take every one of our bodies for their own uses. It was a horror to think about, and it let a gasp escape my lips.

It stepped forward as I stepped back. Something gleamed in its hand.

"Did you fail?" the figure asked. Its voice was low, but somewhat familiar.

If the shadow spellings from my body and seeping into the ground weren't answer enough, I didn't know what to say. But why would a demon ask such a thing if it already knew…

"Ashe?"

He stepped out. His eyes were hooded, dark underneath. His mouth was turned down in a severe frown. He looked so tired. He looked so sad.

"The boys are safe," he said. "They didn't ask many questions."

His tone was conversational, and might have been even lighthearted if not for the dagger in his hand.

"That's good," I said evenly. I swallowed hard. "Why are you here?"

Ashe scuffed the heel of his boot into the ground. The tension in his body eased. "You can't lose me that easily," he said with a smirk. "I told you I'd see this to the very end."

I blinked. "Is this the end, Ashe?"

He lifted one shoulder. "I don't know." He looked at me and held my stare. Our entire history together played out in those green eyes, and I thought I saw a flicker in there. Was he was seeing the very same thing? But then he broke free and glanced at the dagger in his hand.

The dagger was mine.

"You know I don't want to do this," he said.

I lifted my eyes to the sky so the sunlight washed over my face. I had so little energy left, so little that it felt like my life was already draining away. Through the spots in my eyes, I saw Ashe's face: his bright green eyes, his hard jaw.

Abiyaya's voice echoed in my mind: *I see so much pain that it almost kills you.*

I stared at Ashe.

Almost kills me.

My heart beat within my chest.

Almost.

"Ashe." The name choked out of me. His eyes focused on mine.

I told him, "I'm sorry about your father. I'm sorry about your arm. I'm sorry about everything. I never wanted to become a monster. I chose it because I thought I could do good. But I was not strong enough. I am not strong enough."

"You'll always be the bravest person I've ever known." His voice was barely above a whisper. His shoulders slumped forward, bit by bit.

He breathed in deep and lifted his eyes to the sky. His once annoyingly handsome smirking face was now worn and tired. He looked older than he was only months ago when he stood at the thrones of Stormwall and kissed my hand. Forehead crinkled, skin rough and oily, mouth chapped, and hair standing in all directions. "All I ever wanted to see you happy. To see you free."

I looked at the dagger again. The same weapon that killed Rixon and set her free from the Uncanny. "Is that what the dagger is for?"

Ashe's eyebrows sat so low over his eyes, he looked like he was going to fall apart.

"How did you know to do this? Who told you?"

He pulled in a shuddering breath, but did not answer.

"Ashe, tell me."

"The soothsayer showed me what would happen if you lived," he said, his words laced with anguish. "That we would suffer for ages in this world and the next, and you would destroy it. All of it with your rage. I took an oath to protect this kingdom and you, and I won't see you suffer."

As he talked, his face showed a relentless despair. I let out a staggered breath, took one last look at the sky, and closed the distance between us. By now, the demons were already taking hold of my body. My chest heaved and my fingers twitched to wrap themselves around Ashe's throat once more.

But instead of his throat, I grabbed his forearm.

I saw a little boy in Ashe's face. Innocent, uncorrupted by his father. But behind his eyes, I saw the man that he became. A loyal one. A merciful one.

"For Mirosa," he said. His voice broke, and his sadness was right there on his face. How could not have seen how damaged he was? He was utterly lost. He was dying inside.

We stepped closer. He rested his forehead against mine, calm and still.

"Ashe." A great sob escaped me, and a flood of tears gushed down my cheeks. "Gods, Ashe, I am so sorry. I am—"

The dagger came up, pointed straight at my heart.

I grew sad. So, so sad for him. I wished there was another way.

Ashe. Oh, his eyes looked so desperate for a way out of this. *If only there were, foolish prince. If only life dealt us different hands.*

"Don't say it," I said when his mouth opened. "Don't think it. Not now."

He nodded in assent. His chest heaved in and out until he found his composure. With his hands holding his head, he looked at me from beneath his drawn brows. "Think about someplace nice," he said. "A beach. The mountains."

I imagined a beach with rushing waves and gulls overhead. No demons. No fear.

I fell into him, clutching his body tightly. "I won't ever be gone," I whispered into his ear.

He shook his head. He did not believe me.

But I believed. More than ever, I believed in everything.

His fist and the hilt of my dagger dug into my ribs. His body shook.

He plunged the knife into my chest, my life spent.

I counted the beats of my heart.

One.

Two.

Three.

He tore the dagger free, and I crumpled to the ground.

Through my darkening vision, I saw Henry. I heard his voice in my head: *As humans, we still own the rights to our souls.*

I did not know I even had a heart until it began to ache, its essence flowing from me. I did not know if I had a soul to own until I felt it lifting from my body.

Blackness folded over.

Then there was nothing.

CHAPTER THIRTY-TWO

The last few moments had rattled me to my core.

First, I challenged my own pack leader who, by all definitions, was beginning to lose his sanity. I barely survived a rockslide...earthquake? If that weren't enough, at the exact moment of my death, the former king of the Gwylis arrived just in time to pad my fall and carry up the side of a mountain to safety.

I must have been dreaming.

The old wounds sealed over like a scab. But I knew when I looked at him—my father—that at any given moment, he'd peel the scab away and let me bleed.

Which was why I kept my distance and resorted to silence as we scaled the mountain to find the others. At one point, I watched a bird swoop and dip at our heads. I hadn't noticed how high we'd gone up the mountain before the rockslide. Not until I was falling from it.

"Who is in your group?" Aquarius asked. When I failed to respond, he added, "I came a very long way, very fast. I have not slept for three days."

I said nothing. What could I say to the one who'd abandoned the pack? Abandoned me. Should I have felt bad that he hadn't slept? I hadn't slept in years. Not much by any normal standard.

"Sonia!" I called out in a harsh whisper, when we approached the flattened area where we'd all gathered before the quake. The ridge was level enough for me to stand at an angle. I grabbed for the ledge, loose rocks falling all around me, and pulled myself up. A hand thrust down and lifted me to my feet.

Sonia's voice rang out. "Oh, gods, I don't know what I'd do if I lost you."

"Yeah, well, I'm hard to—" I began before Sonia caught sight of what came up behind me. I sensed the alertness of the rest of the group. Their fear from moments ago transformed into confusion. "Look who I found."

My attempt at lifting the mood deemed unsuccessful. Several of the pack stood in a defensive manner. Those who were still wolves dipped their heads and snarled. Neera got in front of her sisters, shielding them from the unfamiliar Gwylis in their midst. The only one who recognized my father for who he truly was had been Branch. His face went slack and his fists curled at his sides.

"It's not true," he stammered. His mouth worked for more words, but none came.

Olio spoke up from his perch on the ground. Sonia must have unbuckled him from her back and shifted soon after the quake stopped. "I said the same thing when Izzy told me he'd changed her into a wolf." He looked past me. "You did change her, right? She wasn't lying?"

Aquarius tensed at the question. "No, why would she—"

I held up my hand to stop him. "Olio's just jesting," I said and wiped the same hand down my face in exasperation.

"How are you here?" Branch asked.

Cas tilted her head. "Who is this? Who are you?"

"That's Aquarius," Neera whispered, as much in shock as the rest of the group. "That is your king."

My lips curled. "*Was* your king."

Mack and Des shouldered past Neera to get a better look. Des snorted. "We have a king?"

"Apparently we don't have king anymore," Olio said from the back of the group. "They either disappear or die. Queens too."

"Olio, shut up, please," Branch said.

"I don't pretend to be your ruler any longer," Aquarius said, his voice low and rumbling like the rockslide we'd all survived. "But Izzy—"

Time slowed to a crawl. "What about Izzy?"

Someone let out a gasp, and the name reverberated from mouth to mouth. *Izzy. Izzy. Izzy.* Like an echo.

"I was on a ship with her and the prince," Aquarius said, sitting on his haunches as if we weren't on a mountain in the middle of nowhere and rather in a warm room sipping tea and eating cheesecakes. "After Stormwall fell, we fled. Izzy had been..." He paused, and my muscles tightened.

"She had been what?" I growled.

"She was sad."

I winced, but quickly recovered. "She was sad," I said in a flat voice.

Aquarius bowed his head. "More than sad, she was angry at me for not coming to her aid until it was too late, although she would not tell you otherwise. The ship was attacked, and the crew and I survived. Izzy and the prince escaped before the worst of it. They were going to Essex."

I heard a murmuring from behind me, but all I could focus on was the old wolf in front of me. For years, I stewed in my anger, imagining a meeting such as this where I would tear the king apart before any explanations could be made. I needed none. I swallowed down a rush of nausea. Revenge was not what I needed right now.

I drew in a calming breath. "Why were they going to Essex?"

Aquarius stared. "You don't know, do you?" He bowed his head. "No, you don't. Of course not. Dal Paratheon kidnapped children and turned them into Gwylis. She learned they were being kept somewhere in that city."

I reeled. "Oh, gods. And she and the prince were going to, what? Rescue them?"

Aquarius said nothing, which was worse than answering.

I closed my eyes as my stomach pitched. My father's words sent a shiver of fear through me. Izzy was walking into a death trap if she were going to Essex. She was only one wolf. One person. The prince had one arms, for gods' sakes!

She'd deviated from the plan. Could I blame her? If I were to put myself in her position, I'd have done the same. Nothing came before children who need saving. She'd been destroyed when Ghetee died. She would not have any more children's deaths on her hands. If I truly knew her, she'd do anything to prevent that. Even give her own life.

"You should have stayed with her." I used a carefully controlled tone, but the anguish washed over me anyway. "She's only one. We are many. We don't need you here." My rage took on an almost physical force. *"You should have stayed with her."*

I smelled my sister's scent near me. "Fray, not here."

I withdrew a few steps, as far as this small area would allow, examining my father. He was so familiar to me, yet so foreign. The past crept up to me, and unbidden, I saw it all:

The battle the night before had broken King Rowan's army. We felt victory. We tasted it on our tongues and wiped it from the tips of our claws and our teeth.

"You fought well."

To be addressed by the king was an honor. I bowed my head as he passed, as did the other wolves who'd fallen in beside me. We felt pride in our bellies. Honor for have fought so bravely. We were still quivering with battle rage, excitement from the kills. The humans did not stand a chance against us. Why did they keep trying?

I'd be glad when they were all destroyed. Every one of them.

"Tomorrow," our king said, addressing the Gwylis army. We were a thousand deep, all fur and teeth and fury. "We will not hold back. Tomorrow will be the end of it all. We have given them chances to flee. No more chances."

"For our people!"

For our people. The last words we'd ever speak again.

But the next morning, after breakfast, when we'd all drunk the water from the wells, we found our voices stolen.

The Voiceless were born. And Aquarius ran in shame.

Now in the present, the same anger returned. "You ran again. You abandoned the only hope we have! We're on a fool's errand here. We're slowly changing into demons, Branch is going crazy, and you left her."

"Is this a fool's errand?" Des's voice came out tiny, like a mouse.

Neera sighed heavily.

"Branch has always been crazy," Olio said.

"It is not a fool's errand," Aquarius said. He looked to Branch and bowed his head slightly. "You were right in leading them to Tamazot. You need an army, and a big one at that. That includes getting back into the gods' good favor." He turned back to me. "You say you're becoming demons? Show me."

My hands trembled as I withdrew the shoulder of my tunic. "Not all of us have it, but Olio over there. He sprouted wings and tried to fly."

Olio blew out a breath. "I didn't do a good job of it."

Aquarius nodded his large head. "I saw winged creatures. They attacked the ship I was on. They were abominations."

"Yes, they are," I said, staring into my father's yellow eyes. "And you did it to us. You've damned us all."

Aquarius's silence spoke volumes, and the ground threatened to give way beneath me. Now was the moment I'd shift and tear out his throat, if my plots of revenge had come to fruition.

But they didn't. Blaming Aquarius felt hollow. I still felt the same. I was only repeating what we all knew. And it would do me no good to keep on with the anger I'd held onto for so long that it became a part of me. What would it be like never to feel that again? I wouldn't know what to do without it.

But before I could say anything else, Branch came forward and relieved me. With my head bowed, I walked into my sister's waiting arms.

I was going to be sick.

"We have to keep moving," someone said. "But it's too steep as a wolf. We must go as a human."

"How are we supposed to carry Olio?" Neera asked.

A deep dread filled the space in my belly. They'd better not suggest leaving Olio behind, or I'd bring this mountain down myself.

But they didn't. Instead, it was Aquarius who answered.

"Let me."

I finally pulled away from Sonia's chest and turned to the old wolf. "You're expended," I said. "I can tell."

I looked to Branch, but he offered no ideas. Fine. That was how it was going to be?

"The rest of you, head up," Aquarius said, standing. "Leave the boy with me."

Olio snorted. "You make me feel so young, Your Majesty."

The group gathered themselves and climbed to the best of their abilities. The rockslide had moved the structure of the mountain, leaving large boulders loose and spitting out most of the footholds. But as we went, I realized how close to the top we truly were. When I pulled myself up for the final time, I kneeled over the edge and caught a glimpse of Aquarius down below.

"Step back," he called up. "All of you!"

I stood and held out my arms to keep the rest of group away from the edge when they ascended. The stillness of the night gave way to a sudden burst of air that shot upward toward us. Olio came with it, bobbing atop the magic and landing safely as our feet.

"That was amazing," Des said.

That was a Gwylis king's magic.

With the group safely together, I took a moment to find Branch. He stood away from the rest, facing the horizon in the distance. The clouds shaded the moon, but there was a spattering of stars above, just enough to remind me that I was not dead yet.

"I shouldn't have challenged you the way I had," I told him, keeping a few paces behind. When he didn't move, I took another step. "It was wrong of me. I am not an official member of this pack, and I should not have—"

"Stop."

My breath stalled. Whatever Branch had planned for my punishment would be well-earned. I was out of place, and because of me, we all nearly died.

"I pushed you," I continued. "It was my fault."

Branch bowed his head. "I said stop. We're here."

I stiffened. "We're where?"

But Branch did not answer. Steeling myself, I approached him and followed his line of sight to, not the top of a mountain, but to the crater of a massive volcano.

Izzy's dead.

The voice came from everywhere, expanding my already heavy core.

There's nothing here but death.

"Do you still not believe in us, Fray Castor?"

An image appeared in my mind. Or maybe I was seeing it in front of my eyes. It flickered in and out, like the night I'd seen Izzy in the bonfire.

I sucked in a breath. Izzy. She was standing in front of the prince. Her head bowed listlessly. Her hair had been shorn off, and stuck up in erratic spikes. She looked exhausted, her shoulders slumped forward. All her fire was gone. "Izzy," I whispered, my heart aching.

As soon as her name left my lips, her eyes glanced to the sky. She moved closer to the prince.

My heart quickened its pace. What was she doing?

"Stay there," I said. "I'm coming for you."

Something disappeared into her chest, and she fell forward onto the prince, slumped as if in death.

I reached out, a scream awaiting in my throat.

I paused, my breath suspended as my eyes latched onto the way she fell. The way her chest stopped rising and falling.

My legs buckled, and I dropped to my knees against the rocky earth. My entire body spasmed with ferocious sobs as the pack watched on, the image fading.

Izzy.

My mate. My love.

Dead.

"No," I sobbed aloud, my heart falling in fragments at my feet. I drew myself back onto both feet. "What was that?"

My question was a plea.

Nobody answered.

"What was that?" I repeated, ice filling my veins, magic thick and potent. "What just happened?"

Are you worthy?

Ice exploded from my fingertips as I raised my eyes to the pack; to Branch, who looked back, his expression dark. "Stop!" I demanded. None of this was real. It couldn't be. "They're fooling with us." The Uncanny were trying to get us to break. "Is that what's happening?"

The voice that answered came from everywhere, all at once. It fell from the sky and rose from the earth. It was the wind and the sky and the earth. And it filled me up.

"That," the gods all spoke at once, "was a sacrifice."

Someone screamed. Maybe one of Neera's sisters. I turned to find Des, Mac, and Cas on their knees. I scanned everybody's faces, registering their shock and terror. Relief poured through, as I hadn't been the only one hallucinating. But as the moments passed, I remained the only one not taking a knee.

"Show me Izzy." My words were cold steel. "Show her to me again. If you're gods, you could do it again."

The sky gaped, parting the clouds like someone opening a book. Although it was still the dead of night, a light broke through. "We do not take orders from human men."

The ground—the volcano—rumbled, and most of the group fell to all fours, steadying themselves. Neera threw herself onto her sisters; Sonia grabbed Olio and wrapped her arms around him. She made a move to grab me, but I stepped away. Only Aquarius and I stood, our eyes skyward.

"I did it," the former king said, his voice low and grated. "Do not punish them for my mistakes."

The world grew quiet, and then, "You all wanted to be gods. The demons below lied to you, as they did when they were not Uncanny. Did you hate us so much that you would give away your very souls?"

The question lined itself with, not anger as I expected, but sadness. It weighed upon our shoulders. Aquarius sank to his belly. "Forgive me."

I drew in a breath. "That is why you came here?" I asked my father. "That is why you followed us? Not for me, but for the gods?"

Aquarius nodded his head warily. "Do not feel envy," he said. "For I have thought of you every day since."

A rush of anger bolted through me. "You're a liar, and the gods will never forgive you, nor will I."

A rustle of wings took my attention from Aquarius. A murder of crows hovered and landed along the lip of the crater behind us. They watched in silence, their heads tilting back and forth.

The tension grew within the group as we watched the crows take flight, forming a great black cloud above our head. They scattered, reformed, and then suddenly, they took shape. With wide eyes, I watched as the birds solidified into a figure descending onto the ground before us.

The woman wore nothing, her dark skin unmarred from head to toe. Her eyes were a pale blue and her hair hung in thick black waves.

The god's eyes roamed over the group before settling on me. When she spoke, it felt like a whisper, tickling my ear. It reminded me of my mother when she'd sing to me when I was very young. "I see nothing has changed, Fray Castor."

I tensed as she moved closer and leaned in. "Your heart is here with me, and she seeks yours in return."

I drew in a staggered breath. Sonia stepped toward me, but the god stopped her with a flick of her wrist.

"Is it true?" I asked, the very thought pricking my skin. "Is she dead?"

"Without her, you are nothing. You walk this earth a blank parchment, brittle, easily burned. Your armies will fall to demons. You will never defeat them. You—" Her light eyes found Aquarius. "You are weak." She looked back to me. "But you have the ability to lead a great force in victory. Humans. Wolves. And those in-between. But if you do not work together, you will fail."

The words faded. The thought of the prince—Ashe Paratheon—killing Izzy immediately rendered my strength useless. What had happened? Why did he take away our only chance at survival?

The word fell out of me. "Why?"

The god tilted her head. "She lingers, here with me. She's waiting for you."

"Then kill me."

Pain bloomed through me as I forced the words out again. I could not bear to think of her all alone. She may be dead, but I was dying here on earth, under the heavens. Without her, what was left for me?

I feel like I don't have a place where I belong, she'd once told me. I knew where she belonged. With me, in life or death.

Let me be with her.

I pushed through the tears, through the gaping horror of my own words. "Take me to her, please."

Let me be with her.

Someone gasped. Sonia, maybe. Or maybe it was my own shock and fear.

"If you want our aid, it requires a great sacrifice. Isabelle Rowan has made her own, as Ashton Paratheon has made his. Are you prepared to do the same?"

I took a tentative step back, prepared to ask for a weapon. Anything that would stop my heart from beating. If it saved Mirosa, if it returned me to Izzy, let it be done.

"She is not gone." The god held my gaze. "If she decides, she will return and raze destruction upon the Uncanny. Her decision depends on yours. We alone can break the demon curse. We can return your souls. I see your look. I know your thoughts: Why didn't we do so before? We created humans with free will, and we vowed never to intervene if not asked. Humans squandered the gifts we gave. You sought to separate from the gods. You found your magic too small. Not powerful enough. And now?"

"Now, we want it back," Neera said. Her sisters whimpered, and she held them tightly. "I don't want to be cursed anymore."

"You cruel things," I hissed through my teeth. "You could have helped us."

"We didn't ask," Neera said. "Not one of us. Not Rixon. Not the elders. Nobody."

Half of us were rendered voiceless. How could we have asked? But I knew better. I wouldn't have come here. I wouldn't have bothered. Being a Gwylis was all I ever knew. I wouldn't know how to be human.

"If we give a sacrifice?" I asked. "Another ritual?"

A slow smile stretched across the god's perfect face. "A life, as payment."

I looked to the ground and nodded, thinking of Izzy. Always thinking of Izzy, even when I tried not to. "So be—"

"No!" Sonia bounded forward, pushing me back and shielding me with her body. "Take me instead."

I grabbed her arm. "Stop. This isn't your decision to make."

"But isn't it?" the god asked. "You are one people, are you not?"

I held onto my sister, gripping her arms. "I won't let you."

"And I won't let you." Her eyes were hard, unrelenting. They mirrored my own.

"I'll do it," Branch said, speaking up for the first time in what felt like hours. "I led you here. I am the leader. It's only fitting—"

I shook my head. "No, you can't."

The god narrowed her vision, her expression impatient. Almost dangerous. "I need only one."

"Stop it!" Sonia cried out. "I'm not losing any one of you."

"Then you doom your people forever. The Uncanny will walk this earth. You doom everyone to death."

I gripped my temples and turned away. "Let me," I hissed to my sister. "Izzy's gone. Let me be with her."

Sonia stood motionless, her arm loose at her side, her eyes watery and bright. She knew better than anyone what doomed love felt like; how the Rowans took our hearts and refused to let them go. Which was why I knew she understood. I could sense it in the way only a brother and sister could. How a wolf could. "I will follow soon after, brother. I will go to war, and I will until my last breath. For you. For Izzy. For Henry. For—" She swallowed a sob and smiled weakly. "For our people."

I returned the smile and looked over the group that had journeyed so far. To Neera and her sisters, who sobbed uncontrollably. To Olio who only gave a tight-lipped smile, ever the friend. To Branch, my leader. Finally, to the god who waited for me. "Finally, I found my place in the world."

Three things happened.

A blade, shining with the light of thousand suns, flashed across my vision.

Someone screamed.

And a peaceful respite coursed through my body.

I stood tall until my eyes fluttered closed and I was falling, falling, falling...

∼

DAYBREAK HAD COME BY THE TIME I'D OPENED MY EYES. I stumbled to my feet into a world of utter silence, fields stretching far into the horizon. Disoriented, I wretched into a pile of bright green grass. I squeezed my eyes closed and went to a place in my mind, listening for anything. A breath. A heartbeat. But there was nothing.

A bird fluttered nearby, and I blinked through foggy eyes. Slowly, someone came into focus. A girl. She wore a gown fitting for a princess. Her hair was unbound, black as a crow's, and her eyes, filled with mischief, flashed to me. She shouldered her bow and winked. "There you are," she said. "Took you long enough."

And then I saw them—or what they wanted me to see. For the gods were not human, but a culmination of the world itself. Light. Dark. The water and the sky. The animals and the trees.

They stood less than fifty meters away, all in row. Hundreds of them. Figures made of the sun, glowing with ethereal wonder. "Do you believe in us now?" they asked.

I blinked rapidly, fighting the tears. I took one step and then another until I fell to my knees. "I never disbelieved," I said softly. "I was corrupted."

"We know the story," they said. "We know everything. We followed our creations—every decision, every mistake, every breath, and every word. We watched the world fall into chaos, and we did not blink. We watched you lose your voice, and we did not weep. But the time has come for intervention. When your lover called on us, how could we ignore it?"

I sputtered my words. "The three jewels, they worked?"

"Not in the way you think. Evocation is more than uttering a few words and thinking the world will again balance itself. Your ancestors bore great power, harnessing the powers of nature to enhance their abilities for good." I bowed my head, filled with shame. "But I am not here to admonish you for the past. You may have been corrupted by the Uncanny, but it does not mean that you are fated to die. You still hold the power of us within you. Lying dormant, waiting for the ones born with the hearts to remember. Separate, you are a force, but together, you are an unstoppable army."

You were born for so much more than this, Sonia had said. Had she known the gods would feel the same way?

"The old gods still protect their land," they said. "We cast away evil from our skies, and we will not let it consume what we made."

"So, you had me killed just to tell me that?"

The mass of gods emanated glow reminded me of a campfire. My body rushed with warmth. "We did not kill you. The girl, Neera did."

A horrible stillness stole over me.

Sounds to me like you're afraid. Neera's words whispered through my ears.

I lowered my chin to my chest. *Oh, Neera, now you must bear that burden.*

"Enough talk." Without saying its name, I knew the figure moving toward me was the god of life, Tyvasi. "We came to you, the girl, Isabelle, and the boy, Ashe because we saw a spark in your hearts, and it made us proud. Unlike the dark powers of the Uncanny, the old gods gave you magic that heals the world around you, and grows through every element. The Uncanny took the buried power inside of you and turned it into something all-consuming. When we remove the curse set upon you, it will leave you vulnerable, and those who have consumed will fail to be free of the demons. You will have to be human. You will have to be strong enough to destroy them. Are you enough?

"Your only hope is the spark in your heart, the love that binds you and strengthens you. The forgiveness for your father and ability to move away from your past and look toward your future and become the man you were meant to be. Are you that man?" I took a deep breath and nodded. "Then you will not fail."

In a blinding flash, the gods all vanished and I stood alone, blue sky above me, green earth underfoot. All at once, my chest heaved, and my belly lurched as the thump of my heartbeat returned. This was not the end for me. I was enough.

"Now, wake up."

CHAPTER THIRTY-THREE

When I arrived in Alaster a week later, I found Derwin and Flea waiting for me, sipping drinks on an outside patio of a restaurant whose sign flaunted "the best eel in the New Kingdom." They did not stand, but looked past me to where someone would be standing if things hadn't gone so completely wrong.

I'd not buried Izzy. I couldn't bring myself to do it. She at least deserved to rest where she was born; a place she fought for to the bitter end. Instead, I wrapped her in my cloak and took care to ride to the nearest town, where I purchased a wagon and a casket, and laid her to rest comfortably. I set the three jewels, her dagger, and Henry's journal atop her chest. I set off for Alaster.

After securing a room at the same inn I'd stayed with Izzy, I left my horse and wagon with a stableman and made my way to the shipyard. After seeing what I needed to see, I went to find the rest.

I managed the entire journey without shedding a tear. Had I gone numb? I now understood how easily people managed to go on with their lives after doing such a thing. My mind made a move to block any and all emotions from seeping through. Thanks to that, I'd managed to make the journey back to Alaster and to the place where I'd assembled a rebellion.

Before I made the journey, I sent a crow to Moora. The same exhausted crow made it back to me within days, informing of the pirate's survival. Moora did not mention much else, but in the words, I felt her fear. I was coming back to Stormwall to finish what Izzy had started.

There would be time for grief, but it wasn't now.

"Izzy is gone," I said as I sat. I took Flea's cup and drained its contents. Water. How disappointing. "It's just us now."

Both men bowed their heads in reverence.

I did not tell them about how she'd died, or that I had transported her body. Or how her lips stayed rosy pink and now, I even imagined her eyelashes fluttered. How would I begin to explain the strangeness of it all?

"More than a hundred ships," Derwin said. "How did you manage such a feat?"

Not without sacrifice, I thought. But instead of answering, I took Derwin's cup and downed the drink inside. Turns out, this one was ale, and it burned its way down my throat. When the waitress passed by, I ordered another. She looked at me strangely, maybe noting how dirty and near death I looked. After nodding to my order, she suggested a nearby bathhouse. I almost laughed.

"She ain't wrong," Derwin said into his cup.

This time I did laugh, and for a moment, it felt genuine. Like things would be all right in the end for a one-armed prince leading a rebellion of humans and wolves.

I laughed, because maybe my time would be nearer.

"There's something different about you," Derwin mused. "Something different about everything. The sun, the moon, the very air I breathe. It feels—"

"Different?" Flea finished.

Derwin shook his head. "No, it feels better. Does that make sense?"

It did make sense, to me. During my journey back to Alaster, something had gone and colored the world a little brighter. Oddly enough, I thought losing Izzy would have bathed it all in grey, but somehow, her death had done the opposite. It changed things.

I tapped my fingers on the table. "Izzy's not dead. She's here, all around us."

I'd done what the gods asked of me, but would I be rewarded? Would I win back the throne that Izzy, and many others, had died for?

Although the world felt different, I did not. I was still a mortal man, not a drop of magic in my blood, but only the strength of the men and women behind me as my weapon.

It had to be enough.

The drinks came and kept on coming, and although the three of us talked about nothing of substance, we still took comfort in knowing we were together, and if we died tomorrow, we would die knowing we tried.

We tried.

When we'd had enough, we put our arms around each other's shoulders and stumbled our way back to the inn. We marveled at the night sky as we went, commenting on the quarter moon and how bright it glowed, even in our drunken state.

"Yes, but look at the stars," Derwin said, dropping his arm from my shoulder to point. "I've sailed the oceans and mapped the stars, but look, those constellations, they're different. The stars have moved."

Impossible, I thought. *Stars don't move.*

Derwin must have seen the doubt in my face. "Don't be an idiot, boy. You know as well as I do that Isabelle did not fail."

Hope stirred in my chest.

"What are you babbling about?" Flea asked.

Derwin shoved a finger to the night sky. "The gods have opened their eyes."

We would leave tonight, under cover of darkness. Talk above stars and gods would have to wait. I needed to meet the men and women on those ships.

Nevertheless, I prayed to the gods. I prayed I would be forgiven for what I'd done; prayed that at least I'd done what they asked of me; and that they had already set me in their favor. And more than that, I prayed that Izzy would get to rest in her home with her cousin and brother who'd gone before her.

Henry, please know I never meant to do her harm.

What would happen if we did win this war? Would I stomach being called a king? I let the thought linger for a moment before shoving it away.

I wouldn't become one if I didn't stop wasting time worrying.

Derwin moved from under my arm and stood to face Flea and me. "I will follow, Ashe Paratheon, to the very edges of the seven hells and beyond. Not because there is a lack of royals around nowadays, but because I trust you. I trust you."

I clasped Derwin's shoulder. "Thank you."

Derwin pushed my hand away. "Thank me when you've taken Stormwall."

~

DERWIN AND I HEADED TO THE DOCKS ON HORSES BEARING THE sun and moon crest of the rebellion, stitched in both silver and red. For the Peek Islands and for Mirosa. A wave of people took us to a large ship with a wild-eyed sea monster as its figurehead. On deck, Derwin shoved a cup of ale into my hands. All around us, the crew raised their own cups, and cheers followed. I clanged dozens of cups and shook hands with people whose names I would forget tomorrow. The excitement had dulled the pain. There were too many lords and ladies sacrificing their men and women for me, and too much riding on our next moves to dwell on the past. I had a feeling it would come at me at breakneck speed once all this was over.

I raised my cup, ale sloshing around and dripping down my arm. "For Mirosa!"

A cacophony echoed my words; every time was like a jolt in my heart. The exhilaration coursed through me as strong as those two words. It slashed any doubts I'd ever had about retaking Stormwall.

I moved across the deck, looking over the ocean and the dark silhouettes on the horizon. Derwin said there were over a hundred ships out there. More than I ever imagined possible. Were the Peek Islands out there?

"Aquarius saved our lives," Derwin said, coming up beside me. The sun was setting, and the evening cooled. "There were these winged creatures, you see, bigger than anything I ever seen in my life, and I've seen some things, let me tell you. That old man, he gave it all he had. I'd never seen magic like that. Once we were safe on the boats, he told me to sail back to Alaster and not to go after you." I turned to look at him and he frowned. "Don't you think I wanted to? That was my queen."

The last four words he spoke in more of a whisper as he looked off to the ocean. I studied his face, his missing eye and turned down expression. He looked anguished.

"Izzy touched a lot of people," I said, rubbing my stinging eyes. I had not slept much in...weeks. Months. Even my bones felt fragile. Sleep was for the weak. Besides, there were too many monsters waiting for me to close my eyes.

Derwin nodded, but said nothing more.

"How long until they notice we're here?" I asked.

A flowery smell hit my senses and I turned, Derwin with me. Moora had stepped onto the deck. She clutched her cloak to her chest, eyes scanning the area.

My heart beat a fast rhythm. Who was she looking for?

She glanced about until her eyes finally found mine. She smiled. As she neared, I noted the shadows beneath her eyes and the pallor of her skin. The closer she got, the nearer I came to being breathless. She'd worked so hard for a cause I had all but abandoned, in hopes it would be there when I returned. She kept it alive.

"I told you I'd see you again," she said, ignoring Derwin. The pirate took the hint, bowed, and left us. "Where is the arm? Have you used it?"

"No, not yet."

"Oh." The word was barely audible over the waves. "But I am glad you returned safely. I worried for you."

"You didn't have to worry about me." My voice grew deep, and cracked in places.

"Ashe, you need rest."

Rest. What a strange word. "What I need is—"

Moora pulled me into her arms, wrapping me tightly in her embrace. "A friend," she finished, and rested her head on my shoulder. My body tensed at first, but then it settled against her, giving in to this quiet moment.

Friend. The word broke through my misery. I had begun to feel like I would never be anything to anyone ever again. That my odds of surviving the coming weeks were horrifically bad.

I was scared. Terrified, even.

Moora took me in tighter. "You are not alone, Ashe Paratheon."

She let her arms fall away and stepped back from me. The wind picked up, whipping our hair into our faces. I let my mind imagine that maybe this wasn't the end for me. When we retook Stormwall, they could vote on whoever they wanted to be their ruler, and then, maybe I could go home. Or I could stay here on a ship like this and sail the waters, discovering new lands.

Now, I knew what Izzy wanted.

Happiness.

And more than anything, a desire to be loved.

CHAPTER THIRTY-FOUR

I felt like I'd been dreaming.

I opened my eyes and found the sky just the way I'd left it, the world the way I left it. The crater. Sonia screaming. Someone crying. And Branch's eyes wide as saucers.

Shit.

I sat up. The wound in my chest had gone, but there was a tear in my tunic and a pink scar as if it had months to heal. But I'd only been gone for minutes, I was sure of it.

Sonia snapped out of it first, falling to her knees and squeezing my fiercely. "I thought I'd lost you!"

I couldn't breathe. "Let me stand."

Sonia let me go, albeit slowly, and helped me to stand. I looked over the group, meeting each set of eyes until they settled on Neera.

"You killed me," I said.

Neera shook her head vigorously. She had her hands behind her back, held by a another Gwylis—Cairn was his name, perhaps? "They told me to do it," she cried. "They said it'd be all right, and that it would save us if I did it. I didn't want to, Fray, believe me!"

The gods had gone, but I still felt their presence; my body was heavy, like a stone slab were on my shoulders. I clutched my fist to my heart and squeezed my eyes closed. *It's not possible. It's not—*

"Fray."

I opened my eyes to see Aquarius, in human form. Someone had draped a cloak over his shoulders. He looked so feeble, like a breeze would blow him over.

I sucked in a breath, not at Aquarius, but at Olio, who stood and cracked his back like he was just waking up. No longer injured. No longer saddled with a curse. "We're humans."

Dawn inched its way up on the horizon. Golden light, surrounding me like a cloak. If I looked hard enough, I could see a shadow in the rising sun, just there at the far edge of the crater. Overhead, crows circled, bursting to and fro like buds greeting the sunlight until they gathered around the figure, solidifying into the shape of a woman. "Now, use your hearts and souls for good," the god said.

"Why me?" I asked. I wasn't special. Not in the way Branch and even Aquarius were in terms of strength and greatness.

"Because you were created with love. You survived on love. You died for love. You were killed for love."

My chest throbbed with the faithlessness I had come to know, and in the truth I could no longer deny.

"The gods are with you now," she said. Sonia held my arm, and Branch pulled up the rear. "We've always been with you."

Black wings took flight, followed by several more until the dawn became a blot of wings. I thought of the crows back at Stormwall, how Izzy had befriended a one named Pax. I remembered seeing crows all along our journey here. Had they been following me? Were they shadowing Izzy just the same?

Maybe crows weren't messengers of the gods, after all. Perhaps they were gods themselves.

"Now that the curse has been broken, you are free to fight as humans will," the god said. "But I must warn you: The Uncanny have taken hold to the weakest, changing them into something grotesque—something we cannot heal. You may have lost your demon magic, but you still have the gifts of the gods."

"Fray!"

I turned to find a blade, soaked in blood. My blood. Branch hefted it from the ground where it lay, as it suddenly emanated a soft light, like a firefly.

"Go west, over the mountains once again, and destroy those monsters. The Uncanny are not weak; they never have been. And you have been given the tools. You only have to be strong enough.

"Your strength is your love for one another. And it will be your salvation." The crows dispersed and disappeared like a puff of smoke. "With love, you cannot fail." Then the world was quiet, a deep inhalation of hope.

I turned to the rest of my pack. "How fast can we return to the Den?"

CHAPTER THIRTY-FIVE

Henry came into my room in the dead of night when only ghosts roam. I'd been awake, listening to the sounds of my father as he raged down the hallway, probably in a fit about something or another. How I'd learned to love the quiet when Mirosa's king was away.

Henry slipped under the covers and nudged me to make room. When I obliged, he draped the covers over us, turned to face me, and began a story.

"In the Land of Ner, there lived a boy named Fern. Fern who once found an injured wolf on his way to a neighboring town. The wolf asked the boy for help, and the boy asked for compensation: a pelt from a wolf in his pack for a new coat. The wolf agreed, and the boy cleaned and dressed the wolf's wound. When the boy asked for his reward, the wolf smiled wickedly, saying, 'Your reward is that I have not killed you.'"

"What is the moral of this story?" I asked.

Henry turned away. "The moral is that when serve evil, be grateful you have not lost your head."

I pondered this for several minutes before speaking.

"I will never serve evil, and you shouldn't either."

"But if you're forced to, don't expect anything from the evil-doers, just suffering."

I couldn't imagine being forced to serve bad people. It didn't seem *like something either of us would ever do. We were Rowans. Nobility and courage ran through our veins. But the doubt crept in and made my skin prickle. I scooted closer to Henry until I felt his warmth and asked, "Why would we be forced to serve wicked people?"*

LIVING IN DARKNESS WAS DIFFERENT THIS TIME. IN MY DEMON-riddled body, at least there was the sun to cast some sort of lightness in my life. But this darkness was so thick, so absolute. I feared no light had ever lived here.

You've come to the end, my daughter. How do you feel?

The voice was airy and came from everywhere. I should have been scared, but there was nothing left to fear. I'd already failed and died. There was nothing much else.

Or so I thought.

I stood in that darkness, or at least I thought I did. Was I part this darkness, with only a subconscious?

That terrified me.

Ashe Paratheon had killed me. He stuck my own dagger into my chest, and in turn stopped my heart and the demons inside of me. I smiled inwardly. I knew that boy was good for something. But oh, would he suffer.

I sighed. I did not want to see him alone, not after all he'd done for me.

For all he'd done for Mirosa.

But he was alone. So was Fray and everyone else I'd ever come to love. There was a war still going on. There was much more to do. So much I had yet to finish.

Are you not ready to leave yet?

"No."

The word was final. Absolute. I was not ready. I still had much to do.

Do you find yourself worthy of the gods?

Did I? I couldn't see how I could ever be worthy. I'd forsaken them by becoming a Gwylis. I'd killed many people. And the one good thing— the light that shone through the darkness—was Fray, and I left him. I might as well have killed him too. I defied my family. I was arrogant and fool-hardy. I gave up the throne, twice. I let those little girls die. I let a lot of people die.

Henry. Lulu. Ghetee. Tyron. All of those children...

Who else?

No, I was not worthy of anything but the death I'd been given.

But I could be.

If I had a body left, I would have probably felt my heart stutter. This wasn't how it worked. Death was death. Ashe killed me. This was not something to negotiate.

The children of Mirosa are worthy.

"The adults, not so much."

The voice sounded as though it were laughing.

Yes, there has been much done to ensure our absence.

Not their absence, but ours.

The gods.

Do you wish to return to the mortal world?

I felt it, the urge to say yes. To beg these gods to bring me back to the land of the living. But what would I do there? I was nothing more than a vessel. If the demons were dead, I had no magic left. How could I save Mirosa then? What good could I do?

I feel the hunger in your heart, daughter. I feel the need for good. No matter what you've done, I know in your soul that you are not the evil you think you are.

A sob wracked my chest. Did I have a chest? Something ached in the place it would be. "I've come so far, and still I failed. We all failed."

No, you didn't. The prince proved his worthiness. The one you love, he also proved that he is worthy our own favor. You, the princess—the queen. You are worthy of our favor.

Was that what all of this was about—the three jewels, Ashe doing what he'd done? It was all a test.

And I had passed.

But it wasn't over. Not yet.

"Will you help me fight the Uncanny, then?"

What an absurd idea. Death was supposed to be an end to my life, an end to any suffering I'd endured in the mortal world. But I did not feel an end to anything. I felt a beginning, and it pulled and pulled.

I found myself in an emerald field. A boy with bright blue eyes and messy brown hair lingered nearby. I saw him clearly in all the ways my mind refused to see him. *There you are*, I thought. *Took you long enough.*

How funny that it could all be so simple. That love was the thing I fought for—the thing I'd suffered for. And no matter how hard I wanted to deny what I felt for Fray, deep inside, it had been the only thing that kept me going. I powered forward, and every step I took was for him.

From the moment he'd carried me from the forest, dying, I'd lived for him.

Death would not keep me from him now. Not after everything.

I snorted, for not even the gods could not keep me away. "Take me back."

Yes, daughter, now wake up.

I OPENED MY EYES TO DARKNESS, MY BODY STIFF AND SORE. My lungs opened, and I gulped in air. The ache centralized there in my chest and turned quickly to an agonizing pain that fired through every limb. I screamed, but it sounded hollow.

I vaguely remembered what had happened. I even felt Ashe's fear and panic as he sunk my own dagger into my heart. He'd only meant to relieve me of my curse and the deal I'd made with the Uncanny. I knew his heart broke and was probably still breaking. I knew even now that he would trudge on and survive.

I talked to the gods, and they told me to wake up. But where was I?

I was so tired, so heavy, that only the lingering pain kept me awake. I took a cautious deep breath and the pain flared again. I lifted my hand only to find something obstructing me on all sides, like I was lying in a box. My hands smoothed over my tunic. Something slid off me and landed somewhere on the side where I couldn't reach. I slid my hand underneath the cloth, against my breast. I carefully found the area of the pain, gently moving my fingers over a large, raised scar.

My breath hitched in my throat, but before I could scream for help again, something snapped within me. Like a thin rope pulled too tight, it finally broke, and a flash of white light lit up the darkness.

A scar.

Pain.

I was human.

Tears burned my eyes. Death had come for me, and it came with a welcome relief. The journey had been long and filled with disappointments, and I'd been so tired that all I wanted to do was sleep. It did not matter what else happened around me. The world could burn, and I would sleep.

But the gods had spoken to me. They gave me life again, and although it was currently full of pain and fear, I felt more alive than I ever had.

Using my reserved strength, I pushed the ceiling above me. At first it didn't budge, so I bent my knees for extra leverage. My lungs seized as I exhausted my air supply. Depending on how long I'd be breathing in here, I knew I didn't have long before I'd fall into a coma. That might be why I was so sleepy. I had to act quickly.

My arms burned and protested, but I kept at it, pushing and knocking against it until finally it gave way. Something clanged, and wood splintered as the lid was thrown off. I threw my arms in front of my face, preparing for the onslaught of dirt, but there was nothing but the fresh taste of air. I hadn't been buried at all.

I carefully sat up. My body felt as though it was filled with air. I moved my legs as slowly as I could, but they still seemed to move too fast. As I stood, my head became dizzy, and I had to brace myself on a nearby wall.

How lonely it would be if the demons ever left me. I'd spent so long in their presence that I'd forgotten what it was like to live without. Was this what I was before I let Aquarius bite me? Was my body truly this fragile?

The floor lurched beneath my feet, and I tilted backwards. I feared this was another side-effect of being human, but the room truly was moving. I noticed a small window behind me. Blinking, I pressed my face against the edge and peered outside.

An endless expanse of blue stretched out before me. I let my body relax as I gazed out at the waves and the pale blue sky. I thought I saw a flash of black soaring above. A crow? Certainly not in the middle of the ocean. Crows didn't belong there.

Did I belong here?

Steeling myself, I turned my sight to the box—the coffin. How strange it was to see the home your body would rest in forevermore. I looked inside to find my dagger, Henry's journal, and the three jewels. Ashe was going to bury me with them. "Such a thoughtful pri—"

I drew in a breath as the door to the room opened.

CHAPTER THIRTY-SIX

"Izzy?"

My legs gave way, and I fell to my knees. Something like a strangled sob erupted from my throat, and before I knew it, I was wrapped in Ashe's arms. He held me as my chest heaved in painful exhales and even more agonizing inhales. I trembled with each one.

We knelt there on the floor what felt like forever. I couldn't let him go. I'd be losing something if I did.

"Izzy," he choked, his eyes shining with tears. "How is this possible?"

It took everything in me to pull away and look into Ashe's face. His eyes were haunted. How long had they been that way?

"The gods said I was worthy." My voice was soft and small. "I remember everything."

Ashe's entire face fell, and tears slipped from his green eyes. "I'm sorry, Izzy."

His sobs nearly broke me, reminded of the last time I saw Fray and how he'd cried over his mother and about everything else he'd kept locked up inside. I hoped this was a release for him. For both of us.

"I thought I lost you." He took my face in his hands and managed a soft smile. "Izzy, gods, I don't ever want to lose you again."

"So, don't kill me again. Deal?"

Ashe's eyes widened with horror, but then his face softened. "Yeah, it's definitely you."

We sat, silently taking each other in, hands roaming across each other's bodies, making sure we were both real.

"Shh," I said, partially to myself. "It's all going to be all right now." I waited until Ashe nodded before getting down to business. "Tell me what has happened."

"You don't waste any time, do you? It's not like you died or anything."

I smiled. "Ashe, I'm human again."

He blinked. "What?"

"The gods broke the curse, for me at least. I'm not sure how this is going to help us, but it happened."

Ashe pushed to his feet. "Say the chant. Do it."

I did, not only to prove my point, but because I had to speak the words that had now become my past. When I got to the end, I spoke clearly and firmly. "I am the beast."

Nothing happened. No stretching of limbs or sprouting of fur. No sharp teeth or long claws. No darkness and no rage. No magic.

With my next breath, I stood with my spine straight and my chin high. "Now, where can I get some food?"

Derwin and Flea sat at the table in the galley while I wolfed down everything they set on the table. Although it was bland, the fish tasted better than anything I'd eaten in a very long time. I slurped water and ale alike until my stomach felt sloshy and my mind cleared.

Flea poked my arm. "You're real? No undead business going on here, right?"

"Have you tried your chant?" I asked Flea. He nodded. "Then this is very real."

The prince proved his worthiness. The one you love, he also proved that he is worthy our own favor. You, the princess—the queen. You are worthy of our favor.

Part of me wanted to question why the gods had chosen me. Had they been following me all this time? What about Henry? Fray? Ashe?

He finally told me what Abiyaya had said to him. Had he been chosen as well?

"How long until we get to Stormwall?" I asked.

"Hours," Derwin replied.

"Then we best prepare."

Ashe's face went hard. He grabbed my wrist as I went to stand. A flash of a memory ignited before my eyes. I saw Ashe and a dozen or more children—all boys—as they played in a courtyard with a fountain in the center, like the one in Stormwall. He wore a crisp uniform, bearing the Bear of Mirosa upon his chest. His hair was cropped short once again. His eyes were happy. The sun warmed his skin.

I gasped at the vision that was not a memory, but a glimpse into the future. I wanted him to have that.

"With the gods on our side, Stormwall is ours," I said. "But we still must fight. The gods can't do everything for us. Ashe, as it turns out, did a lot of the grunt work, so he will lead us into battle."

Derwin sat back in his seat. "What say you, Prince?"

"I say you're all crazy, this one particular." He jabbed a finger my way. "We haven't come this far to turn back now. We have the soldiers, and we have the gods at our back."

The other two men at the table nodded. "And we have the queen," Derwin said, winking his one good eye at me. "Nothing could go wrong."

CHAPTER THIRTY-SEVEN

The chance to revel in my new humanity was short-lived. We began the trek back to the Den faster than the wind could blow us. The faster pack members set the pace, leaving the slower ones such as Aquarius behind. They would meet us soon. For now, we had to hurry.

My muscles ached as I put miles behind me. Sonia and Olio stayed by my side the entire time, stopping little and eating only what we could while we moved. Carefully, we wound our way through the Old Kingdom, aware of our new breakable bodies. Somehow, we still found ourselves traveling mostly at night, like the moon still had a bit of a hold on us.

Perhaps we'd never stop feeling the Uncanny, skittering beneath our skin, clenching our hearts. Would my dreams be haunted by them?

I carried the sword Neera had used to take my life. Now, it glowed with a constant light. A reminder that my old life had been cut away.

A new one awaited.

A day or so from the Den, Olio spoke for the first time in hours, saying, "What do you think we'll find when we pass through the Archway?"

I knew the real question. Would we be alone, or would allies come to our aid?

"I don't know," I said.

Which was all I could say.

We passed the day without any more words. When we came to the gates of the Den, I strode right up to them and howled.

As only a human could howl.

As the gates opened, Sonia drew to my side. "What will you tell them?"

I peered up at the massive wooden doors as they swung open, as if the answer lay there within the cracks. "I'll tell them to fight or die," I said. "Because that's all there is now."

I stalked into the city, taking long gaits.

Fight or die.

CHAPTER THIRTY-EIGHT

It wouldn't have been safe to dock at Stormwall, so we kept a great distance and went a bit further east until we came to the other side of the mountains in a land we used to call the Old Kingdom. From there, we would take small boats and row to shore, entering the new kingdom from the Archway. We would send scouts to the area to make sure the Gywlis had not kept camp in the plains that filled the space between Stormwall and the mountains as they had when we'd first attacked. Knowing Katka, she moved them into the city, and even into the palace itself.

Now on shore, I looked over the massive amounts of men and women who had come to my call. They were all different ages, colors, and sizes, but they had come with one thing in common: to fight.

I walked amongst them, as relief pressed on my heart. Suddenly, a man with a large beard and an old sword took a knee and bowed his head. Several others followed, until hundreds and hundreds of people were paying reverence to me.

Izzy scoffed from behind me. "They didn't even give me a second glance," she said with a snort.

I kept my face neutral. I'd forgotten what it felt like to be a royal and have people respect or even fear you. I did not like that kind of admiration then, and I didn't now.

"How many of you are there?" I said to the bearded man as I gestured for him to stand. He wore loose armor over normal clothes. "Please stand."

"At last tally, we had seven thousand, eight hundred, and sixty-two men and women ready to fight," the man replied.

I bent forward, hands to my knees, breathless. I couldn't believe how many had come. I glanced at Izzy in awe, but she looked away, a small smile on her face.

"Thank you for fighting," she said. "Thank you for being here."

The gods had given us this chance. If I failed now, it would not only mean death for myself, but now, for nearly eight thousand men and women that had come to fight, I could not fail. I would not fail.

THE ARCHWAY WAS AN EERIE SIGHT; ITS MONUMENTAL CURVE reminded me of a mouth wanting to swallow me whole.

The first scouts had returned and reported that the plains were free of any hostiles. It was as I feared. Katka had taken the Gwylis into the city. I imagined what they'd done to it. I feared it was nearly unrecognizable by now.

Days had passed in a haze while we waited for allies to come. The outpouring of camaraderie within my army made my heart swell. I'd done this. I brought Mirosa together. But without the guidance I had, without the rebels, I would not be here. We would not have had a fighting chance.

We made camp beyond the Archway. I watched Izzy as she made her rounds, from tent to tent, campfire to campfire, laughing and embracing and even crying. I took a deep breath, savoring these moments. We'd come such a long way, only to circle back where we started. It was bittersweet.

"You have your thinking face on." Izzy came up beside me, pushing a slice of bread into her mouth. "Who knew death made one so hungry?"

"Please," I scoffed. "You were hungry all the time before all of this."

She met my eyes, a frown on her mouth.

I couldn't help it. I started to laugh.

It took a moment for her to catch on, but when she did, it was relentless. I took her arms and pulled him so close, we were practically dancing. "I never danced with you at the ball."

She threw her head back and chuckled. "That was because I respected you and couldn't bear to give you false hope, Prince of the Peeks."

We swayed together, and for a moment, it felt all right.

"You can let go now, Ashe," Izzy said. "From here on out."

My grip loosened, but not entirely. "Are you sure?"

She nodded and rested her head against my chest. "I'm sure."

Slowly, I released her, but not before gently putting my hand on her cheek. "I am a better man because of you."

"As am I. A better woman, not a man."

My burst of laugher shook my shoulders, and before I knew it, we were both wiping tears from our eyes. Izzy's tears kept coming, long after mine had gone. I dipped my head, concerned. But she spoke before me.

"Thank you, Ashe, for everything."

I lowered my hands and looked away. "Izzy, where does that leave us?" I said. "When this is all over? Do we—"

But before she could answer, a shout cut the air and had us both running toward the sound. A man on a horse came bounding into camp. He jumped from the beast before it'd come to a complete stop. That was when I saw the other body strapped its back.

"They got him!" The scout fell to his knees at my feet and lowered his forehead into the dirt. "My brother..."

I went to the man lying on the horse's back and, with help, lowered the man to the ground. He was alive, but barely. His breathing was staggered. There were deep puncture wounds on his bare arm where his shirt had been torn away. I knew those marks.

I turned to Izzy. "He was bitten?"

The man convulsed so violently that all of us backed away. He cried out in agony, flailing all four limbs. His body arched and fell, arched and fell, and he screamed. Between the sobs of the injured man's brother and the screams, I could not get my bearings.

Part of me knew what this was, but I did not want to believe it.

"Izzy, you know what's happening to that man?"

Her eyes openly stared. "He was bitten by a Gwylis. He is going to change into a wolf."

"I thought the gods broke the curse."

I thought so too. "Looks like the Uncanny got their wish."

I turned to the scout as he watched his brother slowly change from human to monster. "You have to kill him. Now."

The scout's head snapped to face me. But he didn't rebuke the order. He nodded in assent and drew his sword. A moment later, the weapon lay on the ground beside a bloodied dead body with a hole in its chest. The man wept over his brother's body briefly before straightening to face me, his eyes, hard.

"What does that mean?" he asked.

Izzy answered. "It means they were strong enough to take over their bodies. The gods may be with us there in the sky, but the demons are now here on earth."

We stood staring at each other, and our thoughts may have drowned out the cries of the changing man, but they did not fade into the night. For the first time, it occurred to us that we may lose this battle once again.

CHAPTER THIRTY-NINE

In Derwin's tent, I found the pirate hunched over a small table, drinking. It smelled like he'd been going at it all night. The stench of stale breath, body odor, and ale would have certainly made a Gwylis Izzy vomit, but I endured it now.

I sat, and picked cheese and stale bread from the plate set there. Derwin said nothing as he sat back in his chair and stretched his neck until it cracked. He moaned.

"When we win this war, I am going to find the best bathhouse a man can find and live there," he said.

I smiled. "You deserve it."

Derwin grunted. "This doesn't change anything, you know. Demons, men, it doesn't matter. They're in my city, and I don't want them there."

I had to laugh. The way he said made it sound like he was a child, fending off another who tried to take his toy.

"You think this is funny?"

I nodded. "I do, because what I'm about to propose, you're not going to like."

Derwin sighed and leaned forward. "Wait. Don't say a word. Let me guess." I held back a smile and let him speak. "You want to infiltrate the castle, by yourself, and kill Katka, the one you believe is now wholly Uncanny. And by doing so, you bring down her entire army."

I cocked my head. "Close. I want to do all of that, but not alone. I want Ashe and a dozen men with me. I know a way in. The rest of our plan does not change."

Derwin stared at me for a long while. He raised his cup to his mouth. "Eat. Drink. For tomorrow, we fight."

~

I DRESSED FOR BATTLE.

There were no mirrors on the ships nor in any of the tents, but I didn't need one to see my own reflection in the army's eyes. I stood tall, strong and formidable even without demon magic flowing through my veins. I bore the scars of things that tried to kill me.

I was a storm unleashed.

I was human.

Every sense awakened as I prepared. My muscles twitched with anticipation as my heart beat faster and faster, anxious for the battle to be over so Mirosa could start its healing. I may not be the strongest woman to dress for war—sometimes I felt brittle without my magic—but I knew my place was here.

I sheathed Henry's dagger and weighed a new broadsword in my hands. I set it on my lap and ran my fingers over the steel. Something flickered in my heart, fluttering down into my fingertips. Tilting my head, I watched a small bit of light glow and sink itself into the blade.

We fashioned weapons for hunting, formidable and everlasting. We imbued them with magic.

The metal glowed a bright orange, and I smiled. Small magic, indeed.

Outside, the army waited. They were equipped with swords and bows and daggers of all kinds. Some wore armor, while some simply wore the clothes on their backs. They all looked fierce. They all looked ready.

There was no sound save for the wind and the clattering of iron. We marched through the Archway single-file and spread out like a fan on the other side.

I joined Ashe, Derwin, and Flea along with a couple other high-ranking soldiers in the front. I did not know if Katka would have seen us coming, but if she did, she did not deploy the Gwylis. The plains were quiet, and the trees ahead of us, still. I had planned on making these plains our battlefield, but it appeared we could take Stormwall by surprise.

I was equipped with three weapons: a sword at my hip, a dagger on my thigh, and a bow on my back. A thrill rushed through me as my fingers brushed the ends of the arrows. I'd missed shooting. I thought about the last time I'd done it; I'd wanted to feel human again, but a little wolf named Ghetee taught me accepting who you are was most important.

In a quiet moment, with nothing but my breath, I ran my fingers along the bow. *I've missed this.*

That mass of forest at the castle's back always felt like an end. I'd gone out with Fray as I pretended to be some great assassin, but never further until I had abandoned my kingdom entirely. Now, they looked like a beginning.

After informing Ashe of my plan, he immediately agreed, telling me I was crazy, but also the smartest woman he'd ever known. He trusted me. I could not let him down.

"If we mobilize now, we could surround them," he said. "Send back a few ships to take the docks, and file into the city from there."

It was a good plan—a solid plan.

As for me, Ashe, and twelve other men, we'd push further, onward through the forest to a wall surrounding a cemetery where I once spoke to Henry, and where I first got close to a Voiceless servant who showed me the passage in and out.

The hole in the wall.

On the plains, our army stood in formation, swords drawn, shields across their backs. They looked fierce and determined in the dawn. They were here to fight and to die. But mostly to fight.

A crow sailed overhead as we marched. I watched it until it drifted out of sight. I almost called out to the bird, asked it to send a message to Fray. I wanted to tell him that I loved him, but he knew. I hoped he knew.

No more than thirty minutes later, we stood at the treeline of the forest. This close, the tops of the castle reached out like groping claws, its presence like a stone pressing on my chest.

"Ashe," I whispered.

"I'm here," he said.

When the first of the men entered the trees, the fighting began.

It happened too fast. First, I was beside Ashe, close enough that our arms touched, and the next, we both had our weapons drawn. The enemy came charging forward with battle cries and furious swords. Our army formed a tight line in front of Ashe and myself. Before I knew it, bodies were falling, and the scent of blood filled the air.

I loaded my bow; the weight so familiar, like an extension of my limbs. My body tightened as I took aim, breathed, took in the distance. I shot on the count of one, again on two. On three. They each hit their marks. Fast as a rabbit, I kept firing until the arrows ran out and the enemy ceased attacking.

I opened my mouth to say, "I'm retrieving the arrows," when a scream cut the air, and in the chaos, a soldier—one of ours—came running back. He came toward Ashe, who sidestepped. The man fell, and his body shook violently. He got on all fours and threw his head back. Sharp teeth grew in his open jaw. His clothes tore from his body. Everyone gave the man a wide berth as he shifted into what would be a monstrous wolf.

Someone shouted, "Kill it!"

I almost threw myself forward to protect the man, but it would make no difference. He would kill us now that he was bitten. His life or ours. I chose ours.

"He knew the risks." Derwin appeared, and before anyone could say a word, he plunged his sword into the man's half-changed form. Blood formed a pool under the man's body.

There wasn't any time to debate. We picked our way through the forest, shouting for all to hear. "Don't let them bite you!"

The Gwylis charged like wild animals.

I counted at least three dozen dashing forward in a loose formation. They thundered forward, swords flashing, teeth bared.

"Arrows!" The scream ripped through my throat. My hand moved, fluid like water, cutting down the enemy with my sword. These Gwylis were relentless, injured, and dying, but still pushing to their feet. Their calls were wild, sending goose pimples up my arms. *But they're no match for us, not in their human forms.*

Many of the enemy fell, but many more continued to push forward.

I released a battle cry not unlike the screams of the dying around me. The thundering of boots on the ground reminded me of the great storm that surged overhead the day I killed my father. The tremors rattled my bones.

The smell of blood filled my nose as I turned to take note of who was at my back. Ashe was not five feet away, his sword cutting through the enemy with such precision. His boots slipped in the bloody mud beneath his feet. He kneeled as a heap of bodies rose around him. Our fellow soldiers gathered around him, almost protectively. He would have made Henry proud.

We met another wave of attacks mid-way through the forest. Arrows shot through the air and hit our army in a barrage. I heard screams and shouts, our army returning arrows. I could hear the tips of them as they hit metal shields and tree trunks. We had to get through, and now was my chance.

I scanned the battlefield for Ashe, but found Flea instead. He'd wielded a dagger in one hand while the other appeared to be weakened. I spotted Derwin next, pushing through like a wild boar, slicing down anyone that came close until he was beside Flea. Frantic, my eyes finally landed on the sandy-haired prince.

Ashe—on his own by a clearing, battling a monster Gwylis. I swallowed back a scream as the giant wolf knocked away Ashe's sword and barreled into his chest, throwing him backwards against a tree.

The Gwylis shook its ruff, baring its bloodied teeth, and stalked toward Ashe, who lay motionless at the base of the tree.

"No!" I screamed, running forward.

The wolf turned as I closed the distance. I spun on the balls of my feet, my hands closed tightly over the hilt of my dagger. This wolf would have been beautiful—breathtaking, even—if blood hadn't mottled its silver fur and its two triangle ears weren't ripped to shreds.

I squinted against the sunlight as the wolf bounded toward me.

I crouched so low, I might as well have become the ground, and just as the wolf lunged, I gave it all my strength and leapt. Claws snagged my pants, but didn't catch. When my boots found ground again, I found myself behind the Gwylis. With no time to think, I struck the Gwylis before it had time to turn.

The wolf screamed as its body was slowly poisoned by my magic, and turned back human before his body stilled and grew rigid as death took hold.

"Are you all right?" Ashe asked, limping toward me. His pant leg was torn open, but it didn't look bad.

My eyes burned, but there wasn't any time to talk.

Derwin turned the army east, leading the enemy away from the small group peeling away. Upon joining back with the army, Ashe, the twelve soldiers, and myself crouched low and ran. Before we knew it, the sounds of battle faded, and there was nothing but the birds retreating at the chaos and the ground as we marched. We said nothing until we came to the cemetery wall. I let out a breath of relief.

Images played before my eyes of a blue-eyed servant with the angriest of scowls that I wanted to kiss away. My life had changed the very moment I met him, but never did I think it would lead me back to where it all began. When I fell in love with the moon and the night and everything that was supposed to frighten me; everything now felt conquerable. Because he loved me, and I loved him, and love was worth fighting for.

CHAPTER FORTY

The battle had begun by the time we arrived. The sheer number of soldiers crossing into the Archway briefly gave us pause, but when we noted the insignia, we knew they were friends.

After going back to the Den, I'd summoned all able-bodied men and women for battle. It took days for Aquarius and the others to arrive, but when they did, it was short work to pack and head into the Old Kingdom.

A crow soared overhead as we made our way into the rigid formations of what I assumed to be the rebel army. Who was leading them? Some wore simple clothes and thrown together armor, while others bore the crest of the Peek Islands.

So, the prince had a hand in this.

Joined by Branch, Olio, Sonia, and a few other friendly faces, we marched forward. There had been no use for words over the past few days, and no use now. Heaving my sword to my chest, I followed the steps of the men and women who were fighting before me.

Passing through the Archway always gave me a sense of foreboding. Not only was it the passage from one world to another, but it also felt dark and unforgiving, no matter which direction you went.

I registered the battlefield in detail: thousands of swords and shields from allies surging into battle across the fields. I saw the wind and earth magic given to us by the Uncanny and felt a distant tug from somewhere deep within me. Was it the gods, or something far more sinister?

Gwylis fighting one another. It shouldn't have been this way. This was not what Aquarius wanted.

This was not what Izzy wanted.

Izzy.

Her face pushed its way into my mind as I took in the scene around me, as my body tensed, ready for battle.

I'll find my way back to you, I vowed. *Wherever you are.*

I drew in a breath and roared, the sound laden with visceral rage, ugly and loud. It was like a fire burning through me, turning the old Fray to ashes.

Transforming me.

Branch appeared on my left and attacked. We weren't in the thick of it, but we clamored into the enemy nonetheless. Sonia cried out in rage to my right while Olio leapt into the air, delivering a fatal blow to a felled enemy Gwylis.

I engaged and picked my way through the battle, my sword an extension of me. A massive gush of wind passed overhead, and for a moment, I wished for my demon magic, although I'd never truly mastered its power.

I shoved my sword into the enemies' bellies as I pushed forward. The battle grew dense, so much that there was no space to draw my sword, and all sides bumped, shoulder to shoulder, attempting to determine who was who.

Another gust of wind nearly knocked me from my feet. It took me a moment to realize what it was: Gwylis, with wings larger than anything I'd ever seen.

With their inhuman claws, they swooped into the battlefield, picking up rebels and hurling them into the air, only to let them fall. Screams of surprise and horror tore through the air. I elbowed my way through the battle, the glow of my sword growing brighter by the minute.

A scream erupted over the clamor of battle. It sounded like Neera.

A shriek pierced the air at the same moment. I looked up to see one of the monsters with a girl in its talons. Her fire-red hair, her skinny legs.

I noted the exact feeling I felt in that moment—like when I was deep in sleep and I got the sensation of falling, or when I almost missed a step. That chilled fear that shot through me in that split second. I felt it now.

In a messy, horrific display, Cas kicked and cried out, but the demon just flew higher.

And released.

I couldn't look. I didn't have time to chastise Neera for bringing Cas into battle. The demon came back down and slammed through the battle, killing anything in its path.

I barreled away, chasing Neera's screams to find her bent over, her sobs breaking through the violence around her. I sheathed my sword and heaved her to her feet. There wasn't any time to pause and spout words of inspiration. Either fight or die. "Get up. Do you want to die too?"

Neera's eyes went wide and vacant, but she nodded. Her split lip was bleeding bright red, glistening in the light of my sword as I drew it once again.

Visions of those I loved falling dead spread through me. But with that fear, I saw children running through fields of flowers. The sun shining upon marble floors. Smiling faces. Music playing. Izzy...

An arrow sped past me, nicking my ear. I raised my sword. Its power sank into my body, filling up the spaces with warmth. Instinct told me to use this power to prevent more deaths. I ran forward, charging through the battle, ramming like a stag on the attack, my sword cutting like a blade cutting through foliage. Bodies slammed into me, knocking me off my feet. My sword clamored to the ground at my feet. Hands suddenly found my neck, squeezing nearly hard enough to break my spine.

There wasn't any time to think about finding my sword. I turned my head to the side to allow a shallow breath, and then I reached up and broke both of his smallest fingers until the pressure on my throat eased and my airways opened.

Quickly, I gasped and grabbed my sword. I reared and roared as loud as my crushed windpipe would allow and brought my sword down into the man's chest.

There was a moment where the world faded from me. Fear. Panic, like a tangible thing. I almost passed out from the pain.

"Fray!"

Someone grabbed me before I fell. Aquarius.

"Father," I croaked. I could barely eke out the word. My throat ached horribly.

Blood covered Aquarius's face. Even in his old body, he managed to get this far.

He wasn't even supposed to be in battle.

"You're no injured wolf," he told me. "You're my son. Now, get up!"

Izzy's face came creeping before me. Beautiful, so beautiful. When I closed my eyes, I could swear she was right there.

No. It wasn't over yet. I was strong enough. I had to be strong enough.

Besides, you didn't need a voice to take down an army.

CHAPTER FORTY-ONE

The wall was repaired. I realized this with heart-stopping terror.

"Shit," Ashe cursed. "I forgot my father had it fixed when I discovered it."

My heart hammered so loudly against my chest. I feared we'd be given away, but the air remained still. We were alone.

"I'll hoist you up." Ashe stepped into my waiting hands, and I shoved him up until he gripped the wall. He reached down to help me. When I reached the edge, I hopped over and landed on my feet. "Next time, remember those small details, Prince of the Peeks."

Ashe slid down the wall. "Will do, when I'm not busy dodging a murderous father and killing Gwylis."

I led Ashe and the others through the graves, past what was once Henry's. Where there were once guards was now nothing but silence. I let my gaze slide over Henry's empty resting place and away toward the entrance to the catacombs.

I stopped at the door. I closed my eyes, thought of everyone who relied on me, of Fray. All this time, I'd pushed him from my thoughts, but I could not outrun them now. He gave me strength.

I thought of those children we'd saved back in Essex. They would have a future. A home. *Please,* I begged the gods.

I let Ashe take the lead. He opened the door.

We moved through the maze of corridors like ghosts. I brushed my fingers along the cold stone to guide me, for without light, we were traveling by my own memory alone.

A whisper near my ear raised the hairs on my arms. I turned and thought I saw girl with black hair and a long dress.

Lulu?

We entered the dungeons and angled toward the infirmary rooms where I once pestered Pyrus and Pax on occasion. Up a set of stairs and into the main hall.

Once I stepped through, the door slammed behind me, cutting me off from Ashe and the rest. The sound echoed through the massive room, drawing my eye to another sound.

On what was once my father's throne that now sat a tall, blonde woman with two-toned eyes and a grimace.

"You did know that it would all come down to this," Katka said, raising from the throne. She stepped lightly down the dais to where I stood, pounding my fists against the door. Was Ashe all right? I couldn't hear anything. Not screams or iron on iron.

Gods, let them be all right, I prayed.

I turned to face Katka.

"You know," she said, walking slowly toward me. "I regret not killing you back when we first met. I didn't know you'd come for the throne so ardently. You and the prince, I didn't count it."

I slipped my dagger from my boot and charged. I was small by Katka's standards, and I knew I would not reach her throat or even her heart, but I hadn't planned on it. She sidestepped and kicked me until I fell forward on my face, but not before I knocked her leg above the knee and swiped my dagger. The blade made contact along her calf. Blood dotted my face. The momentum slid me across the marble floor. I hit my head hard, and warm blood spilled from my forehead and into my eyes.

The impact knocked the memories free.

Henry. Lulu. Ghetee.

This is all for you.

My lips curved into a grin as I lifted my head. There was no ceremony as Katka's clothes ripped free from her body, the sound of claws clicking on the marble floor.

I sat up and spun around toward the monster. She wasn't a wolf, or any Gwylis I'd ever seen. Her fur was still stark white, but it faded into scaly legs and enormous feet, ending in massive, talon-like claws. She growled, sending saliva down her jutting teeth and long snout. Her two tails curled around her massive frame. I crooked an eyebrow at her, and her body shook with fury.

"My, what big teeth you have."

Her enormous body shed its fur, replacing it with creeping shadows that blanketed her in darkness. She launched herself toward me; her inhuman screams blasting through my ears. I ran forward and slid onto my backside as she sailed over me. I snapped up before she landed, my legs almost folding beneath me. I managed to run toward the kitchen doors and fall through.

The kitchens, much smaller in size than the great hall, would deem a monster of Katka's size to have a bit of difficulty. I ran to the other side of the metal counters, pressing myself against them. I still held my dagger—thank the gods for small favors.

Katka threw open the kitchen doors, but it was not footsteps I heard entering, but claws, click-clacking against the hard floor. I smelled the rot coming from the demon Katka had now become. But it wasn't long before she moaned, first in annoyance and then in pain. A heavy thump sounded, and pots and pans smashed to the floor in heaps.

Huddled there in the kitchens, I finally realized what Wargrave had meant when he said that the world did not bend for me. He didn't mean it would never happen, only that he thought I was too weak to do it.

But after all I'd done, I did move the stars. I changed the course of the world. I would drive the Uncanny to their knees.

I saw it first in my fingertips and then in my hand as I gripped my dagger—light as bright as the sun and just as brilliant.

A tremendous roar echoed from somewhere outside.

A war I needed to end.

I stood up in time to see that I was now bathed in this strange light. Parts of me twinkled like stars, like looking at the reflection of the sun on water. With bated breath, I admired the beauty I never thought I'd become.

I gave a cocky smile.

"How did you do it?" Katka hissed. She was a misshapen wolf with human legs and a double tail swishing below two scaly wings too weak to lift the demon's body off the ground. She hunched over the counter, crying out. "Your weapon."

"My demon killer?" I asked, keeping the wide counter between us. "The gods gave me magic to make it even stronger than before. You'll die before we finish our conversation."

Katka roared. "Poison! You poisoned me!"

"You did this to yourself. You could have gone when Dal died, but you stayed, attempting to take my throne for me. You are nothing but the king's dog, and you will die like the sad beast you are."

Katka dropped her head onto the counter. Black ooze seeped from her eyes and nostrils. Her matted fur and scaly legs shivered with the gods' magic coursing through her, slowing draining the demon's own magic from her body. She would not survive it. I only wished it.

She suddenly straightened and threw back her head, jaw open, revealing several rows of razor-sharp teeth unlike anything I'd ever seen. She spoke, even though her jaw did not move. Demon voices spewed forth all their lies and corruption.

"Shut your demon mouths," I snapped as I held my dagger overhead, prepared to throw it at any moment. "You thought you could control me, but I played your game, and I won."

The demons screamed. They rang out in a cacophony of rage and desperation.

With one swift movement, I snapped my wrist and let the dagger soar. It struck Katka between the eyes.

She spread her arms out wide, knocking over shelves and cupboards. Her legs faltered and she fell, her chin hitting the counter with a sickening *smack*.

The shadows came at once. I leapt onto the counter to meet them head-on. One by one, they came, but one by one the light surrounding me drove them away until they shrunk to nothing but black specks and I heard them crying, sobbing for mercy. But there'd be no mercy.

"Back to the underworld for you." Slivers of light pierced the remaining demons, and then there was silence. I moved to where Katka's body had fallen. It was now human, naked, and small. I bent over to level my gaze. There was no life left in her eyes, although one swam with blackness. I removed my dagger from her forehead, spraying my face with blood, and drove it into the eyeball. "No more demons."

The squishing sound made my stomach lurch, but I gritted my teeth and drove it deeper, and then I pulled it free.

"No more deals."

CHAPTER FORTY-TWO

"Swords at the ready!" someone screamed.

I stopped trying to break down the catacombs door and turned. The tightness of the corridor did not allow me to draw my sword without accidently striking a comrade. But those at the front had already charged forward. Soon, we'd branched out into the adjoining halls, and I was able to arm myself.

Being a prince would not spare me.

I feinted to one side, dodging a killing blow, and crouched low, thrusting my sword upward, joining flesh. The next attack came too quickly, and I nearly fell off-balance, twisting quickly and catching myself along the cold stone wall. The man—Gwylis—began his chant, which gave me room to breathe, but only for a split second. The others were fighting in tight knots up and down the catacombs. From all sides, I could hear screams and iron against stone.

I launched forward and caught the man mid-chant, my sword sinking into his belly. When I attempted to pull my sword free, it only brought the man closer. This close, I could see the life draining from his eyes. *Young,* I thought. *Too young to die.*

"Paratheon!"

The door leading into the main hall of the castle had opened, sending soldiers barreling through. I stumbled into Derwin as I backed away, nearly toppling the man. The act should have been the end of us both, but caused us to miss a straight swish of a blade that would have beheaded us both. I slid onto my butt and kicked my leg out, felling the soldier while Derwin made a killing blow.

"Stay down, princeling," Derwin growled.

I swore aloud as an arrow soared overhead, colliding perfectly with the pirate's blade. Another came and hit me in the meat of my thigh as I tried to find purchase. Not deep, but incredibly painful. My leg went sideways as I stood, nearly sinking to my knees.

"Tight quarters," I muttered, accepting Derwin's hand in standing. He bent down and quickly snapped the arrow so that only a quarter of the thing stayed lodged in my leg. Better in than out.

My muscles pulled so tightly, I felt they may snap at any moment. The fighting went silent as my heartbeat pulsed in my ears. We walked the corridors, stepping over dead bodies, and took inventory of our group. Two dead. I did not know their names.

"They were weakened," Derwin said, wiping spatters of blood from his face. They turned into horrible streaks. "They must have been trained to their breaking point. They knew we were coming."

A terrible keening split the air.

Izzy emerged from a door across the way, her face sprayed with blood. But it wasn't the blood that surprised us.

It was the way a halo of light shone around her body.

"You have it too," she said as she fell into my arms. She pressed her hands against my back. "Wake up."

A shiver passed through me. I pulled away and placed a hand over Izzy's head injury. I did not know what compelled me to do it, but once it was there, I felt the rightness in everything, and after a few seconds, the power ran through me and closed the wound until it was nothing but a pink line, and then nothing at all.

Small magic.

Without a single hesitation, I floated my hand over the wound in my thigh. Slowly, the broken piece of arrow slid free, and with a quick shot of pain, fell to the floor. Through the tear in my pants, I could see the blood beginning to dry and flake apart. All at once, the pain was gone.

"Where's my mother?" Izzy asked, her throat hoarse, like she'd been crying for hours.

The scream I'd heard moments ago turned into howls.

Sad, mournful howls.

Furious, miserable howls.

I glanced in the direction of the dungeon. "That's her. Your mother."

I wrapped my arms around her, denying myself her reaction. I wanted to give her something familiar, something kind before she saw what my father had done to the last family she had left. I hoped my touch would lead to something calm within her, and bring her to a place where she no longer suffered.

But it was too late.

CHAPTER FORTY-THREE

I pulled myself away from Ashe and wiped my dagger on my pants, ridding it of Katka's blood. My chest heaved, but I did not feel the least bit tired. I would rest when all this was over, but for now, adrenaline shocked through me. I shook with the surge of it.

The sounds of battle thundered in the catacombs, muffled and faraway. The battle was drawing nearer and would reach the castle. I knew we were on borrowed time.

If I did not eliminate the last thing keeping me from the throne, we would not win this fight.

"Get back to the others," I ordered. "Tell them I killed their commander."

I found myself running deeper through the catacombs until I reached the dungeons. The keening grew louder, more and more haunting. I stopped, taking in a gulp of air. How many people were being held down here? How many of them were like my mother?

"This is where she was," Ashe said from behind me. He gestured to an open cell. I crushed the palm of my hand to my nose to keep out the stench.

"You need to go," I told him. "Get the word out that Katka is dead. Try—"

"I won't leave you."

I closed my eyes. "Ashe."

But no other words came, for when I opened my eyes and turned away, my mother appeared. She peered through the darkness, eyes like flames. She took a step forward. With a rustle and a squelch, the corridor's air thickened with something sour.

I gasped as my body folded in.

Ashe stepped in front of me, shielding my body, as if I hadn't seen. As if I would ever unsee it.

Instead of letting him protect me, I shoved him away and watched my mother approach. Her once proud and graceful movements, now marred by the thing she'd become. I could no longer see the corsets and the jewelry. I could not even hear her belittling words to me. She was not a queen. Not my mother. That person was dead. There was nothing left of her.

A pang of sadness rolled through me.

Is this what she looked like inside? I thought. My entire life, she'd been nothing but horrible. Catering to my father, even when she knew what he'd done to Henry. Taking men to her bed when he was away. Choosing someone else, always choosing someone else, over her own children. A selfish monster.

She dragged her monstrous body across the floor. Scaly wings stretched out, but could not lift her massive frame.

I could not feel guilt for what happened to her. I refused to feel it. I kept a firm hold on my dagger, poised it to kill my very own mother.

My mother's mouth opened to expose gleaming white teeth and rancid breath.

"Isabelle," she croaked, her chest struggling for breath. Her words, full of anguish. "I...love you."

For a glimmer of a moment, I allowed myself to believe that were true, and that she'd never covered up what my father had done to Henry. My mother, the only one I would ever have, me a mirror of the queen she always wanted me to be. A flare of wanting shot through me.

I shook my head. *NO.* I remembered the day she'd let my father drag me from my room, screaming as he sent me to a marriage I did not want. I remembered how she stood by, watching, saying nothing. I remembered it all very clearly. I would never forget.

My hand trembled as it gripped Henry's dagger, feeling my barriers begin to crumble.

I tensed my muscles, ready to drive the dagger into her heart. I sensed Ashe behind me, but the world spiraled out and away from me.

"Izzy," I heard him say. "This isn't over yet. Even after she's dead. We need you. Stay strong."

Stay strong. It's not over yet.

There was too much death in the world, and I was the cause of much of it. But this awful woman knew nothing about love.

And she was too far gone to learn.

"I wish things had been different." My throat was tight from holding back tears. My voice was little more than a whisper. I felt Ashe's presence behind me, and that gave me courage to step forward.

I drew my dagger and stuck it into her throat.

She made no sound. I stood there, my body against hers, my hand grasping the hilt of my weapon as it sunk into her neck. "Goodbye, Mother."

I withdrew the dagger and let her slump to the floor.

The last of my family, gone.

But I remained.

Sorrow overtook me as I stepped back into Ashe's waiting arms. I remembered the way she spoke of Fray and how she believed so lowly of love. I remembered her words.

Love can hurt in many ways. That's the way of it.

I let loose a staggering breath. *She was right.*

I battled back tears for my mother into the back of my mind. And when I turned back to Ashe, his steely look mirrored my own.

There was no time for grieving. Not yet.

CHAPTER FORTY-FOUR

The battle crashed like thunder.

Alongside Aquarius, I drove through the enemy ranks with my pack behind me, swords ripping flesh, the power of the gods making us light on our feet. Kill, withdraw, repeat.

I'd seen battle before, but never like this. The chaos wringing through this field would be a nightmare I'd never forget.

But I was not afraid. With my pack at my side and the gods at my heels, we pushed onward.

For Mirosa—for the children who lived now and the children to come.

For Izzy.

Dal Paratheon's army—or at least the army he helped create, even if he wasn't commanding it currently, stretched across the fields, standing between the forest and Stormwall.

I couldn't think of the allies who died in our wake. All I could think of was the sword in my hand and the enemy before me. The wolves of the Den—were we wolves anymore after all?—bore iron tinged with light. The magic of the gods seared through the demons who came at us.

Without darkness, there cannot be light. But light will always win.

Still, Stormwall felt so far. There was no longer the claws and teeth of the Gwylis, so I could only rely on my human body, which weakened by the minute. My legs shook, my hands cramped around the hilt of my sword. I ground my teeth together, my throat raw and bruised.

Pain shot throughout my body. I cursed aloud, wishing for a fraction of a moment I had the Gwylis healing abilities. Would the gods heal them? I'd since lost track, pushing the pain from my mind; ignored the blood cooling upon my face.

Kill. Push. Repeat.

The forest was burning. I remembered those trees. I'd snuck out with stolen food almost every night to feed the Voiceless living in camps throughout the area. I'd first seen Izzy there—truly *seen* her. Her determination. Her arrogance. Her kindness.

But mostly, her strength. She would not be cowed by me, not ever. I fell in love with that part of her.

Somewhere above me, a large shadow passed over. Wings like a bat, a body stretched and covered in fur. Human legs dangling like useless appendages.

The thing that killed Neera's sister.

I didn't have a chance to cry out before the demon swooped down and captured a man within its claws. Sonia, at my side, unleashed a barrage of arrows as it soared higher and higher.

The creature bucked and opened its claws, releasing the man and killing him as he fell to the ground. It fell soon after, landing with a heavy *crash* and a throaty cry of pain. My sister slit its throat, but not without a cry of her own.

These were once human, maybe Gwylis. They did not deserve what happened to them.

More shadows lifted into the sky.

I turned to Sonia and to Branch and Olio, who caught up. "The monsters," I said, breathless, every word like a knife in my throat. "We have to take them down."

"They set the forest on fire to keep us away," Branch deducted. He was panting, his face stained with blood. "What we need is—"

I made the sign for rain. Maybe the gods would give it to us.

Giving the felled beast one last look, I turned to Branch. "Carry the order down the line: Keep pushing toward Stormwall."

The battle closed in around us. We only had moments.

"What will you do, brother?"

I glanced at my sword and sneered.

Sonia opened her mouth to shout at me to stop, to roar, but I was already running.

I lifted my sword, letting the glow light up the battlefield like a beacon. *Shine brighter*, I prayed. *As bright as you can, gods dammit!*

I was alone, rushing the field, knocking away the enemy as if they were nothing. They almost parted for me as I darted, away from my friends. Away from Stormwall. As far as I could get.

And the monsters followed.

CHAPTER FORTY-FIVE

"It didn't work," Izzy muttered.

I held my sword at chest level. "What didn't work?"

"I thought killing Katka would stop it."

Oh. She assumed killing the leader would take down the rest. But no, life did not work that way.

Emerging from the catacombs and into the cemetery, we found rain battering on our heads. The forest had been lit on fire. Thick smoke rose into the air, choking the sky.

Patches of enemies formed into small knots here and there. The wall surrounding the cemetery had come down at some point—broken in large chunks like something had taken bites from it—and we were met with weak opposition.

"Your leader is dead!" I called out. "Surrender now!"

For a moment, I thought they would lay down their weapons, tuck their tails, but that hope only lasted mere seconds before the Gwylis army attacked.

I managed to position myself in front of Izzy before fending off the first attack. I guarded, but the man charged again and again, using his sword as a battering ram. The force of the man and his sword forced me through the open doors, back into the catacombs of the castle. I shoved him hard and stabbed him in the center of his belly. I carved a path back to where I left Izzy and the others. She was fighting mercilessly, but I could tell she was exhausted. Her movements were slow, and would get her killed.

We pushed most of the small regiment back, giving us enough space to regroup.

"We have to get back to the others," I told Izzy. The light around her dimmed in and out, like a flickering torch. "The castle is nothing but stone. Let it fall. But not our people."

My words sparked something in her. Suddenly, the light pulsed, and she held out both hands as though she were grabbing for the air in front of her. A scream built up in her chest, the pressure building until it burst forth. It amplified through the air, shaking the ground and the very foundation of the castle at our backs.

The remaining enemies were flung backward by the magic. They stayed on the ground, curled into balls, crying out for help. The wolves shifted back into humans and convulsed on the ground.

Izzy's head snapped to look at me. "Follow me."

She ran, and along with the remaining allied soldiers, darted through what remained of the forest and back toward the battlefield.

We could see it clearly, in excruciating detail.

Our army crashed into the Gwylis army with such force that I could not tell who was winning and who was losing. Swords and teeth and iron and bone. The grass was red with blood.

"Help them."

Izzy's voice was so small that if I hadn't been standing beside her, I wouldn't have heard, never mind whoever answered from somewhere in the skies. Her hands shot forward again, and the light peeled from her body and whisked itself down the battle. But the magic did not kill the enemy. It merely took the Gwylis curse from their bodies. But it became clear that even though they were human again, they would not bend the knee.

"This battle will rage all day," a soldier said from behind me. He sounded choked up, dismal.

We were outnumbered, and the longer we watched, the more of our people died. By the end of it, there would be no one left. Izzy would rule a kingdom of the dead.

"What is that?"

The soldier who'd spoken earlier brushed past me. He pointed. "A light! Look!"

Sure enough, something speared into the sky. From this distance, it looked like a sliver of sunlight creeping through a window in the early morning.

But something so beautiful could never last. Our eyes turned east, where massive demons dove from the sky on wings larger than any bird of prey I'd ever seen.

Great volleys of arrows soared through the sky, blotting out the sun.

The creatures roared with defiance and suddenly banked west, toward the light we'd seen stabbing the sky.

Where was it coming from?

"Gods," Izzy breathed.

I had to join in the fight. But I couldn't seem to move from Izzy's side. Her body trembled and she leaned into me, a frail thing. A human thing. I was bleeding from somewhere on my cheek, and she wiped it away.

The battle ahead was not yet won.

A knot formed in my stomach.

"Izzy."

She made a soft sound that made me want to lock her away safely until the battle was truly over. "No, it isn't over yet, and I promised to end this war."

I brushed the damp hair from her forehead. "Let's help them."

She knew what I meant.

Them.

Our people.

CHAPTER FORTY-SIX

I uttered a small prayer and sent out a surge of magic. We were outnumbered. The enemy was standing their ground despite the death of their leader.

The gods' light surrounded me and bathed the world around me. "Protect them. *Protect them.*"

My eyes followed those giant shards of light in the distance, like slices of sun against the darkening sky.

My hands glowed with pure white light. The gods were with me. I earned their favor, and now I had to use what they'd given to remake this world.

Power coiled inside of me, hugging my very core. With a scream, I let it lose. It sprang free.

The sky above exploded in a white light. I felt it like a wave against my body, and I nearly buckled at the knees. The flash of light followed the wind to the battle below, washing through the enemy and ally alike.

This power, it sang through me.

The mere presence of the gods' magic sent the enemy retreating, but left behind a trail of destruction and death.

The strain of it sent me to my knees, hands clasping at the place where the necklace had once been; the thing I'd looked to for protection from harm. Now, I had nothing but my own strength and courage.

"It's over," Ashe said. "Izzy, it's over."

Ashe's hand found mine and squeezed tightly.

When I looked up at him, there were tears falling from his eyes.

But he looked to the battlefield, not to me.

He looked to where the Uncanny's army of monsters transformed into humans, taking away their power.

He looked to where the sun broke through the clouds and bathed the plains below with bright light.

He looked on as the world became new.

But then something grabbed hold of me and pulled me away, turning my joy into ice-cold darkness.

CHAPTER FORTY-SEVEN

Letting out a shrieking cry, they shot through the sky, one after another. Hulks of abominations soaring through the clouds above.

I could barely breathe; could barely keep my legs from buckling beneath me.

I stopped hearing the battle, stopped seeing anything but the path ahead. If I looked back, I would see the destruction my father had laid upon the land. But what would be the point?

The enemy lines thinned out here. I encountered only one who chose to confront me. I swung my sword, but the man ducked and drove his weapon toward my belly—a searing pain that came and went. It could not stop me from swinging my sword like a whip and taking his head from his neck.

Darkness shrouded the sky. I jabbed the sword into the air, screaming for the gods to listen. The white light flared from my blade, engulfing me its warmth. The monsters cried out, but still they followed. Darkness wanted to destroy light. That was all demons wanted to do. And they'd go to their death to see it done.

I knew with every step, I grew closer to being alone. There was no enemy out here to pick off. The battle raged without me. But I could not let these monsters at my pack.

And I had no intention of surviving this.

But still I went until I could not go any longer. My knees buckled and hit the ground beneath me. I briefly touched my abdomen, and my hand came away soaked with red. Still, I crawled, every inch an inch these monsters followed was a minute closer to victory.

Hoisting myself up once more, I stumbled forward, my muscles throbbing, my teeth gnashed together. A demon dove, knocking me on my side, nearly throwing the sword from my clenched fist. I rolled onto my back, thrusting the sword into the air. The demons screamed, pushed away until they hovered like vultures above me.

In battle, there were always moments of clarity. Maybe it was the presence of death, so near I could almost feel its cold grip on my skin. Whatever the reason, every breath now was a memory, pulsing with the gods' light. An image of my mother singing me to sleep. Of Izzy and of stolen, quiet moments between us. The moments that could never be put into words—that were for me and me alone.

As if realizing their prey was weakening, the monsters opened their wings and let out their hideous cries.

And the skies opened.

I drew in a long breath. Silence fell, and amid the rain beginning to fall, I hoisted myself to my knees and then to my feet. Covered in blood and mud, I began to walk again. Rain would put out the fires in the forest surrounding the castle. We could win. The monsters cried out, desperate to close in on me, deterred only by the glowing blade that dragged behind me like the tail of a cat. *Like moths to a flame.*

Keep going.

Leaking blood like a sieve, I sent my body hurling across the fields. Darkness encroached the edges of my vision.

One last, desperate final push.

"Help me," I choked out, tasting salt and iron. *Help me.*

Finally, as if sensing my end, the light flared again, and the monsters screeched, rose and dove like hawks. I stopped and turned. I could no longer see the battle, nor the castle. The sky had turned a bruised and ugly grey. I blinked raindrops from my lashes and laughed. My chest heaved with it, burned with each exhale. Still, I laughed, for the gods had stayed with me.

Their answering thunder boomed in my very bones, unleashing their power upon the Uncanny.

The sword I carried erupted with power and lit the sky like a thousand suns.

The monsters swooped, and suddenly they diminished into nothing. No longer creatures of claw and wing, they plummeted to the earth in human bodies, too fragile, too weak to survive the fall. They landed all around me, bodies broken and lifeless. I crumpled to my knees and then backwards until I was on my back. One of the cursed fell nearly on top of me, crushing my legs with its weight. But I succumbed to the pain.

"Thank you," I rasped as my tears warmed with the light engulfing me. I couldn't breathe. I didn't want to.

Take me to her.

CHAPTER FORTY-EIGHT

I fell into a world darkness and hit the ground hard as I was taken
from Stormwall and into a place where light refused to touch.

Disoriented, I pushed to my feet and whirled around. There was
nothing. No ground, no sky. No castle. No war.

A voiceless cry echoed in my mind. My heartbeat slammed against
my chest, panic surging as I reached out, desperate to touch something,
anything, but coming up empty.

"Ashe!" I shrieked into the void. This wasn't the heavens of the gods.
This was somewhere terrifying. Somewhere cold and lonely. "NO!"

A chill snaked up my spine, and I trembled within its icy chains.
"*Please!*" I screamed, agonizing for someone to hear me.

*Gods, no. I came back to beat the Uncanny. How could this have
happened?*

I remembered the gods' magic pulsing through me. The Gwylis had
lost, changed back into humans. The curse gone. The demons gone. We
had *won*.

"You are stronger than we imagined." The Uncanny's thick shadows
converged into one blot of darkness. Maybe they had always been one
being with thousands of voices like memories of hate and suffering that
went on and on. I fell to my knees within the void. I'd been here before

in my dreams. But it had never been so vivid. "We will not let you win. You belong to us."

I cried out for Ashe. Was he safe back in Stormwall? Had he seen me disappear? Or was my body lying there, unconscious while I battled here with the demons?

I hung my head. *So, it's come to this. Just me and the Uncanny.*

Nothing could ever be easy, could it?

I'd rallied the gods and we'd won in the world above. They had no foothold on human souls any longer. The gods were back with us. They would never make a bargain ever again.

That is, if history did not repeat itself.

"Who knew," the Uncanny went on, "the gods would return for a measly human like you. You knew not of the power you played with. You could have ruled the world."

Outrage kindled deep in my core. "Yet, here we are."

The darkness making up the demon writhed. Slits of eyes peered through, fire-red. "But we have you, so all is not for nothing."

My body jerked, and suddenly I stood at attention, forced up by some unseen power. A scream waited in my throat, held back only by pure will.

"Now, come to us, Queen of Wolves," the demons hissed.

I took one tentative step. Another. I closed my eyes, shutting out the nothingness around me.

Victory, I had it right there in my hands.

I still had it.

Didn't I?

"It's time to leave, brave girl," the Uncanny spoke. "Your father awaits you here in the fire, and I suspect he has a quite a bit to say to you. Your mother too."

I traced the lines of my memories of my parents and found them blank.

Instead, I saw Lulu, my dear sweet cousin who would have been in the front lines alongside with me, had she survived. Fresh tears stung my eyes at the memory of her face, the bravery in her heart. She'd given it to me.

The ground shifted beneath my feet, and I took a steadying breath to battle back my fear.

"There is another man who wishes to speak to you by the name of Pike—"

I ran a finger along my scar, where the arrow had come through. A reminder that I had endured.

I curled my hand into a fist and bared my teeth.

Opened my eyes.

The Uncanny's writhing had ceased, frozen in time, like an exhale.

The world does not bend for you.

I smiled, suddenly vindicated.

My story would not end here. The Uncanny would not take me. I would not die. I would bend this world to my will.

This will not kill me.

"You are weaker than I imagined," I said, throwing their words back. "You forget that you were cast from the heavens and imprisoned in darkness." My fingers inched toward the dagger sheathed at my hip. "You forget that you are prisoners still."

"No." The word was a gush, like a torrent of wind. "You asked us for help."

A flicker of motion to my left caught my eye.

"I was driven by desperation." I had been no better than Aquarius, who I had judged. But we had made decisions based on what we loved. On what we wished to protect. "I don't regret doing it."

That is what they want; they want me to feel shame and guilt.

A motion on my right.

Determination bolted through me. "I have power within me. I have power at my back. I have the love of my friends and of my family. Nothing can stop that. Not all the deals in the world."

A flash of light and I smiled again.

Surrounding me, stood those who were gone. Lulu. Henry. Ghetee. Tyron and many others I recognized by face if not by name.

I looked closer.

My eyes lingered on one person I had not expected. She was no longer the grotesque beast I'd encountered in the dungeons. She wore a deep red gown, corset cinched in her waist, pushing her chest up. A shiny bauble sat at her breasts, and her stark black hair sat atop her head in an intricate braid.

My mother.

Tears blurred my vision as I lift my hand, palm out. My breath caught in my throat as she mimicked the gesture. She set her eyes on the Uncanny with a fierce determination

Grief charged at my heart, but also pride.

They'd come to me.

Love had my back.

With a battle cry, they charged at the Uncanny, their light engulfing the demons like chains. The darkness, strangled and desperate, cried out.

My past, who I had loved with all my heart, came together at the end.

Because of them, I was not afraid.

Because of them, I would never be afraid again.

And when they begged for mercy, I drew the demon closer and stabbed it in the heart.

The gods' magic bathed me in warmth, searing my skin and ripping a cry from my throat. It pushed through my blade and into the darkness, filling it up. Tearing, ripping, demolishing it all.

The very thing that tried to take my world from me.

I'll banish you deeper, my thoughts raged. *If you return, I will fight you until my last breath. Living or dying. I will be there. My children will be there. We will stand.*

The void exploded in a burst of light so bright, it could light up the world for thousands of years. I crumpled to my knees as my muscles weakened and my magic waned.

Arms outstretched to catch me. To pull me to my feet.

Henry held me tightly. He smelled of musk and iron.

It was always you, I thought as I drifted. *It had always been for you.*

Henry, my beloved big brother, only smiled. "Not anymore, Izzy. Wake up."

CHAPTER FORTY-NINE

I awoke in Ashe's arms with nothing but a flutter of eyes and a small gasp. I buried my face into his chest, and he held me tight.

Together we sat on the battlefield of the greatest war Mirosa had ever seen. Together we let loose the grief we'd long buried. For the lives we'd taken. For the lives taken from us.

"It's over," Ashe said into my hair.

It's over.

Ashe pulled me to my feet. His face, stained with blood and muck, his lips caked in it. He looked very much the warrior prince I'd imagined him to be when he'd first arrived at Stormwall so many months ago.

How far we've come.

He let me lean into him as thunderous booms filled the air. No, not booms. Bells.

A city that had begun celebrating their victory.

I turned to face the castle; my home, and took a staggering breath at the thought of the battle-wrought city and the burials we'd soon attend. So much death. So much..."Don't leave me."

Ashe wrapped an arm around my shoulder and gently nudged my head into his. "After all this time, why would I leave now?"

Because I did not want to be alone.

Because even now, I did not feel victory as I should.

~

No more than an hour later, I was up and trailing Ashe to what I thought would be a council room, but turned out to be the main hall. There we found Derwin, Flea, and two people I never thought I'd ever see again in my lifetime.

I rushed to Olio and leapt into his arms. He caught me quick enough to avoid toppling over. He squeezed tightly. He smelled like rust and blood, no hint of the wilderness on him anywhere. War was hell.

"I can't believe you came," I said as we pulled apart. I looked over his shoulder to Branch, who appeared stoic as always. A large tear in his tunic revealed a bleeding wound that needed to be dressed, but he didn't seem affected by his newfound incapability to heal. He gifted me a nod and then turned toward the doors where Sonia strode in, looking worse for the wear.

"Aquarius is dying," she said. "In the courtyard, just there."

Everything else faded around me, even the lifeless bodies strewn across the floor. I weaved around them and reached the fountain in the center of the courtyard where the gathering grew so thick, I had to shove my way through.

"Let her through!" Sonia shouted. "Let the queen through!"

Aquarius lay on his back with his hands folded atop his chest. His eyes were closed, but his chest heaved. He looked older, if it were possible. The slips of white hair that had hung on were now gone, leaving his head bald. His arms were mere bones, and he shivered. He looked weak. He looked terrified.

He looked human.

I laid a hand on his shoulder, and he opened his eyes slowly, pain reflected in them.

"I thought you abandoned me again," I said, fighting back tears.

Sonia answered. "He led us far into the Old Kingdom to find allies, Izzy. He saved us all."

Indeed, he did. Without him, we might have lost more men and women. I closed my eyes briefly and brought into memory the guilt that riddled the old man for so long, but now I sensed closure. He could die now knowing that he'd redeemed himself, not only in his people's eyes, but also the gods'. "Thank you."

Aquarius did not speak. He did not look at me. Instead, he looked skyward, and whatever he saw there stretched his lips into a smile. *Go, I thought. Be free.* And then he was gone.

I stood and wiped the tears from my eyes. "Hail the king; the king is dead," I said, my voice breaking. I repeated the words, louder and firmer each time until my throat grew hoarse. "Hail the king! The king is dead!"

The words grew like a chant and rippled across the courtyard until I swore I heard it as far as the city and across the plains. *Hail the king! Hail the king!*

A new world had begun.

As I weaved out of the crowd to where Ashe stood with Branch and Olio, a sudden heaviness took hold, and I bent forward. I could have vomited, but there was nothing in my stomach.

"Izzy."

Ashe grasped me under my arms and hauled me to my feet. He whispered, "Don't fail now. They need you."

"Has anyone—" I swallowed and shook the exhaustion from my body. "Have we deployed healers?"

Olio nodded. "The battle ran deep across the plains. Thousands are dead or wounded. It's going to take days to comb through it all."

"What can I do?" Ashe asked.

"Sonia is forming a group to take into the city," Branch replied. "You can aid her. I am going west..."

Their words faded. Their mouths moved, but I heard nothing. I turned to look over the courtyard. A pair of men had hoisted Aquarius's body and were bringing him into the castle to be prepared for burial, I assumed. Some were removing bodies from the ground, piling them in the far end of the courtyard against the hedges. I blinked and saw Sonia pacing. Branch had stopped talking and stared at me. Ashe tilted his head.

"Izzy?"

I looked at them. I looked at each of them.

And asked, "Where is Fray?"

Sonia looked away. Olio closed his eyes. Nobody spoke.

Pressure built within my chest, and my words came out louder. *"Where is Fray?"*

Branch answered first. "We went into battle side by side, but we were separated. He led those flying demons away from the battle."

"Which way did he go?" My voice grew softer and cracked halfway through my question. *"Where is he?"*

In their silence, I recalled Olio's words: *Thousands are dead or wounded. It's going to take days to comb through it all.*

"We're going to find him, Izzy," Olio said, but his eyebrows pinched. He looked close to tears.

"If he were dead, I would have known," Sonia added.

I whirled toward her. "How would you know?"

She lifted her shoulders and froze them there, stunned at my reaction.

Oh gods. Oh gods.

"Let me go," I said, locking eyes with Branch. "Let me go with you."

Ashe shook his head. "No, we need you here. You're the queen now, Izzy. You have to address the people."

Address the people, while Fray lay out there dead or dying? Not one part of me wanted to wrap my head around such a thing. I pulled at my hair. Sweat broke out on my temples.

What should I do?

Olio and Sonia closed around me, their arms wrapping around my shoulders. "We're going to find him," Sonia whispered. "Trust us."

Before I could answer, I heard someone calling for me. No, not my name, but my title. Couldn't it wait? The blood had not yet dried, and they wanted to place a crown on my head, for what reason? I turned toward the voice to see Pyrus walking toward me, my mother's crown in his hands. I shook my head.

"Izzy, do it for the people," Ashe said. "They need to see you."

A massive crowd had formed. It came from the courtyard, from the main hall within the castle and up, stretching along the king's road as far as my eyes could see. They were my people. My kingdom.

They needed me.

As I stepped toward Pyrus, my eyes caught sight of a crow soaring overhead. It curled like a buzzard, gliding over the tops of the crowd. I looked at Pyrus, then to the crown, and felt like nothing mattered.

Finally, nothing mattered, except Fray.

I missed the way he'd always scowl, even when he was happy. My moody wolf with the attitude problem. I missed the deft movement of his fingers when he signed and the way his muscles moved beneath his clothes. I'd been falling since the first time we'd met, plummeting down, down, down.

"Isabelle Victoria Rowan, we crown you Queen of Mirosa," Pyrus said, loud enough that the words traveled as people spoke them. He lifted the crown. He lowered his voice. "You're supposed to bend at the knee, Izzy."

Awwwwwwwwk!

The crow landed on Pyrus's shoulder. It tilted its head as Pyrus shrugged it off.

"Pax?" I whispered, my heart stuttering.

Pax took flight again, flapping incessantly near my head, ruffling my hair. I shook my head and turned back to Pyrus. My mind told me to move, to bend, to accept this crown, but something in my heart told me to lock my knees.

AWWWWWWWWWK!

Something broke inside of me, a dam against a raging river. I backed away. One step and then another, until I pushed through the crowd, weaving my way around the side of the castle.

Fray wasn't dead. I knew this in my heart.

Pax led the way, cawing as he flew overhead.

I ran as fast as my human legs could go, through the charred forest and onto the battlefield.

Bodies as far as the eye could see. So many dead. Healers walked amongst them, slowly, using swords to kill the wounded enemies and find the living.

I told him not to come for me. But he did. And he may have given his life because his stubbornness could not keep him away. *Stupid man*, I thought. *Stupid, stupid man.*

Pax screamed for my attention and bolted forward.

I shoved through, tripping over bodies. I had to look at it. To make sure. My eyes clouded over with tears. Sobs cracked my chest in half.

How did it come to this?

If I don't find him, I will break, and I will keep breaking until there is nothing left of me.

I loved Fray Castor, and I would love him for the rest of my life, here, now, and what else comes after.

The screams of the dying and those calling for friends filled my ears. My body fell into a panic. I stumbled across the field, holding a hand to my nose to block out the smell. *If I were a wolf, I could run faster,* I thought. *I could smell him out.*

Pax called out, begging for me to focus.

I knew coming here was doing the impossible. There were thousands of bodies here. Blood soaked the fields, and daylight waned. It looked endless. It looked futile.

I called out for him as I moved, albeit slowly. Pax cawed relentlessly, but I had to keep eyes on the ground. Walking slowly, I scanned the faces of the dead, begging the gods that he wasn't among them. I pawed furiously at my tears and set my jaw.

I ran.

I crashed through healers, tripped over bodies. Eyes forward, not down. Pax led the way, flapping furiously, glad that I'd finally caught up to him.

Crows were the messengers of the gods. *Follow me,* he said. *Hurry!*

"Fray!" My screams were drowned out by the chaos around me, by the patches of fighting still raging, by the sound of Pax crying, and by the people calling out as I ran past.

It couldn't be the end. It couldn't be.

RUN.

I could not wear the crown, not until Fray was safe and home with me. Not until he stood beside me.

"Fray!" My scream felt small, building up to something horrible that waited to be unleashed.

But I wouldn't let it. I ran and ran.

"Fray!" My throat burned like hot coals, but I screamed his name. I would until my voice was gone entirely.

Please be here. He had to be here.

I screamed for him once more before stopping to catch my breath. A tremendous sadness built up in my body. A desperation. The plains were a graveyard, and I stood in a sea of the dead. *I can't do this without you. Not without you!*

AWWWWWWWWWK!

I plunged back into it, further and further from the heart of the battle. I bit down on the pain igniting my legs and the sheer exhaustion threatening to upend me. I came finally to a place where the bodies were scattered far enough to see the grass. They were not my soldiers, but the enemy Gwylis. Some had even died in their monster forms, as if they'd been killed so quickly, they did not have time to revert. I followed the trail of them. There were so many.

I tried to run fast enough.

I wasn't running fast enough.

"Fray!" His name came out in a rasp. Was it possible that he had survived and was already on his way back to the castle? He could already be there, looking for me!

AWWWWWWWWK!

"You're wrong, Pax," I said. My throat felt as though it would start bleeding at any moment. "He's not here."

But Pax protested. He lowered himself and dug his feet into my back. *Come,* he told me. *A little further.*

I did, but my pace slowed, every step permeating despair. Until suddenly, Pax landed.

And a voice called my name.

Fray lay on his back, a sword still in his hands as he tried to reach out. My name fell from his lips in a cracked sob. He lay dying not ten feet away.

His free hand came to clasp mine as I fell to my knees beside him. His entire body was soaked with blood. This was not like the injury he'd endured back at Stormwall. These were not gashes that split his skin, but a cut from a sword that left his belly leaking blood so badly, I thought he shouldn't be alive.

He lifted his head, but it fell back onto the ground. His hair plastered against his forehead. Blood painted his face. His voice a wet rasp. His blue eyes lightened as his life seeped from his body.

Like Lulu. Like Ghetee.

NO.

I tore the fabric of his shirt, ignoring Pax's cries as he fluttered around me, and pressed my hands to the open wound. He must have healed a little by the way the skin had begun to stitch itself in the corners, but the wound still gaped, like a mouth split into a sinister smile. I saw bone and muscle. My stomach flipped.

"We need help." My next words were a sobbing scream. "*We need help!*"

But we were too far from where the healers were making their way through carefully. I'd passed all that. They wouldn't find us for hours. Days.

He swallowed, and it sounded painful. He opened his mouth to speak again, but no words came out. An ugly bruise spread across his throat.

"Don't," I told him, pressing my hands to his belly. "Don't speak. You've fought long enough."

He lifted one hand, and then the other dropped the sword, and he tried to sign, but I clapped them with my own bloodied palms and shook my head. His face radiated agony. His mouth twisted with so many unspoken things I did not need to hear.

"I don't need your words," I told him. "I just need you."

He groaned and his look softened.

No, don't leave me.

I dropped his hands and pressed mine to his wound once again. I did not know how the small magic worked, but I summoned the same thoughts I thought when I'd shielded the battle from my balcony. The love I had for Fray was not just in my heart, but in my very soul.

"Fray Castor." I focused on my magic and my words, which were a prayer. "Until the day I die, I will love you. You are part of everything that I was and everything that I am now. I know we were not soulless because you are my soul and always have been."

His breath came in staggered rasps. His heart stuttered, and his eyes slowly closed.

"No!" I cried out. "Open your eyes. *FRAY!*"

Don't let this be the end. Please.

His body stilled, although his chest rose. Fresh blood leaked over my hands until I saw nothing of my skin, only red.

Gods...

"Save him." My words were firm and clear despite the agony ripping through my body. "Save him. *Now.*"

I didn't know what my magic would do, but I knew I could not lose him. *I don't want to know what it's like to live in a world without him in it.*

I focused everything on the wound, and along with my pleading to the gods, a soft light glowed from my hands and immediately encased Fray's body within. I wasn't ready to let him go. I wished for him to live more than I wished for anything.

I kept on begging the gods as the light brightened like a second sun. I could no longer see Fray's body, but I knew it was there beneath my palms. His abdomen contracted and his legs kicked out, and beneath my hands, the wound knitted itself together, little by little.

Making him whole.

Suddenly, he cried out in pain. I kept going until the light dimmed and I'd run out of energy to keep my body upright. I fell beside Fray's body, hoping that if he died, the gods would take me too.

A gentle quiet flowed through the world, and I closed my eyes.

An intake of breath opened them again.

I turned my head to look at Fray, and he'd done the same. We laid there, staring at each other as if we could hardly believe the other were alive. I took a deep breath and let it go, and then I closed my eyes.

"Don't go," I whispered. I turned my body and fit myself against him. One hand pressed to his chest. To his heart that beat steadily.

He reached a hand to touch my cheek.

And I slept.

CHAPTER FIFTY

Stormwall stood as a husk of its former glory. Rubble cascaded the streets, and shattered windows glittered in the morning sun. The air smelled of blood and rot. People stood around, gathering up what they could salvage, sweeping and hauling away the rest.

But the city was alive. They would rebuild. I would help them, every step of the way.

Izzy sat up from her bed when I entered her bedroom. It didn't look as though she'd been awake long by the bewildered look on her face.

"Get out," she said.

I did the opposite, coming to sit at the edge of her bed. "Like old times, huh?"

She held her head in her hands. "How long have I been asleep?"

"Two days."

She pursed her lips and nodded. "Water?"

I pointed to her bedside table. "Just there."

She gulped down the entire glass, and I flinched when she looked at me again. Her eyes are hard and filled with something I couldn't describe. Determination, perhaps? "We have made efforts to reunite families and rebuild," I told her. "We have a proper coronation planned—"

"No."

"No?" I leaned forward with my elbows to my knees. "I'm not sure I follow."

"I am happy with what I am," she murmured. "I am happy, and therefore I am not sure that I can be a proper ruler for Mirosa. I want a life. I want freedom."

"What are you talking about?" My voice sounded alarmingly edgy. She appeared to be awake and fully aware of her surroundings. Was she still sleeping? I went to poke her when she swatted me away.

"I want you to wear the crown, Ashe," she said firmly.

I opened my mouth. Closed it again. The only way I could think that I would sit on the throne would be if I married Izzy or she abdicated the throne. Was it possible that *I* was dreaming?

Izzy smiled warmly and scooted closer. "I considered you, Ashe, but I cannot marry you. I do wish you will marry someday and have lots of children."

"Mostly boys?" I jested.

Izzy tilted her head. "Ashe, I'm giving you the crown. Don't make it weird."

The crown? I could see Izzy wearing it; I could see her ruling, and she would be better than her father before her. But I could also see her in a quiet place living in a world that she'd remade, that she could watch grow from afar.

I finally saw Izzy for who she always was. What she always wanted.

"Are you sure?"

Izzy nodded. "I don't want to be queen. I thought I did, but when it all ended, I felt as if I had done everything I could do. It's time for somebody else to take the reins."

This journey had taken so much out of Izzy. I wasn't quite sure how long it would take her to recover. How long it would take us to recover. But I saw the bravery in her, and that would never change. Not for anything.

"I think Mirosa needs a new beginning," she said. I could see the future she saw reflected in her eyes. "No more Rowans."

"No more Paratheons."

She smiled. "How about Paratherowan?"

I laughed. "Don't give me false hope."

She only smiled, her look forlorn.

"I don't know if I can do it..." I faltered, thinking of everything I was and how much I'd yet to discover. Could I be the king that Mirosa needed?

"You can," Izzy said, coming to sit beside me. She rested her head on my shoulder. "You'd do anything for your kingdom. I saw it firsthand."

"What about you?" I asked.

"I'll go somewhere where I can watch the ocean. Somewhere Henry would be happy."

I stared at my hand. "I will be king if you want."

Izzy pushed me playfully. "Let it be whatever *you* want, Ashe."

Did I want to become king?

I would have ruled beside Izzy, had she chosen me all those months ago, so the thought was not a foreign one. I thought about what I could do with uniting both kingdoms, as well as the islands. I knew it would take time, but time was what I had.

Yes. I wanted to become king.

I stood up and bent at the waist. "I accept."

Izzy stood up, drew me into an embrace, and held long and tight. "Take me to him?"

I nodded into her hair. "Will I see you after this is done?"

She pulled away and met my eyes. "I won't be far. I'll always be there for you. Always."

A strange mix of emotions flooded through me. Sadness. Anxiety. Excitement. Fear.

Hope.

"All right. Let's go see that boy of yours."

CHAPTER FIFTY-ONE

Fray was not in the infirmary, but in one of the guest rooms on the same floor as my own. There were no guards at his door or anywhere in the halls. But there was destruction at every turn. Burned carpeting, broken accents, and scorched walls. I tried to ignore it all, but it was impossible.

Fray lay on a large bed, body under the covers, arms at his side, eyes closed. I whispered his name, and his eyes opened. There were angry gashes on his forehead; his throat wrapped so he could not turn his head to me.

I walked over to him and pulled up a chair.

"I know you're resting, but I wanted to see how you were. Pyrus told me that, along with the injury of your stomach and your throat, your leg was crushed very badly and that your recovery will be slow, but you will walk again, with a limp perhaps."

There was a weariness in his eyes. His frown deepened as he tried to sit up.

"Let me."

But the moment I tried to help haul his body up, he rejected me, brushing my hands away. With a grunt, he managed it on his own and signed. *We won? Is it over?*

I swallowed the lump in my throat. "Yes."

You left me.

"Yes."

What else could I say? I had my reasons for leaving and doing what I had done. But I could not give excuses to Fray. I could not make him understand, because it was over.

Until Fray's hand found mine.

I leaned over. Our faces were so close, I could see the specks of yellow in his blue eyes. Blood still crusted the wounds littering his beautiful face. Gashes like claw marks on his brow and jawline. The bruise I'd seen on his throat peeked from the bandage, angry and dark.

He stared into me, and I thought about the Fray I had once known. This was not the one who saved me from dying by a poisoned arrow and who tried to hunt down my would-be assassins. This was not the Fray who gave me his heart. He was no longer a beast. He was breakable.

I signed, *I'm sorry.*

I watched him read my deft hands, the way he used to when he was Voiceless. His careful demeanor melted. His hand in mine tightened before straying to my shoulder, to my scar, my cheek.

I shut my eyes at his touch, suddenly overcome by how much I had missed him; how I missed the feel of his skin and the way he loved me so unconditionally. He knew me beyond the royal title, beyond any title at all. I knew him by the downturned lips and the way his brow lowered when he was thinking too hard. I knew him by how he defined me and how he defined love.

I felt it now, with his hand on my cheek—the sum of everything we never got to say and everything we would ever be. I put my hand over his and met his eyes, silently telling him that I could not have lived without him if he had died. *I do not exist if you don't.*

Our first meeting played out like a song in my head, a story on my lips. An unconventional romance burdened with fear and loss. I'd remember it always, the way he'd come into my life and how I refused to admit it before, but I felt his absence like a hole in my chest.

He robbed breath from my lungs, seeing him now—as he always did.

He pulled his hand away if only to sign, *Seeing you hurts me.*

I'd learned that sometimes in life, you felt pain before the blow was dealt. An anticipation, perhaps, a memory of an injury. Your mind prepared you before the hit came.

In this moment, my body tensed as though a blade were soaring toward me.

I swallowed back emotion rising in my throat. I did not own Fray. I could not control him. He'd had a whole life before me. But the thought of being without him crushed me. "No, I know. I can't take back what I've done to you."

Are you all right?

A weight loosened from my shoulders. "Yes, I'm all right, for now. Whatever all right truly is."

I thought you were dead.

I thought of what I'd seen when I died and the horror when I was living. I thought of all those I lost and whose memories would never fade. *I am of this earth, and I will bear its strife.*

A shadow passed over his face. *Our friends?*

"Alive."

The prince?

"He kept me alive, in a sense. I wouldn't be here if not for him."

My hand strayed to the scar over my heart.

"I think we have much to talk about, Fray Castor, but now is not the time." I paused, thinking of the right words. "I don't know if there will ever be a right time, but for now, we heal, however long it takes."

Will you stay here?

"In Stormwall?"

He nodded.

"No. I abdicated the throne to Ashe, and before you retort, just let me tell you how much it makes sense. I want my name to belong to something else. Something better."

Fray smiled. *I missed you.*

The tears finally came. I swiped at them furiously. "I'd hug you if you didn't look like a terrible mess."

A bigger smile pulled at his lips.

This was the most I was getting out of him, I decided. As soon as Ashe was coroneted, I would leave Stormwall. There would be no turning back when it came to my decisions. I would go, with or without Fray.

Better with him.

But here we were again, saying goodbye.

Fray clicked his tongue to get my attention. *I can't sleep. I'm afraid to sleep. I see—*

"Demons."

He nodded, and my heart wrenched.

"They're not gone, just contained," I said. "But the gods are here, and they will protect us now."

Fray's hands moved quickly. *It feels strange not being a wolf.*

"Do you still remember the way it felt?"

Fray swallowed, and his face scrunched up with pain. *It was all I ever knew.*

How long would it take the Gwylis to forget their curse? Would they ever get used to being human, so fragile and breakable? Would they ever stop trying to run, or point their noses to the moon?

I tucked a stray hair behind his ear, and his eyes met mine. My heart jumped into my throat at the memory of his lips; a sweet and bitter memory, knowing I may never feel them again. We'd start over as people. Love changes, ever shifting with ebbs and flows. But my love of him would never be silenced.

The door to the room opened and a nurse came in, carrying fresh bandages and a jug of water atop a tray. Our time was up. I stood up and made for the door without another word when I heard Fray struggle for breath as he choked out my name.

"Isabelle."

I turned. "Don't speak, Fray. You'll hurt yourself."

He shook his head and even tried to get out of bed before the nurse caught him before he stumbled. Settling him back into the bed, she scolded him as I watched from the doorway, forcing myself not to run to his aid. To protect him.

"He wants to speak; let him speak," the nurse said to me. "He won't do any more damage than he already has."

"Speak, Fray, but keep it short."

"You..." He paused, sniffing and shaking his head in frustration. "You...are...everything."

I covered my mouth with my hands, containing the giddy sob breaking through. "You are *my* everything," I said through joyful tears.

I did not need a throne, not when I had the love of a boy lovelier than a golden crown. No matter where we went in the days to come, no matter how dark the night or how frightful the dreams, I had him, and that was everything I needed.

CHAPTER FIFTY-TWO

I took a deep breath, held it, and counted to three.

In the small room behind the thrones, I itched at the fabric against my skin. Pedoma had insisted I wear the dress since she'd been working on it since the day I left Stormwall after Dal Paratheon had taken over. I hadn't worn a dress in so many months; I'd become a different person. Still, the old Izzy smiled, and the new one endured it. After today, I wouldn't have to wear dresses if I didn't want to. I never had to do anything I didn't want to do.

"You look beautiful."

I turned to see Ashe. His hair was shorn as short as the day we'd first met. He wore a uniform: black pants with a matching jacket capped with silver buttons. My eyes snagged on the insignia stitched where his heart lay beating.

The moon and the sun and the stars. A new symbol for a new world.

He stood straight and tall, almost kingly. Gone was the weariness that weighed him down. He was every inch the man I used to know.

All except for the past swirling behind his eyes.

He must have seen the way my face had fallen. He pursed his lips and tilted his head away from me. "Time will tell just how strong we are to forget."

I knew right away how every word about that was wrong. Strength had nothing to do with it. As humans, we were bound to our memories just as the stars were bound to the night sky. We would never forget, no matter how strong we were.

The silence stretched between us, broken only by Lile, who came to stand beside Ashe. The young boy had grown since I last saw him. The hardness in his eyes had stayed, but his loyalty had brought him here along with several of the boys we'd rescued from Essex. With parents either dead or missing, they came to stay at Stromwall at our invitation. Lile had proven himself something of a shadow to Ashe, trailing him at every turn.

"I'm too young to be a father," he'd said a week ago. "I can't care for these children."

I had smiled, not because I found it funny, but because I knew Ashe wanted them more than anything in the world. I saw it in the way he'd gather them up at night to tell them stories. In the way he always made sure they were accounted for at meals. I saw it in the way his face lit up at the very mention of the boys.

I smiled now, because Abiyaya had been correct in her prediction. Ashe had become a father. Everything felt right.

In the weeks since the war ended, Stormwall had begun a transformation. The servants my father employed—the ones I'd grown up knowing—all returned, and with new titles. They would not serve the king and queen, but work with them. They could come and go as they pleased. Laws were changed and people were punished. There had been a great inquiry into what had happened in Essex, and a new lord had been chosen to oversee its reconstruction.

"Ashe, you look like a light breeze would blow you over," I jested. I worked closely with the new council to reunite families and arrange burial for the dead. It had been a daunting task, one that kept me awake most nights, so this day was supposed to push all the sad stuff to the side. Today was to be a day of celebration. "You're nervous as a baby rabbit."

Ashe laughed, but quickly sobered, taking a steadying breath.

"The crowd has gathered as far as the city streets," Lile informed us. He looked handsome in a crisp uniform. He stood with his hands clasped behind his back, like Ashe, and even cut his hair similarly. "Are you ready?"

I was in a dream. In another life, I would have been where Ashe stood now, but I did not regret a thing. He took a steadying breath and moved to go beyond the curtain separating us from the thrones. His head turned to look at me, but thought better of it. He held it a moment and stepped beyond my reach, Lile trailing behind him.

As the curtain fluttered behind him, I caught a glimpse of the waiting crowd. I spotted my aunt and uncle, Lulu's parents. Pedoma and Crim. Derwin and Flea and lords and ladies from other cities. I saw Olio, Branch, Sonia, and Rini. I saw a joining of worlds.

But mostly, I saw humans.

Many of the people that had gathered either in the castle or outside had spent part, if not most, of their lives fighting. Those we once called the Gwylis lived their lives in fear that one day, they would have to defend their home at any given moment. Some lived hiding like mice while others hid in other ways, pretending they were human and that their souls had not been tainted with a curse. Now human, they could choose to be whatever they wanted, but they no longer had to be afraid.

I hoped things could stay this way for a long time to come.

Within the confines of the small room, I listened to a man speak. "It is customary to first crown the king or queen before they get to speak, but on this occasion, which is an occasion unlike any other, we are throwing customs to the wind."

The crowd gave a low laugh. Ashe cleared his throat.

"I should not be here," he said plainly. "But I have come a long way to find that the places we think we are meant for may not always be the places you end up. I am here because I killed a man who should not have taken your kingdom from you. I am here because another king had made some bad decisions. I am here because an entire line of rulers have wanted nothing but to destroy. I am here to bring these worlds together and banish evil once and for all."

I closed my eyes and counted the steady, slow pulse of my heartbeat. Never had I heard Ashe sound so confident and so firm. I smiled as I moved the curtain aside just enough to see Ashe kneeling in front a white-robed man. The man set a crown atop my friend's head, a crown made from Henry's dagger and set with emerald, ruby, and celestite. With the crown, Ashe became King of Mirosa.

Ashe glanced at me, and I chastised him with a look as I pinched the curtain to my mouth to thwart my tears. The crowd erupted with cheers.

I closed the curtain and snuck away, tears of joy flowing faster than a heartbeat.

~

I DID NOT WANT TO BE QUEEN. I'D THOUGHT ABOUT MY MOTHER and the other women that had worn the crown and wondered how they could have sat and watched as history played out before them and done nothing to stop it. These daughters of lords, mothers to princes and princesses. All of them who let men destroy, who turned a blind eye and bit their tongues. I thought about Lulu, who had dared take a courageous step to fighting for what she believed and was struck down for it.

No, I did not want to be queen. Not if they remembered the Rowan name.

The celebration poured from the castle and into the courtyards, where music filled the air and food filled our bellies. Torches blazed and wavered in the light breeze. The grounds were packed to bursting. Everyone had come to see Ashe's coronation.

But everyone stared at me.

"Dance with me." Ashe smiled gallantly as he bowed slightly and offered a hand. The metal one. "You owe me."

I snorted and took his hand. He pulled me into position with gentle hands on my back and danced with the sure-footedness of a king. "They're all looking."

"Of course, they are. They think you're going to be my queen."

"I can imagine that ending very badly for us," I said, suppressing a smile.

The musicians kept on playing, and I swayed along with Ashe. Women giggled as he twirled me effortlessly and brought me back into his arms. Their stares clenched my heart. I knew he'd end up with someone eventually, but part of me wanted to be there when he did so I could tell his woman of choice I'd sooner eat her than see my friend's heart broken. But that part of me no longer existed. No longer was I the murderous and vengeful Izzy. Now I stuck to simple emotions, like jealousy and sorrow.

I imagined what I would see if I'd turned and looked back at Ashe Paratheon, the sadness and the regret. There weren't any words to cure any of us of the past. We'd live with our demons forever. But Ashe and I would have a bond that only came when two people shared a terrible ordeal, and we may have woken up screaming with the memories of it all, but we weren't alone.

But Ashe stared past me, and his face open and resigned.

"Ashe?" I asked. I turned and followed his gaze to what caught his attention. Fray. He dressed exquisitely in a black uniform, loosened at the neck, and his long hair brushed and tied back. He crossed the hall toward us, his limp barely there, but noticeable. He stopped briefly, his face not scathing for seeing me with Ashe, but filled with admiration.

I felt Ashe's eyes on me. "The only other man to lose his breath over you."

"You're joking about that time I tried to kill you, aren't you?" I slapped his arm. "Behave. You're a king now. Oh, who's she?"

A woman with long amber hair pulled to one side, wearing a simple cream-colored gown stood behind Ashe. She looked to be holding in a growing smile.

"Someone you know?" I asked, waggling my eyebrows.

Fray reached us and bowed. "May I cut in?"

I embraced Ashe tightly and whispered in his ear, "Be a good king. Build a good kingdom."

A kingdom where love could stand.

I stepped from his arms and turned toward Fray.

Fray put his hands on my waist, and I reached up to set my hands on his shoulders.

"You clean up rather nicely."

He licked his lips and smiled. "I've always thought you did."

We swayed from side to side, moving our feet slowly. It was just as well, seeing as Fray had two left feet, and with his injury, he probably shouldn't even be dancing at all lest he take out all my toes. I spotted Ashe and the girl in the cream dress dancing not far from us. If I knew any better, there was a certain flush to his cheeks. *Oh, Ashe, you deserve it.*

"I saw that your horse being made ready," Fray said. "As soon as you are."

In the weeks that had followed, Fray recovered, and we said very little to each other. Everybody kept to themselves, if only for a time as to gather their thoughts and settle themselves down in their new lives. There had been so much work to do. By the end of the day, I'd peeked in on Fray to whisper goodnight and fallen into sleep, only to wake up hours later in a panic. It took several minutes to remember where I back in Stormwall and not in the center of a battle.

When Fray could speak again, he told me what had happened. He spoke about falling from the mountain—volcano, he told me afterward— and how Neera and her sisters begged to sacrifice themselves to the gods. He told me, in great detail even for a man, how he felt when I had left and the sadness that had threatened to overwhelm him.

We all had pasts that hurt us, and it would take a long time to heal those wounds. Right now, we all had to work on healing ourselves.

"I had them prepare another horse," Fray continued.

My heart seized, and I took a gulping breath, going over every possibility how this moment could end; fearful there was an enemy to evade, a shadow ever growing at our backs. I felt like I was at the center a firestorm and I couldn't breathe, I couldn't breathe...

You're all right, Fray signed. He nodded, jaw tense, a hard look in his eyes. *Everything is all right.*

Slowly, ever so gently, he leaned in. I gasped against his mouth, obliterating all the sadness and grief I'd kept inside. Every muscle in his own body tightened; I felt the tentative way he brushed his lips against my own, feather light. He'd been through so much. This simple act of connecting to another was now foreign to us both.

"I miss you," I said when he drew back. His eyes danced across mine, searching. "I don't miss what we were, because we never had a chance.

"We were together in secret before leaving Stormwall, and at the Den, we had our own set of new challenges. We never had time to discover one another; to get to know who each of us were."

We never had a chance to grow to love one another truly.

"I miss you too," Fray said.

Moving with fluid grace, he stepped back and took my hand. He nibbled his lower lip, and with my hand still grasped in his, turned in a complete circle and then pulled me into him. He didn't say a word. He held me and looked me in the eyes as I smothered a smile. I brushed back a strand of hair that had come undone and tucked it behind his ear.

"We're going to be okay," I said. "I need to know if you can forgive me."

A crease formed between his brow, his lips pinched tight. "I never blamed you, not really, but if you want forgiveness, you have it."

My throat constricted. I held him closer, feeling his heart against mine. "It just...it hurts sometimes. It *hurts a lot.* Everything—"

"I know." He took both hands and cupped my chin. "It hurts for me too. I never wanted to hurt you. I never wanted anything bad to happen to you. The first time I saved you—the first time, I beat myself up for not getting there in time. For giving you that scar—"

"Fray."

He took a sharp breath.

"None of it was your fault. None of it was my fault. We were given a broken world. We did what we could to put it back together. My scar, it's a part of me. I do not regret anything. Not anymore."

"Not even meeting me?" he asked.

"I'd meet you a thousand times over. There's no life without you."

Fray's chest heaved. "It's going to take a lot of work."

I touched his face, his lips, his cheeks, his brow. "And we have a lot of time. We're stronger now. We'll get even stronger in time."

I pulled my face to his and kissed him as the music faded around us and the only two people on this floor were me and the boy I loved. His mouth was warm against mine, his heart beating in time with mine. He tasted like the forest, like new buds and spring. He held a promise in those lips, and I trusted it.

"Thank for you saving me," I whispered into his ear.

"Thank you for saving me," he said with a laugh.

"Fray?"

"Izzy."

I rested my head on his shoulder. "Don't ever leave me."

"Never." He bared his teeth and fiercely drew me against him. "Not ever."

And he leaned down and pressed his lips to mine, and we slipped from the hall, away from the music and the people to the dimly-lit corridors, and into the darkness I no longer feared.

CHAPTER FIFTY-THREE

The morning after the coronation, I went to Branch's room to find it already occupied with both my sister and Olio.

"Did I come at a bad time?" I asked Branch, who shook his head. Sonia and Olio drew me into their arms. Their embrace felt like a good-bye. "You're leaving?"

Sonia pulled away while Olio lingered, his arms wrapped around my neck as I tried to shove him away. "We were going to tell you later this morning at breakfast," she said. She bit her lower lip and chuckled. "Since we didn't see you last night, of course."

I rolled my eyes. "When will you return?"

"When will you?"

I held my sister's gaze. "You're right. I didn't tell you I was leaving with Izzy. In my defense, I didn't know I was until yesterday." Olio finally released me, and I stretched my neck. "Will you return to the Den?"

"For a while," Branch said. A week ago, we'd agreed, Izzy and Ashe included. The Old Kingdom would have its separate government. And whenever they were ready, they'd name a king. The Peek Islands, on the other hand, pledged their allegiance to Mirosa the day after the war ended. Small steps. "There are many who wish to make a home there once again. A new home."

Sonia made a bid for my attention. "We're going to move Henry's body and bring it home."

I let loose a sigh. Izzy would be glad to hear the news.

"It's still there." Olio sank down into one of the two plush chairs occupying the room. "I feel it sometimes, weak, but—"

I nodded, feeling the same sliver of darkness. Like a shadow, always following. "Still there."

"You look tired, brother," Sonia said.

"Courtesy of dying, nearly twice."

Olio guffawed. "I can't wait until history writes you in. The great Fray Castor of the Den, former kitchen slave and mute, saves the day by leading a bunch of weird monsters away from battle with a glowing sword. Also, he gets the girl, and a bunch of cool scars."

THAT AFTERNOON, I BADE GOODBYE TO BRANCH, OLIO, MY SISTER, and the remaining pack as they traveled past the Archway once more. One by one, I embraced them, and there were words of inspiration and thank yous all around. When I got down the line to Neera and her sisters, she smiled and pulled me away.

"You know what they're calling you?" she asked, speaking low into my ear. The crowd forming in the courtyard had grown double its size and grew by the minutes. So many wanted to come and see off their heroes.

"Please don't say cute kitchen servant with the glowing sword," I said.

Neera frowned.

"Forget it."

Neera shrugged. "If it means anything to you, they're calling you their king. Don't look so surprised. You are Aquarius and Rixon's son, and the gods did speak to you."

I nodded. "Glowing sword."

Neera grinned. "Glowing sword, indeed." She sobered up and looked past me. "Will you not come with us?"

I shook my head. "I was never made to lead, Neera. I only did what I had to survive."

"That's what leaders do, Fray."

My lips thinned as I peered at my leg. "I'm done fighting. I think a few years of sitting around, watching the sunset with Izzy will do me a lot of good."

I thought of Cas, and how Neera now had only two sisters left. I wished her peace, if it were any comfort.

She took me into an embrace and knocked the wind out of me. "I'm happy you found your love again," she said into my hair. "I knew you would, Fray."

"Thanks in part to you," I said as we pulled away. "I wish you the best, Neera."

"And you, Fray Castor." She nudged my shoulder with her fist. "Don't be a stranger."

I wanted to tell Neera that I didn't think I had it in me ever to go back to the Den ever again; a certain part of me was dead and gone, even if it lingered in tiny spurts every now and again. I knew it would fade, and years from now, my past would be nothing but a hazy memory.

I wanted to tell them all to forget me, but would that have been fair?

So, I stood there watching my friends and my sister walk away. Even the king had come to see them off. He stood on the other side of the fountain, met my eyes once, nodded, and looked away.

Out of the corner of my eye, I spotted a black-haired girl with a bow across her back, wearing a gown and sporting an arrogant smile. I knew there would never be any goodbyes. Nothing could ever be forgotten.

EPILOGUE

Spring gave way into summer, and the world began anew.

I sat on the beach in Alaster watching the layers of colors stack in the dusk. Golden beach, turquoise water, with the golden sun presiding over it all. I watched the tide and dug my bare toes into the sand. Was this the place my brother Henry used to dream about?

The evening air was cool and sent prickles to my skin. I breathed it in, knowing my brother would have been happy here.

I bought a house on the other side of a patch of tall grass overlooking the ocean. From my porch, I could see the beach where Ashe and I had washed up and the inn where I'd rubbed life back into him. I laughed at the memory. Would the rest of my memories do the same? But I woke up each morning gasping for breath before realizing I was safe. I was alive.

I was a princess no longer. A wolf no longer. I just was.

I smiled as I imagined a shivering naked prince and stood, drawing my cloak tightly around myself. From somewhere above, a crow cawed.

Any other time, I would have dismissed such a thing, but I knew better than anyone: If there were a crow around, it was important.

I raced up the beach to find the bird perched on the railing of my porch. I kicked sand from my feet and approached it tentatively. It wasn't Pax, but a small female with shorter wings than her male counterpart.

"What news from Stormwall, I wonder. Perhaps Ashe finally asked Moora to marry him." I took the small letter from her leg and gave her back a stroke. "Thank you, pretty girl. Will you stay for dinner?"

The crow cawed and hopped away in search of insects or small reptiles.

I sat on the porch and drew a cloak around me so it acted as a blanket. I set the letter in my lap and looked out at the ocean. The sun was lowering now, and I was losing light. I flicked a finger to the lantern hanging on the wall of the house behind me, and it came to life.

I'd received many letters these past few weeks, most from Olio, who seemed to not only like the sound of his own voice, but also knowing I had to listen to it even from this far away. Sprinkled between those were missives from Ashe and occasionally Pyrus and Crim with one lone one from Wargrave, who told me he'd been wrong, and that the world had bent for me after all.

I never saw Abiyaya again. But with each crow soaring overhead, I knew she was watching in some way.

Late one night, I'd received a crow from Branch telling me they'd brought my brother's bones back and buried him properly in the grave underneath the willow tree in Stormwall. I'd wept long into the night.

I'd wept a lot.

I'd wept for things long passed and things forthcoming. But mostly, I wept because I was alive, and I had everything I ever wanted.

I breathed in the night air and listened to the soft roll of the waves. When was the last time I had this sort of peace? This freedom? How long would it last?

Ashe and the lords of Mirosa had a long road of rebuilding. Integrating the Gwylis of the Old Kingdom deemed a hefty task. Not everyone saw eye to eye with their new king, but I trusted Ashe would win them over in time. Nothing was perfect. We had a war to recover from, and those wounds may never have closed for those who saw it with their own eyes.

The crow hopping in the shrubs beside my little house caught my eye, and my hand closed over the letter. "All right, Olio," I said. "What shapes did you find the clouds today?"

I went still, my fingers slackening from the parchment as I read the familiar scrawl.

"Sonia," I whispered.

I nearly lost the letter as a wind blew through. I moved my hair from my face and stood to call Fray back from the beach. He came right away. Closer, closer I saw him. He wore loose pants and his feet were bare. He favored one leg and, in his hands, he carried his boots. His hair had been tied back, but some strands came loose in the coastal winds.

But I turned away. I merely wept into my hands until the letter came up soggy. Suddenly, I had no control over my own feet. Perhaps it was a dream, but it was a dream I would run to and not away from. I came to a stop a breath away.

"Read it." My voice was breathless, still unbelieving.

Fray took the soggy letter and spoke the words aloud. "We hope you will come, and we wish for you both to be part of our children's lives." He looked at me, bewildered. "There's no beginning; it's all wet and runny. Izzy?"

I drew in a breath. "It's from Sonia. She said she's marrying and that she's pregnant."

Fray's eye widened. "Pregnant? My sister?"

The tears came again. I spoke through my sobs. "We have to go visit."

"You don't have to say it. I'm already there."

I blew out a gust of air, still in shock. "A nephew, or a niece, can you believe it?"

Fray ran a hand down his face. "We'll have to teach them, Izzy. Let them know how amazing their mother is. I'll have to be the big, strong uncle. Gods, when is a good time to start buying them everything?"

He drew me close and held me against his body. He twined his fingers into my hair and placed a kiss my forehead, my chin, and then softly to my lips before whispering in my ear, "I love you, Izzy."

We had been through so much together. We had cried together, failed together, and shed blood for each other, and interwoven in that was bravery and understanding. Love.

And love was carrying one. In Sonia and all the others, it was thriving.

I pulled away, wound my fingers in his hair, and looked over his face, from his downturned mouth to his gently sloping nose to his bright blue eyes. I placed a hand to his belly, and he momentarily staggered back, only to come closer a moment later. Two of the cuts to his face left scars. I traced my finger along them, feeling sad.

"They're reminders," he said.

"Of what?" I asked. War? The struggles we'd endured?

"That I'm human."

Wounds healed, but scars would always remain. We would remain.

The evening breeze cooled my tears, and we sat and discussed our plans and our future, not with fear, but with hope, relief, trust that things would be all right for a girl who loved all the wrong things.

"So, what now?"

"What now?" He smiled, with dimples and his face opened. "Now, we stay together. We fight our demons together. We do everything brave and everything stupid together, and if you ever want to leave, you tell me and I will make arrangements for your comfort, and if you will it, I will come with you. Wherever you want to go. Whatever you want to do. I will—"

He swiped at his eyes, and suddenly, I found myself lifted in the air and cradled in Fray's arms.

"—be there." His voice cracked through his own emotion. He carried me toward the house and set me down past the threshold. "Through all your suffering and all your accomplishments. I am broken. You are broken."

He signed the last part. *Together, we can be unbroken.*

I thought of all the children like Ghetee who never had a chance to grow up, and those who would remember. But also of Sonia's child, who would grow up in a world without curses. There may be war—there would always be war—but right now, we could hope that the world would let them be. The gods' light would shine on them. And I would make sure, as long as I lived, that light never dimmed.

That night, we lay with one another and as the candles reflected off Fray's sleeping form, I hoped his dreams were hopeful images of running wolves, and stolen kisses, and gods who smiled down on us.

And of children who never thought they could move the stars, but did.

ABOUT THE AUTHOR

Celia Mcmahon is a devourer of books and coffee. If she's not busy buying more books than she can read or discovering new ways of being tired, you can find her scouring the world army-wife style for book ideas.